MW00380385

Blood of the Earth

Sovereign of the Seven Isles: Book Four

by

David A. Wells

BLOOD OF THE EARTH

Edited by Carol L. Wells

www.SovereignOfTheSevenIsles.com

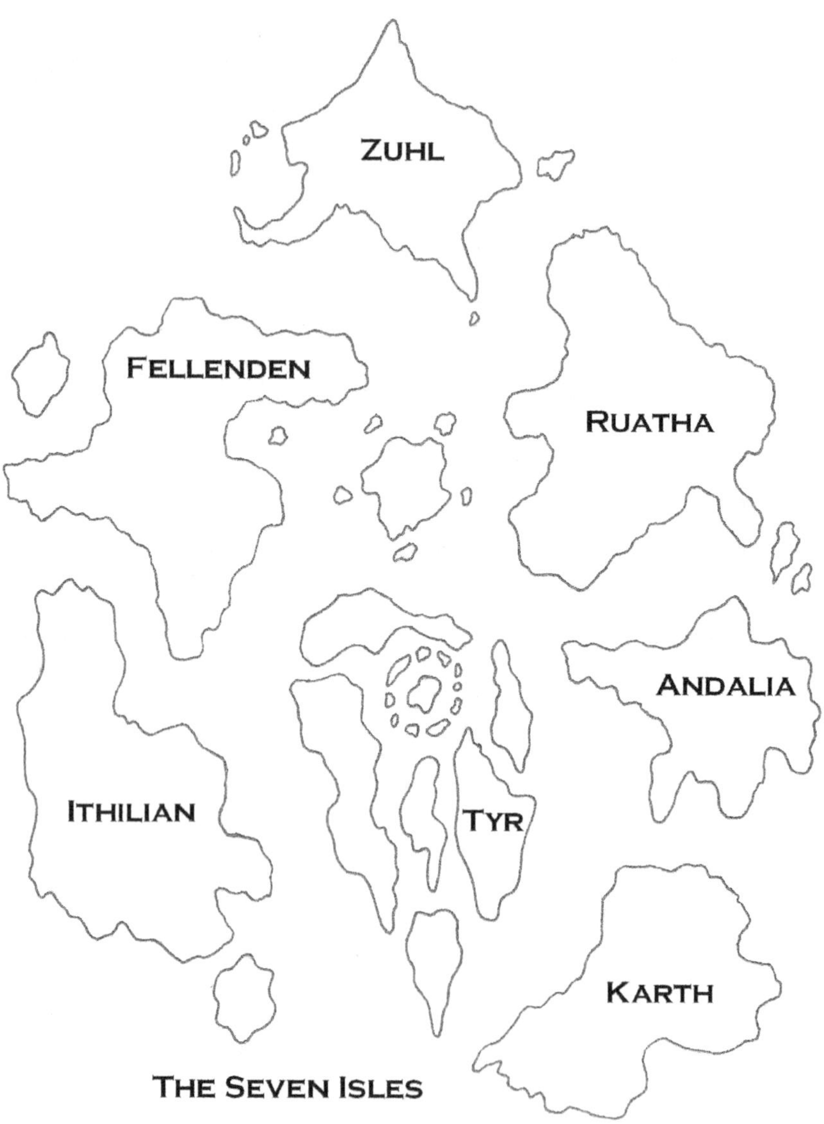
ZUHL
FELLENDEN
RUATHA
ANDALIA
ITHILIAN
TYR
KARTH
THE SEVEN ISLES

Iron Oak
Shipyard
11
8
9
10
12
2
1
7
6
3
5
4
Isle of Fellenden
1 - Fellenden City
2 - Bristol Bay
3 - Shoalhaven
4 - Sochi
5 - Suva
6 - Val'daran
7 - Val'Sinj
8 - Ellesmere
9 - Wakefield
10 - Breden
11 - Irondale
12 - East Reach

Blood of the Earth

Chapter 1

"Darkness comes, My Love," Chloe said, spinning into a ball of light.

Alexander scanned the debris field for any sign of a threat. Rubble lay in every direction. The wreckage was scattered haphazardly within the walls of the ancient city. Piles of broken buildings were interspersed with a dozen large craters where Mage Gamaliel's terrifying weapons of utter destruction had fallen.

Northport was completely obliterated. The devastation was so thorough that Alexander felt the weight of guilt bear down on him as he surveyed the remains of the once great city.

Over the generations, countless thousands of people had made this place their home, and in one moment of need Alexander had ordered their homes, shops, and communities destroyed.

And destroyed they were.

Little worth salvaging remained. The lumber was reduced to splinters and kindling, useless even as firewood. The stone was pulverized into gravel or dust. Scarcely a stone larger than a man's head could be seen anywhere within the uneven field of broken homes.

All that remained intact was the outer wall.

In the distance a man stepped up on a high place in the field of detritus. His colors screamed out an alarm within Alexander's psyche that was at once visceral and terrifying. It looked like a man and a creature of the netherworld inhabiting the same space. Alexander knew of only one such creature.

A shade.

Alexander drew the Thinblade and pointed toward the advancing enemy with his impossibly sharp sword.

"Enemy!" he shouted. "I think it's a shade."

Isabel gasped, then tipped her head back and closed her eyes, linking her mind to Slyder.

"There're two more," she said.

Suddenly, the man mixed with darkness disappeared, leaving just a hint of black smoke where he'd stood.

A fraction of a moment later, he reappeared about twenty feet closer. Alexander couldn't quite be sure what he was seeing.

Then another man appeared on top of another pile of debris. He had the same tortured colors as the first man—like a man possessed by darkness.

A moment later a third man appeared just as the second man disappeared and reappeared almost instantly about twenty feet closer.

Alexander had seen magic, but this was something altogether different. He watched, mesmerized, as the three men advanced toward them, taking a few steps, then disappearing and almost instantly reappearing closer. They covered the distance quickly.

He'd decided to survey the damage done to Northport before returning to Blackstone Keep. The bulk of the army was moving north under his father's command with only a legion of Rangers held in reserve on the outskirts of Northport.

Alexander intended to rebuild the vital port city, and quickly. The Rangers would play an important part in organizing the timber crews along the northern edge of the Great Forest. They knew the woods better than anyone, knew which trees to take and how to transport them from the forest to the city.

Mage Gamaliel had accompanied him to survey the damage, partly to see the results of his weapons and partly to lend his advice concerning the resources that would be necessary to rebuild. Mage Landi and Wizard Sark were there as well, along with Lieutenant Wyatt and the dozen remaining battle-tested Rangers that had served Alexander so well during his voyage to the Reishi Isle and Ithilian.

Jataan P'Tal and Boaberous Grudge shadowed Alexander, following him wherever he went, whether he asked them to or not. They remained quiet and unobtrusive, in the background, observing and protecting.

Isabel hadn't left his side since the terrifying battle with the scourgling. While the weight of the world bore down on him and the war raged throughout the Seven Isles, he occasionally found himself feeling profoundly grateful for the terrible responsibility he'd been given, for the simple reason that it had brought Isabel into his life.

After having been separated from her for several months, he found that every moment he shared with her was a gift. Her presence soothed his soul and filled him with a deep and abiding joy.

As the enemy advanced, Isabel nocked an arrow.

"Why would all three shades come here?" Jack asked, frowning. "What do they want with us? Aren't they supposed to be searching for the keystones?"

He'd been quietly observing from the background, as usual. Until Chloe's warning they'd all been sharing a somber moment, taking in the utter destruction around them.

Alexander shook his head. "I don't know, but all three of those men look like they have a demon inside them."

Wizard Sark and Mage Landi started casting spells. Lieutenant Wyatt assembled his Rangers into a firing line; they waited with arrows at the ready. Jataan sauntered out in front of them all and took his position between danger and his charge, hands clasped lightly behind his back.

Boaberous dropped his war hammer and drew a javelin. Mage Gamaliel took out a slingshot and loaded it with a stone the size of a plum.

The three men drew nearer, each disappearing, leaving only a wispy hint of black smoke in their wake and then reappearing twenty feet closer, taking half a dozen steps before doing it again.

"Fire!" Lieutenant Wyatt commanded. His Rangers loosed a dozen arrows, dividing them evenly between the three men. All three took direct hits to the torso.

Kill shots.

All three shrieked with a mixture of human agony and demonic glee. Then all three disappeared and reappeared twenty feet closer. The arrows were gone and their wounds were healed.

"This might be a problem," Alexander muttered.

Isabel sent an arrow at the possessed man in the middle and hit him cleanly, but he simply disappeared and then reappeared closer without so much as a trace of injury.

"I've never read an account of a shade wielding such magic," Mage Gamaliel said, shaking his head. He quickly whipped his slingshot around twice and released the plum-sized stone at the nearest enemy. The stone sailed true and somewhere in midflight grew to the size of a pumpkin. It hit the enemy in the chest, crushing his ribs like a stone hurled from a catapult. He went down for a moment, but Alexander could still see his colors: darkness mingled with the living colors of a man.

Then he disappeared. Half a heartbeat later he reappeared, only closer, and without any damage from the punishing attack he'd just been dealt.

They were only a hundred feet away now. Boaberous threw a javelin, but before it found its mark, his target vanished, then reappeared closer.

Isabel dropped her bow and started casting a spell. Jack tossed his hood up and vanished from sight.

As one, the three enemy drew long, black daggers. Alexander saw at once that the blades were enchanted with some form of dark magic, though he couldn't discern its purpose.

Blink, they vanished.

Wizard Sark transformed into a whirlwind.

Blink, they reappeared, only closer.

Fifty feet now.

Alexander could see the smug, tight grins they wore … like they knew something he didn't.

Chloe spun into a ball of light. "I'm afraid, My Love," she said in his mind.

"Be brave, Little One, and stay out of sight," he replied through the link born of their bonding.

Mage Landi brought forth a creature like nothing Alexander had ever seen before. A luminescent cloud of white smoke eight or ten feet across. Lightning rippled and crackled within it, occasionally dancing across its surface in impossibly complex patterns. Landi directed it toward the advancing enemy. For a moment the cloud seemed to hesitate but then it moved with terrible speed, elongating into a horizontal column of smoke and shooting toward the nearest enemy like an arrow, engulfing the man mixed with darkness completely.

The struggle that ensued was a contest between light and dark. The silhouette of the enemy could just be seen within the cloud creature. He struggled to blink away, only to reappear within the cloud. Electricity played across the silhouette, and a distant shrieking could be heard from within.

The other two ignored the plight of their companion.

Sark, in the form of a whirlwind, bounded to the nearest one, drawing him up into his vortex, spinning him around and around and then throwing him violently away into the rubble. Before the man crashed into a mound of broken rock and splintered wood, he disappeared and then reappeared not fifteen feet in front of Jataan.

The man smiled at the battle mage with unrestrained malice.

"Master sends his love," he said and then disappeared, leaving only wisps of blackness that quickly faded.

He reappeared behind Commander P'Tal and tried to stab him in the back, but Jataan was too quick. He whirled, catching the enemy's hand by the wrist and driving his blade to the hilt into the man's heart. The man's eyes opened wide and he looked like he was trying to scream, but no sound came from his open mouth … then he disappeared.

The third enemy walked straight toward the line of Rangers. Lieutenant Wyatt ordered his men to fire; a moment later, the enemy was peppered in the chest with a dozen arrows, any one of them a kill shot, but he simply vanished, only to reappear unharmed behind their line. Alexander caught the look of maleficent glee that ghosted across the man's face as he plunged his dark blade into the back of the last Ranger in the line. Yet another of Lieutenant Wyatt's men had fallen defending Alexander.

The enemy who had tried to stab Jataan reappeared behind Isabel. When Alexander saw him come into existence, he lunged toward his wife but she was too far away. Racing toward her, he saw the look the man gave him as he raised his dagger for a deadly downward stroke into Isabel's back.

In that moment, he knew their purpose. These men mixed with darkness weren't here just to kill him—Phane had sent them to hurt him. These men were here to deliver revenge to Alexander for killing Kludge.

The man stabbed down toward Isabel's back. Alexander was helpless to stop him. He watched the blade descend on his love and felt a mixture of unmitigated terror and furious rage tighten around his soul. When Isabel saw the look on his face, she spun to meet her attacker. The blade came down hard but was turned aside when it met the magical shell of her shield spell. She thrust her sword into his belly and twisted it for good measure.

Alexander felt relief wash over him like a cool breeze. The thought of losing Isabel again was more than he could bear.

The man on the end of Isabel's sword disappeared.

The one who had just killed the Ranger reappeared behind Alexander. But with his all around sight, Alexander saw him come into existence and spun to meet the attack. The man stabbed at him with his dark blade in midturn, but Alexander's dragon-steel shirt saved him yet again. He completed his turn and brought the Thinblade around in a sweeping arc across the enemy's body, cutting him cleanly in half—his hands came free at the elbows and his torso toppled off his trunk. But instead of crashing to the ground, he vanished.

Alexander was dismayed at the seemingly indestructible nature of these men. They wore the stylized R of the Reishi Army Regency on their leather armor and they were men, flesh and blood, yet they were more—much more. Some dark magic had infused them with power beyond Alexander's understanding.

The man that Isabel had just run through appeared behind another Ranger and stabbed him in the back, driving his long dagger through his right lung and out the front of his chest, only to disappear before the next Ranger in line could counterattack.

The one Alexander had just cut in half reappeared behind Jataan, whole and smiling wickedly. The battle mage turned to meet the attack, easily defending against the enemy's knife and slicing his throat cleanly in one deft and inhumanly quick stroke, when the second man, the one who had just killed a Ranger, appeared behind Jataan and stabbed him in the back.

Jataan stiffened with a look of shock and surprise. He had killed many men with a blade; this was the first time he had ever been stabbed himself. Always before, he'd been able to avoid injury. These two men, enchanted with darkness, had just bested the battle mage. He slumped to his knees as the two men disappeared, laughing.

Alexander couldn't believe it. He'd come to think of Jataan as nearly invincible. Yet he lay bleeding on the battlefield before him. Alexander wanted to rush to his side, to see if he would live. He'd come to value Jataan as a protector and even considered him a friend in spite of past circumstances. He'd forgiven him for sending the assassin who killed Darius, even though the loss of his brother still pained him.

With a gesture, he ordered Boaberous to tend to Jataan. The giant reached his commander quickly and went to work staunching the flow of blood and assessing his injury.

Everything was happening so fast. The enemy seemed to be beyond all but the most powerful magic. Only Mage Landi's conjured cloud of electrical light had any effect on these men and then it was only holding the one enemy in place.

The other two appeared on either side of Mage Gamaliel and stabbed at him in unison. His dragon-steel plate armor easily turned their blades aside. Both of the men shrieked inhumanly at seeing their attack so easily thwarted.

Kelvin didn't cast a spell or use one of his many enchanted items to counterattack; instead, he unceremoniously slugged the nearest one in the side of the head with his large, gauntleted fist. His attack wasn't driven by magic but simply by the strength of his arm and the weight of his large frame. The man mixed with darkness fell unconscious to the ground like a sack of beans.

Alexander seized on the hope that these terrible new enemies could fall. It suddenly occurred to him that he hadn't even drawn Mindbender. The Thinblade was a sword of unparalleled sharpness and terrible power, but Mindbender gave him an edge that the Thinblade couldn't match. Through Mindbender, he could see into the thoughts of his enemy during battle. He drew the blade with his left hand, point down, and stretched out with his mind.

The remaining enemy disappeared, but Alexander knew where he would materialize.

"Mage Landi! Behind you!" Alexander called out, a moment too late.

The man mixed with darkness appeared, stabbing in the same moment, driving his blade through the conjurer's heart. Bright red blood sputtered from Mage Landi's mouth and the light of his aura faded quickly. As he slumped to the ground, his attacker disappeared and the cloud of light that had been holding the third enemy at bay faded from the world of time and substance.

The enemy that had been trapped by the cloud of light disappeared. The one that had just killed Mage Landi reappeared behind another Ranger and killed him with a single thrust. Wyatt stabbed the enemy but he simply vanished off the lieutenant's blade.

The one who had been in the cloud of light disappeared, then reappeared a moment later behind Alexander, but this time he knew what to expect. He'd heard the enemy's thoughts as they formed and knew where the enemy would appear. He also knew how to counter the attack. Mage Gamaliel had shown him their weakness.

Even as the man mixed with darkness materialized behind him, Alexander spun. He brought the Thinblade around high and caught the man at the temple, cleaving the top several inches of his head cleanly off with one swift stroke.

This time the man didn't disappear.

Half of his head slipped free and thudded to the ground, spilling brain in a bloody jumble. His body followed more slowly as gravity claimed him.

They could be killed.

Another Ranger fell.

Isabel unleashed a blinding ray of light from her outstretched hand that burned a hole through the chest of the last remaining enemy as he stood over the dying Ranger. He looked at her with shock and pain for a moment before disappearing.

Mage Gamaliel produced a metal collar of polished silver inlaid with magical symbols in burnished gold and fastened it around the neck of the unconscious enemy.

The last one reappeared behind Isabel but his thrust was again turned aside by her shield. He disappeared again and reappeared half a moment later behind Lieutenant Wyatt. Before he could stab the Ranger in the back, Jack stabbed him instead.

The man stiffened with a startled shriek and disappeared again, reappearing behind Mage Gamaliel.

Isabel was ready. She was waiting for a clear shot at the enemy. Instead of her light-lance spell, she unleashed her Maker's light at the man mixed with darkness. He screamed with such agony that Alexander almost felt sorry for him. The light didn't kill him or even injure him, but Alexander could see the darkness within him writhing around in shock and pain. He disappeared and reappeared twenty feet away, running from the battlefield. Three steps later he disappeared again, reappearing twenty feet farther away.

He was headed toward the legion of Rangers encamped outside the walls surrounding the remains of Northport.

Chapter 2

Alexander produced a healing draught from his pouch and handed it to Boaberous without a word.

"Lieutenant Wyatt, transport Jataan and our prisoner to the camp," Alexander commanded as he turned to Isabel. "Let's go, we have to stop him before he gets to the Rangers."

She nodded, following him at a dead run toward their horses.

"We'll never catch him before he gets to our troops," Isabel said as they mounted up. "He's almost to the walls already."

"I know," Alexander said, "but we have to try." He kicked his mare into a gallop, pushing her to run as fast as he dared, given the uneven footing of the bombed-out city. They reached the gate and coaxed their horses into a sprint. The man mixed with darkness had a commanding lead and was gaining ground. Every three steps or so he would disappear and reappear twenty feet farther from Alexander and closer to the Rangers' encampment.

The Rangers at the perimeter of the camp had seen the enemy and raised the alarm. Dozens of arrows met him but he either disappeared before the shafts struck home or shortly after, only to reappear closer without any trace of injury. It was as if his body was made whole each time he teleported.

Then he was inside the camp.

A Ranger fell.

The enemy vanished and reappeared.

Another fell.

Alexander spurred his horse into a reckless sprint, closing the remaining yards.

The Ranger in command of the perimeter guard ordered his men to stand back to back once he saw the nature of the enemy. Alexander was impressed with the quick thinking and calm decision making of the young man in the face of such an impossible threat.

The man mixed with darkness appeared to the side of a pair of Rangers and stabbed one, though not fatally, before the other stabbed him. He cackled with malice and disappeared.

Alexander charged into the camp with Isabel at his side. He drew Mindbender and stretched out with his mind to listen for the enemy's thoughts. He guided his horse in the direction of the next target. The man mixed with darkness was moving deeper into the camp, striking wherever he could.

Another Ranger fell. His partner stabbed the enemy. He didn't disappear right away but instead stepped into the blade, driving the length of it through his gut and then stabbed the Ranger in the heart. Alexander rounded a tent just as the man mixed with darkness disappeared.

"Isabel, on your left!" Alexander called out in warning as the man appeared just in front of Isabel and to the left of her horse's path. He thrust his dagger into her horse's throat. The animal squealed in pain and crashed to the ground, taking Isabel with it.

She flew forward over her horse's head and tumbled to the ground. The man mixed with darkness looked at Alexander and smiled, then disappeared.

He heard the enemy's thoughts through Mindbender and knew that Isabel was his target. She lay stunned on the ground, her shield long since dispelled, helpless.

Everything slowed down for Alexander. He was in a fight and he had a sword in his hand, but not just any sword. He held Mindbender. A weapon fashioned by an adept wizard to be wielded by an adept wizard. A weapon of surpassing power.

He formed the image he wanted and released it into the sword, even as the man mixed with darkness reappeared standing over Isabel, only the enemy didn't see what he expected to see. When he looked down, he didn't see Isabel at his feet, where she truly was. Instead, he saw Isabel sprawled out on the ground a good ten feet away. Alexander had projected a simple illusion to deceive the enemy.

Confusion stole across the man's face and his confidence faltered as Alexander slipped off his horse.

A nearby Ranger drove an arrow into the man mixed with darkness. He disappeared and reappeared behind the Ranger, killing him with a single thrust to the heart.

Again, Alexander created a false vision of reality and released it into the sword. Mindbender had substance only as a blade but it was powerful beyond words, for it could create belief within the mind of the enemy.

Belief was all powerful.

The man mixed with darkness stopped and looked around with wary confusion. The Ranger encampment was gone, Isabel was gone, the horses were gone. All he could see was Alexander in an open field on the outskirts of Northport.

The man mixed with darkness shrugged off his confusion and fixed his murderous glare on Alexander before vanishing. Alexander knew where he would reappear, Mindbender told him his enemy's thoughts even as they formed. He stepped to the side and brought his blade up to strike.

When the man mixed with darkness reappeared, he slashed at Alexander with his dark blade, tearing into his left arm, slicing deeply across the outside of his bicep. Alexander drove the point of Mindbender into the man's right eye socket and out the back of his skull. A tremor ran through the man as the darkness released him and he slumped to the ground, dead.

Alexander raced to Isabel, ignoring the sharp pain of his fresh wound. She was just regaining consciousness when he reached her side. She looked up at him and tried to smile through a wince of pain.

"Did you get him?"

"I got him. Now lie still, that was quite a fall. Does anything feel broken?"

She frowned, taking a mental inventory of her injuries before shaking her head. "No, just banged up and bruised." Then she noticed the blood coating his left arm.

"You're bleeding—let me heal you," she said as she sat up with a grimace.

"I'll be fine," Alexander said, "nothing a little healing salve won't fix."

"Nonsense," she said as she gently put her hand over his wound and opened her connection to the realm of light. She focused on her love for him and released the healing energy of the Maker's light into his wound.

Nothing happened.

Isabel frowned, shaking her head in confusion. "I don't understand. It worked on Abigail and Anatoly."

Alexander looked at his wound and the sight staggered him for a moment. He felt his breath catch and a thrill of fear course through him.

There was a taint of darkness in the gash on his arm. He looked quickly at the long dagger on the ground near the corpse of the man mixed with darkness and saw in a glance what he feared. The enemy had used dark magic to enchant the blade.

Rangers had gathered all around them, providing a cordon of security. The quick-thinking perimeter commander deliberately cleared his throat, drawing Alexander's attention.

"Lord Reishi, I'm Lieutenant Doyle," he said. "Can we expect more enemy or was this the only one?"

"This should be the last of them. Have your men stand down and send word to the camp physician to expect wounded."

"Very good, My Lord," Lieutenant Doyle said with a crisp salute.

"Lieutenant, I need a bandage," Isabel said before he could attend to his duties. He nodded and gestured to another Ranger who produced a field dressing from his pouch and handed it to Isabel. She went to work cleaning and wrapping Alexander's wound.

***

Alexander stood in the gloom of late evening, watching eleven funeral pyres burn as he struggled to keep his attention away from the throbbing pain in his left arm. He'd applied a generous scoop of healing salve, but it seemed to have no more effect than Isabel's healing light.

Eleven more people had died for his cause. Ten Rangers and Mage Landi—eleven more families torn asunder.

He pulled Isabel closer.

Mage Gamaliel and the Rangers had carefully transported Jataan back to the Ranger encampment. Boaberous reported that he'd given the battle mage the healing draught but it had no effect. The camp physician had worked on him for over an hour, cleaning and disinfecting the wound and then bandaging it.

His report to Alexander wasn't optimistic. The injury was deep and the damage was great. He gave Jataan P'Tal even odds of surviving unless some form of magic could be found that would aid in the healing process.

Boaberous had stoically stepped into the position of Alexander's protector, shadowing him without request or permission, but Alexander knew that as big and formidable as Boaberous Grudge was, he wasn't equal to the battle mage.

Jataan's injury had shaken Alexander—not just for the hopefully temporary loss of his protector, but because it had happened at all. He had come to believe that no mortal swordsman was a match for Commander P'Tal. Alexander's experiences fighting beside the battle mage had only served to confirm that belief.

But this enemy was different—they were created to take those closest to Alexander, and they had succeeded in besting two mages in battle. One dead, the other gravely injured. But they hadn't succeeded against the Guild Mage.

He'd knocked one of the three men mixed with darkness unconscious, revealing their weakness, and he'd put a magical collar around his neck that confined the darkness within. The prisoner was locked in a cage, awaiting transport to Blackstone Keep.

The funeral fires burned down. Alexander looked at Isabel. He'd come close to losing her today. The thought still made his soul quail. He needed her more than he needed air.

"We should go have a chat with our prisoner," Alexander said.

She nodded.

Kelvin frowned. "I believe you should have adequate security present. The magic within these men is beyond my understanding and the collar I put on the prisoner may not prevent him from transporting himself outside of the cage.

"When you sent word of the shades," Kelvin continued, "I conceived of the collar and designed it to act much as a magic circle does—preventing darkness confined within from escaping. My hope was to be able to imprison a shade within a single victim. I never envisioned a creature such as this. However, the prisoner doesn't seem to be able to wield the magic he used so effectively during the attack."

"You think he's just waiting for the right time to strike?" Jack asked.

"Perhaps," Kelvin said. "Mostly, I'm proceeding with an abundance of caution."

"You'll get no argument from me," Alexander said. "Give me a minute, I have something I need to do before we go have our chat."

He went to Lieutenant Wyatt and invited him to walk with him. Once they'd strolled out of earshot of the other mourners, they stopped and watched the fading light of the funeral pyres in silence for a moment.

"You and your men have paid a heavy price for volunteering to accompany me," Alexander said quietly.

Wyatt nodded somberly and fell silent. He was struggling with fresh grief. Alexander gave him the time he needed to find his voice.

"For myself, I'm proud of our service to you and your cause," Wyatt finally said. "I believe my men are, as well."

"I have no doubt of that, but you've borne more of this burden than most. I know it's a small consideration but I'd like to offer you and your men any posting you want: Glen Morillian, Southport, Blackstone Keep, wherever you'd like."

"That isn't necessary, Lord Reishi," Wyatt said. "We all understand, better than most, what we're fighting for. For myself, I want to be on the leading edge of this war and that means standing right next to you, come what may."

Alexander smiled sadly and nodded. "Well, think about it, talk it over with your men. The offer stands for each of them. Let me know what you decide."

"Thank you, I will," Wyatt said.

Alexander clapped him on the shoulder and left him to grieve the loss of his men. He walked with Isabel and Mage Gamaliel to the tent where the prisoner was being held. Jack and Boaberous trailed along behind.

Anatoly was heading toward Blackstone Keep with Lucky. His injury during the battle with the scourgling wasn't life-threatening because of Isabel's healing light, but he still needed time to recuperate. Abigail had flown with Mistress Constance and a wing of Sky Knights to the aerie in Blackstone Keep to help them get settled in. Isabel's wyvern, Asteroth, had gone with her. The rest of the Sky Knights had returned to the fortress island to apprise the triumvirs of the battle.

Before Alexander entered the tent where the prisoner was being kept, he drew Mindbender and shifted his mindset. This interrogation was a battle that he had to win. Information was power and he needed to find out everything he could about the new threat Phane had sent against him. He felt the weight of the sword in his hand and the familiar calm of battle settled over him. He stepped into the tent and locked eyes with his opponent. He was in a fight and he had a sword in his hand. Everything else faded away.

Alexander reached out with Mindbender and listened to the thoughts of the man mixed with darkness. He heard the prisoner think of where he wanted to appear. He flickered in place for just an instant, wisps of darkness surrounded him briefly, but nothing happened. The collar he wore flared with the colors of active magic.

Alexander smiled, "Looks like your collar is working, Kelvin. He just tried to blink behind me but couldn't."

The Guild Mage nodded with satisfaction.

Alexander stepped closer, but not too close. "What are you?"

The man smiled with malice. "I am wraithkin. Master made me more than I ever was when I was just a man." His voice was raspy and ever-so-slightly unhuman.

"I take it Phane is your master."

"Prince Phane is everybody's master, even yours, usurper."

"That remains to be determined," Alexander said. "How many wraithkin did Phane make?"

He shrugged. "There were almost a hundred of my brethren when we were dispatched to kill everyone that you love."

The wraithkin smiled as his statement settled into Alexander. He felt a little chill race up his spine.

"How many of your kind are on Ruatha?" he asked.

The wraithkin smiled but said nothing.

Alexander stared at him, waiting for an answer. "One way or another I'll get an answer to my question."

The wraithkin shrugged again. "I doubt it. I will answer many questions but none that will help you."

"Perhaps another line of questioning is in order," Jack suggested, "if I may?"

Alexander nodded.

"How were you made?" Jack asked.

Kelvin leaned in with greater interest.

"I was once just a man," the wraithkin said, "but then Master asked for volunteers to become much more than we once were. He called forth a creature from the netherworld and blended it into my being." He shuddered with pleasure. "You have no idea the power Master gave me."

"Not enough to get you out of that cage," Isabel said.

"Not enough to get the job done, either," Alexander said. "We killed the other two."

The wraithkin shrugged. "We took several of those who serve you. One by one we will take everyone you care for. You will know the pain of loss so completely that when we come for you, you will welcome the touch of our blades."

"Doubtful," Alexander said. "I am curious about those daggers of yours, though."

The wraithkin smiled knowingly as he looked at the bandage on Alexander's arm. "Your wound will heal slowly and magic will do nothing to speed the process. Does it hurt?"

Alexander snorted and shook his head. His worry for Jataan increased. With magic to aid in healing, he would be back on his feet in a week, but without it, he might never recover.

"I'll ask my question again," Alexander said. "How many of your kind are on Ruatha?"

The wraithkin drew himself up and smiled at Alexander silently.

"Maybe I can persuade him," Isabel said. She opened her connection to the realm of light and let the Maker's light pour into her, then began casting a spell. Pure white light arced forth from her hand and hit the wraithkin in the chest. He shrieked with such horror and agony that Alexander felt a little thrill of fear race through him from the sound of it alone. He hadn't heard anything like it since he'd faced the revenants on Grafton Island.

The wraithkin collapsed to the ground and writhed around in abject torment for several minutes before he regained enough of his senses to stand up. He looked slightly afraid when he faced them again.

"How many?" Alexander said.

The wraithkin started trembling but said nothing.

Isabel smiled humorlessly. "I can cast that spell again and again. And I have to tell you I really wouldn't mind spending the rest of the night torturing you. You killed several good people today, some were my friends. Answer the question."

He held his tongue until Isabel started whispering the words of her Maker's light spell again.

"Nine," the wraithkin said. "Master sent nine of us aboard the fleet from Andalia. I don't know how many made it to shore after our ships were sunk. I found the other two and we came here to find you."

His colors, although tainted by the darkness within, revealed that he was telling the truth.

Chapter 3

They retired to a command tent to discuss what they'd learned.

"At least we know what Phane's been up to," Alexander said. He was tired of being on the defensive. Since Phane had awoken, Alexander felt like he'd been back on his heels trying desperately to stay one step ahead of an untimely death. He wanted to find a way to strike back.

"Indeed," Mage Gamaliel said. "These wraithkin are a significant threat. Loose in an encampment or a city, they could kill countless people before they could be brought down. Fortunately, they're vulnerable when struck in the head. We should send word of this weakness to all of our forces."

Alexander nodded. "I'll have the Rangers send riders north to the main army and south to General Talia and Kevin. When you get a chance, I'd like you to take a look at the daggers they carried, see if there's any way to magically heal a wound caused by one." He took a deep breath and let it out slowly. "I'm worried about Jataan. He was hurt pretty badly. Without magic, it will take him months to heal."

"I've collected the blades and will study them briefly this evening but I suspect I'll need the equipment in my workshop to make a full assessment." Mage Gamaliel shook his head. "I've never heard of such an enchantment. If I'm able to determine how they function, I may be able to construct a counter to the magical taint they leave in a wound."

"If we assume the worst case, there are still six wraithkin wandering around Ruatha," Isabel said. "Maybe we should consider sending out teams of hunters to find them."

"That's not a bad idea," Alexander said, nodding. "My father tells me they've been training a company of soldiers for special operations. They might be ideally suited to the task."

"I would concur," Mage Gamaliel said. "I spent most of the time you were away fashioning armor for the Strikers from the dragon scales we recovered in the Blackstone aerie. They would be better able to defend against the wraithkin than any other soldiers within your army."

"Good, once we catch up with the main force, I'll talk to my father about it," Alexander said. "He might have a suggestion or two. Until then we should probably keep the one we captured alive. He might know something useful about Phane or his army."

"I agree," Kelvin said. "While I'm loathe to bring him inside Blackstone Keep, it would give us an opportunity to study him and perhaps learn how he can teleport and heal so quickly. With sufficient understanding, we may be able to undo their power. If there are nearly a hundred wraithkin serving Phane, we'll need some means to meet the threat."

"Do you think a magic circle would contain the prisoner?" Jack asked.

"I assume so since the collar works on the same principle, but perhaps it would be wise to test our theory prior to taking him inside the Keep," Kelvin said.

"That's probably a good idea," Alexander said. "We can build a circle within the encampment at the base of the Keep and contain him there.

"Once we get to the Keep, I'm going to hold a King's Council with as many influential people as possible in attendance. I've already sent invitations to the triumvirs of the Sky Knights, and I'd like to have as many of the territorial governors of Ruatha at the table, as well as King Abel. We need to plan our next moves. We have more than enough enemies and not enough resources to face them all. I want to make sure I'm not missing anything before we decide on a course of action."

"That's wise," Kelvin said.

"And politically savvy," Jack said. "There are bound to be some questions about the Sovereign Stone amongst the nobles. Some may question your ability to be both the Sovereign of the Seven Isles and the King of Ruatha at the same time. Others may be reluctant to support anyone claiming the Reishi name. An open council meeting with all in attendance will give you an opportunity to provide them with the assurances they need to remain loyal."

Alexander frowned. "To be honest, I hadn't thought about that. Given the history of the fall of the House of Ruatha because of their allegiance to the Reishi during the war, I can see how some might find it difficult to support anyone claiming to be the Reishi Sovereign.

"As for being both the Sovereign and the King of Ruatha, it never even occurred to me that I can't do both, but I think you're right, Jack. I'll have to give it some thought."

Isabel put her hand on his. "The Regent of Northport may have some harsh things to say about the destruction of his city."

"Can't say I'd blame him," Alexander said. "I'm still not sure it was the right thing to do."

"It was," Jack said. "Consider the alternative—a fortified city with eight enemy legions supported by two or three mages awaiting reinforcements from Andalia. War without end. You made a hard decision. Ultimately your choice saved a great many lives at the cost of stone and timber. Not a bad bargain."

"I agree with Master Colton," Kelvin said. "The damage done turned my stomach but the alternative was much less palatable."

"How many of those weapons do you have left?" Alexander asked.

"One large one like the ones we used on Northport and three small ones like the ones used in the battle for the Gate," Kelvin said.

"As much as I don't want to have to use them, we may find they're the best weapons we have for certain circumstances," Alexander said. "Do you have what you need to make more?"

"No," Kelvin said. "Each requires a very small quantity of Wizard's Dust and I've used all that we had. Incidentally, six of the seven candidates for the mana fast have survived and become novice wizards. The seventh was lost to the firmament."

Alexander sighed. He remembered the trials and felt a pang of pity for the one lost. It wasn't a good way to go—if there was such a thing.

He opened his pouch and removed his five remaining vials of Wizard's Dust and placed them on the table before the Mage.

"We found more in the Reishi Keep," Alexander said. "Lucky has a small quantity with him as well, but not enough for a mana fast."

Kelvin smiled in wonder. "I had not hoped to mentor more than one or two wizards through the mana fast for the rest of my life. Our order is reborn, Alexander."

"Use it as you see fit, but I think we might need some more of those weapons," Alexander said. "I gave enough Wizard's Dust to the guild on Ithilian for three new wizards, and I gave three vials to the Reishi Coven. Isabel used one and Magda is holding one for Abigail if she wants it. I suspect they'll use the third to induct another member into their order, if they haven't already."

"Very strategic thinking, I see," Kelvin said with an approving smile. "Not only have you given priceless gifts to a guild of wizards and a coven of witches, thereby engendering goodwill, but you've created the impression that you are the most likely to triumph in this conflict because you alone possess the secret to magic.

"Alexander, I am reluctant to ask, but it is a question that has plagued me since I learned that you had bonded with the Sovereign Stone." Kelvin hesitated. "Does it hold the secret?" he whispered intently.

"It does," Alexander said, "but I can't make use of it yet. On the advice of Balthazar Reishi, I've decided that the secret should remain a secret for now. I don't know what it is and I don't intend to ask until I can put it to use."

Kelvin smiled and nodded to himself. "I have often dreamt of the day when the secret of wizardry returned to the world, but I see the wisdom in your caution. Just know that every wizard in my order stands ready to help you make whatever preparations you require."

"Thank you, Kelvin," Alexander said. "I understand how much this must mean to you. Once we return to Blackstone Keep, I'll set my plan in motion, and hopefully, we'll have the ability to make Wizard's Dust for ourselves by year's end."

"All of the threats we face seem to diminish in the face of that knowledge," Kelvin said.

***

Several days later they reached the main encampment of the Ruathan army located between the Reishi Gate and Blackstone Keep. It was an imposing sight. Tens of thousands of soldiers spread out across the plain in the shadow of the Keep.

Horns called out his arrival as he approached the perimeter defenses, and a squad of soldiers rode out to meet him.

"Lord Reishi," the squad sergeant said, saluting crisply, "General Valentine posted us to watch for your arrival. He would speak with you."

"Very good, Sergeant, lead the way," Alexander said, then turned to Lieutenant Wyatt. "You're welcome to join us after you see to your men."

Wyatt turned to the commander of the hundred-Ranger honor guard that had accompanied Alexander from Northport.

"See to the men's quarters and horses, then find them a hot meal," Wyatt said before nodding to Alexander.

They wound through an ordered maze of tents and paddocks. The soldiers were mostly busy with their tasks, some cleaning and repairing equipment, others sharpening weapons. Many turned to look as Alexander rode by—some cheered, while others looked at him as if he had brought war into their lives. Even though the army was comprised of forces from many different territories, they were organized and disciplined, no doubt as a result of his father's stern leadership. Alexander knew all too well that his father expected much of those around him and even more of himself.

The sergeant brought them to an inner area of command tents surrounded by a perimeter fence guarded by a force of Rangers. They pulled the fence aside when they saw Alexander approach and put it back in place the moment his party had entered.

Duncan came out of the command tent to greet his son. "I hear you had some trouble," he said, gesturing to the bandage around Alexander's left arm.

"Seems Phane's been building a small army of very dangerous assassins," Alexander said. "We killed two and captured one." Alexander pointed at the wraithkin mounted on a horse and shackled to the saddle.

"Has he said anything interesting?" Duncan asked.

"He was reluctant at first, until Isabel persuaded him." Alexander smiled at his wife as she dismounted, handing her reins to a nearby Ranger.

"Apparently, he came to Ruatha with eight others," Isabel said. "Hopefully, the other six drowned during the naval battle off the coast of Southport, but we probably shouldn't count on it."

Duncan smiled over at Alexander. "You did well with this one, Son. I've always said, hope for the best, but plan for the worst."

"The perimeter guard said you had news," Alexander said as he pulled his father into a hug.

"I do," Duncan said. "The army is coming together. Most of the command structure of the individual legions has been reorganized into a single unified command. It's taken some doing but we should be ready to move within a few weeks."

Alexander nodded, listening to his father as they walked toward the command tent. He knew Duncan was putting on a show of a report without getting to the important news, but he didn't know why. His father was a cautious and deliberate man by nature, but he didn't spook easily.

Alexander started to worry. He'd noticed the additional security around the command tents but didn't think much of it, until now.

The oversized tent enclosed a stone slab with a magic circle inlaid in silver and gold reaching nearly to the sides of the stone square. Within the circle was a large table surrounded by a number of general officers, including Kern and Markos, and a few wizards, Sark and Jahoda among them.

All stood when they saw Alexander enter. He looked to his father for an explanation.

Duncan frowned and shrugged. "Recent events have made an abundance of caution prudent." He motioned to the chair at the head of the table.

Alexander took his seat with Isabel at his left and Duncan at his right. Jack and Kelvin took empty seats at the table, while Boaberous took a position near the door and stood watch. Before Alexander could ask his question, Chloe appeared in a ball of light and floated gently down onto the table in front of him.

Several of the men at the table sat up a bit straighter when she appeared.

"All right, why the extreme measures?" Alexander asked.

Duncan nodded gravely. "For the past three nights, there've been murders within the camp: two men the first night, five the next, and three last night. Last night we got some measure of confirmation about the threat. A squad of Buckwold infantry were sitting around a cook fire when one of their own stood up abruptly, drew his sword and killed his two closest friends in cold blood. The rest of his squad was stunned by the sudden turn of events and sat speechless, staring at their fellow soldier. All six men independently gave the same account of what followed." Duncan paused and shook his head.

"Apparently, the soldier said, 'I am Shivini and my master, Prince Phane, has promised me the souls of any who do not bow before him.' Then he cut his own throat and fell into the fire."

Alexander took Isabel's hand and shared a look of stricken horror with her. He knew what she was thinking: together, they had loosed the shades on the world.

"At least we made the right choice in retrieving the Sovereign Stone," Alexander whispered as he closed his eyes.

Once again he was facing a threat sent against him by the Reishi Prince, and Phane was probably dining in comfort and safety inside the walls of the palace on Karth. Alexander felt like he was being forced to react to Phane's threats without ever having the chance to choose his next move. He remembered another of his father's many lessons on strategy: He who controls the initiative controls the game. From the day Phane woke, Alexander had been reacting, scrambling to stay alive. He'd made gains, more than he would have thought possible, but he was coming to see that he couldn't match Phane on his terms. He needed to change the rules of the game. But how?

He took a deep breath and let it out slowly before drawing himself up and facing the scrutiny of those arrayed before him. The people at this table needed him to be strong, even if he didn't feel up to the challenges that lay before him.

"All right, one thing at a time," he said. "First, Phane has created a new kind of enemy called a wraithkin, a man blended with a creature from the netherworld. They have the power to teleport short distances and heal nearly any injury they've sustained each time they disappear and reappear. They're armed with daggers that taint the wounds they cause with dark magic, preventing our healing magic from having any effect." Alexander gestured to the bandage on his left arm. The gash still hurt but he'd learned how to deal with pain. Just six short months ago, this wound would have had him mewling in agony—now it was just a minor distraction.

"Phane sent nine wraithkin to Ruatha to kill everyone close to me," Alexander said. "I'm afraid I made it personal for him when I killed his familiar. He wants revenge and he knows the surest way to hurt me is to hurt those I love."

"I'll order bodyguards for Bella and me as well as Hanlon and Emily," Duncan said. "Lucky, Anatoly, and Abigail are probably safe inside the Keep, but I'll send word to Erik just in case."

"Good, I'd also like to assemble several teams of hunters," Alexander said. "I think Captain Sava's new unit, augmented by a few wizards, might be the best-suited for the job."

Duncan nodded thoughtfully. "We can field four platoon-strength units from his company," he said, turning to Kelvin. "Can you spare four wizards, one for each platoon?"

"Yes, in fact I already have a very short list of the best candidates for the job," Kelvin said. "Once we return to the Keep, I'll make the arrangements."

"I would recommend a Ranger or two be attached to each platoon," Lieutenant Wyatt said. "They can serve as trackers and scouts."

"I agree," Duncan said. "General Markos, I'd like you to oversee the formation of these units and coordinate their operations. Captain Sava will report directly to you."

"Understood, General Valentine," General Markos said.

"So now to the shade," Alexander said. "From the nature of the attacks, it's clear that the intent is to undermine morale and create fear within the ranks. As damaging as that might be, I don't for a second believe that's its only mission. If Phane has bound it to his will, then he sent it here for something. Other than the Sovereign Stone and my head on a platter, what might Phane be after?"

The table fell silent. After a long moment, Kelvin ventured a guess.

"Perhaps Phane knows of something within the Keep that we are unaware of. He fought at his father's side against Mage Cedric for many years. He may be after some relic of that struggle."

"That's unsettling," Jack said. "There's no telling what's in there."

"Maybe it's time to do some more exploring," Alexander mused. "Mage Cedric said there were things of power and danger locked away under the Keep. Unfortunately, he wasn't more specific than that."

"I would like to accompany you," Kelvin said. "I may be of some assistance."

"I was hoping you would," Alexander said. "Do you have another one of those collars?"

"I'm afraid the one around our prisoner's neck is the only one. It will take over a week to make another."

"All right," Alexander said, turning to Wizard Jahoda. "We're going to need another magic circle built at the base of the Keep. I don't want to risk taking that wraithkin inside Blackstone, and we need to get that collar off him so we can use it against the shade. I considered executing him, but he might still provide some valuable information."

"I'll begin at once," Jahoda said. "I believe there's a suitable space within the encampment of the garrison guarding the road."

"I need to talk to Conner," Alexander said, standing up. "Anyone know where he might be?"

"He's making the rounds through the Ithilian Infantry," Duncan said, "trying to calm their nerves after the shade's attack."

Alexander appraised the soldiers of his army as he made his way through the encampment. Isabel and Jack accompanied him with Boaberous trailing along behind. Alexander could see the fear in the men's colors. The shades were creatures of legend, monsters from a dark period in history. They were feared, and for good reason. The fact that one was loose in his army worried him, that it was serving Phane was more troubling still.

It was a good bet that the Reishi Prince knew about the Nether Gate. That made finding it a greater priority than ever. That familiar sense of urgency started to build within his gut. He'd only just returned to Ruatha and he was already planning to leave, but he needed to get counsel first.

He found Conner standing in a small group of soldiers. They all came to attention when Alexander approached.

"Relax, gentlemen," Alexander said. "I'm afraid I need to talk with Prince Conner for a moment."

They all nodded and melted back into the encampment.

"Lord Reishi," Conner said, "it's good to see you. The soldiers are a little nervous, so I've been trying to ease their fears, although I'm not really sure what to tell them."

"At this point, I'm not sure either," Alexander said. "We're working on a way to contain the shade, but it'll probably be a few days before we're ready and even then implementing the plan will be difficult."

"At least you have a plan," Conner said. "That alone will give the men some hope."

"Conner, I need to send you back to Ithilian with a message for your father," Alexander said. "I'm holding a council meeting with everyone I can get on such short notice. I'd like him to attend."

"I can be ready in an hour," Conner said.

It was nearing sunset when they arrived at the Gate. Conner had an honor guard of a hundred Ithilian infantry, and Lieutenant Wyatt had volunteered to accompany Alexander. His Rangers were fanned out, watching the empty plain as if it might attack.

Alexander touched the Island of Ithilian on the map carved into the Gate. The stone shimmered for a moment and abruptly opened to the plains of Ithilian.

A dozen men stood guard, awaiting word of the campaign on Ruatha.

"Prince Conner," the sergeant said with a salute, "your father is anxious for word. He's here in the encampment."

Chapter 4

Before Alexander closed the Ruathan Gate, he set both it and the Ithilian Gate to accept commands from the wielders of the Thinblades.

It was well after dark by the time they made it back to the command area of the army encampment. As he rode through the neat and orderly rows of tents, Alexander reflected on how large his army seemed to him. Before this ordeal had begun, he'd never seen so many people in one place. But he knew with terrifying clarity that his army was tiny compared to Phane's, and he didn't even like to think about the vast horde of battle-hardened warriors serving Zuhl.

There would be blood and dying before this war was decided, and lots of it. Alexander focused on figuring out how to make sure it was the enemy's blood that ran freely. He couldn't hope to defeat either of his foes in a direct conflict. He had to be smarter. He had to find a way to attack without wasting his army in a futile engagement. He hoped his war council would help him formulate a sane and sensible strategy.

His mother was waiting in his tent when he and Isabel entered.

"Alexander, it's good to see you. Have you eaten?"

"Actually, I haven't had time for dinner," Alexander said, giving his mom a hug.

"Well, you have to eat," Bella said. "You need your strength and a clear head. They told me you'd been injured."

Alexander grimaced slightly, motioning to the bandage on his arm.

"Well, sit down and let me have a look."

Bella maneuvered him to a chair at the field table and lit another lamp before carefully unwrapping the bandage.

Isabel sat down across from Alexander.

Bella turned to her with a warm smile. "Hello, dear, I hear you had some excitement at Northport. They tell me these wraithkin don't like your light very much."

Alexander chuckled.

"No," Isabel said. "The one we captured wasn't afraid of anything until I hit him with my Maker's light spell. That got him talking."

"Well done, Dear," Bella said, then turned back to Alexander's wound and frowned, pursing her lips as she examined the gash. It was healing poorly, if at all. Blood still oozed from the laceration and it wasn't clotting as it should.

"I don't like the looks of this at all," Bella said with a hint of worry in her voice as she turned back to Isabel.

"I'm told you used your healing magic and it had no effect," Bella said.

Isabel nodded gravely. "I don't understand why, either. It worked on Abigail and Anatoly. It certainly should have worked on Alexander."

"Not necessarily," Bella said. "Dark magic can counter healing magic. Did you notice any difference in the way your healing spell felt when you cast it on Alexander?"

Isabel thought for a moment and nodded slightly. "It felt colder. The first two times, I felt a gentle warmth within, but when I cast it on Alexander, I felt a hint of deathly cold in the center of my chest. I didn't think much of it at the time because I was worried about Alexander and confused that my spell hadn't worked."

Bella sighed and shook her head. "These weapons may be more dangerous than we first thought. Have you tried your healing since then?"

"No," Isabel said. "Why do you ask?"

"It's just a hunch, and I hope I'm wrong," Bella said.

Alexander felt a little thrill of fear when he saw his mother's colors. She was afraid. Bella Valentine was a strong woman, a witch with considerable wisdom. She didn't frighten easily.

"What is it, Mom?"

"It may be nothing, or it may be something very serious. I can't know for sure just yet."

Alexander took a deep breath to calm the urgency that was building in his gut.

"Tell me what you think it is."

Bella held her son's eyes for a moment.

"The magic of the dagger may have tainted Isabel's connection to the light or to the firmament when she tried to heal you."

Alexander looked at Isabel intently, scrutinizing her beautiful colors. She looked as clear and bright as ever.

"I don't see any difference in her colors."

Chloe buzzed into existence in a ball of scintillating white light and flew in an orbit around Alexander's head once before landing in the middle of the table.

"I don't sense any darkness in Isabel, nor in Alexander, even though his wound is tainted with it," she said.

"The magic may take time to work," Bella said, "or it may only advance when she casts a spell … or I could be completely wrong."

"Is there any way to know for sure?" Isabel asked. She had only recently become a witch, but she felt a sudden vulnerability at the possibility of losing her magic.

"Perhaps, but it may just make matters worse," Bella said.

"How so?" Alexander asked.

"If Isabel uses her magic, you may be able to discern if the taint has spread from your wound to her through her colors, but it may cause the taint to grow."

"Knowing for sure would be worth the risk. What spell should I cast?" Isabel asked.

"I don't know your repertoire, Dear, but I'd suggest something defensive that doesn't rely on your unique connection to the realm of light."

Alexander had spent several days with his family while the army prepared to move from Northport. During that time Isabel and Bella had talked a great deal about witchcraft and magic. Bella had slipped easily into the role of mentor and Isabel felt a greater willingness to be forthcoming with her about her magic than she did with even Magda. She trusted the triumvir but not nearly so much as she'd come to trust Bella. Alexander was happy to see them becoming friends. He valued his mother's opinion a great deal. That she genuinely liked and respected Isabel meant a lot to him.

"I learned a shield spell," Isabel said. "I'll start with that."

She stepped away from the table and began the casting. The spell depended on anger. Alexander watched her colors closely as she formed the emotion necessary to defend against the firmament. He marveled at her passion and emotional control. From the intensity of her colors, he was certain that he couldn't match the controlled rage she was able to call so easily. The spell succeeded and a shimmer of magic enclosed her in a protective shell. Then the anger she had called to cast the spell drained away.

He looked closely for any hint of darkness within her aura, but saw none.

Shaking his head, he said, "Maybe there's nothing wrong with her."

"I hope you're right, Son, but we have to be sure," Bella said. "Can you make a connection with the realm of light, Isabel?"

Isabel nodded and closed her eyes for a moment to center herself, then touched the passage within her psyche that led to the realm of light. She had come to view her connection with the light as the most potent magic she had at her disposal. She cherished it all the more because it had been created through the birth of Sara, Alexander and Chloe's fairy daughter.

Isabel felt the light flood into her as the warm, loving creativity of it engulfed her.

Then Alexander cried out, "Stop! I see darkness in your colors."

Isabel slammed the passage shut in a rush of fear and loss. She loved the light. It filled her with calm, loving purpose every time she touched it.

"The darkness is gone now. I'm so sorry, Isabel," Alexander said as he drew her into a hug. She sobbed gently against his chest for several moments. Once she'd composed herself, she turned to Bella.

"How do we fix it?"

"I don't know, but I'm sure some of the wizards may be able to help," Bella said. "In the meantime, you must refrain from using magic that requires you to touch the realm of light."

"My healing and my Maker's light are the most powerful magic I have," Isabel said. "What if I need to use them?"

"Be sure there's no alternative," Bella said. "Darkness is not to be trifled with. A taint such as this was undoubtedly constructed deliberately, most likely as a secondary attack against any healers within our ranks. Also, I fear Phane wanted to ensure that those injured by these blades died slowly and painfully."

"Don't risk it, Isabel," Alexander said, still holding her beside him with an arm around her shoulders. "We'll find another way. Until we figure out how to undo the daggers' magic, you can't cast those spells."

She nodded wearily.

"We'll figure this out, Dear," Bella said with a reassuring smile.

"Let me call for some food and then I'll sew up that gash."

"My Love, you should put a pinch of fairy dust into the wound," Chloe said. "It may help with the taint."

Alexander looked to his mother for advice.

Bella shrugged. "Fairy dust is powerful magic. If you have some, I doubt it could hurt."

Alexander sat down and carefully opened the vial of fairy dust, took a small pinch and sprinkled it into his wound.

At first he felt a warm tingling as the iridescent powder dissolved into his blood. The warmth spread throughout his body. He began to relax and feel heavier. Then he felt a stab of pain in his chest. A moment later he felt like he was on fire. He tensed up, losing all muscle control as he toppled out of the chair.

Isabel and Bella both raced to his side. He heard Chloe whimpering in despair and apology within his mind, but the unmitigated agony coursing through his body wouldn't allow him to form a single thought to comfort her. He felt himself on the floor, every muscle clenched in an uncontrollable spasm. He couldn't make his lungs work and felt an especially keen burning in his chest. As he struggled to gain a breath, the darkness began to close in.

The last thing he heard before the darkness claimed him was Chloe's voice in his mind, "Please don't leave me, My Love."

Chapter 5

Lacy Fellenden was tired, hungry, and absolutely terrified.

She crouched in the corner stall of a stable behind a stack of hay bales and struggled to calm her breathing, lest it give her away. She'd been running ever since the enemy had come to her country and thrown her quiet little life into turmoil. All she knew now was fear. The kind of fear a small animal must feel when a predator is on the hunt.

In the first days after Zuhl and his terrible, brutish army arrived, Lacy had tried to nurse a righteous anger at the injustice being done to her people. She had tried to hold on to the fierce rage she felt at the idea of evil being done to her family. All of that was gone now.

The world had gone mad and she was lost and alone. At first, she'd had the counsel and protection of Wizard Saul, her father's court wizard, but he had been possessed by something out of a nightmare and now he was hunting her as well. It was all so beyond her. She was a princess, accustomed to maidservants and fancy dresses. Decisions of importance had always been made by others, and yet her father had entrusted her with the legacy of her family, though she didn't even know what that was, except that others of great and terrible evil wanted it—and they wanted it badly.

To Lacy, what mattered most was that her father, now almost certainly dead, had entrusted this most important of tasks to her in his hour of greatest need. That he had no one else to burden with the duty didn't matter. Lacy knew her father loved her. She knew he doted on her and would have done anything for her. What she didn't know, until it mattered most, was that he believed in her. That simple realization had come upon her in the night like an epiphany.

She would not fail him, no matter what.

She didn't even know what was in the little box she carried. It was black as night with no markings, keyhole, or hinges. The only clue she had about its contents was learned on the night Wizard Saul had been possessed by a creature he called a shade—the one named Rankosi.

He had demanded that she give him the keystone.

She had no idea what that might be but she knew with terrifying certainty that neither the shade nor Zuhl's horde could ever be permitted to have it.

Unfortunately, she was alone, in unfamiliar territory, with enemies closing in on her and no one to turn to for help. She almost yelped when the door to the stable opened.

"Lacy," Rankosi said, "I know you're in here. It's only a matter of time before I find you. Come, Child, hand over the bauble and I will let you go—for now." His voice morphed from cloying and sweet to strained rage. "Come out now! If I have to find you, I will flay the flesh from your bones and make you watch."

Lacy froze, half deliberately and half from wild panic. She dared not breathe. Straining to listen, she held her breath and remained stock-still. Rankosi stood in the doorway, sniffing the air like a dog.

She heard horses coming up the road, then a muted curse as Rankosi turned to meet the squad of Zuhl's hunters. All of her enemies were coming to her at once. She inched around the bale of hay and snatched a peek just as Rankosi turned away from the stable to confront the approaching soldiers.

When she heard him begin casting a spell, she made her move. Carefully and quietly, she crept toward the door on the far side of the stable. A few horses rustled as she passed, but Rankosi was too busy with his spell to notice.

As she slipped through the door, she took a quick look across the stable at the possessed man who had once been her protector. All around him, shards of translucent blue force began appearing, slowly at first but then more and more rapidly. They hung in the air, growing in sharpness, until they looked almost solid. With a word and a forceful gesture, the conjured shards darted forward, tearing into the approaching enemy. Men and horses fell to the magical onslaught, leaving only two soldiers still alive out of a dozen.

When Rankosi turned slowly and looked directly at her with a menacing smile, she ran. It was dark and the ground was uneven. She stumbled and faltered, but still she ran with all the strength and abandon of wild terror. She dared not look back for fear that the wizard-turned-demon would be there.

She reached the fence to the paddock and clambered over, daring to glance back only when she was on the far side. Rankosi was walking through the pasture toward her. The two remaining soldiers had fled the wizard's attack, no doubt to deliver a report about the enemy they had encountered.

More soldiers would be coming.

Lacy raced into the village, winding through the small houses and shops that made up the little community. She didn't think about where she was going, she just ran, hoping her erratic path would be enough to throw off the shade, but she knew it wouldn't. It was only through luck and good fortune that she'd managed to stay ahead of it this long.

She rounded a corner and ran headlong into a man in the dark. Stumbling back, she turned to run but stopped when he spoke.

"I'll help you, if you'll let me," he said.

Lacy was desperate and terrified. She didn't know who this man was. She'd been betrayed by other villagers recently, only barely escaping with her life. She'd lost her horse when she trusted a family that let her sleep in their barn for the night. Once she was bedded down, they told the soldiers where she was. Her recently acquired skill for light sleeping was all that allowed her to escape with her life. That incident had cost her a horse, her saddlebags, and her bedroll. All she had left was her pack and her belt pouch, which held a few silver coins and even less gold.

She looked at the man warily, but then she heard Rankosi in the distance.

"All I want is the keystone, Child," the shade said into the night.

She nodded urgently to the stranger. He motioned for her to follow. He wound through the village until he came to a little house. A man was waiting there with a horse. The stranger motioned for Lacy to remain in the shadows while he went and talked to the man. He handed over a small purse and the man mounted up and spurred his horse into a gallop through the village.

When the stranger returned to Lacy, he motioned for her to remain silent and to follow him. Behind another house, he pulled open a trapdoor to a cellar and led her into the dark. She followed cautiously, her hand on the hilt of her dagger. Once they reached the base of the stairs, she noticed a low-burning lamp on the far side of the room. He took the lamp and led her through a door before turning up the light.

"We should be safe here," he said. "I'm Drogan. You would be Lacy Fellenden, yes?"

Her wariness flared. "Who sent you? How do you know who I am?"

"I was sent by a friend to help you escape Zuhl and the creature of darkness that hunts you," Drogan said. He was a big man, easily over six feet tall, with a barrel chest and broad shoulders. His hair was black as night and his full beard matched it. He wore a long, dark, leather riding coat and a broad-brimmed hat. He took a seat at the little table in the center of the room.

"You might as well get comfortable," he said. "We should stay here for the night. If my ruse worked, the demon hunting you will be a long way from here when it realizes you're not the one on the horse."

"You sent that man on the horse as a decoy?" Lacy asked, hopeful and horrified at the same time.

"It was the only way to throw the demon off your trail," Drogan said. "I have some experience hunting things from the dark. They don't let go of a trail until they catch the one making it. By then we'll be long gone."

"What about the man on the horse? What will happen to him?"

Drogan shrugged. "That's less important. You can have the room through there. It has a bar on the door, the bed's comfortable, and there's some food, if you're hungry."

Lacy was starving. She nodded tightly as she made for the door, giving Drogan a wide berth.

"I'll be here if you need anything," he said, gesturing to a pallet covered with straw mats pushed up against the wall.

Before she closed the door, she stopped for a moment and looked at Drogan, trying to size him up. He accepted her scrutiny without affront.

"Thank you," she said, then closed and barred the door. She made a quick search of the room before helping herself to the bread, cheese, and fruit laid out on the table. She hadn't eaten a decent meal in days. Once she'd eaten her fill, she collapsed on the bed and fell asleep. She didn't know for sure why he was helping her, but that didn't matter for now.

For the first time in weeks, Lacy Fellenden felt safe.

***

Phane smiled broadly as he swirled his goblet of dark red wine. He was sitting in his Wizard's Den, looking through his enchanted mirror into the little room where Lacy slept.

"It seems your agent has been successful in making contact, General," Phane said.

"Drogan's a good man, My Prince," General Hargrove said. "Now that he has the girl, I recommend we send orders for him to kill her and return with her possessions."

Phane shook his head absently, deep in thought.

"Tempting, General, but ultimately counterproductive," Phane said. "If I'm correct, and I usually am about these things, the item she carries can only be opened by one of her bloodline and then only while not under duress.

"Have Drogan bring her here, but only through persuasion. He is not to use force or threat against her in any way. We must win her over so that she chooses of her own free will to do as I ask. Only then will I gain my prize."

"As you wish, My Prince," General Hargrove said.

"That will be all," Phane said, as he stared into his goblet, gently swirling his dark red wine.

Chapter 6

Alexander came awake gradually. At first he was only dimly aware of anything at all, then he floated in that half-dream state where he was still asleep but aware at the same time. When he heard the soft crying, he woke with a start.

Chloe buzzed up over his face from the place on his chest where she'd been sitting and looked intently into his eyes. Alexander blinked the sleep away and tried to focus on her.

She clapped and suddenly burst into a ball of scintillating white light, buzzing toward the ceiling.

"You're awake!" she said out loud.

As Alexander began to come to his senses, he tried to speak but couldn't make his mouth work, so he thought his question to Chloe.

"What happened?"

"I'm so sorry, My Love," Chloe said, floating down closer to his face. "I suggested you use fairy dust to combat the taint left behind by the wraithkin's dagger."

She landed on his chest and sat down, burying her face in her hands.

"I thought I'd lost you, My Love," she said in his mind. "You died." She sobbed into her hands, releasing all of her pent-up fear and worry.

"Died?" he mumbled.

She nodded, her face still buried in her hands.

"You haven't lost me, Little One," Alexander said without speaking. "I'm right here."

He glanced around at his surroundings. From the looks of the stone walls, he was somewhere within Blackstone Keep. He'd recognize the seamless, smooth-cut walls and perfectly straight lines of the Keep's stonework anywhere. He was lying in a big, four-poster bed with a thick, feather mattress and finely woven linen sheets. The room was large with one closed door to his left and an open door leading to a water closet on the wall opposite the bed. To the right was a series of heavy red curtains that looked like they blocked out the light from at least five arched windows. There was a small table in one corner with four chairs pushed in under it and a set of two comfortable, cushioned chairs next to the bed with a small table separating them.

Isabel was curled up in one of the chairs, sleeping.

"We've been so worried, My Love," Chloe said, after she finished sobbing. "You've been unconscious for three days."

Alexander was suddenly alarmed. There was no telling what might have transpired in the three days he was out. He shook his head; it felt like it was full of cotton. He couldn't quite make his mind work right.

"What happened?"

"You started shaking violently after you used the fairy dust," Chloe said, and then started crying again. "I almost killed you, My Love. I'm so sorry. Can you ever forgive me?"

Alexander almost laughed. "Chloe, there's nothing to forgive. You were trying to help me."

She was sobbing into her hands again. Through his bond with her, he could feel the weight of guilt she had taken upon herself.

"Look at me, Little One."

She sniffed and looked up at him.

"I love you, Chloe. You didn't hurt me. The wraithkin did. All you tried to do was help me. I don't blame you for anything and I hope you won't blame yourself. You don't deserve that."

"You mean it?"

"Every word, Little One."

She swallowed and sniffed again.

Her mood lightened a bit when Alexander smiled at her.

"Now, tell me what happened."

"After you used the fairy dust, you fell out of your chair and every muscle in your body spasmed at once. You shook for several minutes. Your heart was racing and you stopped breathing. Your mother said it was because the muscles around your lungs weren't working right."

She swallowed hard and looked him in the eye.

"Then your heart stopped. I was so afraid. I can't lose you, My Love. I can't." She started to lose her composure again.

"Hush, you haven't lost me, Little One. It's all right. Just tell me what happened next."

"Isabel used her healing light on you."

A thrill of fear raced through Alexander. He looked over at Isabel quickly and scrutinized her, then closed his eyes with a feeling of dread when he saw a hint of darkness tangled up in her beautiful colors.

"She's all right, My Love."

Alexander shook his head. "No, she's not. The wraithkin's taint is infecting her magic."

"Oh, My Love, I'm so sorry. She said she felt fine."

Alexander nodded with his eyes closed.

"Her light brought your heartbeat back and healed the cut on your arm."

Alexander opened his eyes with a frown. "So the fairy dust worked … it just killed me in the bargain."

Chloe nodded. "Lucky said he thinks the conflict between the fairy dust and the wraithkin's dark magic unleashes too much power. It caused all of your muscles to clench uncontrollably until you ran out of air. You only relaxed once your heart stopped."

Isabel moaned softly as she woke from the sound of their conversation. Alexander watched her with a gentle smile. With all of the trouble swirling around him he was at peace just knowing that this amazing woman loved him. With her at his side he could face any challenge.

She came awake with a start and scrambled out of the chair and onto the bed, kneeling beside him and putting her head on his shoulder as she started crying softly.

He put his hand on her back and caressed her gently.

"I'm all right, you saved me—both of you."

"Don't ever scare me like that again," Isabel said. "When your mom said your heart had stopped, I felt like the world was ending."

"Come here," he whispered.

She lay down beside him and put her head on his shoulder.

"I'm grateful that you saved me. But now the wraithkin's taint is growing inside you," Alexander said.

She tensed a little but didn't say anything.

"You have to promise me that you won't use your light again until we figure out how to undo whatever the wraithkin's magic did to you."

She nodded. "I don't feel anything. Are you sure it's really there?"

"I'm sure," he said.

"I promise I won't use it unless it's the only way to save you," Isabel said.

"Isabel, we don't know what's happening. The wraithkin's taint could kill you."

"I know," she whispered.

"You can't risk yourself for me," Alexander said.

She lifted herself up so she could look him in the eye. "I can and I will," she said, her green eyes flashing. "When I was lost in the darkness, you risked yourself to save me. You can't ask me to do any less. I love you just as much as you love me. Losing you would be the most horrible thing that could ever happen to me."

Chloe nodded, still sitting in the middle of his chest.

Alexander sighed and shook his head. "I just don't want you to get hurt."

"I know," Isabel said.

He relaxed and let himself drift off. When he woke an hour later, Isabel was resting with her head on his shoulder, and Chloe was curled up asleep on his chest. He yawned and both of them woke.

"Are you hungry?" Isabel asked.

"Now that you mention it, I'm starving."

"I'll have Adele make us some breakfast and send word to your parents and sister that you're awake," Isabel said, as she got up.

"Adele? From New Ruatha?"

"Yep, she volunteered to serve as your house manager. She's the one who got these quarters cleaned and furnished for us. In fact, as I understand it, she went to Erik demanding to know why he hadn't assigned a staff to attend to you when you were in the Keep. He was a bit flustered at first. I can't say I blame him since he's been busy coordinating the supply operation for the army. When Adele offered to take care of our quarters, he gladly assigned her the job."

Alexander chuckled and shook his head. "I don't blame him, either. He's got more important things to do than worry about where we're going to sleep. Besides, I thought we had rooms off the paddock."

"Alexander, you're the Sovereign," Isabel said, smiling at his discomfort. "It wouldn't do for you to stay in the barracks with the soldiers."

Alexander shook his head. "One of these days, I expect everyone to realize that I'm just a ranch hand and throw me in the dungeon for impersonating a king."

"You are much more than a ranch hand, My Love," Chloe said, standing in the middle of his chest with her hands on her hips and looking at him sternly. "I know your heart, maybe even better than you do yourself. You are every bit the king that the people need. Without you, they don't stand a chance against the storm that's coming. Through you, they may yet live to see a world ruled by justice rather than ambition."

Once again, Alexander felt the weight of his burden settle into place. He set aside his dream of a simple life with Isabel and accepted the world as it was. He was the Sovereign of the Seven Isles—and he had a war to win.

"Let's go get breakfast."

He opened the door leading from his bedchamber into a large circular sitting room. There was an arch on the opposite side leading to an entry hall with a door on the far side. To his right was an arch that opened into a large formal dining room with three crystal chandeliers hanging over a long oak table. On his left was a heavy bound oak door. The sitting room had a fireplace in the center with a stone chimney rising into the ceiling. On one side of the fireplace was a low table with couches on two sides and overstuffed chairs on the other two. Colorful tapestries, probably from New Ruatha, hung over the black granite of the walls. Brass lamps stood at intervals between the tapestries, providing ample light.

Boaberous stood when Alexander entered.

"Lord Reishi, it's good to see you well again."

"Thank you, Lieutenant. Report," Alexander said.

"Your rooms are secure. There's only one entrance from within the Keep," he said, motioning toward the door in the entry hall. "The balconies are inaccessible except by flight. I've posted two Rangers at the door and four on platforms above your balconies.

"Commander P'Tal is still incapacitated, but the healers tell me he's mending. I'm aware of only one immediate threat. The Rangers reported that a serving girl was murdered last night within the Keep. They're investigating."

"It's always something," Alexander said with a frown.

Adele came bustling in and smiled broadly when she saw Alexander.

"Lord Reishi, it's so good to see you. We were all worried sick that you wouldn't wake up. I'll send word to your mother right away." She turned and called out into the other room, "Lena."

A young woman of about nineteen came into the sitting room. She wasn't quite as tall as Isabel, had dark brown hair and soft brown eyes, clear skin, and a timid smile. She was beautiful but still unsure of herself as a woman. Her colors were clear and bright, vibrant with life but also revealed the nervousness and uncertainty of youth.

"Yes ma'am?"

"Lena, this is Lord Reishi," Adele said, turning back to Alexander. "With your permission, Lord Reishi, Lena will be your maidservant. She is well-trained and has served on my staff for many years."

"I trust your judgment, Adele. Pick your staff as you see fit," Alexander said, then turned to Lena. "Hello, it's a pleasure to meet you."

"Thank you, Lord Reishi," she said.

"Lena, run and tell Lady Bella that her son is awake," Adele said.

Lena nodded and headed out the door in the entry hall.

"You must be famished," Adele said. "I'll have the chef start breakfast right away. I suspect your family will be joining you shortly, so I'll be sure he makes plenty. Is there anything in particular you'd like?"

Alexander shrugged with a smile, "Maybe some eggs."

"Of course, I'll get breakfast started and be back with a pot of tea," Adele said, as she whisked out of the room.

"I'm not sure I'll ever get used to that," Alexander said. "It just doesn't feel right having people waiting on me."

"You have more important things to worry about," Isabel said.

Alexander and Isabel were sitting on a couch sipping tea when Duncan and Bella arrived.

When Bella saw her son, she put her hand on her chest and closed her eyes to fight back tears. She hugged him fiercely and then held him by the shoulders at arm's length.

"How do you feel? Are you having any light-headedness, dizziness, or confusion?"

"I feel fine, Mom, just a little hungry."

"You had us all pretty worried, Son," Duncan said, "especially after Esmer died."

"Who's Esmer?"

"He was one of Kelvin's wizards, a healer," Duncan said. "He tried to heal Commander P'Tal with a spell but it didn't work. We found him dead the next morning."

Alexander looked at Isabel again, examining her colors more closely.

"I'm fine, Alexander. Stop worrying. My healing magic works differently than most others'. I've already talked with Kelvin and Magda about it. They said Esmer died because the wraithkin's taint kept his connection to the firmament open. When he went to sleep, he got lost in the firmament in his dreams. That's why he never woke up.

"Since my healing doesn't come from manipulating the firmament, Magda thinks the taint will attack my connection to the realm of light instead. I might lose my ability to use the light but not my other magic."

"What's Kelvin think?" Alexander asked.

"He's not so sure," Isabel said, reluctantly. "He's afraid that the taint will go to work on my connection with the firmament once it's overpowered my link with the realm of light."

Alexander frowned. "We have to get rid of that taint, and sooner would be better than later."

"We're already working on it, Alexander," Bella said.

The door in the entry hall opened and people started filing in. Abigail and Jack, with a young waifish girl trailing behind them, looking timid and wide-eyed, came first, followed by Anatoly, Lucky, Kelvin, and Magda.

Abigail went straight to her brother and hugged him, then stepped back and said with a smile, "Be more careful!"

"You're looking well for a man who's just recently died," Jack said with a sparkle. "It's good to have you back."

"Quite, my boy," Lucky said. "Looks like your wound has mended nicely."

"I hear you got two of those wraithkin," Anatoly said. "Not bad. I went to see Commander P'Tal yesterday. They hurt him pretty bad. The healers say he'll be out of commission for a few months, at least."

"You look like you've recovered well," Alexander said.

"Isabel's magic fixed me up better than I had any right to expect," Anatoly said. "I thought I was gone for sure when that scourgling hit me. Felt like every bone in my chest was shattered."

"That's because they were," Lucky said. "You were far beyond my talents. Without Isabel, you would have died."

"So you keep reminding me," Anatoly said.

Lucky smiled impishly.

Kelvin shook Alexander's hand. "Glad to have you back. We have much to discuss and your leadership is sorely needed."

Alexander sighed and nodded. "Can we have breakfast first?"

Kelvin chuckled, nodding.

"Hello, Lord Reishi," Magda said. "I'm glad to see you're well. I feared the worst when I arrived to the news that you'd been unconscious for two days."

"Thank you, Magda. I'm glad you could come to Blackstone for the council meeting," Alexander said with a deferential nod to the triumvir.

Then he turned to the young girl and smiled. "You were sitting with Isabel and Abigail when I looked in on them at the fortress island. Thanks for keeping them company. I'm sure your friendship was a comfort to them. I'm Alexander."

She swallowed hard and curtsied as if she just remembered she was supposed to be on her best behavior. "I'm Wren, Lord Reishi. Thank you for having me as a guest in your home."

Alexander smiled and chuckled. "You're most welcome. Any friend of my wife and sister is a friend of mine."

"Wren is a treasure," Jack said. "Abigail introduced her to me when she arrived with the triumvirs yesterday. It seems that Wren wants to sing. We bards are always on the hunt for new talent, so I listened to her for a few minutes. I have to say, I've never heard anyone with more natural talent and passion for the craft. With a little coaching, I expect her to be one of the greatest singers in all of the Seven Isles."

Wren blushed furiously. "I'm not really that good," she muttered.

Adele came bustling into the sitting room and stopped short when she saw the crowd. "Ah, breakfast is ready. There's plenty for everyone."

They ate a leisurely meal, enjoying the food and talking of little things. When only Lucky was still eating, Alexander sighed contentedly and looked to Isabel. She nodded.

"So tell me, what's happened since I've been out?"

"The army is staged near the Gate," Duncan said. "We've been using the magical larders in the Keep to produce supplies for them. I estimate we have sufficient food for a two-month campaign without the need to resupply. I've received word from Kevin and General Talia. Southport has assimilated many of the refugees from Northport and is busy building fast-attack boats and sending raw timber to Kai'Gorn. General Talia is rebuilding the city and he's started building boats using Kevin's design. Between the two of them, they should have over a hundred built and crewed by winter.

"Andalia has been quiet. Talia sent scouts to take a look and it seems they're working on boats of their own. He says he has a plan to move a legion of infantry to Andalia if need be. The people of Kai'Gorn enthusiastically came around to our side once they realized that we meant it when we said they would be governed according to the Old Law.

"Duane is still up north keeping an eye on Rake and his legion of troublemakers. They've holed up in the mountains and are busy fortifying their position. I'm not too worried about them, except that they're keeping a legion of Rangers occupied that I could use elsewhere.

"The shade is still loose in the camp and killing three to five men every night. Morale is starting to suffer and there've been some desertions. The men are afraid and I'm not sure what to do about it," Duncan said, shaking his head in frustration. "Also, another wraithkin showed up last night at dusk. It attacked openly and killed twenty-three men before disappearing into the darkness. Captain Sava is hunting it as we speak."

Alexander nodded somberly and looked to Kelvin.

"The wraithkin prisoner is safely contained within a magic circle at the base of the Keep," Kelvin said. "He hasn't responded to questioning since our initial interrogation. I've removed the collar and carry it with me in case we have need of it.

"Their daggers are a most interesting design. They don't carry the magic that produces the taint themselves. Rather, they allow the dark magic of the wraithkin to flow through the blade and into the wound of their victim. So far, I've been unable to devise a counter to the taint, but I do have a number of wizards working on the problem. They're pursuing several lines of inquiry that might lead to a solution."

"Boaberous tells me there's been a murder in the Keep," Alexander said.

Anatoly nodded. "A serving girl was found dead. She was killed pretty savagely. We have little to go on right now, but Erik has assigned one of his best constables to investigate."

"Anything else?" Alexander asked.

"King Abel is set to arrive today, and Lady Buckwold will arrive tomorrow," Duncan said. "She has a letter from Duke Warrenton authorizing her to speak on his behalf. Regent Samuel of Northport arrived today and Regent Cery is on his way, should be here by dark."

"Good, we'll hold the council meeting day after tomorrow," Alexander said.

Chapter 7

Alexander took Abigail aside after breakfast and walked her out onto the balcony that opened from the dining room. They were high up on the south side of Blackstone Keep and could see the central plateau of New Ruatha rising like a bump on the plain and the green of the Great Forest coloring the horizon beyond.

"I have something I need you to do," Alexander said quietly. He knew Abigail wasn't going to be happy with his plan, but there was no other way.

"All right," she said with a shrug.

Alexander hesitated, trying to find the right words, wishing that if he did, it would make the enormity of what he was about to ask of his sister less of a burden, but knowing that it wouldn't.

"What is it, Alex?" Abigail asked. "You're starting to make me nervous."

"Abigail, I need you to become the Queen of Ruatha," he said quietly but intently.

She looked at him for a moment, then burst out laughing. When Alexander didn't laugh, she stopped and stared at him like he'd just grown a second head.

"You can't be serious," she said.

He nodded sadly. "There's no other way."

"Tell me you're kidding, Alex."

"I can't do both. I need to be the Sovereign. You're the only one who can wield the Ruathan Thinblade besides me and Dad. He's already had his children, so that leaves you."

She shook her head ever so slightly, backing away from him.

"I don't want that sword. I don't want to be queen. I don't want any of this," she said, motioning to the Keep around them.

"I know," Alexander said, looking down sadly. "If there was another way, I would gladly choose it, but there isn't. Ruatha needs a leader—and it can't be me."

"Why not? You found the Thinblade. You're the one with that cursed mark on your neck. The nobles have accepted you as their king. What makes you think they'll accept me? I'm just a farm girl."

Alexander shook his head. "You're much more than that. You're Queen Abigail Ruatha."

"No, I'm not!" she shouted, a tear slipping from her eye. "You can't do this to me, Alex. Please don't do this to me."

When he didn't relent, she sobbed and then turned away from him and left his quarters, crying.

The others were still in the dining room discussing the enemies they faced. When Abigail stormed through in tears, they all stopped, looking toward Alexander as he came in from the balcony.

"What's wrong with your sister?" Bella asked.

Alexander sat down heavily in his chair and sighed.

"I just told her she's the Queen of Ruatha," he said.

"What?" Bella snapped.

Jack closed his eyes in sorrow.

Duncan took a deep breath and nodded slowly.

"It's the only way," Alexander said, more to convince himself than to explain it to the others.

"I agree," Magda said. "I had intended to bring the matter up during your council meeting."

"Abigail doesn't want to be queen," Bella said.

"I know, but she's the only one who can wield the Thinblade and I can't be both King of Ruatha and Sovereign of the Seven Isles," Alexander said.

"I'll go talk to her," Isabel said, reassuring Alexander with a hand on his shoulder as she stood.

He nodded to her with a smile.

"There has to be another way, Alexander," Bella said. "Please don't do this to your sister."

Alexander swallowed the lump in his throat and looked down at the table in misery. He loved Abigail. She was his best friend. This was the last thing he wanted to do to her, but he couldn't see another choice.

"Alexander's right, Bella," Duncan said. "I hate this as much as you do, but it must be someone from the House of Ruatha, someone who can wield the Thinblade. I can't wear the crown … you and I have already had our children. Ruatha needs an heir."

"But she's my little girl," Bella said, stifling a sob. "She's not ready for this."

"I disagree," Magda said. "In the time Abigail and Isabel spent with us, I came to know your daughter as a strong and formidable woman. You have cause to be very proud of your children, Lady Bella, more so because they both seem reluctant to accept the mantle of authority. In my experience, the best leaders are those who do not desire power. Abigail will make a fine queen."

Bella closed her eyes tightly, as if shutting out the unwelcome reality she faced, tears slipping down her cheeks.

"I'm proud of you, Son," Duncan said. "I know how hard this decision must be for you, but you've put your duty first. That's a rare quality in a leader."

"If it's such a good idea, then why do I feel so bad about it?"

"Because you love your sister," Duncan said. "She'll come around. Just give her time."

"Your father's right," Anatoly said. "She'll see the necessity of your decision and stand by you just like she always has."

"I hope you're right," Alexander said. He took a deep breath and let it out slowly. As much as his mind wanted to dwell on the pain he'd just caused his sister, he had other matters to attend to. He pushed his emotional distress aside and dredged up a mental list of the other problems he faced.

"Lucky, do you have those books we found in Grafton?"

"Of course," Lucky said as he started rummaging around in his bag. Even in the Keep, he carried the magical bag Kelvin had given him. By now it was probably overflowing with all manner of odds and ends.

He produced the books one at a time, stacking them on the table before him.

"Kelvin, I'd like you to assign someone to study these and identify the subject matter of each. I'm hoping one or more of these volumes will contain information about my calling that might be helpful."

"I have just the man for the job," Kelvin said, taking the first book and carefully leafing through it.

"Good, that just leaves a murderer loose in the Keep," Alexander said. "I'm going to find Erik and see where the investigation stands."

"I'll come with you," Anatoly said.

"Me too," Jack said.

Boaberous fell in behind them as they left.

At first Alexander was a bit disoriented. He'd been carried to his quarters when he was unconscious and had no idea where he was in relation to the rest of the Keep. Then he remembered the Keep Master's ring—when he was within the Keep, it was almost like the fortress was an extension of his own body. He could see the layout of the entire massive structure in intimate detail in his mind's eye and command any of the Keep's defenses with a thought.

Erik was in the offices he'd set up to administer the workings of the Keep. Alexander grinned as he appraised the room. It was big enough to be a conference room. The large table set in the middle was littered with papers, reports, and maps. The walls were covered with rosters, work schedules, and supply requirements. A modest desk was set in one corner so that it faced into the room. Erik sat behind it studying a report. Two of his subordinate officers were standing across the room looking at a duty roster posted on the wall.

Erik looked up and smiled. "Alexander, it's good to see you up and about," he said as he stood.

"Thanks, Erik," Alexander said, extending his hand to his brother-in-law. "I wish I could say I just stopped by to say hi."

Erik nodded with a frown. "You've heard about the murder."

"I'm told a young woman was killed pretty gruesomely."

Erik signed. "I saw the body, Alexander. She was beaten to death. It looked like her killer toyed with her for a while before finishing it."

"I hate to ask this, Erik, but I have to," Alexander said. "Is there any chance one of our soldiers did this?"

"I haven't ruled it out, but I doubt it. We're interviewing the victim's friends and family, but so far we don't have much to go on. I've asked Kelvin to help and he offered the services of Wizard Ely. He's busy preparing a divination spell to see if he can identify the murderer."

"Hmm," Alexander said, "I may be able to help with that."

"Anything you can do would be welcome," Erik said. "I have Constable Ward investigating the matter. He's meticulous and thorough, but he didn't find any leads at the crime scene and his interviews have turned up nothing so far."

"What do you have in mind?" Jack asked.

"I may be able to use my clairvoyance to find the killer," Alexander said. "I can usually find the person I'm looking for if I know who they are. I might as well see if I can find this killer based on his activities rather than his identity."

"I won't pretend to know how your magic works," Anatoly said, "but I'm willing to give anything a try at this point. I don't much like the idea of a killer loose in the Keep, especially with all of our allies coming here for a war council."

When they arrived at his quarters, he stopped in the middle of the room with a frown.

"I need a magic circle," he muttered, turning around, just as Adele came into the room.

"Is there anything you need, Lord Reishi?" she asked.

Alexander smiled and said, "I don't suppose you have a magic circle handy."

"Of course," she said, happy to be able to help. "When I took responsibility for furnishing your quarters, I consulted with Mage Gamaliel to see if there were any items you would require. He was most helpful."

She bustled through the room to the door opposite the archway leading to the dining room. It opened to a hall lined with several more doors.

"You have a study, a personal library, a meditation chamber equipped with a suitable magic circle, and a training room stocked with an assortment of weapons."

She motioned to each door as she spoke.

"Thank you, Adele, your efforts are greatly appreciated," Alexander said with a warm smile. He hardly knew this woman, but she had taken it upon herself to provide all of the little things that he didn't have the presence of mind to think about until they were needed. He reminded himself how important it was for him to succeed against his enemies so that people like Adele would be spared the pain, suffering, and death that Phane, Zuhl, and the shades represented.

She smiled at his praise and her colors swelled with pride.

"If there's nothing else, I'll leave you to your duties, Lord Reishi."

He went into his meditation room. It was a simple square room with windows on one side covered with heavy curtains. A brass lamp stood in each corner, and a ten-foot-diameter magic circle inlaid in gold and silver was set into the floor. In the center of the circle was a cushion. Otherwise the room was empty.

"I have to go for a while, Little One," Alexander said to Chloe.

She buzzed into view in a ball of light and flew in an orbit around his head before coming to float a few feet from his face.

"I know, My Love. I'll watch over you. Hurry back—I get lonely when your mind is elsewhere."

Alexander sat down and cleared his mind. As he'd done so many times in the past, he acknowledged each stray thought and then let it go until his mind was quiet. Then he was floating on the firmament. He could feel the collective angst of the world in the limitless expanse of the present moment as it unfolded in countless lives across the Seven Isles.

He narrowed his focus and thought of the murderer loose in the Keep.

Nothing happened.

When he tried again, he still couldn't focus on the person he wanted. It seemed he needed a name or at least a passing acquaintance with his target in order to find him. So he decided to focus on his worst fears instead. A single man acting alone would be a nuisance but not a significant threat. He was far more worried about creatures from the dark.

He focused on Jinzeri. He felt a sensation of impossible speed as his awareness coalesced in a large cave. There was ample light in the natural cavern from several clusters of glowing crystals jutting from the ceiling. Along one wall was a jet-black fragment of stone, uneven around the edges but polished to a mirror sheen on its face. It stood about twelve feet tall and was eight feet wide at the base.

The Nether Gate.

Twenty feet in front of it was a magic circle surrounding a stone pedestal cut from the same jet-black stone.

Sitting with his back to the pedestal was Rexius Truss.

He was possessed by Jinzeri and he was eating a rat—bones, fur, and all.

Alexander watched for a moment until Jinzeri turned and looked directly at him, smiling with rat blood smeared around his mouth.

Alexander moved straight up through hundreds of feet of stone until he came to the surface, rising higher still, until he was floating many thousands of feet over the Reishi Isle. He made a mental note of the location in the rugged northwestern mountains of the island and then faded back into the firmament.

Next, he focused on Rankosi.

His awareness coalesced over a road cut through pasture. A lone man was walking briskly like he had a purpose in mind. He was older, with white hair and a white goatee. He was dressed in the simple robes preferred by so many wizards. Alexander floated around in front of him to get a better look, when the man stopped and smiled at him.

"Hello, Alexander," Rankosi said.

Alexander was taken aback. He couldn't imagine how the shade knew his name, let alone how he could see him. Not for the first time, he wished he knew how to speak through his clairvoyant presence.

"Of course, I know your name," Rankosi said. "You and your woman brought us into this world … and without binding us to your will first." He laughed with maleficent glee. "In all of eternity, we never imagined that anyone would be so foolish. As a reward for such a priceless gift, my brothers and I have decided to spare you until the end, so you can watch the results of your carelessness. We are going to ravage your world and there's nothing you can do to stop us."

Alexander wanted to scream. All of his worst fears about the shades were coming true. He took a firm grip on his turbulent emotions and rose high into the sky directly above the shade until he could make out the form of the Isle of Fellenden. He marked the position of the shade and faded back into the firmament.

Finally, he focused on Shivini.

His fear spiked when his awareness coalesced within Blackstone Keep.

A possessed Ranger stood over the broken and mutilated corpse of another maidservant, savagely beaten to death.

The shade turned from his victim toward Alexander.

"Master has sent me to undo your alliance," Shivini said. "It was so good of you to summon all of your allies to one place. But there'll be plenty of time for that. At the moment, I'm very focused on the more important work of beating innocent young women to death. The taste of their fear when they realize they're going to die is exquisite."

Alexander was repulsed and infuriated. He drew his awareness up through the Keep to get an idea where Shivini was, then slammed back into his body and bolted to his feet.

"Little One, go find Kelvin and guide him to me," he said to Chloe without speaking.

She buzzed up and kissed him on the cheek before spinning into a ball of light and disappearing into the aether.

"Be safe, My Love," she said in his mind.

He came out of the meditation chamber at a run, racing through the sitting room as Anatoly, Jack, and Boaberous scrambled to their feet.

Alexander reached into the Keep Master's ring as he ran, searching for the location where he'd found Shivini and then looking for the quickest route there. The shade was in one of the areas designated as quarters. Alexander searched for any shields nearby and found three, one at each of the access points to that particular section of the Keep. He raised the magical barriers to prevent his enemy from escaping.

He heard Anatoly bark an order to the Ranger standing sentry outside his quarters. The man ran in the opposite direction to get reinforcements.

Alexander wasn't sure what he was going to do once he found Shivini, but he wasn't about to let the shade roam the halls of Blackstone Keep killing people at his whim. He was confident that he could kill Shivini's host, but he also knew that wouldn't stop the shade from taking another. Still, he had to do something.

He raced through the halls until he reached the area where Shivini had been. He slowed his pace, stretching out with his all around sight into the rooms on either side of the hall, searching for the shade.

He rounded the corner and saw the Ranger possessed by Shivini savagely backhand Wren.

Chapter 8

She was caught by surprise and fell hard.

Shivini laughed.

Wren recovered her wits quickly, scrambling away from her attacker.

He didn't seem to be in a hurry as he sauntered toward the terrified young woman.

Alexander dropped the shields around the section of quarters, so Kelvin and his reinforcements could get through. Then he pulled his throwing knife from the sheath on the back of his belt. Just as Alexander threw the knife, Shivini turned toward him. The knife hit the shade in the shoulder and buried to the hilt.

Shivini laughed.

"This body isn't mine, you fool. You can't kill me."

He pulled the knife out and licked the blood coating the blade with a malicious smile.

"I do so love that taste," he said.

Alexander closed the distance quickly, drawing Mindbender as he ran.

Shivini stood his ground and spread his arms wide.

"Kill me," he said tauntingly. "I've always relished the fear of a dying host."

Alexander stopped just outside of striking range, leveling his sword at the enemy. He was at a loss. The Ranger possessed by the shade was innocent. He didn't deserve to die, yet Alexander couldn't let his body be used to commit murder. He decided to stall.

"Have you found Kelvin?" Alexander asked Chloe silently.

"Yes, My Love. We're nearly there," she replied.

"I just spoke to Rankosi a moment ago," Alexander said to the shade. "How is it that you're serving a master and he's free to do as he pleases?"

Anger contorted Shivini's face. "Phane discovered my presence and bound me to his will. In the end, it won't matter," he said with a shrug. "Once we open the Nether Gate, Phane and everyone else will be at our mercy … and we have very little."

"That's never going to happen," Alexander said.

"You still don't understand, mortal. We will live forever. Even if we can't dominate this world during your lifetime, we will eventually. It's only a matter of time."

"Not if I destroy the Nether Gate," Alexander said.

"Such limited thinking," Shivini said, shaking his head. "Now that we know such a device is possible, we can always build another. All it takes is the right host, one with the proper foundation of experience and knowledge for us to build on." He smiled at Alexander's growing realization.

"You've doomed the world, Alexander. And the part that I find the most delicious is that you did it all for love." Shivini started laughing maniacally just as a squad of Rangers approached from the other end of the hall.

Anatoly motioned to Wren, and two Rangers cautiously approached with weapons drawn, guiding the young woman back down the hall and away from the shade. The squad lined up across the hallway, blocking Shivini's retreat.

The shade looked over his shoulder and shrugged. "Perhaps it's better this way. Once her story spreads through the Keep, all of the young women will be even more terrified of me. It's always more satisfying when their fear rises into unbridled panic."

Kelvin approached from behind with Chloe.

"Alas, I'm afraid I still have a few tasks to carry out for my temporary master," Shivini said. "I've enjoyed our conversation. Trust that we will have other opportunities to chat in the future."

Shivini sliced his host's throat with Alexander's throwing knife. Alexander saw the shade leave the man's dying body, the Ranger's expression changing from malevolent glee to stark terror as his consciousness reasserted itself.

The shade floated toward the squad of Rangers. They held their ground, but Alexander could see the fear in their colors. Shivini passed into one. There was a struggle between the shade and the Ranger, then Shivini passed out of him and into another. After a momentary struggle within the second man, Alexander watched the Ranger's colors change as Shivini possessed him.

The shade stabbed the Ranger who had resisted him with a gleeful giggle, then turned and ran down the hall.

"Do you have the collar?" he asked Kelvin.

"Of course," Kelvin said, handing it to him. Alexander raced after the shade, with his friends right behind him.

The shade led him through the Keep, always staying ahead but not too far. It seemed as if he was deliberately drawing Alexander after him. When Shivini passed people in the halls, he stabbed or slashed at them gleefully, leaving a trail of injured people in his wake. Alexander raced past the fallen, trusting that Anatoly would assign Rangers to tend to them.

Shivini took the most direct route to the Hall of Magic. When Alexander recognized where the shade was going, he erected the shields surrounding the long hallway.

They reached the first shield and Shivini transitioned his host into the aether for just a moment, just long enough to pass through the shield. He looked back at Alexander with a grin and raced on down the hall.

Wizard Hax came out of a room just ahead of the shade.

"Shade!" Kelvin bellowed in warning.

Hax muttered a quick string of words and Alexander saw his colors swell momentarily. When Shivini passed, slashing with his sword, the blade met a magic shield that saved Hax from injury. Shivini ran on.

Alexander dropped the shields around the Hall of Magic and continued the chase. He was getting tired, his lungs burned and his heart pounded, but he raced on. When he saw Shivini turn down the corridor lined with summoning chambers, his blood ran cold.

Again the shade shifted into the aether just long enough to pass through the shield Alexander kept in place across the entrance to that hallway. There were still a few demons trapped inside magic circles within that section of the Keep. It was one of the things on Alexander's very long to-do list. He never felt comfortable having those demons trapped in there, but he also didn't want to fight them if he could help it. Now he might not have a choice.

He dropped the shield to the hall and raced after Shivini. The shade passed a door leading to a chamber that Alexander knew housed a very unpleasant-looking demon and continued to the next door, which led to another imprisoned netherworld beast. Shivini stopped just long enough to giggle with maniacal glee before he entered the room. Alexander was out of breath, but he'd managed to close the gap somewhat. He was only thirty feet behind Shivini when the shade entered the room.

He stopped and drew the Thinblade in his right hand and Mindbender, blade down, in his left.

"Demon!" he called out over his shoulder to his friends as they caught up to him.

Boaberous stepped up on one side and Anatoly took a position on the other. Jack tossed up the hood of his cloak and faded out of sight. Kelvin produced a blue glass orb about an inch in diameter and whispered an incantation over it. Three Rangers were still behind Alexander, the rest had stopped to help the wounded. They drew weapons and stood ready behind Kelvin.

Alexander raised the shield at the entrance of the corridor to keep anything from getting out.

"The darkness is free, My Love," Chloe said in his mind. "It comes." He could feel her fear.

"Stay away from it, Little One," he said without speaking as he braced himself for the battle that was about to unfold.

The creature that came into the hallway was a walking nightmare. It stood nine feet tall and had black, leathery skin stretched tight over powerful-looking muscles. It walked like a man and had two arms ending in long taloned fingers. Its head was similar to that of a goat, except its jaw unhinged, opening impossibly wide as it roared. Its horns swept back from its temples, spreading wide behind its head. Its eyes were smoldering red, the color of hot coals, and they radiated hate and malice. From the back of its shoulders sprouted two tentacles, easily twelve feet long, ending in barbed bone spikes that flailed about over its head.

Shivini stepped out behind it and smiled at Alexander, then once again cut his own throat. The Ranger fell to the floor gurgling blood as Shivini slipped free of the body and slid through the air toward Alexander and his companions. As the shade slipped past him, Alexander maintained his focus on the monstrous demon before him, but watched Shivini with his all around sight as the shade possessed one of the three remaining Rangers.

Shivini turned and ran for the Hall of Magic, leaving Alexander to contend with the demon. He was torn. He couldn't abandon his companions to face this beast on their own, but he dared not lose Shivini if he could help it. There was no telling what the shade intended and he could easily have more information about Blackstone Keep than Alexander did.

The demon in front of him roared and settled the debate within his mind when it started forward. Alexander knew better than to use Mindbender to touch the demon's mind. As powerful as the sword was against men, it was just a blade when facing a creature from the netherworld.

Boaberous raised his war hammer high and charged toward the demon. It snapped both tentacles forward with terrifying speed. The first wrapped around the haft of the hammer and ripped it out of the giant's grasp, sending it skittering down the hall behind the demon. The second jabbed into the giant's shoulder and jerked him forward. Boaberous set his weight against the strength of the demon, crying out in fury and pain from the wound.

Alexander raced forward, slashing at the tentacle with the Thinblade, cleaving it cleanly with one stroke. The demon roared and sent its other tentacle at Alexander, striking him in the chest and sending him sprawling backward. Anatoly pulled him to his feet.

"Get clear of it!" Kelvin bellowed.

Boaberous retreated a few steps out of the tentacle's range and Kelvin pronounced the command word that activated the magic of his glass sphere. A shimmering blue orb of magical force about twelve feet in diameter enveloped the demon, imprisoning it within.

It roared in rage, flailing against the magic sphere, but the barrier held.

"How long will that hold it?" Alexander asked, rubbing his chest. His armor shirt had saved him again but the force of the blow left him sore and bruised.

"Indefinitely, as long as I remain in proximity," Kelvin said.

"Good. Stay with it," Alexander said. "I'll send a Ranger to get help." Then he turned and ran toward the Hall of Magic, dropping the shield at the entrance to the summoning corridor along the way. Shivini had shifted through the aether past the shield and fled down the Hall of Magic toward the sentinel and the central tower. Alexander didn't know what the shade intended but he was certain it wouldn't be good.

He raced toward the central tower with Jack and Anatoly trailing behind him. As he approached the archway sealed with stone, the sentinel was facing the blocked doorway as if it was confused.

"Stand down," Alexander commanded the sentinel, before dismissing the stone wall blocking the archway. Then he slipped into the large circular room that formed the foundation of the wizard's tower rising high over Blackstone Keep.

"Can you tell which way he went, Little One?" Alexander asked as he stopped to catch his breath.

Chloe buzzed into a ball of light and vanished, reappearing a few moments later.

"He went down the stairs, My Love."

Alexander didn't hesitate. He bounded down the circular staircase, stopping at the secret passage leading to the Bloodvault.

"Wait here," he said to Anatoly and Jack, as he dismissed the stone wall sealing the chamber and entered carefully, his night-wisp light held high and his all around sight extended to the limits of its range. The chamber was cold and lifeless, just as he'd left it.

He sealed the entrance and motioned for his companions to follow him as he continued spiraling deeper into the dark and unexplored bowels of the fortress. The air was cold and heavy, but it was also thrumming with power, as if some ancient magic was at work in the dark.

They reached the base of the spiral staircase, breathless and exhausted, slick with sweat in spite of the chill air. The stairs ended on a landing that extended ten feet farther and abruptly stopped at a smooth wall. Alexander reached into the Keep Master's ring with his mind and found the place where they stood. It was deep within the center of the stone mountain that made up the foundation of the ancient fortress, but the map in his mind's eye ended with the landing. No rooms lay beyond.

He placed his hand on the wall and sent his all around sight through to the other side. His vision passed through the heavy stone wall and entered a dark chamber. He could only tell that there was a space beyond from the quality of the colors that the stone of the Keep itself generated.

"Can you pass through this wall and see what's on the other side, Little One?"

"Of course, My Love," Chloe said before she spun into a ball of light and vanished into the aether. A moment later he heard her voice in his mind. "It's a square room with three doors leading out, two are normal oak-bound doors, but the third is spelled with a shield."

"Thank you, Little One," he thought back to her. "Don't go any farther until we get through."

Alexander held up his night-wisp light and inspected the wall and surrounding area until he found what he was looking for. Along the right side of the stone wall was an indentation that looked like a perfect fit for his ring.

He took a deep breath and pressed the black stone set into the Keep Master's ring into the receptacle. A moment passed. Then another.

Abruptly, the wall vanished, revealing a simple stone room twenty feet square. There were large oak doors at the center of the left and right walls. Directly across from the entrance was an open passageway barred by a magical shield of a quality that Alexander hadn't encountered before. Where most shields had a slightly blue aura, this one was the color of blood and it glowed, even to his normal vision.

"That looks dangerous," Jack said.

Alexander nodded as he sent his mind into the Keep Master's ring, searching for the barrier but he still found nothing past the threshold of the room where he stood.

"Little One, can you tell which way Shivini went?"

"There is darkness beyond the shielded passage, My Love."

With a frown, he started to reach for the shield but Anatoly caught his hand.

"Are you sure that's wise? Maybe start with something you don't need quite so much … like a knife," Anatoly said, handing him a throwing knife.

Alexander grinned at his old instructor as he took the blade. Carefully, he brought it into contact with the magical field. As it passed the plane of magic, it vaporized, leaving nothing but half a blade and a wisp of noxious smoke.

"I wish I'd spent more time studying that book Mage Cedric left me," Alexander said. "There's no telling how to deactivate this shield or if I even need to. I may be able to pass right through it because of the ring, or it could do to me what it did to that blade."

"For my part, I'd rather you didn't risk it," Jack said.

"I tend to agree," Anatoly said.

"Shivini is in there … and he's up to something," Alexander said.

"Yeah, and you won't be able to do a thing about it if that shield kills you," Anatoly said.

"There has to be a way through," Alexander said. "If not with the Keep Master's ring, then how?"

Anatoly shrugged. "I couldn't tell you, but the only way you're going to find out is by risking at least a finger."

"You're right," Alexander said, facing the shield and carefully extending his left little finger toward the red plane of magic. He braced himself for the pain but felt only a warm tingling sensation as his finger moved through the field. He pushed through to the other side and turned back to his friends.

"I don't like this, Alexander," Anatoly said.

"Me neither," Jack said.

"What choice do we have? Shivini has to be stopped."

Anatoly clenched his jaw, but remained silent.

"Be careful, Alexander," Jack said. "There's no telling what's down here, but it seems clear that Shivini knows something we don't."

Chloe buzzed into a ball of light over Alexander's head, facing Anatoly and Jack.

"I will protect him," she said.

Alexander smiled as he started down the dark corridor with Chloe flying in an orbit around his head.

Chapter 9

Isabel followed Abigail through the Keep, asking passersby for directions at every turn. At first she wasn't sure where her sister was going but it didn't take long to realize her destination. Isabel quickened her pace. She knew Abigail was upset, she only hoped she wasn't so distraught that she would leave the Keep by herself.

Isabel reached the aerie just in time to see Abigail launch from the flight bay on Kallistos.

"Abigail!" she shouted into the wind, but her sister either didn't hear her or chose to ignore her.

Isabel knew she could impose her will on Kallistos and force him to fly back to the aerie whether Abigail wanted to or not, but she wasn't willing to usurp Abigail's free will like that. She had come to love and respect her new sister, but even more than that, she valued their friendship.

Mistress Constance approached.

"Lady Reishi, Abigail saddled Kallistos and was prepared to launch before we realized what she was doing," she said. "Against my counsel, she left the Keep alone. I'm readying two Sky Knights to fly escort as we speak."

"Good, saddle Asteroth as well," Isabel said without looking away from Abigail as she descended to gain speed.

Isabel tipped her head back and found Slyder preening himself on the balcony of her quarters. With a thought, she sent her familiar after Abigail. At least she would be able to watch over her through Slyder's eyes.

The Sky Knights were doing the work of wyvern handlers, so the job took longer than normal. The aerie was just beginning to come to life. With the assistance of the Rangers, they had been busy cleaning and preparing for the arrival of many more wyverns, handlers, and Sky Knights, but for the time being, the place was operating on a skeleton crew.

Isabel paced as Abigail disappeared into the distance, flying south toward New Ruatha and the Great Forest. Isabel had no idea where she was heading. It could be that she was trying to get as far away from the war and her unwanted responsibility as possible. Isabel hadn't known Abigail for all that long, but they shared a bond of friendship forged in hardship and shared danger. They were close and Isabel ached for the pain she knew Alexander had caused her, but she also knew that Alexander was right.

He had made the hard choice yet again.

She was proud of him and worried about the emotional toll his choice would exact. It was one thing to accept the burden of responsibility upon yourself, but quite another to place such a burden on one you loved. She knew he would struggle with the consequences of his decision, especially if Abigail was hurt in the bargain.

Mistress Constance returned.

"The escort riders are ready," she said. "Shall I hold them until Asteroth is prepared or send them now?"

"Send them," Isabel said. "I'll catch up. Also, send a Ranger to Alexander with a report."

"Right away, Lady Reishi," Constance said.

She watched the two escort riders launch. Both were experienced Sky Knights riding mature wyverns with countless hours in the air. They slipped over the edge of the launch bay and tipped into a shallow dive to gain speed.

Not long after, several Sky Knights led Asteroth onto the flight deck. He was saddled and eager to take to wing. Isabel linked her mind to the big wyvern and soothed the beast with assurances that they would soon be airborne. It didn't take her long to change into riding armor and lace herself into the saddle. Once she was secure and had done her checks, she urged Asteroth into the air. With one thrust of his wings, he gained ten feet, the second thrust propelled them out over the edge of the flight bay. Isabel savored the exhilaration of flight as she leaned into Asteroth's neck and urged him into a gentle dive.

She caught up to Abigail within the hour. The two escort riders were above and behind, watching over their charge. Abigail ignored them.

Isabel pulled up alongside her sister and signaled to turn around. Abigail shook her head vigorously, wiping tears from her eyes. Isabel resigned herself to follow wherever Abigail led. They flew for the better part of the afternoon, floating high over the Great Forest. The vast expanse of wild lands seemed to stretch on forever.

Isabel had grown up in the forest and knew it well, but even she was awed by the true dimensions of the forest blanketing the world below her. The trees stood tall and proud reaching high into the sky for the light raining down on them from above. The aura of life was so palpable that Isabel almost imagined she could see the colors of the trees the way Alexander could.

She'd often wondered about his magic. It was such a simple thing, seemingly without great power and yet it had carried him so far.

The power to see.

Insight into the nature and motives of those he faced. Isabel had power to cause harm: her light-lance spell could kill a man at a distance with unerring precision, yet she found herself humbled by Alexander's ability to see. His magic gave him knowledge of his enemy and guided his decisions in a way that no other power could match.

His unique power, coupled with his essential goodness, made him just the right man for the hardest job in all of the Seven Isles. He had proven that once again when he tapped his own sister to be the Queen of Ruatha, knowing full well that such a decision would cause him pain and her despair, but also knowing that it was right and necessary. He hadn't flinched or stalled. He made his decision and carried out his plan in spite of the personal consequences.

He was the right man for the job and she would support him come what may. In this case, it fell on her to convince Abigail of the necessity of accepting her duty. She was the right woman for the job of leading Ruatha. Isabel knew her strengths as well as anyone. They had stood shoulder to shoulder against many enemies and Abigail had never wavered. She would make a fine queen … once she accepted her duty.

Isabel intended to see to it that she did just that. She knew Abigail wouldn't like it. She would resist, but in the end she would come to understand and she would live up to her brother's trust.

It was late afternoon when they floated past the edge of the Great Forest and into the southern plains of Ruatha. Abigail banked sharply when they came to the road leading from Southport to Highlands Reach. She followed the road for a while and then began to descend. Isabel followed.

When it became clear that Abigail intended to land, Isabel gave a hand signal to their escort riders to fly overwatch. They broke off and settled into a wide orbit.

Abigail landed near the burned-out ruins of a large manor. Isabel followed and set down near Kallistos. She dismounted and followed Abigail to the husk of the house.

Abigail stood in the center of what used to be the courtyard of a stately manor house at the center of a ranch estate. Several of the outbuildings were still intact, but the place seemed abandoned.

She was holding her stomach and sobbing, tears steaming down her cheeks.

Isabel approached slowly.

"It's not fair," Abigail said through her tears.

"I know," Isabel said.

"My whole life has been taken away from me. My big brother is dead. My home is burned to the ground—and for what?" Abigail slumped to her knees and cried.

Isabel knelt beside her, cradling her head silently, holding her sister as she cried. After a while Abigail sniffed back her tears and sat down. Isabel sat next to her, but still said nothing.

"We grew up here," Abigail said. "This was home and now we can never go back."

Isabel just listened.

"My room was right up there," Abigail said, pointing to a place that no longer existed. The house was a shell of its former form, just stone and charred timbers.

"That was Lucky's workshop. He always had something on the stove. We used to stop by in the afternoons for a snack. He was always happy to feed us and listen to stories of our latest adventure, even though our mother would scold us for ruining our appetite before dinner."

She picked up a handful of dirt and let it slip through her fingers in the gentle breeze.

"Everything that went before is dust."

She fell silent as she stared at the broken remains of her former life.

"We were happy here. We grew up surrounded by people who loved us and watched out for us in a world filled with possibility. The greatest dangers we ever faced were always the result of our own poor judgment. We don't deserve this."

"I know," Isabel said.

"What am I going to do?" Abigail pleaded, close to tears again.

Isabel turned to her sister and waited until she was sure she had her full attention.

"You're going to make certain that no one else has to suffer the way that you and your family have suffered. You're going to do your duty, Abigail."

She closed her eyes against more tears and shook her head.

"Why does it have to be my duty? I don't want responsibility for other people's lives. What if I make a bad decision and people get hurt? I'm not ready for this." Then she whispered, "I'm just a farm girl."

"There's where you're wrong," Isabel said gently. "You are a queen and a Sky Knight. You've stood by your brother this long. Are you really going to abandon him when he needs you most?"

Abigail looked up sharply and sniffed back her tears.

"I'm not abandoning Alexander. I would never do that."

"I know," Isabel said with a smile. "He isn't doing this because he wants to, he's doing it because he has to. The other island kings won't accept him as both the Sovereign and the King of Ruatha."

"There has to be another way," Abigail whispered.

Isabel sat in silence while Abigail worked through her feelings and the demands weighing on her.

"I don't know how to be a queen," she said in a very small voice.

"Me neither," Isabel said.

Abigail frowned, deep in thought.

"You didn't ask for this either," Abigail said. "How is it that you've accepted it so easily?"

Isabel shrugged with a smile. "I got Alexander in the bargain."

"How do you do it, Isabel? How do you make the right choices when there aren't any good options to choose from?"

"I'm not sure I do," Isabel said. "I just try to make choices that will help Alexander the most. He has the weight of the world on his shoulders and sometimes I think he feels like it's more than he can bear."

"Sometimes I wonder if it's more than anyone can handle," Abigail said. "I worry about him. He's had just as much taken from him as I have. I worry that one day he's going to lose something so dear to him that he'll break."

"I know what you mean," Isabel said. "He told me about the day you and I were taken by the Sky Knights. Without Chloe, I'm not sure if he would have made it off the Reishi Isle. He said she gave him hope and love when all he could find within himself was despair.

"Don't you see, Abigail, he needs us, all of us. He's just one man standing against terrifying enemies. And he isn't doing it because he wants to. He's doing it because it's the only way to have the life he wants."

"I don't have any choice, do I?" Abigail asked.

"You always have a choice," Isabel said. "It's just that in this case, the only choice you have that's consistent with who you are, is to support your brother."

She was silent for a long time before she nodded and rubbed the tears from her face.

"It's getting late," Abigail said. "We should probably be going."

Chapter 10

Alexander cautiously moved down the corridor. In his right hand he held the Thinblade, in his left, a vial of night-wisp dust. The corridor ran for several hundred feet from the shield before it ended with a staircase leading down, deeper into the heart rock of the Keep.

Alexander descended the stairs, straining the limits of his all around sight to prevent Shivini from surprising him. The shade had promised to let him live so that he could witness the horrors he had unleashed, but he didn't believe it for a moment. Shivini had been bound to Phane's will. If the shade had a chance to kill him and take the Sovereign Stone, he would. Alexander had no doubt about that.

He slowed when he saw light coming from the base of the staircase. The landing opened onto a platform at the edge of a giant room, which was shaped like a toroid and measured at least two hundred feet across and forty feet high at the highest point. The center of the room was occupied by two formations that would have been a stalactite and a stalagmite in a natural cave but here they were clearly cut with exacting precision.

Suspended in the space between the two stone points was a giant spinning crystal shaped like an elongated diamond. It was easily six feet tall and two feet wide at its widest point. It spun with such speed that it almost looked like it was standing still.

Colors of magic poured off the crystal, flowing into the stone of Blackstone Keep. Alexander had never imagined such a thing, but he knew instinctively that the Keep's magic was powered by this spinning crystal. Waves of energy flowed outward, filling the toroid with heat and light. He realized with a jolt that this place had to be in the exact center of the mass of the Keep.

Shivini was climbing toward the crystal. He was halfway there already and slowly inching his way up the artificial stalagmite. Alexander had no idea what would happen if the crystal was disturbed and he didn't want to find out. He was sure that it had been spinning in perfect balance for over two thousand years.

He slipped over the edge and slid down the gently sloping wall to the floor, then raced across the room toward Shivini. The shade saw him coming and tried to climb faster, but he could gain little purchase on the smooth pillar. As Alexander neared, Shivini slipped and slid to the ground. He drew his sword and faced Alexander with a grin. His nose and fingertips were grey from frostbite.

"Looks like moving through the aether is taking its toll on you," Alexander said.

"Not on me," Shivini said, "on my host. But he doesn't matter, Alexander. Even if you destroy this host, I'll just take another and come back to finish my work."

"What's your plan?" Alexander asked, leveling the Thinblade at his enemy.

Shivini shrugged. "I'm going to destroy your Keep, kill you, and take your fancy necklace to Phane, not necessarily in that order."

"You're more forthright than I would have expected," Alexander said as he tried to formulate a plan.

"As a general rule, I prefer to lie unless the truth will cause more fear," Shivini said. "Here's another truth, Alexander. You can't win. You and everyone you love were doomed the moment Phane bound me to his will and sent me to destroy you.

"Did you know that we've never failed to accomplish a task we were assigned? Over the decades that we were summoned and pressed into service by Malachi Reishi we always succeeded, every single time. It's no wonder he came to rely on us so heavily when he could have summoned many others from the darkness.

"Face it, Alexander. You've lost. Embrace the despair growing within you. Give in to the hopelessness."

Alexander laughed bitterly. "You don't really expect me to take your advice, do you?"

"I guess not, but it's always worth a try. Next to fear, my favorite human emotion is despair. It nourishes my very soul. Or at least it would if I had one."

"The way I see it—you've lost," Alexander said as he edged closer to the shade. "Now that I know your target, I can stop you from ever getting down here again."

It was Shivini's turn to laugh. "I can float right through the stone and take one of your sentries at my leisure. You can't hope to guard this place against me."

"There's where you're wrong," Alexander said as he attacked. He slashed off the first two feet of Shivini's sword, then brought the Thinblade back up, taking off his hand and forearm. It thudded to the ground, blood flowing onto the floor. Alexander wasn't trying to kill him … in fact, he needed him alive, but he also needed him defenseless. In the back of his mind, he mourned the loss of yet another Ranger to his blade, but this time it was necessary.

As Shivini recoiled from the sudden attack, Alexander kicked him in the chest, sending him sprawling onto his back. He dropped the Thinblade and jumped on Shivini's chest, pummeling him in the face several times.

Shivini laughed.

Using his attack as a distraction, Alexander withdrew the collar Kelvin had fashioned for just this purpose and snapped it around Shivini's neck. As it clicked into place, Alexander saw its colors swell with power as the enchantment was invoked. He rolled off the shade and retrieved the Thinblade.

Shivini sat up with a look of alarm, then he howled with rage as he bolted to his feet and charged toward Alexander in wild fury. Alexander sidestepped and tripped the shade, sending him sprawling to the floor again.

He was trapped.

He got to his feet again and faced Alexander with growing awareness, but then he broke into a malicious smile. Before Alexander could react, Shivini snatched up his bloody forearm and threw it at the spinning crystal filling the chamber with light and power.

It hit with a thud. Blood splattered against the crystal, and the arm ricocheted with terrible force across the room, smashing into the wall so hard that it left nothing but a clump of bloody mush that slowly slid toward the floor, leaving a streak of gore in its wake.

The blood staining the crystal smoldered and burnt, sending a spiral streamer of smoke radiating away from it.

Shivini laughed, pointing at the almost imperceptible wobble in the balance of the crystal.

"I told you, Alexander. You can't win. Even this rather ingenious collar will do you no good. I'm quite sure I will be free the moment this host dies."

With that, Shivini charged toward Alexander again. His attack was sloppy and left him vulnerable, but Alexander didn't take the bait. He danced out of the way, sheathing the Thinblade before turning to attack Shivini with his hands.

Shivini fought with reckless abandon, not caring about the body of his host, indeed trying to get himself killed, but since he was missing a hand, Alexander was able to wrestle him to the ground and bind his arms behind his back with his own belt. With Shivini restrained, Alexander began dragging him toward the entrance to the toroid-shaped room.

Shivini cursed and struggled, but Alexander was able to drag him up the sloping wall to the entrance platform. He was thankful that there was a series of steps cut into the stone or else he would have been hard-pressed to climb out of the room himself, let alone drag Shivini behind him.

It was slow going with the shade struggling all the way, but Alexander managed to drag him to the shield … where he stopped cold.

Anatoly and Jack were waiting for him. Boaberous had joined them, a bandage wrapped around his shoulder where the demon had injured him.

Before Alexander could voice his dilemma, Shivini began to laugh.

"I keep telling you to give up, Alexander," Shivini said. "You can't win. The moment you drag me through that shield, I'll be free again. I'll just take another body and finish my work, and even if I don't manage to get back down here, it won't matter in the long run. The heartstone of the Keep is unbalanced. It's only a matter of time before it fails and then all of the magical protections, shields, weapons, and capabilities that make this place so powerful will fail along with it."

"What's he talking about?" Jack asked.

"There's a giant spinning crystal in the room down there that's giving off more magical power than I've ever seen before. It looks like it's feeding the Keep with energy. Shivini threw his arm at it—after I cut it off mind you—and now it has a slight wobble. If I had to guess, I'd say the crystal is what's powering all of the magic in the Keep. Shivini may have just destroyed Blackstone Keep."

The shade laughed.

"The other problem is this shield," Alexander said. "I'm pretty sure Kelvin's collar will only work on a live host. Once the host dies, Shivini will be free again."

Shivini's laughter turned maniacal as he surged to his feet and bolted toward the shield. Alexander caught him, struggling to pull him back, but the shade extended his head toward the deadly plane of magical energy, and with a final lunge, succeeded in thrusting the top four inches of his skull through the shield. It vaporized in an instant. Alexander watched the dark colors of the shade come free of the dead host and float straight toward him.

He felt a thrill of icy cold deep in the recesses of his soul as the shade searched his psyche for a way in. Alexander saw images of everything he'd ever done wrong flash across his mind's eye one after the other with impossible speed.

Shivini seemed to be looking for anything that would evoke a feeling of guilt or despair, anything that he could leverage into a belief that Alexander deserved to be punished, that he deserved to suffer for what he'd done.

He faced the memories of his life with calm confidence. He'd been through an experience like this before when he bonded with Mindbender. He wasn't afraid. He knew that he'd never done anything that warranted relinquishing his free will to Shivini.

With deliberate intent, Alexander brought his love for Isabel into the forefront of his mind. Shivini shrieked silently and fled from him, through the shield and up the spiral staircase into the safety of the shadows.

Alexander shook his head and sighed as he knelt down to remove the collar from the dead Ranger's neck. Another victim, another family shattered.

"At least we know the collar works," he said, tucking it back into his shirt and stepping through the shield.

"How's the shoulder?" he asked Boaberous.

"Master Alabrand put some healing salve on it," Boaberous said. "It'll be fine by tomorrow."

Alexander nodded. "How's Kelvin doing with that demon?"

"It's still contained in the blue sphere, but they're not sure what to do with it since they can't get it through the door into the summoning chamber again."

Alexander thought about it for a moment before sending his mind into the Keep Master's ring and tracing a route through the Keep. He was looking for a series of passages leading to the paddock big enough to accommodate the sphere. When he found a route, he smiled mirthlessly.

"I know how to take care of that demon without risking anyone else. Have you taken a look behind these doors?" he asked, motioning to the two oak-bound doors on either side of the little room.

"They wouldn't open," Jack said. "And they don't have a lock to pick, so we figured we'd wait until you returned. They'll probably open for you."

"Let's hope you're right," Alexander said as he pulled on the heavy brass ring on one of the doors. A shimmer of magic raced over the surface of the pull ring and the door swung open easily, revealing a corridor leading into the darkness.

With night-wisp light in hand, he proceeded down the hallway for several hundred feet until the corridor opened into a room made entirely of crystal. It resembled the room they'd found under the ruins of the adept's keep in Grafton.

It was about twenty feet across, cut in a perfect half-sphere. The crystal walls were polished to a sheen and the floor had a ten-foot magic circle inlaid in gold set into it. Otherwise the room was entirely empty.

"I really wish I knew what these crystal rooms were good for," Alexander muttered.

"Perhaps one of the books we found in Grafton will shed some light on that," Jack said.

"I hope so," Alexander said. "It seems like someone went to an awful lot of trouble to make this place. It really ought to do something interesting."

They retraced their path back to the central chamber and closed the door. Then Alexander opened the door on the opposite wall. Again they were met with a corridor leading into the dark. When they reached the room at the end, Alexander was so stunned, he just stopped and stared, slack-jawed.

It was easily two hundred feet square with high ceilings supported by broad pillars.

The entire room was filled with treasure.

There were boxes, bags, and barrels filled with gold coins, jewelry, and loose precious stones of all manner and variety. It was the most impressive collection of wealth that Alexander had ever seen.

His friends entered, staring in disbelief as well. As far as the light of their night-wisp dust would let them see were mounds of gold, silver, and assorted treasures, enough to buy a country, enough to buy an entire island.

Alexander scanned the room for any sign of magical colors but saw nothing. It was all just ordinary gold and silver in staggering abundance.

"Well, I was wondering how we were going to pay people to rebuild Northport," Alexander muttered.

"This is the kind of treasure hoard I would expect to see a dragon sitting on top of," Jack said.

Anatoly chuckled. "We can certainly use this. Duncan mentioned he was worried that we were depleting the coffers of New Ruatha with payroll for the army. I'd say this eliminates that worry as well."

"Blackstone Keep certainly doesn't disappoint," Alexander said. In spite of his defeat against Shivini, he couldn't help feeling a sense of hope in the presence of such wealth. Money was power, different than magic or armies, but power just the same. This treasure would go a long way toward accomplishing their goals.

Alexander picked up a handful of gems from a nearby cask and let them fall through his fingers. Most were semiprecious stones but there were a few diamonds, rubies, and emeralds mixed in. He found an emerald the size of his fingertip that matched Isabel's eyes nearly perfectly and slipped it into his pocket with a smile.

"We should probably go see how Kelvin's doing with that demon," Alexander said.

They closed the door to the treasure room and it magically sealed itself behind them. Alexander pressed the Keep Master's ring into the recess in the wall and the stone barrier reappeared, sealing the entry chamber closed again.

The climb back up to the Hall of Magic was arduous and long. Alexander's legs burned and ached from the strain of climbing so many stairs. He was exhausted once they finally reached the large circular room at the base of the tower.

The sentinel was standing where he'd left it.

"Sentinel, go to the base of these stairs," Alexander commanded. "Kill anyone who approaches except for me."

The sentinel nodded and began the long descent.

They found Kelvin where they'd left him. He was staring at the demon imprisoned within the blue magical sphere.

"Alexander, it looks like things went well with the shade," Kelvin said, motioning to the blood on his tunic from wrestling with Shivini.

"Yes and no," Alexander said. "I'll explain more later. Right now, I have a plan for this demon."

"Good, I've been thinking about that," Kelvin said. "So far, the best I've got is cutting a wider doorway into the summoning chamber with the Thinblade so we can put it back into its circle."

Alexander shook his head. "No, we're going to kill it."

He motioned to a nearby Ranger from the squad standing by to provide any support Kelvin might need.

"Yes, Lord Reishi," the sergeant said.

"Have two of your Rangers crawl past the sphere to the other side and roll it down the hallway into the Hall of Magic."

Not long after, they were navigating through the halls of Blackstone Keep along a route that Alexander had plotted for the size of the corridors. It was a circuitous path but it beat the alternative of trying to fight the demon.

An hour and a half later, they rolled the very agitated demon into the paddock. It screamed in rage when the sunlight hit it. The Rangers rolled it to the bridge abutment and out into the sky. As it slipped over the edge and sailed out into the open air, Kelvin shattered the little glass sphere against the stone wall, releasing the magic of the sphere imprisoning the demon. Everyone went to the low stone wall to watch the demon plummet to the ground. When it finally crashed into the plain thousands of feet below them, it didn't move again.

As Alexander watched the demon to be sure it was dead, a breathless Ranger ran up to him.

"Lord Reishi, your wife and sister have left the Keep mounted on their wyverns. Mistress Constance has sent two Sky Knights to provide escort."

"What?!" Alexander said.

Chapter 11

Alexander reached the wyvern aerie with his temper barely held in check, anger driven more by fear than anything else. He couldn't lose either of them again and they were vulnerable away from the Keep.

He marched straight to Mistress Constance, who was speaking with Magda.

"Why did you let them leave?" he demanded.

Constance frowned. "It was not my place to stop them."

"They aren't safe out there," Alexander said. "You should have stopped them."

Magda started to interrupt but Constance held her ground.

"Lady Abigail saddled her own steed and launched without warning," Constance said. "Your wife demanded that we saddle Asteroth. She is both Lady Reishi and a triumvir of the Reishi Coven. As such, I am duty bound to obey her."

Alexander took a deep breath and calmed his anger. He couldn't fault Constance and he knew his anger was misplaced.

"You're right," Alexander said. "I'm sorry I took my anger out on you. Do you know where they went?"

"They headed due south," Constance said.

"Send word the moment they return."

"Of course, Lord Reishi."

Alexander went back to his quarters. He was exhausted from the injury he'd only just recovered from and from his day of climbing stairs but he still had things to do. Before attending to anything else, he needed to know that his wife and sister were safe.

He went to his meditation chamber. It didn't take long before he was floating on the firmament. He found them flying south over the Great Forest. Abigail led the way and she looked distraught. Isabel and the escort riders followed. Alexander decided they were safe enough, so he returned to his body.

He sat for several moments brooding over the enemies, both immediate and distant, that threatened to undo his world. It all seemed so much bigger than he. Once again he took refuge in the thought that he was a simple ranch hand, that these challenges were both unfair and more than he could hope to overcome. It wasn't long before his mind was flitting from one problem to the next seeking refuge from one danger by facing the next, only to find it as insurmountable as the last.

Chloe broke his brooding when she buzzed into a ball of light a couple of feet in front of his face. She floated closer with a stern look.

"Stop that!" she said.

Alexander was both startled and bemused by her tone.

"You are not a ranch hand. You are Lord Reishi, Sovereign of the Seven Isles. I know your heart, I have seen your soul. You can overcome these challenges, but not if you sit here brooding over the problems you face. Stop looking back at the past, forget what you used to be, let go of what you wanted for your life and embrace what your life is now. You are the focus of hope for all those who want freedom. You have great power at your disposal and you have something precious that none of your enemies will ever have."

Alexander frowned questioningly.

"You are surrounded by people who love you, people who will do anything for you. Do you think Phane has one single person in all the world that he can trust with his life? Do you believe that any of the people in Zuhl's court think for one second that Zuhl would risk anything of value to preserve them?

"You have people all around you who would sacrifice their lives for you without question, people who know without doubt that you would risk your own life for them. That's why I know you will be victorious. Love will triumph. It has to."

"I love you, Little One. Thank you," Alexander said with a soft smile.

Chloe buzzed up and kissed him on the cheek.

"I love you too, Alexander."

"Will you watch over me while I talk to the sovereigns?"

"Of course, My Love."

Alexander touched the Sovereign Stone and his consciousness translated into the timeless place that was the Reishi Council Chamber.

Balthazar stood. "Alexander, when last we spoke you were preparing to do battle in Grafton province. What has transpired?"

Alexander took his seat with a sigh. "A great deal, I'm afraid. I have need of your counsel. It seems that every time I succeed in one area, the enemy makes inroads in another."

"Such is the nature of war," Balthazar said. "You can never be strong in all places. The key to victory is knowledge, both of one's self and of one's enemies."

"We succeeded at Grafton," Alexander reported. "Ithilian is free of military forces loyal to Phane, although there's no telling what his agents are up to. Phane's army on Ruatha has been destroyed with minimal loss on our side, except for the city of Northport." Alexander took a deep breath and let it out slowly. "It's been completely razed."

Five of the six sovereigns sat forward with alarm. Malachi smiled with interest.

"How many lives lost?" Balthazar asked.

Alexander shook his head. "A few thousand on our side, those who refused to heed the order to evacuate. The vast majority of the population was relocated to other cities."

"So just the wood and brick of the city was lost?" Darius Reishi said.

Alexander nodded. "I ordered the Guild Mage to deploy a dozen weapons he created. The devastation was staggering. The city is nothing more than a wall surrounding a field of rubble."

Balthazar said, "Brick and timber is easy to rebuild. A single life lost is gone forever."

"Oh, there was great loss of life," Alexander said. "My father tells me there were more than eight enemy legions within the walls when we attacked. They all fell."

"War is a horrible business, Alexander," Balthazar said, "all the more so for those with a conscience. I take it you are on Ruatha now."

"Yes, I'm in Blackstone Keep and there's a shade loose here: Shivini. He says Phane has bound him to his will and ordered him to destroy the Keep, kill me, and take the Stone.

"So far, I've had one confrontation with him and survived, but at great cost. He led me to a giant spinning crystal in the heart of the Keep that seems to be feeding the fortress energy. Shivini damaged the crystal's balance. It's wobbling now and I don't know what to do about it."

Balthazar took on a very serious expression and thought for a moment. The other sovereigns waited for him to proceed.

"This is grave news indeed," Balthazar said. "I built the Reishi Keep and invented the concept of the heartstone. It's the power source of a magical keep. In essence, it's an artificial wizard."

Alexander frowned in confusion.

Balthazar nodded with understanding as he donned the mantle of the teacher. "A human wizard links his mind with the firmament and injects his will. The heartstone is designed to form a permanent link to the firmament for the purpose of injecting a very specific set of predetermined spell forms into the firmament when triggered by the occupants of the Keep.

"It must spin with perfect balance to function correctly. Once it's thrown out of balance, there's little that can be done to correct it without re-enchanting the heartstone itself."

The magnitude of the damage settled on Alexander. "What happens when the heartstone fails?"

"It will fall and shatter," Balthazar said. "The Keep will lose all of its magical protections and weapons, but it will retain its natural fortifications."

"How long?"

"Depending on the degree of wobble, a few months, maybe a year," Balthazar said.

"Will it degrade gradually or will it all go out at once?"

"Bits and pieces will begin to fail, sometimes sporadically until the heartstone topples and shatters. Everything will stop working at that point."

"What would it take to fix it?"

"An arch mage enchanter with the right instruction," Balthazar said. "I can provide the instruction, but you must provide the enchanter."

"The Guild Mage is an enchanter. Can you help me help him become an arch mage?"

"If you have a sufficient quantity of Wizard's Dust," Balthazar said.

"I don't at the moment. But Lucky is a master alchemist," Alexander said. "How can I help him become a mage so we can make the Wizard's Dust we need?"

"That is much easier, although not without challenge. I can teach you a series of exercises for him to perform that will expand his understanding of his link with the firmament. If he practices diligently, he will be able to advance."

"Good, let's start there," Alexander said.

Balthazar taught him a single exercise and drilled him until he could repeat it verbatim without error.

"When you leave here, go to a quiet place and write this exercise down for your friend. Once you've related the task to him and he's practicing the exercise, I will provide the next in the series."

"Very well, although I may need to leave Lucky to his studies here in the Keep," Alexander said. "If that's the case, I'll need all of the exercises before I depart."

"Of course, but these things are best done at a measured pace and in the correct sequence," Balthazar said.

"Lucky knows what's at stake, he'll do what he must."

So much had happened since he last spoke with the council. He wanted to make sure he consulted them on every matter of importance. Their counsel might provide some vital bit of knowledge but it all hinged on giving them complete information and asking the right questions.

"Isabel has become a Sky Knight and one of the triumvirs of the Reishi Coven," Alexander said. "She's brought the forces of the fortress island to our side in this war and they've already proven invaluable. They helped sink a fleet of Lancer transport ships from Andalia and they delivered the weapons that destroyed the legions dug in at Northport."

Balthazar smiled with satisfaction. "Well done, Alexander. Choosing the woman you will spend your life with is the most important decision any sovereign, indeed any man, will ever make. It sounds like you've chosen well."

"She's the best thing that's ever happened to me, but that's not why I've mentioned her. Prior to being taken by the Sky Knights, she had been poisoned. We used a potion made with fairy dust to stay the poison for a time but it wasn't a cure. Mage Gamaliel found an item in the stores within Blackstone Keep that he believed was her best hope and had it transported to the fortress island.

"It was made by an arch mage named Desiderates."

Both Constantine and Darius sat forward with increased interest.

"As Isabel explained it to me, the item was a wish spell."

Constantine tipped his head back and laughed with pure joy.

"He was finally successful? After all those years of failure," Constantine said, shaking his head. "He never did know how to give up. I always admired that trait in him."

"He asked Isabel that I relay a message to you that he won your bet."

Constantine laughed again.

"He was never satisfied with success until others knew that he had succeeded," Constantine said. "I am curious about the workings of his spell."

"Apparently, he bound the essence of his consciousness and soul to a small box. When Isabel invoked the spell and opened the box, she found herself within a place out of the world of time and substance where she had a conversation with Desiderates. He looked into her mind and then offered to help her in every way he could.

"He cured her poison. For that I'm forever in his debt. But he did much more. The Guild Mage had given Isabel a necklace that allowed her to talk to animals with her mind. Desiderates amplified the power of the necklace and bound it to her so that she can not only communicate with animals but command them as well.

"Unfortunately, during the journey to the Valley of the Fairy Queen, we were attacked by a demon possessing a big cat. Once the cat was killed, the demon possessed Isabel's horse. When she tried to calm her horse through the power of her necklace, the demon touched her mind, opening a rift to the netherworld within her unconscious and drawing her into the darkness. I followed her in and brought her back out, unknowingly freeing the shades in the process, and leaving the rift to the darkness present in her mind."

The sovereigns stared at him silently.

"Desiderates gave her conscious control over the passageway so that she can keep it closed and prevent the darkness from using her ever again."

"A connection to the netherworld is as dangerous as it is powerful," Balthazar said. "Has she attempted to use it for anything?"

"No. Magda, one of the triumvirs of the Reishi Coven, warned her to keep the passage closed."

"Good, I would suggest you reinforce her warning," Balthazar said. "No good can come from the darkness, no matter what the denizens of the netherworld promise."

Alexander nodded. "There's more. When I became bound to Chloe, the Fairy Queen demanded that I sire a fairy child through Isabel. The conception opened a conduit within Isabel's psyche to the realm of light. Desiderates made this conduit accessible at will, rather than only subconsciously."

The Reishi Sovereigns sat in dumb silence for a moment before Constantine smiled and shook his head. "I'd say my old friend outdid himself."

"I would tend to agree," Balthazar said. "An active connection to the realm of light has the potential to be magnificently powerful."

Alexander nodded. "After Isabel survived the mana fast, she was able to tap into the realm of light to heal others and even created a spell that channels the Maker's light into a beam capable of banishing a scourgling."

"Impossible!" Malachi protested.

"She saved my life with it," Alexander answered. "I'm telling you all of this to provide background so you can help me save her. Phane has been busy. He's created a unit of soldiers bound with creatures from the netherworld—they're called wraithkin.

"These men have powers like nothing I've ever faced before. They can teleport short distances, healing any injuries they've sustained instantly each time. I've only succeeded in killing them by attacking the head. They bested the Commander of the Reishi Protectorate, a battle mage, and killed another mage in our first encounter, not to mention nearly a dozen Rangers.

"I was injured during that fight and Isabel tried to heal me, but failed. We've since come to understand that the wraithkin's daggers are enchanted to infect the wound of those injured so that any attempt to magically heal the wound will fail. Ultimately, I was healed through the use of fairy dust, but they tell me it stopped my heart for a time before the taint was eliminated.

"More importantly, healers who attempt to use magic on the injured are infected with some form of dark magic. We've already lost one wizard who tried to heal an injured soldier."

Alexander took a deep breath and held it for a moment before letting it out all at once.

"Isabel's colors are tainted with darkness. It doesn't seem to have any effect on her connection with the firmament but her link to the realm of light has been compromised. I'm terrified that the taint might spread."

Malachi started to laugh slowly and deliberately. "My son will be victorious in the end. He's taken your Keep. He's taken your woman. It's only a matter of time before he takes your life and the Sovereign Stone with it."

Demetrius sat forward, scowling. "You are my own son, Malachi, and I count Alexander as a far better addition to this council than you."

Malachi started to protest but Alexander stopped him with a raised hand.

"You've caused so much suffering, so much pain, so many lives lost and all for your petty self-importance. Be silent. Nobody cares what you think anymore."

Malachi sat back, brooding with rage, but said nothing.

"Have you examined the weapons responsible for her condition?" Balthazar asked.

"Mage Gamaliel has. He reports that the dagger acts as a conduit for the darkness within the wraithkin rather than causing the taint itself."

Balthazar frowned. "Dark magic is insidious. When I first became aware of its potential, I began to study the netherworld but quickly discovered the cost of such magic. Once I realized how dangerous it was, I stopped my studies, destroyed all of my research, and forbade all Reishi-trained wizards from pursuing any form of dark magic.

"Unfortunately, it would seem that my precautions have rendered me ignorant of the capabilities and workings of netherworld magic. I'm afraid I can't offer any insight into the nature of the taint within Isabel. I'm sorry, Alexander."

Alexander nodded slightly as his gaze fell to the table. He needed something—anything to help Isabel. The men at this table had more collective experience and magical knowledge than Kelvin's entire guild. If they couldn't offer a solution, or at least a line of reasoning that might lead to a solution, then no one could.

His eyes came up quickly when the thought occurred to him. He turned toward Malachi with a humorless grin.

"You know something about this, don't you?"

Malachi's face contorted with rage but he answered nonetheless.

"Of course I do, you simpleton! Who do you think taught Phane the dark arts?" Malachi spat with open derision. "His knowledge is so far beyond you that I could explain it to you in minute detail and you still wouldn't even understand it, much less be able to help your wench."

Malachi started to laugh at the look of smoldering anger clouding Alexander's face.

"She will die badly, which I suspect is Phane's plan. He was always one for making his enemies suffer before he dispatched them."

Alexander reined in his anger to clear his mind. This was no less a battle than any sword fight he'd ever been in. The world faded away and the details of the battlefield came into sharp focus. He needed the information that Malachi possessed but he was quite certain that the Sixth Sovereign would resist at every turn, offering him no information that he wasn't specifically asked for and Alexander had no idea what questions to ask.

As he thought over his dilemma, a smile spread across his face.

"Malachi, I command you to answer fully and truthfully any and all questions posed by any of the other sovereigns at this council table."

Malachi snarled a curse as Alexander turned to Balthazar.

"Question him and obtain the information necessary to offer me a solution to Isabel's condition. Take all the time you need and be thorough in your interrogation."

Balthazar smiled, openly appraising Alexander for a moment before turning to Malachi.

What followed was nearly incomprehensible to Alexander. The five sovereigns loyal to the Old Law interrogated Malachi for several hours, extracting esoteric and complex magical concepts from their reluctant subject, asking questions in multiple ways to ensure they had a complete understanding of the idea they were attempting to understand before discussing each concept amongst themselves.

Alexander was patient, even though his emotions bubbled under the surface. The complexity and intricacy of the ideas these ancient arch mages were discussing simply surpassed him. He would need a lifetime of study and experience to begin to grasp the concepts being bandied about, let alone employ them in any meaningful way, and that was assuming he had the necessary calling in the first place.

He began to feel a weight of despair settle on him as he realized the magnitude of the magic that created the taint working within Isabel. At first, the five sovereigns struggled to understand the principles of dark magic they learned from interrogating Malachi, but after some time and discussion they began to seem more sure of their understanding.

While Alexander didn't comprehend much of what they said, he tried to follow their line of reasoning as much as possible. The despair he was feeling began to morph into a kind of visceral terror as he realized that Isabel was once again at risk of being claimed by the darkness, not simply killed but taken heart and soul.

He pieced together a few details but reserved judgment because he was out of his depth. He trusted Balthazar and the other sovereigns. If there was a solution to the threat Isabel faced, they would find it.

The interrogation ebbed and flowed, sometimes the sovereigns peppered Malachi with questions one after the other, other times they discussed what they'd learned, piecing it together with what they had already surmised.

After they were confident that they had drawn all of the necessary information from Malachi, they began to discuss options for healing Isabel of the netherworld magic. Alexander listened with rapt attention. They argued and debated possibilities until they finally had a working theory.

The table fell silent and Balthazar fixed Alexander with a firm but empathetic gaze.

Chapter 12

"I must preface what I'm about to say with the caveat that this is all speculation, albeit quite informed speculation."

Alexander nodded for him to continue.

"We do not believe that the wraithkin could exist and function as they do in the world of time and substance without an active connection to a creature of the netherworld ... specifically, a wraith.

"Wraith are insubstantial creatures that feed on the life energy of their victims. It is for this power that we believe Phane has summoned a wraith and bound it to his will to be used in the creation of his wraithkin. How he has accomplished such a thing is beyond our understanding, but one thing is certain, the taint of the wraithkin's magic draws its dark power from the presence of the parent wraith within the world of time and substance. Eliminate the parent and you will undo both the wraithkin and the taint they've left through their daggers."

"How do I destroy it?" Alexander asked.

"Much like a shade, it cannot be killed, only banished," Balthazar said. "There have been many spells created for just such a purpose but most require the power of a mage to be successful."

"Where can I find a banishing spell?"

"There were three variations contained within the private library in the Reishi Keep," Demetrius said.

Malachi chuckled but said nothing.

"Why do you laugh?" Alexander demanded.

"I moved all of the spells capable of combating dark magic out of the Keep and into my Wizard's Den," Malachi said with a smirk. "You have exactly what you need dangling from your neck and yet it's quite beyond your grasp."

Alexander felt frustration begin to build within him again, but he shoved it aside with ruthless severity. He needed to remain calm and focused.

Be driven by emotion but ruled by reason.

"How long before I can access the Wizard's Den?" Alexander asked.

"That I do not know," Balthazar said. "It has been different for each of us, but in each case it required a period of several months after bonding with the Sovereign Stone. You will know the time is near when the Stone begins to pulse with light. Within a day after it first pulses, the Wizard's Den will open spontaneously. You will be able to control it at will from that point forward."

"How long does Isabel have?"

"We cannot know," Balthazar answered. "The taint could work very quickly or take years to do its damage. Much depends on Phane's intent when he created the wraithkin. Most likely, the taint will advance more quickly if she uses her magic and especially her link with the realm of light."

"Is there any way to cure her without destroying the wraith?"

"Perhaps, but it will require much and may not work in the end," Balthazar said.

"Whatever it takes."

Balthazar nodded with understanding. "I believe a potion could be concocted that would banish the darkness from within while preserving the flesh. In the past, most such potions have failed, killing the subject in the process. In Isabel's case, given her unique connections to the light and the dark, it is impossible to know how such a potion would affect her."

"I'd rather banish the wraith but that may prove impossible," Alexander said. "I have no doubt that Phane's taken precautions against such an attack and I'm no match for him."

"I'm not sure I agree," Constantine said. "With Mindbender, you may be able to defeat Phane in a direct confrontation. However, I doubt he would ever risk such an engagement."

"Regardless," Alexander said, "I need to be prepared for the possibility that I can't banish the wraith. What do I need to create this potion and why is it so dangerous?"

"Darkness is insidious," Balthazar said. "When it invades a person, it works its tendrils into their very soul. Power great enough to rip it free and cast it away is also powerful enough to leave the victim's soul in tatters and their consciousness scattered in the firmament. However, it has been done.

"As I neared the end of my reign, a distant cousin of mine, Reishi-trained and quite powerful, began dabbling in the dark arts. I discovered his treason and destroyed him but not before he tainted one of my nieces with darkness. She was young and innocent, which is, I'm quite sure, why he chose her. Darkness loves nothing more than to corrupt the pure of heart. His curse didn't allow a demon to possess her but instead opened a passage into her unconscious mind through which voices from the darkness could whisper to her.

"I was able to restore her through a very potent potion. The ingredients are quite rare and difficult to obtain, and the risk is great because the nature of the darkness within Isabel is undoubtedly different, as is her nature."

"Ultimately, the decision will be hers, but I want to give her every possible option," Alexander said.

"Very well, you will need a quantity of Wizard's Dust equal to the amount necessary for a single mana fast," Balthazar began. "You will need a generous pinch of fairy dust and the powder from one pouch-like blossom of a deathwalker flower. You will need three drops of nectar from the flower of the vitalwood tree and you will need a single drop of blood of the earth. The remaining ingredients are commonly available."

Alexander blinked and then frowned.

"I have the Wizard's Dust, deathwalker powder, and the fairy dust, but I don't even know what a vitalwood tree is and I've never heard of blood of the earth."

"That's understandable," Balthazar said. "Both are closely guarded secrets of the Reishi Sovereigns. We've only revealed the existence of each to the next sovereign through the Stone, and then only at great need. We never told Malachi, and he didn't suspect enough to ask."

Malachi scowled. "I discovered the vitalwood tree without you."

Demetrius smiled and cocked his head. "Did you meet the guardian I placed there for you?"

"You did that?" Malachi said incredulously.

"Of course, my wayward son," Demetrius said. "I saw the darkness growing within you even then. My greatest failure was not killing you before I died. I just couldn't bring myself to do it."

"That's too much to ask of any man," Balthazar said, "even a sovereign."

"Where is this vitalwood tree?" Alexander asked. "And what is the guardian?"

Balthazar deferred to Demetrius.

"The vitalwood tree is located in the northwest mountains of the Reishi Isle," Demetrius said. "It grows on a small island in the center of a deep mountain lake surrounded on all sides by sheer cliffs. It's only accessible by flight or through a maze of caverns that pass beneath the mountains.

"As for the guardian, I summoned a Lord from the realm of light named Selaphiel and beseeched him to guard the vitalwood tree. He was charged with preventing anyone from entering the grotto where the tree grows. I revealed my fears of Malachi to him and he agreed to protect the tree."

"Do you think he'll still be there after all these years?" Alexander asked.

"Of course. He is a being outside of time," Demetrius said. "He does not need to remain at the location of the tree in order to be aware of its surroundings and prevent any from approaching."

"How will I get past him?"

"That may be difficult," Demetrius said. "He is a kind and gentle soul but surpassingly powerful. If he is not moved by reason, then I fear you will have little chance to reach the tree."

"Why is this tree so important?" Alexander asked.

"It's the last of its kind," Balthazar said. "The fairies tell tales of the forest that used to blanket the Reishi Isle. It was alive and sentient, not in the same way as people are but self-aware nonetheless. The vitalwood forest was said to be the birthplace of many magical species that inhabit the Seven Isles. It was under the shelter of these great trees that the first dragons were spawned. It's said that the fairies chose to leave the realm of light itself and take mortal form so they could frolic under the magical beauty of these trees.

"The vitalwood tree naturally draws Wizard's Dust to it and concentrates it within its trunk, limbs, and bark. But more than that, it's a natural conduit to the realm of light. It's been speculated that the vitalwood are the means through which creatures native to the realm of light can exist indefinitely within the world of time and substance. The vitalwood trees live forever unless killed and are a potent source of magic.

"I've included vitalwood nectar in the list of ingredients because it will cleanse Isabel's link to the light while stabilizing her connection to the firmament."

"If these trees can't die, then where did they go?" Alexander asked with a touch of dismay. He remembered the beauty of the Great Forest and could only imagine a truly magical forest blanketing the world.

"They were killed in a war that raged across all of the Seven Isles long before humanity came into preeminence," Balthazar said. "Little record exists of that time, only that the forest was destroyed save for a single tree preserved by those loyal to the light. They secreted it away from the rest of the world."

"Why didn't you plant more?" Alexander asked. "Doesn't it produce fruit or nuts?"

Balthazar sighed. "No, it is forever in flower but doesn't produce any type of seed. I spent years trying to reproduce the tree but failed. The fairy legends say it has chosen to lay dormant until it feels it's safe to spread forth into the world again."

"I'll have to ask Chloe about it," Alexander said. "What can you tell me about the blood of the earth?"

"Much less I'm afraid," Balthazar said. "I discovered it in my later years and studied it quite extensively, finally deciding that it was simply too potent. It is a thing of permanence. I'm speculating, but I believe it to be the thing that informs the firmament as to how to create the stone and earth of the world itself from one moment to the next.

"As you know, the firmament underlies reality and creates each moment anew according to how the previous moment existed. I believe the blood of the earth is the place where the world remembers what it is supposed to be.

"It exists in a dual state, both within the firmament and the world of time and substance, but it does not tolerate the light or the darkness. I have included it in the list of ingredients to banish the taint of darkness within Isabel left by the wraithkin's magic."

Alexander frowned. "If it's so powerful, why not just use it alone to get rid of the taint?"

"Precisely because it's so powerful," Balthazar said. "Everyone who has consumed the blood of the earth by itself has died. I believe it is naturally connected with the firmament at all times so that it can impart its deep, timeless, and silent understanding of how the structure of stone and earth must be created in the next moment. This unrestrained connection is imparted to any who consume it."

Alexander started to wonder if this was such a good idea after all.

"So what's to stop it from killing Isabel?"

"The other ingredients," Balthazar said. "The vitalwood nectar will stabilize and regulate her connection to the firmament while shielding her link with the light from the effects of the blood of the earth. The fairy dust will protect her body and soul from harm while the potency of the blood of the earth washes away the taint. The deathwalker root will render her deeply unconscious so that she doesn't inadvertently project a thought into the firmament while she has an unrestrained connection. The Wizard's Dust will allow the alchemist who concocts the potion to impart an intention upon the mixture to perform the desired task. All ingredients will work in concert to produce a favorable result—provided I'm right. If I'm wrong, Isabel will die."

Alexander sat silently, trying to absorb the magnitude of what he'd just learned. His love was at risk and the only options for saving her were bad and worse. For a moment he lost focus and allowed his anger at Phane to seep into his psyche. All of this fear and danger could be placed squarely at his feet. Before it could boil over into rage, he reined it in and refocused his mind on the task at hand.

"Where do I find the blood of the earth?"

"I discovered it in a chamber deep under the central volcanic island of

Tyr," Balthazar said. "It was collecting in a small crystal bowl in a room cut from a vein of gold and quartz.

"I must caution you, Alexander. Take only a very small quantity and do not allow it to touch your skin. Tell no one of this place and be extremely cautious with the sample you remove. Above all, do not allow it to fall into Phane's hands. There's no telling what he may be able to do with it. I know that I could have easily unmade the world if I had so desired using the thimbleful that I took to study."

If Alexander was worried before, now he was alarmed.

"How can that be?"

"Even one drop seems to be as potent as the whole. It's as if every drop of the blood of the earth is part of the same entity, all sharing one quasi-sentient consciousness. Where a wizard's link with the firmament is capable of affecting the world of time and substance in their general vicinity, the link with the firmament created by the blood of the earth exists everywhere there is stone and earth. A clearly visualized outcome injected into the firmament through such a link could affect the whole of the Seven Isles. Of course, anyone who was a party to such a link would most certainly be drawn into the firmament and scattered into oblivion.

"Do not attempt such a thing. I cannot stress this enough. There is no way to know all of the ramifications of such an action. Such power is better left unused."

Alexander nodded as the terrifying possibilities swirled around in his mind. He took a deep breath and centered himself, bringing his awareness back to the present moment. He had a plan to help Isabel but there were still other concerns to address.

"Can you offer any suggestions for dealing with Shivini?"

Balthazar shook his head slowly and shrugged helplessly.

"The shades are creatures of the netherworld that were never summoned during the centuries of Reishi Sovereignty prior to Malachi's reign. I'm afraid he's the only one at this table with the necessary experience to answer your question."

Alexander turned to face Malachi. He wanted to slap the smirk off his face but it would do no good—the Sixth Sovereign was already dead.

"How do I banish the shade?"

"I don't know," Malachi said. "I never tried."

"How do I contain it?"

"Again, I never tried."

"How did you control it?"

Malachi hesitated for a moment, as if he was trying to figure out how to answer the question without providing any useful information.

"I made a bargain with each shade I summoned to perform a specific task and then return to the netherworld," Malachi said. "In exchange, I offered them the souls of one hundred children."

Alexander was aghast. He had no idea the price of such a summoning. Malachi sat back with a self-satisfied smile.

"The shades have a preference for innocent souls," Malachi said. "Rankosi once told me that they taste better."

Alexander struggled to regain his composure. The magnitude of the depravity that Malachi Reishi had embraced was staggering—simply beyond Alexander's capacity to imagine.

"How would Phane bind a shade to his will once it was already free in the world?" Alexander asked with a somewhat unsteady voice.

"How should I know?" Malachi said. "I never tried such a thing."

"If a shade were loose in the world, how would you go about binding it to your will?" Alexander pressed.

"I'd take precautions to ensure that it didn't possess me, then call it to me and offer it a bargain," Malachi said. "Of course, since they're already free in the world, I doubt they would make any bargain that would include returning to the netherworld."

"This isn't getting me anywhere," Alexander said as he turned back to Balthazar.

"How can I contain Shivini?"

"That is a complicated question," Balthazar said. "I believe it's possible, but it would take an arch mage to construct the necessary device. A variation of a Wizard's-Den spell could create a pocket of space that exists outside of the world of time and substance. Getting a shade inside such a place would be another matter."

"It seems that the solution to every problem I face is just beyond my reach," Alexander said. "What about trapping a shade within a person? Mage Gamaliel created a collar that acts as a magic circle. When placed around the neck of a possessed person, it contains the shade within the person for as long as they're alive. How can I keep the host alive when the shade is trying to kill the host to escape?"

"I suppose rendering the host unconscious might keep the shade confined for a time," Balthazar said.

"The spell that Phane used to escape retribution at the end of the Reishi War would keep the host alive indefinitely," Demetrius said. "Of course, it too requires an arch mage to cast."

A smile slowly spread across Alexander's face as an idea came to him.

"Is there any way to close the door to a Wizard's Den that was left open after the caster died?"

Balthazar nodded in thought for a moment before responding.

"I believe there is, provided you have some remnant of the casting wizard's body. A transference potion would give you brief access to limited pieces of his knowledge and allow you to act as his proxy with regard to spells he cast."

"So I could command the door to the Wizard's Den to close and anything inside would effectively be removed from reality."

"Not technically, but for all intents and purposes, yes," Balthazar said.

"How complicated is the potion? Do I need any exotic ingredients?"

"Not really," Balthazar said. "A pinch of Wizard's Dust and a piece of the dead wizard's flesh or bone are the most difficult to obtain. The rest are commonly stocked ingredients within most alchemical laboratories."

"Outstanding!" Alexander said. "Finally, a solution I can put into action. How do I make the potion?"

Balthazar explained the recipe for the transference potion. It was fairly complex but Alexander listened carefully, paying close attention to the details. He knew he could always come back and ask questions if necessary, but he wanted to have enough information to get Lucky started working on the potion right away.

Once he'd committed the ingredients and preparation for the potion to memory, he sat back and went through his mental list of concerns. He had answers to most of his pressing questions—not the answers he wanted, but answers nonetheless.

"I have another enemy that I haven't mentioned yet," Alexander said. "A tyrant named Zuhl. He's a powerful necromancer and he commands the largest standing army in all of the Seven Isles. When I took possession of the Sovereign Stone and the Reishi Gates became active, he used the Gate on Zuhl to move ten legions into Fellenden. He's pillaging the island as we speak and has begun construction of a giant shipyard on the western coast at the southern edge of the Iron Oak Forest. He's building a fleet."

"The ambitious, self-important, and narcissistic are always the ones to gravitate to power," Balthazar said with disgust. "It would seem little has changed in the hearts of man over the past four millennia."

"It's a shame," Darius said. "The House of Zuhl was noble and honorable during my reign. They upheld the Old Law with diligence and wisdom."

Several of the other sovereigns nodded agreement.

"Do you know anything of the relationship between Zuhl and Phane?" Balthazar asked. "Have they formed an alliance against you?"

"I can't be certain, but I doubt it," Alexander said. "Zuhl is probably the oldest man alive. He created a spell that keeps him young by sacrificing an innocent life every year. For over seven hundred years, he's been spreading the story that all of the hardship and suffering experienced by the people of Zuhl is the fault of the Reishi. Commander P'Tal tells me that Zuhl hates the Reishi and wants to establish a tyranny over all of the Seven Isles in his name."

"Good," Balthazar said. "Play one against the other."

"That was my thought as well," Alexander said. "I was wondering if there's a way to open one Gate to another from the master Gate Room in the Reishi Keep."

Balthazar shook his head with resignation. "I'm afraid not. Once the Gates were built and functioning, I realized how useful such a capability might be. I consider the lack of that feature to be the greatest design flaw in the entire Gate system. The only way to open one Gate to another is to physically go to one and touch the symbol of the island you wish to travel to."

"That complicates things," Alexander said. "I was really hoping I could open the Karth and Zuhl Gates from the Reishi Keep and let them fight it out while I build my strength."

"That would be ideal, but I'm afraid it's simply not possible," Balthazar said. "If you wish to open those Gates you will have to travel to one island or another yourself. The good news is that once open, the Gates will remain open until you close them from either Gate or from the Reishi Keep."

"I'm going to have to think about that a bit before I make a decision," Alexander said. "For now, I have more than enough to worry about. One other thing. I found a crystal chamber under Benesh's keep in Grafton and a similar chamber deep inside Blackstone Keep. Do you have any idea what they do?"

Balthazar frowned but Constantine sat forward.

"I believe I do," he said. "Benesh often spoke of the power of crystal as a focusing agent for magic. He may have used the crystal chamber you spoke of to project his illusions much farther than would have been possible on his own.

"His keep was rumored to be enchanted. Some reported seeing it fly, others said they saw it disappear altogether. I discounted these stories because I knew my brother, but I suspect he was using the crystal chamber you found to extend the range and scope of his illusions."

"I would suggest you experiment with this chamber," Balthazar said. "Attempt your clairvoyance while in the chamber and note any differences. Also, have another wizard cast a spell or two within the chamber and see if there are any increased effects. Such a capability could prove useful, especially if you find yourself besieged."

Alexander nodded and stood up.

"Thank you, gentlemen, your advice is greatly appreciated."

With that, he left the council chamber and opened his eyes. Chloe was sitting on his knee watching him.

"Did you learn anything of value, My Love?"

"Quite a bit, actually," Alexander said as he got up and stretched his legs.

"You've been gone for many hours, My Love."

He pulled the heavy curtain aside and saw that it was fully dark outside.

"Are Isabel and Abigail back yet?"

"No, My Love. Boaberous guards your door. I told him to disturb you only if they returned."

Alexander frowned and sat back down. "I'll be back soon, Little One. I just want to see where they are."

It took several minutes to focus his mind and empty his thoughts before he was floating on the firmament. Then with a flick of thought he was in a dark stone room. There were two beds and the door was barred and locked. He looked at the figures sleeping in the beds and could see Isabel from her colors at once. Abigail was in the other bed. He drifted up through the ceiling and found himself within a keep. He rose straight up into the air over the city until he recognized it as Southport.

With a sigh of relief he returned to his body. They would be safe in Southport and could exchange information with Kevin. Good enough.

Chapter 13

"Over the coming weeks and months, I have a set of tasks I need you to focus on," Alexander said to Lucky.

They were in his private study along with Kelvin and Chloe. She was sitting cross-legged on the armrest of Alexander's comfortable chair. They had just finished breakfast with Jack, Anatoly, and Alexander's parents. Nearly everyone had arrived at the Keep for the war council. Erik was coordinating the guests' lodging and providing additional security for each of them. Alexander knew that bringing in more men wasn't the way to defend against a shade but he had to do something even if for appearances. He had a busy day ahead of him. There was much to be done, especially considering that he was planning on leaving the safety of Blackstone Keep within the week.

"Of course, Alexander, whatever you need, but I thought I would be accompanying you on your journey," Lucky said.

"It's that obvious I'm planning a trip?"

"I've known you since you were a boy," Lucky said with a genuine smile. "You have that sense of urgency about you again."

Alexander nodded. "I guess I do. There's so much to be done and too little time. I plan to leave a few days after the war council."

"And you'd like me to stay here?" Lucky asked. His tone was measured but Alexander could see a sense of loss swell within his colors.

"I'm afraid so, Lucky. I think you'll understand in a minute, but before I explain, I need to impress upon you both the necessity of keeping this conversation and everything related to it a complete and total secret from everyone."

Lucky and Kelvin became more serious, both nodding agreement.

"Making Wizard's Dust requires an arch mage of any calling or a mage alchemist," Alexander said. "Lucky, I need you to become a mage."

Lucky was uncharacteristically speechless. Kelvin nodded somberly.

"If we had the necessary quantity of Wizard's Dust, I would suggest that you attempt the mage's fast, Kelvin, but we don't, so I need you to help Lucky with his studies and mentor him through the process."

"Of course," Kelvin said.

"We have a few problems that need to be addressed," Alexander continued. "The heartstone of the Keep is imbalanced. The sovereigns tell me that it will eventually fail, leaving Blackstone Keep without its magical defenses. The only way to repair the damage is for an arch mage enchanter to re-enchant the heartstone and set it spinning correctly again. So, if you're willing, Kelvin, I need you to prepare for the mage's fast in anticipation of the time when Lucky can create Wizard's Dust."

"How long until the heartstone fails?" Kelvin asked.

"There's no way to know. It could be anytime now or sometime next spring. One thing is certain though, it will fail. And without magic, the Keep will be vulnerable to all manner of attacks by Phane and his minions."

"I'll be ready when the time comes," Kelvin said. Alexander could see a slight tremor of trepidation ripple through his colors. The mage's fast hadn't been attempted in centuries. The last few to attempt it had died in the process.

"I have no doubt of that, Kelvin, but I'll still ask the sovereigns for guidance to help you through the process. They have knowledge that will help ensure success."

"I certainly welcome their advice."

Alexander turned to Lucky. "The sovereigns gave me an exercise to start you out with, Lucky. It should help you expand your link with the firmament."

Alexander spent the next half hour teaching both Lucky and Kelvin the exercise until they had a firm grasp of the process.

"Practice diligently. The ability to make Wizard's Dust may be the deciding factor in this war," Alexander said.

"I will devote myself to it," Lucky said.

"Good, but before you do, I need you to make a transference potion for me."

Lucky frowned. "I'm unfamiliar with such a potion. What's its purpose?"

"It will allow me to close Mage Cedric's Wizard's Den," Alexander said. "I plan to trap the shade inside and close him away forever."

Kelvin sat back, his mind on fire. Lucky broke into a broad smile.

"I was wondering how we were going to defeat him," Lucky said.

"You'll need to sacrifice the collar I created to make your plan work," Kelvin said. "I'll begin fashioning another immediately."

"Good. I'd like to take one with me when I leave," Alexander said.

Alexander spent several minutes explaining the process of creating a transference potion, recalling every detail of Balthazar's instructions with exacting precision. Once he'd explained the basic process, Lucky started nodding with understanding as his experience began to fill in the blanks. After they were both satisfied, Lucky smiled approvingly at Alexander.

"And so you have become the teacher."

"More like the messenger, in this case," Alexander said but he smiled at his old mentor nonetheless.

"Do you have a blowtube with sleeping powder?" Alexander asked. "You once described such a thing to me when discussing deathwalker root."

"Of course," Lucky said as he began rummaging around in his bag. "Ah, here we are." He handed Alexander three small tubes, each not more than four inches long and sealed on either end with paper.

"Just blow hard on one end and the dust will be propelled into a cloud about five feet in front of you. One whiff and your target will fall unconscious. Be careful to wait a few moments for the powder to settle before approaching your target or you may find yourself asleep as well," Lucky said with a little smile.

Alexander nodded, tucking the vials away into his pouch.

"All right," he said, standing up. "I'm heading to the top of the wizard's tower. I was hoping you'd accompany me, Kelvin. I need to clear out Cedric's Wizard's Den and I could use your help."

"Absolutely, just let me make a stop in my workshop to give my assistants instructions so they can begin preparations for fashioning another collar."

"Good. Meet me at the base of the tower in an hour or so," Alexander said. "I have an errand to run in the meantime."

***

Alexander opened the door quietly. Boaberous had guided him to the chamber where Jataan was recuperating from his grievous wound. The battle mage lay on his side, facing the door. He appeared to be sleeping but opened his eyes when Alexander stepped into the room.

"Lord Reishi, forgive me," Jataan whispered hoarsely.

Alexander shook his head as he drew a chair up next to the bed.

"There's nothing to forgive, Jataan. The enemy got the best of you. It happens."

"Never before to me," Jataan said.

"No, I don't imagine, but that's not important. What matters now is that you heal."

"The wound is slow to mend," Jataan said. "The healers speak encouraging words, but I can see in their eyes that it is beyond their ability. In truth, I may not survive."

"Nonsense," Alexander said. "It will take time but you can and will heal."

"I've heard them whispering of dark magic bound up in the wound."

Alexander nodded. "The wraithkin leave a taint in the wound that prevents magical healing. The only thing that's proven effective is fairy dust but it nearly killed me. In fact, they tell me my heart stopped for a time."

"I would have you give me fairy dust," Jataan said. "I would rather risk death than fail to stand in my place between you and danger."

Alexander smiled sadly and shook his head.

"The healers tell me it would almost certainly kill you. My wound was just a gash on the arm; yours is life-threatening and it's drained your strength."

Jataan hesitated for a long moment.

"I have killed many men with a blade, but this is the first time in my life that I've felt the pain of a serious wound. During the many hours I've had to myself here, I've been wondering what the last moments of my victims must have been like for them. My conscience weighs on me."

"My conscience weighs on me, too, Jataan."

"For most of my life I thought that I served the Old Law, but I've come to realize that I saw the Old Law and the Reishi as one in the same. I believed that serving the will of the Reishi was service to the Old Law, even when I violated the life, liberty, or property of others. I've come to see things differently since I met you and I find that I have guilt where once there was certainty."

"We can't change the past," Alexander said. "We can only learn from it. If you feel guilt for things you've done, then face it and own it because it truly does belong to you, maybe more than anything else in the world. But also learn from it. Let it guide you to act in a way that doesn't lead you to feel guilty ever again."

Jataan nodded slowly, thinking about Alexander's words.

"It would seem that I will have plenty of time to reflect on my past and come to terms with the things I've done."

"Take the time you need to heal," Alexander said. "Don't push yourself too much or you'll reopen your wound."

"I will do what I must to recover quickly, so that I can stand with you again. But while I'm recuperating, I plan to reorganize the Reishi Protectorate. For centuries, we've been a far-flung and loosely organized group of largely independent operatives that shared information and sought out potential threats to the Reishi. Now that the line has been reconstituted, we must become more than we were."

"I agree," Alexander said. "I'd like you to create a number of small teams, three to five highly capable people each, who can be sent on important tasks. There always seems to be too many things to do, so it would be helpful to have reliable people to assign some of the more difficult jobs."

"I'll begin immediately," Jataan said. "Is there anything else I should focus on?"

"Healing," Alexander said. "I'll be leaving soon and I plan to take Boaberous with me."

"I assumed as much," Jataan said. "May I ask where you'll be going?"

"Truthfully, I'm not entirely sure of that yet," Alexander said. "I want to take counsel from all of our allies before I decide where to focus my attention. We have too many enemies and not enough resources to face them all at once."

"I would like to attend your war council," Jataan said. "I may have insight into Prince Phane's thinking that would prove useful."

"If you feel up to it, I'd like to have you there," Alexander said. "But only if the healers think you can be moved without aggravating your injury."

Boaberous was standing in the corridor outside Jataan's room when Alexander opened the door. His face and colors revealed concern for his commander. The giant of a man was typically stoic and only displayed emotion in the heat of battle, but Jataan's injury had shaken him. The battle mage was a match for most mortal enemies but the wraithkin had bested him. Alexander suspected that Lieutenant Grudge was worried that he wouldn't be able to defend against Phane's unnatural creations.

Grudge fell in behind him as he headed for the tower. Alexander tried to organize the enemies he faced as he walked, giving them each a priority based on both the immediacy and magnitude of the danger they represented. He had a pretty good idea where he would focus his attention but he still wanted to hear the counsel of his allies before he made any decisions, if for no other reason than to include them in the decision-making process so they would buy into his plans more fully. He realized he was thinking like a noble and felt a brief sense of revulsion. He hated the idea of manipulating people, but the stakes were simply too high to allow any advantage to be wasted. He needed every single edge he could get.

When he arrived at the entrance to the tower, Kelvin was waiting for him. Alexander dismissed the stone wall sealing the doorway and they began the long climb. Alexander's legs burned from the exertion, especially after all of the stairs he'd climbed the previous day, but he pressed on through the pain and reached the top of the tower relatively quickly. The little room just below Mage Cedric's meditation chamber was just as he had left it, just as it had been for thousands of years. He left Kelvin and Boaberous there and pushed through the shield that guarded the highest room in the entire Keep.

He carefully gathered up Barnabas Cedric's dry and brittle bones, wrapping them in the blanket from the little bed inside the Wizard's Den. Next he took the books from the bookshelf and carefully moved them to the top of the staircase. Finally he dragged all of the furniture from the room, leaving nothing but a bare stone room that existed in its own dimension.

He spent the next several minutes moving everything down to the room below. Alexander didn't see an aura of magic in any of the items, but he asked Kelvin to examine them just the same.

"Nothing is enchanted, but several of these books are quite interesting," Kelvin said.

"How so?"

"This one appears to be a treatise on the creation of a magical keep including the enchantment of a heartstone," Kelvin said. "This one is a spellbook detailing the creation of a Wizard's Den, and this one is a spell capable of calling forth a mountain range. I suspect he used this spell to create Glen Morillian. Of course, all three of these spells can only be cast by an arch mage. These other books contain a variety of spells that can be cast by master- or mage-level wizards. Some are quite powerful. Most are known spells but I believe a few of them are unique."

"Take the ones you can make good use of but leave the Wizard's-Den and the mountain-range spells here," Alexander said.

They carefully wrapped the spellbooks in a bed sheet and began the long descent. When they reached the level with the bridge leading to the wyvern aerie, they stopped for a break. Alexander watched the horizon, hoping to see his wife and sister returning from their outing. He wanted to be angry with Abigail for leaving without warning but he was more concerned for her well-being and worried about burdening her with power. She wanted to live a simple life and he was asking her to give that up. It wasn't fair and he knew it, but he also knew with certainty that it was necessary.

He waited for an hour or so, until about noon, when he saw them in the distance. He breathed a sigh of relief as he started across the long bridge spanning the distance between the tower and the aerie.

He was standing on the platform when they floated in for a gentle landing. Isabel pulled her release strap, unbuckling her armor from her saddle, slipped off Asteroth and went straight to Alexander. She hugged him without a word, then said, "I'm sorry I left without telling you."

"You were helping Abigail. I'm just glad you're both safe."

Abigail dismounted and faced Alexander with a mixture of defiance and chagrin. She knew it had been foolish to leave the Keep, but she was still angry that he was asking so much of her.

"Did you find what you needed?" Alexander asked.

She nodded with resignation.

"Our home is gone, Alex. Burned to the ground. I guess I always thought we'd be able to go back to our lives once this was over, but I can see now that the lives we had are gone. I don't like it, but I accept it. Deal in what is, not what if, right?"

Alexander smiled softly and hugged his sister.

"I seem to remember hearing that once or twice when we were children," Alexander said.

"Anything happen while we were away?" Isabel asked.

Alexander's mood darkened as he nodded.

"Quite a bit actually," Alexander said. "Shivini is loose in the Keep. He killed two young women and attacked Wren, beat her up pretty good, but nothing that won't heal."

"Where is she?" Isabel asked.

"Safe in her quarters. Her wounds should be mended by now. That's not the worst of it, though. Shivini has damaged the Keep. It's only a matter of time before Blackstone loses all of its magical protections and weapons."

"Dear Maker," Isabel whispered.

"There's more," Alexander said. "I consulted the sovereigns and they believe you're in great danger from the taint left by the wraithkin. They gave me two possible solutions but both are difficult, to say the least. For now, it's important that you don't use your link to the realm of light."

"What do we have to do to get rid of the wraithkin's taint?" she asked.

"Either kill the wraith that Phane summoned to create the wraithkin in the first place or make a potion with some very difficult-to-obtain ingredients that might kill you anyway."

"I vote we kill the wraith," Abigail said, "whatever that is."

"I tend to agree," Alexander said. "Unfortunately, we don't have a banishing spell and the thing can't actually be destroyed."

"We may have a banishing spell," Kelvin said, hefting the load of books he was carrying. "One of these books deals with combating dark magic. It will take some study to be certain, but I'm hopeful."

"That would be a relief," Alexander said. "The sovereigns believe that the wraithkin will be stripped of their powers if the parent wraith is eliminated."

"What do we need to make the potion?" Isabel asked. Alexander could see the trepidation in her beautiful colors. It made him angry. Phane would pay for doing this to her.

"We already have a number of the ingredients," Alexander said, thinking quickly. The sovereigns had told him to keep the existence of the blood of the earth a secret from everyone, and he was inclined to take their warnings seriously.

"We need nectar from the vitalwood tree and the tears of a dragon," Alexander said, lying about the last ingredient. He hated lying to those he loved and trusted the most, but it was necessary. Phane had eyes and ears everywhere. Isabel was infected with his dark magic and, as much as he hated to face it, she might be turned against him. He couldn't afford to let the secret of the blood of the earth slip, not to anyone, but least of all to Phane.

"What's a vitalwood tree?" Isabel asked.

"How are we going to make a dragon cry?" Abigail asked.

"The vitalwood is an ancient tree that lives on the Reishi Isle," Alexander said. "As for the dragon's tears, I'm working on that."

"Killing the wraith sounds like it might be easier" Abigail said. "Do you remember Tanis? We've faced a lot, but nothing like her."

"I know," Alexander said. "I'm hoping we can reason with Bragador, but it would be good to have a backup plan."

"I'll have Wizard Ely study these books immediately," Kelvin said. "For now, I must return to my workshop to begin the task of creating another collar, and Lucky will need those bones to begin formulating the transference potion."

They returned to the tower and made their way down to the Hall of Magic. Kelvin went to his workshop, sending one of the new wizards to find Wizard Ely, while Alexander went to Lucky's workshop.

When they entered, Lucky was busy setting up glassware on a table. He smiled at Isabel and Abigail. "I'm glad to see you've returned. We were all worried about you."

"I know, I'm sorry I left without telling anyone," Abigail said, giving Lucky a hug.

"You should probably go find your mother," Lucky said. "She was worried more than most, even if she tried to hide it."

Abigail nodded, dutifully heading for the door.

"You should also find Jack," Alexander said with a knowing smile.

She was blushing slightly as she left the room.

"I have Barnabas Cedric's bones," Alexander said, placing the bundle on the floor next to the table.

"Ah, excellent, I should have the potion complete by evening."

"Good. We'll be ready for him tomorrow," Alexander said. "I expect him to make trouble at the war council."

"I'm sure you've thought of this but I feel it needs to be addressed," Lucky said. "You will have to kill his host in order to be rid of him."

"I know," Alexander whispered. "I wish there was another way, but he has to be stopped, no matter the cost."

In the back of his mind, Alexander worried that Shivini would possess someone dear to him and feared he would be forced to make a terrible decision. Worse, he knew what his choice would be. He had to eliminate the shades. They were the greatest threat of all. If they succeeded, everything for all time would be lost. If Phane or Zuhl won out, the Seven Isles would suffer a thousand years of tyranny, but at least the world of time and substance would survive. The shades represented the end of all things. They had to be defeated.

"I don't understand," Isabel said. "How do you plan on killing a shade?"

"I'm not going to kill him, I'm going to put him in Cedric's Wizard's Den and close the door. He'll be trapped forever. Unfortunately, whoever he's possessing will also be lost."

"Oh Alexander, what a terrible choice to have to make," she said, putting her hand on his cheek.

He nodded, looking into her piercing green eyes and hoping selfishly that the price would be bearable.

Chapter 14

After a quiet lunch with Isabel, Alexander went back to his meditation room and sat down. He needed all the information he could get prior to the war council. It took longer than usual to reach the firmament. He was distracted by his worry for Isabel. After finally clearing his mind and acknowledging each stray thought, he was able to reach the place of empty-mindedness that led to the firmament.

He floated there, trying to absorb the mood of the world in the midst of such strife. People were afraid, many were suffering terribly. Their emotional distress was reflected in the infinitely complex music of the firmament.

He brought his awareness into focus over his head. With a thought, he shot high into the sky until he was floating many thousands of feet over the Seven Isles. He located the Isle of Fellenden and focused on a point over the Gate. The world rushed past as his awareness flitted thousands of miles in a blink. Two heavily armed legions were encamped around the Gate. Alexander made a mental note of their strength and rose higher into the sky.

From his vantage point, he could see the swath of destruction carved into the countryside by the passage of such an enormous army. They cut a straight line to the city of Fellenden. He had visited the city with his clairvoyance before and found it to be devastated. Now there were a few inhabitants but they lived in the dark places, taking shelter and picking the bones of the city for what sustenance they could. For all intents and purposes, the city was abandoned.

He followed the trail of Zuhl's army as they made for the coast on the northwestern edge of the Isle of Fellenden. He found about half of Zuhl's forces encamped around a massive shipyard on the southern edge of the Iron Oak Forest. They were busy falling the ancient trees and dragging them to the many mills set up nearby to cut the trees into boards for use in the construction of the giant ships for Zuhl's fleet.

Zuhl had ten berths with the beginnings of a warship starting to take shape in each. Alexander moved in closer and saw the scope of what he faced. The ships would be enormous, easily capable of transporting a thousand troops each. The first ten were more than half complete. Alexander had no idea how many ships Zuhl planned to build but an armada of just ten of these ships would easily tip the balance of power in his favor, especially with such a massive army at his disposal.

Alexander spent some time surveying the operation and the defenses of the shipyard. He estimated about four legions held the area with at least as many slaves working in the giant operation. He rose into the sky again and went in search of the remaining soldiers in Zuhl's army. He found them one legion at a time.

Each of the four remaining legions was systematically pillaging the entire island in search of supplies, slaves, and any magic they could find. The people of Fellenden were totally at the mercy of the marauding soldiers. They were suffering terribly. The corpses of thousands were scattered in the wake of each legion as they moved about the island searching for plunder.

The magnitude of the devastation sickened Alexander. Even Phane hadn't caused such suffering. The wantonness of the scorched-earth war Zuhl was waging kindled a rage within him that nearly interrupted his connection to the firmament.

With a mental effort he calmed his mind and went looking for any other sign of activity on the island. A few streamers of smoke rose from deep within the Iron Oak Forest. With a thought, he was floating over the ancient trees. Their colors screamed of life and potency to his second sight. They were undoubtedly descendants of the vitalwood trees that Alexander had only recently learned of.

He sent his awareness into the canopy of the trees and found extended camps of Fellenden soldiers and refugees. The people who had escaped Zuhl's rampage across their homelands were preparing to wage what war they could against the invaders. Alexander felt a swell of pride within his soul. Even against impossible odds there were always those willing to risk everything to preserve a world worth living in. These people were his allies even if they didn't know it. He decided that he would help them in any way he could.

He slipped back into the firmament and then focused on Jinzeri. The world rushed by in a blur and he found himself in a cave somewhere on the Reishi Isle. Jinzeri, in possession of Truss's body, was still waiting near the Nether Gate. He looked bored as he cruelly tormented a doe that he had hogtied. He looked up at Alexander and smiled with malice.

Alexander drifted up through the stone of the cave and into the sky overhead. He spent several minutes searching the area until he found the entrance to the cave system that Jinzeri was holed up in. With a start, he realized that it was the same cave system that led to the grotto of the vitalwood tree. He went to the secluded little lake and descended slowly toward the tree.

It was a magnificent deciduous tree with broad limbs and wide, bright green leaves. Colorful flowers bloomed all over the outside branches. To Alexander's second sight, the colors of the vitalwood tree were bright and pure, filled with life energy and ancient potency. Before he could get any closer, a being appeared and faced Alexander.

"I have been charged with protecting this tree against all trespassers," he said. "I ask that you leave of your own free will."

The creature stood ten feet tall and looked like a man, except he was made entirely of pure white light that pulsed softly. His aura was radiant, complex and powerful, easily surpassing that of Tanis or Ilona. Alexander surmised that this was Selaphiel and withdrew, not wanting to risk the ire of a Lord of the realm of light.

Next, he went to the Reishi Keep and into the master Gate Room. The tentacle demon was nowhere to be seen but there was plenty of evidence of its past presence. The walls and floor were scorched with demonic acid where its tentacles had touched. Alexander withdrew from the Gate Room and searched the Keep. It was an odd sensation. He found that he knew the layout of the Reishi Keep in the same way that he knew the layout of Blackstone Keep. Even through his clairvoyance, he was able to navigate through the fortress with unerring precision.

He found the tentacle demon suspended from the rafters of the throne room, lying in wait for some unknown prey. He floated up into the sky again and located the central volcano on the Isle of Tyr. With a thought he was there.

The caldera was bubbling and sputtering with bright red-orange lava. Acrid smoke rose into the sky, leaving a pall hanging overhead. He descended into the caves and caverns of the giant volcano and found the dragons. There were hundreds of the ancient magical beasts. They resembled Tanis, though not as large and their colors were different. Where Tanis had been golden brown, these dragons displayed a variety of colors from reddish black to deep green to bright red, all with a hint of iridescence in the hue of their scales.

Alexander searched through the maze of volcanic tunnels and chambers that permeated the mountain and found the Temple of Fire deep within. It was mounded with treasure all around and several very large dragons slept fitfully atop the heaping piles of gold and silver coins.

The temple itself was less impressive than he imagined it would be. It was a platform of stone fifty feet square with a single large pillar at each corner, easily five feet in diameter and rising fifty feet into the air. In the exact center of the platform was a pit of fire. It burned brightly as if it had been recently stoked with fuel. There was no other structure, not even an altar.

The cavern the temple occupied was huge, rising two hundred feet overhead and spanning five hundred feet at its widest point. Several large passageways led out, each big enough to accommodate a dragon.

Alexander searched deeper within the mountain and after nearly an hour, he finally found the chamber he was looking for. Far underground, accessible only through a winding series of passages fraught with risk from dragons and flowing lava was the tiny chamber where the blood of the earth accumulated within a crystal basin. The colors of the blood of the earth were so vibrant and powerful that Alexander had difficulty looking directly at it even through his clairvoyance. It screamed of power, deep and ancient. As he drifted toward the sky through the stone of the mountain, he thought that no one should have that kind of power. No wonder Balthazar had warned him to keep its existence a secret.

He sent his awareness to the southernmost island of Tyr and found the abandoned ruins of the Reishi Protectorate keep. After a few minutes of searching, he found a number of smaller, better-fortified castles built on higher ground that were still inhabited. They looked crowded and the people had the colors of fear about them. Everyone seemed on edge, though Alexander couldn't discern why.

He searched out the surrounding smaller islands of Tyr and found them inhabited by petty pirate lords and brigands. The islands seemed to be a haven for criminals, thieves, and cutthroats. There was no government, save the whip of the powerful. The Old Law was nowhere to be seen.

At a narrow point between two of the islands, he saw a battle taking place between two small fleets, each flying different flags. Several ships were burning, a few were listing, and at least one was sinking.

He visited Andalia next. It was a nation of enforced poverty and tyranny. Those who served the King of Andalia lived well—everyone else paid for it. Lancers strutted through the streets of the capital city, sending anyone in their path scurrying for the gutter. Businesses were few and poorly stocked. Food for the people was scarce and of limited quality and variety while those in government ate well.

Alexander spent several minutes searching for the forge underneath the city. The sovereigns had told him that it was where the force lances were made. He wanted to destroy it, but it was very well protected and heavily guarded.

He found the Andalian king, wearing his jewel-encrusted, golden crown; it looked like the gaudy, ostentatious type of crown Alexander had read about in stories when he was a child. The king was obese and slovenly. A swarm of servants and sycophants surrounded him, attending to his every whim. He clearly enjoyed his comforts.

Alexander looked around the island at the force strength of the Lancers and estimated their total numbers to be around two hundred thousand, an army easily capable of destroying all of Ruatha if they could make it across the channel.

When he found the shipyard on the northern coast, he was shocked to see that they were building the exact same type of fast-attack boat that Kevin was building in Southport. They were also building over two dozen troop-transport vessels capable of moving Lancers along with their rhone mounts. These transports were of a different design. They looked like they were capable of running aground on the beach and unloading their cargo of Lancers into the surf very quickly. Alexander started to get worried. If the Andalians didn't need a port to unload their rhone, they could make landfall anywhere. As soon as these ships were seaworthy, Ruatha would have another wave of Lancers to contend with.

He sent his awareness to Karth and searched the island for nearly an hour. He found an enormous army barracked all around the central city. Supplies flowed in from the outer territories to provision the massive number of soldiers. Along the coast, he found several shipyards busy building large, oar-powered ships capable of transporting a couple of hundred soldiers each. The scope of the preparations being made to destroy everything he knew and loved was daunting.

Alexander cautiously searched out the main fortress of the Reishi Army Regency. It was a huge, sprawling complex of fortified buildings surrounded by a giant stone wall. Unlike Blackstone and the Reishi Keep, this fortress had been built by men and not magic. At least there was that, Alexander thought.

He searched deep under the fortress until he found what he was looking for. It was a set of three magic circles suspended in the air by heavy chains. Each was made of silver and inlaid with gold symbols. One was suspended horizontally and two were vertical, each at a right angle to the other. Within the sphere of magical circles was a creature of darkness that made Alexander's soul squirm.

It had no distinct form. Instead, it was a haze of blackness staining the air. Its colors were dark and hateful, seeming to communicate a craving for the living energy of those who existed in the world of time and substance. Tendrils of dark power stretched away from it through the aether, reaching out across the Seven Isles to each of the wraithkin.

The room was accessible through a single series of passageways that were spelled and trapped and heavily guarded. Even if Alexander could get to Karth undetected and make his way into the fortress without being discovered, he doubted that he had the ability to bypass all of the security measures Phane had in place to protect his new pet. Alexander felt a little thrill of fear at the building certainty that he would have to risk using the potion to save Isabel, placing her life in jeopardy in the process.

Finally, Alexander sent his awareness to the Isle of Zuhl, where he saw an army of nearly a million battle-hardened and brutish soldiers sprawled out across the tundra surrounding the Gate. They were beginning to move some of their number to the crescent bay on the southwest coast of the island. Alexander understood immediately that Zuhl was putting his forces in place so he could bring them aboard his ships as soon as they were seaworthy. Once his navy was built, the Seven Isles would fall to him. Alexander was certain of it.

He faded back into the firmament and gently returned to his body, then sat staring at the wall for several minutes until Chloe buzzed into a ball of light and came to rest floating a few feet from his face.

"What troubles you, My Love?"

Alexander shook his head in dismay, unable to put words to what he'd just witnessed. He felt like a pretender. His enemies were well ahead of him in all ways. The feeling of defeat started to take root in his soul.

"I had no idea the magnitude of what we face," he whispered. "I knew they had more soldiers than we do, but they're both building huge navies capable of moving thousands of soldiers. Once their fleets are seaworthy, we'll be at their mercy."

"You will find a way to defeat them, My Love. I have faith in you."

"I wish I did," Alexander muttered. "I have no idea how to withstand such power. We simply can't win in a fight."

"Then find a way to defeat them without fighting them, My Love."

Alexander shook his head silently as the weight of impending doom settled on him. If it was just one of his enemies, maybe he could defeat them, but he didn't stand a chance against everything he faced. The entire world had gone mad and he felt like the only voice of reason arguing against the insanity. It felt so futile.

"Do not despair, My Love. More than anything else, despair feeds the darkness. Hold on to love and hope even in the face of certain defeat. With love in your heart, anything is possible. Without it, nothing else matters."

Chapter 15

Alexander sat brooding over what he'd seen with his clairvoyance. It was nearing dark and he was still in a foul mood. The war council was scheduled to begin the next morning, and he was afraid that once he reported on the magnitude of the threats they faced, his allies would quail in fear. The odds seemed insurmountable.

Isabel had made a few attempts to cheer him up but finally decided to let him be alone. She was coming to understand her husband's moods and knew that sometimes he just needed time to work through his feelings. After a long day of flying back from Southport, followed by several hours of work preparing the aerie for the arrival of many more Sky Knights, she had gone to bed early. There was much still left to do and never enough time to do it.

With his all around sight, Alexander saw Lena come into the room from the dining hall. He knew in a glance at her colors that Shivini had her. A jolt of fear coursed through him but he mastered it quickly and schooled his expression, pretending to be absorbed in his thoughts even as he reached out for Chloe with his mind.

"Shivini is here, Little One. Go and warn Isabel."

"At once, My Love."

Lena, possessed by the shade, gently cleared her throat and Alexander turned with a feigned start.

"Oh, you startled me," he said. Deception was the most potent weapon on the battlefield. It could often carry the day when nothing else would lead to victory.

"I'm sorry, My Lord," Lena said. "Would you like some tea?"

"That would be nice," Alexander said with a forced smile.

"You seem tense, My Lord," Lena said. "Perhaps I could relax you." Her suggestive smile communicated more than words. Shivini was trying to seduce him. If he hadn't been so filled with wariness and fear, he might have laughed. Instead he decided to play along to buy time.

"I am feeling a bit anxious," Alexander said. "I would welcome a distraction. There are so many people depending on me and I really don't know how to help them."

Shivini savored despair and hopelessness. Alexander used that knowledge to his advantage, giving the shade what he most wanted to hear.

Lena poured his tea, leaning over deeply to give him a clear view of her breasts. She stood with a warm and inviting smile, just a bit too close.

"If you'd like to come to my quarters we could be alone," Lena said. "I could give you a massage … or anything else you'd like."

Alexander did his level best to play along. He furtively glanced down at her breasts, then quickly back to her face and nodded slowly.

"I'd like that, but I have to make sure my wife is asleep first," he whispered.

"Of course, My Lord, I'll be waiting for you," she said with another suggestive smile and a flip of her hair.

The moment Lena left the room, Alexander bolted to the door of his bedchamber. Isabel was just strapping on her sword. She was wearing her armor and was ready for battle.

"Shivini tried to seduce me," Alexander whispered, still a little taken aback by such a tactic. He couldn't understand why the shade had opted for that approach, and his lack of understanding worried him.

"Chloe, can you find Lucky and see if he's finished with the transference potion."

"Of course, My Love," she said as she flitted up to kiss him on the cheek. "Be careful." She buzzed into a ball of light and was gone.

"The shade invited me back to Lena's quarters for a massage," Alexander said.

Isabel frowned. "What game is he playing? What could he possibly hope to gain?"

The realization hit Alexander like a sledgehammer.

"He wants to corrupt me so he can possess me," he said. "Remember when Lucky told us about the shades. They need their victims to feel guilt or despair before they can possess them. He's trying to set me up so he can take me."

"That's pretty calculating, even for a shade," Isabel said.

"Yeah, but it makes sense."

"All right, so what do we do?"

"I go to Lena's quarters and play along until I can get the collar around her neck."

Isabel grimaced. "Lena's such a sweet and innocent young woman. I hate to sacrifice her."

"Me too, but we have to stop the shade," Alexander said.

"You're sure there isn't another way?"

"No. But I'm out of ideas," Alexander said. "I don't want to do this either, but we can't afford to let the shade roam free. It's too dangerous."

Isabel reluctantly nodded agreement.

She and Boaberous waited around the corner from Lena's door as Alexander knocked softly.

Lena opened the door wearing a nightgown that was more revealing than Alexander would have liked.

"Come in, My Lord," she said with a breathy voice. "I've been waiting for you."

Alexander smiled even as he surged forward and snapped the collar around her neck in one quick motion. Her eyes went wide and then she snarled as she tore free of Alexander's grasp and bolted for the balcony. Before he could stop her, she leapt over the railing, plummeting thousands of feet to the plain below.

Alexander was stunned by the sudden turn of events. He'd been so sure of his plan, but Shivini had turned the tables on him yet again, and Lena had been lost in the process. Alexander swallowed hard at the realization that he'd played a part in her death. If he'd thought through his plan more carefully, she might have survived, or at least her death would have meant something. This was so pointless.

Then he realized he would have to tell Adele about her death. He dreaded causing her such pain.

Isabel and Boaberous came up behind him.

"What happened?" Isabel asked. "Where's Lena?"

"She jumped off the balcony," Alexander said. "I killed her."

"Oh, Alexander, I'm so sorry," Isabel said. "But you didn't kill her. The shade did."

"I played a part," Alexander said. Lena's death seemed like the last straw. After seeing all of the forces arrayed against him and then watching Lena die for no good reason, he felt like something snapped inside him. Despair flooded into him, filling him with emptiness. He'd only felt such a crushing feeling of hopelessness during the mana fast … except this was worse because it was real.

He returned to his quarters in a fog, not really knowing where he was going or why. He let Isabel guide him and simply put one foot in front of the other until he was in his sitting room.

"Alexander, are you all right?" Isabel asked as he slumped into a chair.

"I'm fine," he said without emotion.

"Don't let this get to you," Isabel said. "You aren't responsible for her death, so don't let it weigh on your conscience so much."

"But I am," he mumbled. "She's dead because I couldn't stop the shade from killing her, just like I can't stop Phane or Zuhl from bringing war and devastation to every corner of the Seven Isles."

"You must fight the despair, My Love," Chloe said. "It is as much your enemy as Phane and it will defeat you just as completely if you let it."

"Look, I know you're both trying to help, but I just need to be alone right now," Alexander said as he got up and shuffled off to his meditation chamber.

He kept playing the scene over and over in his mind. Lena was an innocent young woman with her whole life ahead of her and his decisions had led to her death. He knew in the back of his mind that Shivini had been the real cause, but he was so distraught by all that he'd seen in his clairvoyant reconnaissance that he couldn't seem to make reason count. All that mattered was the insurmountable odds he faced.

It all seemed so hopeless.

He found himself surrendering to the despair, embracing it as if that would make him feel better.

It didn't. He slipped into an emotional malaise where he simply couldn't bring himself to care about anything. It was almost like his psyche was defending the despair by keeping all those things in his life that he was genuinely grateful for out of his mind while allowing all of the things that he feared to run rampant through his thoughts.

One terrible possible future flashed through his imagination after the next—and all of them were his fault: for not stopping Phane, for not stopping Zuhl, for not stopping the shades. A part of him railed against what he was doing to himself, tried to argue reason against the emotional onslaught, but reason had no power in the face of the guilt and fear and despair he was feeling.

He felt numb and dead inside. He felt nothing except emptiness and loss.

Suddenly, quite unexpectedly, he was scattered into the firmament. With a rush of fear, he scrambled to find a place of safe harbor where he could take refuge against the abrupt dissolution of his consciousness across the wave of creation.

If he'd never experienced this before, he might have been lost, but he'd faced it in the past. All of the despair and hopelessness he'd been feeling just moments before evaporated in the face of the need to survive.

He withdrew a single scrap of his essence into the place of calm stillness within his psyche, the place where the witness lived. From there he searched out the rest of his memories, experiences, and personality traits—carefully and painstakingly reassembling himself into one cohesive consciousness. Once he felt whole again, he spread out across the firmament looking for anything he might have missed, but he found nothing more of himself lost in the ocean of creation.

He was whole once more.

With an act of will, he tried to return to himself, but couldn't. Fear coursed through him as he was repelled from entering his own body. He coalesced his awareness over himself and saw himself talking with Boaberous.

"Go find the Guild Mage," he heard himself say. "The shade has Isabel. She can't be trusted. Tell the Rangers to capture her and hold her until I return."

"Lord Reishi, my place is with you," Boaberous said. "Send another to fetch the Guild Mage."

"No!" he heard himself shout. "Go now! It's Isabel's only hope."

Boaberous hesitated for a moment before he nodded and ran down the hall.

Alexander's fear spiked when Shivini, in possession of his body, looked up at his disembodied consciousness and smiled.

Alexander sent his awareness into his bedchamber to find Isabel. She was strapping on her armor. Chloe was flying around in a circle.

"Hurry, I can't find his mind," she said. "I fear the worst." His fairy familiar sounded distraught.

"You're sure he's still alive?" Isabel asked with a hint of panic.

"I would know at once if he'd been killed," Chloe said. "He still lives, but his mind is elsewhere."

"Chloe, go find Lucky," Isabel said. "Tell him we need a way to put Alexander to sleep without hurting him."

"At once," Chloe said, then buzzed into a ball of light and vanished into the aether.

Alexander thought furiously. He needed to find someone who was sleeping. With a flick of his mind he was floating in Abigail's quarters. She was breathing deeply, sound asleep. He carefully but urgently insinuated his awareness into her mind. In her dream, she was standing on the watchtower of Valentine Manor, looking out over the range land at an approaching thunderstorm. She always liked to watch the lightning … she said it looked like the gods were fighting.

She was startled momentarily when Alexander materialized beside her.

"Abigail, I need your help. Shivini has me."

Her eyes went wide with fear, and Alexander was abruptly ejected from her mind as she sat bolt upright and went to her armoire. Within moments she was dressed and pulling on her boots. Alexander sent his mind back to his body and saw himself heading with haste toward the paddock.

Shivini glanced back at him with a knowing smile.

"Feels so helpless, doesn't it?" He paused as if waiting for an answer. "Oh, that's right, you can't respond because you don't have a body anymore. I must say, Alexander, I've never taken one such as you before. Usually I can hear my victims screaming from deep within, but you are silent. Pity."

He watched the shade order a horse made ready. The Ranger tried to argue, tried to suggest an honor guard, but Alexander ordered him to saddle just his horse, stating that he was leaving on an urgent mission that he alone must attend to.

A few minutes later he was riding across the ribbon of a bridge spanning the chasm between the paddock and the bridge platform. As he passed under the arch onto the platform, the bridge vanished.

Alexander heard a woman yelling from the paddock and sent his awareness over to the altercation. Three Rangers were attempting to restrain Isabel.

"Let go of me!" she screamed at them. "Shivini has Alexander. You're letting him get away."

Boaberous was there. Kelvin came into the paddock a few seconds later.

"Shivini, we will find a way to drive you from Isabel," Kelvin said with an undercurrent of anger.

"I'm not Shivini!" Isabel railed at them as they held her arms. "Alexander's left the Keep. You have to let me go after him."

"Lord Reishi himself told me that Lady Reishi is possessed by the shade," Boaberous said. "Her word is suspect."

"I agree," Kelvin said. "If you truly are Isabel, then I apologize and I trust that you will understand as well as any the necessity of such precautions."

Isabel suddenly realized that she was on her own. Shivini had used the most powerful weapon on the battlefield against her to devastating effect. A simple lie had bought the shade the time he needed to get to the Gate with Alexander and the Sovereign Stone before they could stop him.

She stopped struggling and sent her mind to Asteroth. Her wyvern steed came awake with a start as she called him to her. In the distance she heard a roar. The significance of it was lost on her captors.

"You're making a mistake, Kelvin," Isabel said calmly, "a mistake that could doom us all."

"I hope you're wrong," Kelvin said, "but I have to believe Alexander's word. Lieutenant Grudge was sent to warn me of your possession. Until we can be sure that you're not under the shade's control, we have to hold you."

"If Alexander sent you to warn the Mage, then where is he?" Isabel asked Boaberous. "Aren't you supposed to be protecting him?"

A Ranger was quickly approaching from the stables but before he could arrive, Asteroth landed in their midst with a roar. Everyone was stunned by the sudden noise and the presence of the giant wyvern … everyone except Isabel.

In the moments before her steed landed, she had called up a powerful anger born of need and fear, focused her mind, and cast her shield spell. The two Rangers holding her arms were repelled as the shield took on form and substance. Isabel didn't hesitate. She bolted toward Asteroth in a headlong sprint.

Kelvin whipped his hammer off his back and brought it down onto the paddock, sending a shock wave through the ground that knocked Isabel sprawling.

She hit hard and was momentarily stunned, but her shield protected her from the brunt of the impact. She rolled onto her back and unleashed a light-lance spell at the Guild Mage. She took care to aim for the center of his chest, knowing that his dragon-scale armor would protect him from the damage while still sending him to the ground, dazzled and stunned.

He fell back as the light stabbed out at him. Boaberous tried to reach Isabel, but Asteroth whipped his tail around and smacked him hard with the flat side of his bone blade, sending the giant hurtling to the ground.

Isabel was up in an instant, racing for her steed. She mounted, not caring that she wasn't wearing her riding armor or that Asteroth wasn't saddled. She desperately needed the speed that only he could give her.

With a thought, she commanded Asteroth to launch, sending dust swirling all around the paddock. She goaded her steed toward the edge of the paddock and the open sky, clinging to his neck for her very life.

Abigail raced out onto the paddock just moments after Isabel disappeared over the edge, trailing Lucky and Chloe behind her.

"Alexander, where is he?" she demanded.

A Ranger ran up just as she shouted her question.

"Lord Reishi commanded that we saddle a horse for him and forbade us from accompanying him as he left the Keep," the Ranger reported.

"Alexander told Boaberous that Shivini had Isabel," Kelvin said with a building sense of alarm.

"No!" Abigail cried out as she spun and raced back into the Keep.

Lucky stopped, trying to catch his breath. "Alexander came to Abigail in her dreams and told her that Shivini has him," he said around his heavy breathing.

"Dear Maker," Kelvin said. "Isabel has gone after him on her steed. We thought the shade had her so we tried to stop her."

"Resourceful, isn't she?" Lucky said. "I suggest we send riders after them."

Kelvin nodded to the Ranger, who raced off to saddle horses and raise an alarm.

Alexander trailed along behind himself, helplessly watching Shivini take him toward the Gate and certain defeat. Once he opened the Gate to another island, there was virtually no hope. He remembered that only moments before Shivini had taken him, he'd felt totally hopeless, like nothing could get any worse. He would have laughed bitterly if he could have.

***

Isabel held on for dear life. Asteroth was flying steady and fast, losing altitude in a gradual dive toward the Gate. She wasn't sure if she would even be able to see Alexander from so high in the dark, but she reasoned that the most important thing was to stop him from opening the Gate. If she could keep him on Ruatha, then there was still hope. If he managed to get though the Gate, then he would be lost to her forever.

She descended to an altitude of about a hundred feet and settled into a glide, scanning the plain below for any sign of him. As she neared the Gate, she saw him riding as fast as his horse would carry him. She banked hard and started to slip off Asteroth. Her steed compensated and landed quickly to give her the chance to regain her balance. Alexander gained ground, looking over his shoulder with a triumphant grin.

Isabel reached out to the horse with her mind and commanded him to stop—and stop he did. He came to a halt so suddenly that Alexander went over the horse's head, tumbling to the ground. Shivini bounded to his feet, running toward the Gate.

Isabel was helpless to stop him. She couldn't get to him quickly enough to prevent him from opening the Gate. Once he was through the Gate, all would be lost. Phane would have the Stone, the Gates, the Thinblade, Mindbender, and most importantly to her, he would have Alexander. She would never see him again.

With grim resignation, Isabel touched her link to the realm of light. It was her only hope. She didn't know if it would work, but of all the powers available to her, it was the one that might succeed where all others would surely fail.

Love flowed into her and filled her with calm certainty. She whispered the words that served to focus her mind and helped her form the necessary images, then unleashed her Maker's light spell at Alexander. It stabbed through the night from her outstretched hand and struck him full in the back, sending him sprawling to the stone of the Gate platform.

The scream that followed sent chills up her spine and left her blood cold. She froze, fearing that she had just killed her one true love. Alexander lay still as a corpse. She couldn't see if he was breathing. Cold terror gripped her. One moment she was frozen in place and the next she was off Asteroth and running with every ounce of strength and speed she could muster, driven by fear and need.

She reached him and rolled him over, searching his face for any sign of life.

When he gasped for breath and sat up, she nearly fainted from relief.

Still reeling from the emotional turmoil of almost losing him, she managed to take his face in her hands and look into his gold-flecked eyes.

"Alexander? Is that you?"

He swallowed hard and nodded just as Chloe spun into a ball of light from the aether, rising higher with each spin.

"You're back!" she shouted with triumph.

Isabel sobbed, collapsing into his arms as all of her terror broke over her.

"It's all right," Alexander whispered. "You saved me again."

"Always," Isabel said, but even as she spoke, she heard from somewhere deep in her unconscious mind the bubbling up of laughter that embodied both malice and madness. The portal to the realm of light was blocked and the passage to the netherworld was once again open in her mind … but this time it was different.

She started crying as the magnitude of the danger soaked into her. Yet, when she thought of the alternative, of losing Alexander, she knew in her heart that she had done what she must and she wouldn't do anything differently, no matter the cost to herself.

"It's all right, I'm safe," Alexander said.

"I'm not," she said, sniffing back her tears. "I can feel the darkness awake within my mind again, and the light is gone."

"Dear Maker," Alexander whispered as he closed his eyes and pulled her to him. “We’ll find a way to help you, no matter what it takes,” he said, stroking her hair.

Kallistos landed nearby and Abigail dismounted quickly. She raced up to her brother.

“Alexander, are you safe?”

He nodded as he held Isabel to his shoulder while she wept in fear. Abigail frowned questioningly. Alexander shook his head to stop her from asking. There would be time to discuss the problem later. For now, he just wanted to comfort Isabel. She had saved him again and risked her soul in the process, risked the horror of the darkness.

Within minutes, a platoon of Rangers led by Boaberous and Kelvin surrounded them as Isabel tried to gain control over her fear.

An hour later, Alexander was guiding her back to their quarters. It was late and they were both exhausted.

Sometime in the middle of the night, Alexander was awoken by a scream. Isabel sat bolt upright and screamed again before she woke and realized she was dreaming. She collapsed into his arms and wept.

Chapter 16

Alexander woke with the light of dawn, just a bit at first—hovering in that half waking state where everything is soft and distant. His bed was comfortable and Isabel was warm in his arms. Contentment filled him and surrounded him, but there was something nibbling at the edge of his awareness.

He opened his eyes and the truth of his reality flooded into him. Today was the day of his war council. He had called together all of the most powerful and influential leaders from all of his allies to hear their counsel. There was much that he needed to tell them, to be sure, but he was hoping that one or more of his guests could offer suggestions for confronting the threats they faced.

Isabel stretched and nuzzled in closer to him. He looked down at her disheveled chestnut-brown hair and kissed her gently on the top of the head as she used his shoulder for a pillow.

"Good morning," she mumbled, still half asleep.

He kissed her again and stifled a yawn as he slipped out of bed.

When they emerged from their quarters ready for the day ahead, they found Adele waiting in the sitting room. Her eyes were red and puffy from crying.

Alexander realized with a start that he hadn't told her about Lena; she must have found out by other means. He went to her without a word and hugged her gently.

"I'm so sorry, Adele."

She nodded against his shoulder and then stepped back, sniffing her tears away.

"I have breakfast ready."

Alexander nodded dumbly and followed her into the dining room. During breakfast he went through all of the things he needed to accomplish during his war council. There were so many threats. He was almost afraid to reveal to his allies the true nature of the enemies they faced lest they lose heart.

Jack and Abigail arrived after breakfast to accompany them to the council chamber. Alexander hadn't actually inspected the large room that had been cleared out and transformed into a meeting hall, but Jack assured him it would be suitable. Boaberous seemed to materialize as they left their chambers and fell in behind Alexander without a word.

They talked of small things on the way to the war council, avoiding more serious subjects. Alexander smiled and nudged Isabel when he noticed that Jack and Abigail were holding hands. She smiled radiantly and stifled a giggle. Alexander felt a sense of calm wash over him. Even in the face of all the darkness, his sister had found love.

"I believe you might be right, Little One," he said in his mind. "Love will triumph."

"Of course I am, My Love," Chloe replied impishly in his mind.

Jack nodded to the Rangers standing guard outside the large double door. They pulled the doors open simultaneously to reveal a giant room with an oversized table filling the center.

The arched ceiling was fashioned of multifaceted panes of glass that diffused the daylight, casting a warm glow over the entire chamber. The walls were adorned with bright, masterfully woven tapestries, no doubt brought from New Ruatha. The room was filled with people, all standing around in small circles talking to one another and enjoying the refreshments being served from tables set up along the sides of the room. Rangers were stationed along the walls to provide security, but no one seemed to be worried about a threat given the collected power within the room.

Alexander knew differently. He scanned the room with his second sight, looking for the telltale colors of the netherworld but saw nothing unusual.

Jack stepped up to the threshold of the room and nodded to a Ranger standing next to a pull cord. A bell tolled once, drawing everyone's attention. Jack seemed to revel in being the focus of attention, even if he was simply announcing Alexander and Isabel.

"Assembled guests, Kings, Wizards, Triumvirs, Nobles, and Generals, I am pleased to announce Lord Alexander Reishi and Lady Isabel Reishi."

As they entered, people found their seats. Alexander took his place at the table with Isabel at his right and Abigail at his left. Chloe spun into existence and took her place in front of Alexander, silencing the room with her entrance.

Everyone else who mattered most to him was there: his parents, Isabel's parents, Anatoly, Lucky, Kelvin and several other wizards, Sark and Ely among them. The guests included King Abel, Prince Conner, Mage Dax and Chancellor Breton from Ithilian, Magda and Cassandra from the Reishi Coven, Regent Cery from New Ruatha, Lady Buckwold, Regent Samuel of Northport, General Markos and General Kern as well as Jataan P'Tal. Alexander had also asked Lieutenant Wyatt, Captain Sava, and Erik Alaric to attend.

"Thank you all for coming," Alexander said. "We have much to discuss and much to decide. We face many enemies.

"Phane controls Andalia by proxy and Karth by force. He has two hundred thousand Lancers on Andalia and half a million infantry on Karth. Both islands have numerous newly constructed shipyards busy building attack boats and transport vessels.

"He has created a new form of soldier by blending men with wraith … how we don't know, but they are dangerous in the extreme. We believe he has nearly a hundred such agents. In addition, he has control of one of the three shades loose in the world.

"The other two shades are working to find the three keystones that unlock the Nether Gate, so they can open it and flood the world of time and substance with darkness. They've located the Nether Gate itself and they already have one of the keystones.

"Zuhl has invaded Fellenden with an army of ten legions and is waging a scorched-earth war against the people. Many cities have been lost. Farms and livestock have been either destroyed or taken to feed his men. He has built an enormous shipyard on the northwest coast near the Iron Oak Forest and is building ships capable of transporting a thousand men each. In addition, he has nearly a million battle-hardened soldiers on Zuhl awaiting the completion of his fleet.

"We are at war."

Alexander stopped and surveyed the room. He was looking at the faces of his friends and allies but he was also scrutinizing their colors, gauging their resolve and commitment. Most, certainly those closest to him, were steadfast. A few showed fear at the stark assessment of what they faced.

"I will not surrender to any of these enemies or the futures they have planned for us. I will fight them with my last breath. I hope I can count on all of you to do the same. The future is counting on us. If we fail, our descendants will know only darkness."

There was a general murmur of ascent from the room. Alexander took a deep breath and stood up. He deliberately unbuckled the Thinblade from his belt and held it by the scabbard, extending the hilt to Anatoly.

"Grasp the hilt and tell me what you feel," he said.

Anatoly took a careful grip on the hilt of the ancient sword but didn't draw it from its scabbard.

"It feels like a snake trying to wriggle out of my hand," Anatoly said.

Alexander nodded and extended the hilt to Regent Cery.

Cery took hold and a look of confusion ghosted across his face and he let go, staring at the sword. Alexander extended the hilt of the sword to the Baroness of Buckwold and Regent Samuel of Northport. Each released their grip quickly.

"I recovered the Thinblade from this very Keep," Alexander said as he slowly walked around the table. "It was left for me by Mage Cedric and serves as the badge of office for the King of Ruatha. I have since recovered the Sovereign Stone, and so now I am faced with a dilemma. I can't be both Sovereign of the Seven Isles and the King of Ruatha … I must abdicate the throne of Ruatha and relinquish the Thinblade."

Those in the room who didn't know this was coming were shocked, to say the least. The political leaders of Ruatha were stunned speechless. Such a thing was unheard of. Nobody gave up power, least of all when it was tied to one of the most potent magical swords ever created.

Alexander stopped in front of Abigail. He could see the uncertainty and discomfort in her colors, but she stood nonetheless. When he extended the hilt of the sword to her, she grasped it and drew the blade as though it belonged to her.

The room fell silent.

"Abigail Ruatha, I name you the rightful Queen of Ruatha," Alexander said, as he handed her the scabbard.

She sheathed the Thinblade and bowed formally to him.

"Lord Reishi, I swear loyalty to the Old Law and promise to defend the life, liberty, and property of the innocent."

Alexander stood aside and held out his open hand toward Abigail.

"I give you the Queen of Ruatha."

There was a brief celebration as the room rose in applause and then the guests circulated around to congratulate Abigail on her very informal coronation. After half an hour or so, everyone returned to the table. Alexander brought them all back to the business at hand.

"General Valentine, what is the state of our army?" he asked his father.

"We have a total of sixteen legions in northern Ruatha," Duncan reported, "including nearly four legions of Ithilian infantry. Nearly all are massed at the Gate. South of the Great Forest we have three legions—two in Kai'Gorn and a legion of Rangers in Southport. Glen Morillian has a single legion holding the forest road, and a single legion of Rangers guards the north against Elred Rake and his cavalry in the northern wilds.

"Many of our soldiers are inexperienced but they're learning quickly. We are well provisioned thanks to the magic of Blackstone Keep and we're ready to move on command."

"Excellent. King Abel, what news do you bring?"

Abel Ithilian nodded deferentially to Alexander.

"I have mustered another four legions—three of infantry and one of cavalry," Abel said. "They are encamped at the Gate. We have news from Fellenden that confirms your report. The island is being pillaged and the people are suffering horribly. I have ordered my fleet to ferry evacuees from the southern coast to Ithilian, but many more are lost than saved.

"In addition, I've ordered an armada to be assembled on the northern coast. My naval commanders estimate that they can muster sixty-three combat-worthy vessels.

"One report tells of Princess Lacy Fellenden. She was sent by her father to recover a family heirloom given to their house by Mage Cedric. She was supposed to have come to Ithilian, but as yet, she has not arrived. We fear the worst."

Alexander's mind raced, hoping and fearing that Princess Lacy might be carrying the one thing he needed more than any other, the one thing that would eliminate the threat of the Nether Gate, but he didn't voice his thoughts. If she did have a keystone in her possession, she was in great danger, and the fewer people who knew what she might be carrying, the better.

"Mistress Magda," Alexander said, turning to the triumvir, "have you anything to add?"

She nodded formally to Alexander.

"We have long been loathe to become involved in the affairs of the larger world, preferring to remain secluded and to focus on our self-appointed task of guarding the Sovereign Stone. Sitting here, seeing the Stone around your neck, I can't help but conclude that our purpose must change.

"While there are many within the Reishi Coven who are still wary of allowing the Stone to remain in your care, I have come to believe that you are best suited to carry the burden. Furthermore, we too have looked on the enemies you speak of and agree that they must be stopped. The Reishi Coven and the Sky Knights stand ready to aid you in any way we can."

Isabel smiled radiantly, her colors swelling with pride. Alexander gave her hand a squeeze. She had been taken hostage by these people and had turned them into allies, a triumph worthy of story and song.

Alexander turned to Kelvin and nodded for his report.

"We're working diligently to understand many of the items we've discovered within the halls of Blackstone Keep. We also stand ready to support the army in a variety of capacities and we're training the new additions to our ranks. I have a number of very capable wizards ready to deploy with the army as needed."

"Very good," Alexander said. "We know what we face and we know what we have at our disposal. I've called you together to hear your counsel. King Abel, what say you?"

"Fellenden is an important trading partner and her people are longtime friends and allies of Ithilian," Abel said. "Their plight pains me greatly. I would choose to aid them in every way possible.

"Phane is a dangerous and treacherous enemy … I know this from personal experience. But at the moment he is distant, and the islands he controls are beyond the power of our forces.

"As for the shades, they are beyond me. I have neither the knowledge nor the power necessary to defeat them and so I choose to face those enemies that I can stand against.

"I say we destroy the forces that have invaded Fellenden and capture Zuhl's shipyard for our own use."

Alexander smiled slightly. He had similar ideas but he wanted to hear the suggestions of all those present.

"General Valentine?"

"I tend to agree with King Abel," Duncan said. "The sheer numbers of soldiers on Karth or Zuhl place both islands beyond our capability. The Lancers on Andalia are also more than we can afford to face. Add that to the toll of human suffering being inflicted on the people of Fellenden, and I believe that to be our best objective.

"Additionally, we will be faced with multiple fleets of transport vessels from the south within the coming months. King Abel's suggestion that we capture Zuhl's shipyard is a sound strategy for adding to our limited naval capability."

"Any objections?" Alexander asked.

The table fell silent. Alexander scrutinized the colors of all present. A few had misgivings about the plan but none voiced an objection.

"Very well, our primary military objective will be to retake the Isle of Fellenden, capture Zuhl's shipyard and utterly destroy his invading army. No quarter will be given in this campaign. I have seen the wanton devastation they've inflicted on the people of Fellenden and I judge them guilty of violating the Old Law. We will make them pay with blood."

"When do you plan to depart?" Bella asked.

"I won't be leading the army into Fellenden," Alexander said.

Chapter 17

There was a moment of shocked silence before everyone started speaking at once. Alexander held up his hand to silence the room so he could explain.

"I have to stop the shades. Phane and Zuhl will impose a thousand years of tyranny if they're victorious, but the shades will unmake the world of time and substance itself. They have to be stopped and I intend to do just that."

"Who will lead the army against Zuhl?" Abel asked.

"I will," Abigail said before Alexander could answer. He looked at her sharply. She was his little sister and best friend. He hadn't expected her answer and he didn't want her off fighting a war, especially if he wasn't there to protect her.

"You made me the Queen of Ruatha. The majority of our forces are Ruathan, so it stands to reason that I should be the one to lead them into battle."

"Abigail, think this through," Bella said, clearly worried for her daughter's safety.

"There's not much to think about," Abigail said. "I'm the queen now … my place is with our army."

Alexander smiled sadly at his sister. "I'm proud of you, Abigail."

"I'll accompany you," Duncan said.

Abigail shook her head. "No, Dad, you need to stay here. Ruatha needs a leader here who can command the respect of the other generals and the nobles in case Phane manages to land more troops or sends something else we haven't even considered."

Duncan frowned but bowed to her authority.

"Anatoly, I'd like you to go with Abigail," Alexander said. "She needs someone watching her back that she can trust absolutely."

Anatoly nodded slowly. "Who will be watching your back?"

"Isabel, Chloe, and Boaberous," Alexander said.

"With your permission, I would accompany you as well," Jack said.

Abigail looked at him with a mixture of surprise and dismay. Alexander held his tongue.

"I'm sorry, Abigail," Jack said. "I want to be with you more than anything but my duty is with Alexander."

"We'll talk about this later," Abigail said coolly.

"Aren't you going a bit light?" Duncan asked. "You could take Lieutenant Wyatt and his men; they've served you well in the past."

"There's no question about that, but I'm eventually going to wind up standing in front of Bragador and I don't want to come knocking on her door with a small army."

"That's wise," Kelvin said. "Bragador is reasonable, to a point, but she does not take kindly to unannounced guests, especially those who look like they came for a fight."

"You plan to visit the dragons of Tyr?" Magda asked, a bit taken aback.

"I have good reason to believe that she has one of the keystones to the Nether Gate," Alexander said. "I plan to ask her for it."

"Surely you jest," Magda said. "Dragons do not part with treasure easily and they can be most unpleasant when they choose to be."

"I need that keystone," Alexander said. "I'd much rather bargain for it than steal it, or worse, try to fight her for it. One way or another, I have to get that keystone."

"You play a very dangerous game," Magda said.

"The most dangerous there is," Alexander replied. "But I'm not a fool. I'm going to the Reishi Isle first to see if I can find the Nether Gate and destroy it outright. Barring that, I plan on taking the keystone from Jinzeri."

Magda frowned with alarm. "Please do not speak the shades' names aloud. They can hear you. To be honest, I'm not sure which path is more dangerous, confronting a shade or trying to bargain with a dragon for a trinket from her hoard."

"I'm open to suggestions," Alexander said.

"I'm afraid I have none at the moment," Magda said. "Perhaps with time to consider the challenges we face, we may be able to offer a better alternative."

"I'll listen to any ideas you have, but right now that's my plan," Alexander said. "Given the threats we face, how would you suggest we deploy the Sky Knights?"

Magda and Cassandra shared a look before Magda took a deep breath and let it out slowly.

"For centuries we have maintained a careful limit on the number of wyverns in our force. We believed we had sufficient strength to defend the Reishi Isle while remaining consolidated within the fortress island. Given the current threats we face, it's time to begin breeding more wyverns and training more Sky Knights.

"I've inspected the aerie within this Keep and it can easily house two flights. Each of the other four fortress islands can house four flights. I would like to move one flight here and another into the northernmost fortress island to begin building another outpost there.

"Additionally, I believe a flight should accompany Lady Abigail to the Isle of Fellenden in support of the battle against Zuhl's forces. I would like to accompany her as well. I may be able to offer some advice or insight that could be useful. Cassandra will return to the fortress island and coordinate the deployment, Bianca will take command of the northern fortress island, and Constance will remain here to command the flight assigned to Blackstone Keep."

Alexander grinned slightly as he appraised her before he spoke.

"You have been very reluctant to take action until now. What changed?"

"Always before, we had the luxury of time and safety," Magda said. "Now, we have neither. War is upon us, and while careful deliberation is our habit, we realize that bold action is required. We intend to do our part."

"Outstanding," Alexander said. "I agree with your plan completely, but, in addition, I'd like to use the Blackstone flight to offer support to General Talia in southern Ruatha. Your Sky Knights are uniquely suited to engage any naval assault out of Andalia or Karth."

"Of course," Magda said. "I would suggest sending two wings south.

That will leave nearly fifty Sky Knights here for any contingency that might arise."

"Good, I'd like to use those remaining here to support Duane in the north," Alexander said. "It's about time we dealt with Elred Rake."

"I can send another legion north to assist," Duncan said. "It would be good to eliminate all enemy forces on Ruatha."

Alexander nodded. "We also need to discuss ways to destroy enemy ships from the air. The Sky Knights who are also witches can use their magic, but we need a nonmagical way for the others to sink enemy vessels."

"Simple firepots would be effective," Lucky said. "Although magical weapons would be much better, especially against the larger vessels you described being built by Zuhl."

"We've tried flame-based weapons in the past," Magda said, "but we've always had trouble igniting them in flight."

"I have just the thing," Lucky said. "Conventional fuses would be useless in flight, but I have a formula for an igniter that flares on impact."

Magda and Cassandra both sat forward.

"Fire would be a most welcome addition to our arsenal," Cassandra said.

"What's needed to make firepots?" Alexander asked.

"Mostly just clay pots, lamp oil, and a glass ampoule filled with an igniter," Lucky said. "The most difficult part is the igniter. It requires a careful mixture of less-than-common ingredients, but it can be made without magic."

"Good. Let's get a team of people trained to make them and start production immediately," Alexander said. "I'd like to get the Sky Knights armed with firepots as quickly as possible."

"For the larger ships," Lucky said, "I can think of a number of compounds that would be highly effective, although somewhat dangerous for the Sky Knights using them. Liquid fire, of course, and a few more caustic forms of magical acid I know how to concoct."

"Those will require your direct involvement to create, won't they?" Alexander asked.

"Yes, there are no other alchemists within our guild, and those concoctions require magic to create."

"Let's focus on the firepots for now," Alexander said. Lucky had other assignments of more importance.

"We have two master alchemists in the Ithilian guild," Mage Dax said. "I'm quite sure they would be happy to create the weapons you speak of."

"Excellent," Alexander said.

"I have a few thoughts on the matter as well," Kelvin said. "I can create a much smaller variation of the explosive weapons we used against Northport and design them to detonate on impact rather than on command. A direct hit should be enough to sink nearly any vessel."

"You're already stretched pretty thin," Alexander said. "If you have the time, do what you can, but don't make it a priority over some of the more pressing projects you're working on."

"If I may," Regent Samuel said.

Alexander nodded.

"Since the Guild Mage mentioned it, I would like to discuss the disposition of Northport."

"Of course," Alexander said.

"I must say I was most distressed by the destruction of our city," Regent Samuel said. "It has been a terrible loss for our people. Many innocent citizens lost everything in your attack—their homes and possessions are gone. Thousands have been reduced to refugees in other cities, forced to rely on the charity of others to survive. What I'm trying to say is that you had no right to do what you did. That was our city and you destroyed it."

"Yes, I did," Alexander said. "While I regret having to make that decision, it was necessary."

"Perhaps, if Northport had been your home, you wouldn't have been so quick to wield such terrible power against it."

"Our home was burned to the ground by the enemy," Abigail said coolly. Alexander stopped her from continuing with a gesture.

"Northport's loss is terrible," Alexander said, "but not as terrible as losing half of our army in a pitched battle against the enemy forces that had taken refuge within your city. We are at war, Regent Samuel. Some of the decisions we must make are a choice between a bad option and a worse option.

"What's done is done. Northport has been sacrificed and I understand the loss that has caused for you and your people. But now is the time to focus on rebuilding for the future."

"Honestly, I'm not sure the city can ever be restored to its former glory," Regent Samuel said.

"I have no intention of restoring it," Alexander said. "I intend to rebuild it better than before. A legion of Rangers is already working to clear the rubble within the walls, salvaging any materials that can be of use and cutting the timber necessary to rebuild.

"What I need from you, Regent Samuel, is to call your people home and put them to work. My father will have access to sufficient gold to pay the workers and will also provide the assistance of the army.

"The first order of business is rebuilding the shipyards and roads. As soon as the shipyards are operational, they will begin producing warships while the rest of the city is rebuilt. All of this is going to happen with or without you. I would like your input and your assistance, but I don't require it."

Regent Samuel blinked and his colors flared with anger and indignation, but he held his tongue, clearly thinking better of challenging Alexander and risking his power. Instead he nodded his assent and remained silent.

"Good," Alexander said. "Coordinate with General Valentine. He will oversee the rebuilding effort."

"As you wish," Regent Samuel said, his colors revealing inner turmoil. Alexander understood the man's feelings but he couldn't do much about it, so he moved on.

"Commander P'Tal will be calling the Reishi Protectorate to Blackstone Keep and reorganizing his forces into a military cadre and an intelligence force. I've asked him to form several teams of highly capable operatives who can be sent on missions of the most sensitive nature and highest importance. Commander P'Tal will handpick those who demonstrate the skills and abilities he needs. Wizards, witches, Rangers, Sky Knights, and soldiers are all welcome to apply."

"I suspect a number of my order would welcome the opportunity," Kelvin said.

"Mine as well," Magda said.

"All right, I believe the final order of business is the Reishi Keep," Alexander said. "There are stores of knowledge and magic within the Keep that might be invaluable. Unfortunately, there are also some very dangerous creatures within and even more living on the Reishi Isle.

"I intend to send a regiment of soldiers through the Gate to begin constructing a wall around the Keep just inside the wood line to prevent anything else on the island from entering. Once the wall is built, we'll begin systematically clearing and restoring the Keep."

"Wizard Jahoda is uniquely suited to lead the construction of the wall," Kelvin said. "I estimate it would take a month or six weeks to build a complete defensive perimeter wall, if he's provided with sufficient manpower."

Before Alexander could respond, Chloe spoke within his mind.

"Darkness is near, My Love."

Chapter 18

Alexander tensed slightly and focused his all around sight, searching for any sign of the shade. He had expected, even counted on Shivini showing up during his war council.

One of the Rangers standing guard beside the door stepped forward past Boaberous, drawing his sword, and tried to stab Abigail in the back, but Alexander saw the attack coming. He put his foot on the edge of Abigail's chair and shoved her over just moments before the thrust that was meant to take her life. She tumbled to the floor and came up quickly, drawing the Thinblade and scanning the room as Alexander came up as well, drawing Mindbender.

Boaberous grabbed the Ranger possessed by Shivini by the back of the neck with one giant hand and hurled him backward into the wall so hard that the man lost consciousness.

The Ranger who had been standing guard with him knelt next to his fallen friend as Shivini slipped free of the first Ranger and into him. After a brief struggle for dominance, Shivini stood up in his new host with a malicious smile and drew his sword. Before anyone could react, he stabbed the unconscious Ranger in the heart.

"You know, Alexander," Shivini said, "you're the only one who's ever escaped me. In fact, it's a point of pride for me. Every single person I've ever possessed has died by my hand, so to speak, except you."

Boaberous started to advance toward the possessed Ranger.

"Hold," Alexander commanded.

Boaberous stopped but remained poised to strike.

"Oh, come now, Alexander, let the giant strike me down," Shivini said in a mocking tone. "I do so relish that moment when the soul of my possession slips free. You know, they can hear and see and even feel everything. I make sure of it. The fear and hopelessness of being trapped within one's own body as death nears, being unable to do a single thing about it as their life comes to a violent end, it's positively intoxicating."

"Maybe we should try this again," Alexander said, holding up the collar.

Shivini started casually strolling toward Abigail. She stood still, but ready, with the Thinblade between her and the possessed Ranger. Erik had taken command of the remaining Rangers in the room with hand signals and directed them toward the head of the table. Isabel was muttering the words of a spell under her breath. Alexander could see the flare of anger in her colors.

Magda and Cassandra had joined hands and were both in the midst of casting spells as well. Wizard Ely was muttering under his breath, Kelvin was inching closer on one side of the table while Sark approached from the other.

Shivini shook his head sadly. "Tsk, tsk, Alexander, you should know better than that by now. I'm disappointed in you. I'd hoped that you would have come up with something else—equally as useless, of course."

Alexander ignored Shivini's taunting. "I need him alive," he said.

Boaberous didn't hesitate for an instant. His war hammer came off his shoulder with terrifying speed and smashed the Ranger on the left shoulder, crushing him to the ground but leaving him alive.

As Boaberous advanced, Shivini laughed. Before the giant could reach him, he cut his own throat and his maniacal laughter transformed into a sickening gurgle. Before the Ranger could take his last breath, Alexander watched the shade slip free of his latest victim and into Boaberous. The giant froze as the shade struggled to dominate him. Everyone in the room held their breath, then Boaberous turned and Alexander saw Shivini in his eyes.

"Don't you see, Alexander?" Shivini said from within Lieutenant Grudge. "You simply can't win. You were doomed from the moment you released us into this world."

"You don't belong here, shade," Isabel said.

"Ah, but of course I do, Mother," Shivini said.

Before Isabel could find the words to protest, Shivini continued.

"You brought us into this world, gave birth to us, in a manner of speaking. We belong here as much as you do."

"I'll find a way to send you back, Shivini," Alexander said, advancing toward the shade. Abigail flanked him on his right, Isabel on his left.

"Enough of this," Shivini said. "As much fun as this is, I've come with a more important purpose. My master would address your war council."

Shivini pronounced a word from some long-dead language and Phane materialized, standing in the middle of the table. Everyone froze for just a moment before they began making preparations to attack.

"Hold!" Alexander commanded again. "It's just a projection."

"Some projections can do harm," Kelvin said.

"My dear Guild Mage," Phane said with mock indignation. "I have no desire for unpleasantness. I only wish to be heard by this esteemed council."

Alexander caught Erik's eye and pointed to Boaberous. Erik nodded, directing his Rangers to surround the giant. Once Shivini was cordoned off, Alexander turned to face Phane.

"How can he do this?" Abigail asked.

"I don't know," Kelvin answered with a frown.

"My dear Abigail, are you referring to how I managed to penetrate Blackstone Keep's security or how I'm projecting an image from so far away?"

"Both," Abigail said.

"He must be using an enchanted item of some sort to relay the projection," Kelvin said.

"Very good, Mage," Phane said. "You could yet serve me. In fact, I would be willing to accept the surrender and fealty of everyone in this room, save Alexander, of course."

The room fell deathly silent for a moment before Isabel started laughing softly.

"You won't turn any of us, Phane," she said.

"Don't be so sure, my dear. All it would take to end this war for everyone on Ruatha is Alexander's head in a bag and the Sovereign Stone delivered to me. I would even let dear Queen Abigail rule in my name."

"You must have actually loved that imp of yours," Alexander said.

Phane lost his composure, his face contorting in a mask of rage and sorrow for just a moment before he reclaimed control.

"You should never have murdered Kludge, dear cousin," Phane said. "Before that, I would have killed you quickly, or even allowed you to rule in my name—didn't matter to me, so long as the Sovereign Stone was surrendered to me. But now it's personal."

"It was personal the day you killed my brother, Phane," Alexander said.

"Oh, but I never killed your brother," Phane said innocently. "Your protector, Commander P'Tal, was the one who ordered your brother killed, and yet you have forgiven him."

"He sent an assassin to prevent Darius from threatening you," Alexander said, "but it was always about you."

"If you'd had the good sense to die two thousand years ago, none of this would be happening," Isabel said.

"Perhaps, my sweet, but I didn't want to die," Phane said with a shrug, "and I usually get what I want."

"Did you really go to all this trouble to try and turn my friends and family against me?" Alexander asked.

"Oh no, dear cousin, I wanted to tell you what's going to happen next," Phane said with a boyish smile. "You see, I created the wraithkin with a very specific purpose: vengeance. I know about Isabel's rather unique magical abilities. Quite impressive really; she will make a formidable Lady Reishi, once I've turned her, of course."

"That's never going to happen," Isabel said.

"Oh, but it's already begun," Phane said gleefully. "The taint left by the wraithkin's blades was meant for you. In a way, you should be flattered. You have no idea how much trouble I went to. You see, I knew you would attempt to heal those injured by my wraithkin, especially after more conventional means of magical healing failed. When you did, the hook was set. Now Azugorath, the wraith queen, has her tendril into you and there's nothing you can do about it. The transformation will take some time, but it *will* happen and it can't be stopped by any power within your grasp. I'm afraid, dear Isabel, that you will become a wraithkin as well, and when you do, you will give yourself to me willingly."

Phane laughed at the stunned looks worn by everyone in the room.

"Of course, there is a solution to your dilemma, Alexander," Phane said, "one that would save you Isabel's inevitable betrayal as well as rid the world of the shades. Kill her now, and the shades will be drawn back into the netherworld through the closing passageway within her mind. Of course, they'll also claim her soul in the bargain.

"Either way, I will have my vengeance."

Chapter 19

Isabel was dumbstruck. Alexander's eyes glittered with smoldering rage. The rest of the room was too stunned to speak.

"You're wrong, Phane," Alexander said. "I know about your wraith queen, I know where she is, and I'm coming to kill her. I sincerely hope you try and stop me."

"Dear cousin, I would draw you a map," Phane said. "It would save me the trouble of coming to get the Sovereign Stone. Of course, I don't really believe you will ever leave the room you're standing in."

Phane faded away with a malicious grin and Boaberous, possessed by Shivini, attacked the cordon of Rangers surrounding him, smashing the first to the ground with a single stroke of his war hammer. The Rangers attacked as a group but Boaberous swept his hammer across them, knocking several to the ground in a jumble.

Alexander spun to face the possessed giant as he tossed the collar to Jack, who caught it and flickered out of sight. Boaberous knocked Isabel out of the way with a backhand stroke that hit her shield spell with enough force to move her aside as he headed for Alexander.

Alexander raised Mindbender to meet Shivini's attack when Jataan, still sitting, threw a knife at the charging giant. It buried in the side of his chest, piercing his lung, but it didn't slow him down. Shivini slapped the blade of Mindbender with such force that it sliced his hand nearly in half lengthwise but also knocked the sword from Alexander's grasp, sending it clattering to the floor under the table.

A moment later Shivini launched himself at Alexander, crashing into him in a diving tackle. They both started to fall to the ground … and then they were both gone. One moment they were there and the next they were simply gone.

Alexander felt the sudden burn of cold like nothing he'd ever imagined. There was no air and the world had gone strangely translucent. In a moment of terrible realization, he remembered seeing the world like this once before—when he'd bonded with Chloe.

Alexander was in the aether.

The chill penetrated into him with such force that he was paralyzed by it. His lungs burned with need of air. For just a moment, Boaberous was there with him and then he was back in the world of time and substance, leaving Alexander trapped in the aether like Malachi Reishi. He fell back onto the floor but felt a strange lack of sensation. Instead, he felt only an all-encompassing cold and a desperate need to breathe. Within moments, the strangely translucent world started to go dark. Just before he lost consciousness, a ball of light flitted up to him and then suddenly he was back in the world of time and substance, gasping for breath.

But everything was still dark.

"Are you all right, My Love?" Chloe asked urgently in his mind. "Was I fast enough?"

"I'm alive," Alexander said to her. "Thank you, Little One."

Through his all around sight he took in the turmoil surrounding him. Everyone was shouting in confusion as they mustered a defense against the rampaging shade. Boaberous had rolled to his feet and immediately turned and hit Hanlon hard. The Forest Warden went down, unconscious. Regent Cery scrambled to get out of Shivini's reach but Boaberous was quick, despite his size. He grabbed the Regent by the arm and flung him across the room into the wall.

Anatoly vaulted onto the table and dove headlong at the giant, tackling him and driving him to the floor. Boaberous would have been more than a match for Anatoly, except for the magical belt of strength he wore. They grappled for a moment before Anatoly wrenched the giant's arms around behind his back and pinned them in place.

Shivini started to laugh but stopped abruptly when Jack snapped the collar around his neck. Jack stepped back from the flailing giant, held fast by Anatoly, just as Magda released her spell.

An arch of amber light leapt from her hand and struck Boaberous in the head. In a blink, he was completely encased in amber light, paralyzed by the spell. Anatoly disentangled himself from the immobilized giant and got to his feet.

Isabel was at Alexander's side a moment later.

"Are you all right?" she asked.

He nodded tightly. "I think so—except … I can't see."

"Dear Maker," she whispered, helping him to his feet.

He stood stiffly in spite of the preternatural chill that still ached within his bones. His normal vision was gone—the cold had damaged his eyes.

He was blind.

Focusing on his all around sight, he made his way to the immobilized giant, trying not to think about his lost vision. He examined Boaberous through his all around sight, scrutinizing his colors. He was dying. The wound inflicted by Jataan's knife was fatal, barring some form of extraordinary healing magic.

"How long will this spell hold him?"

"Only for a few minutes," Magda said.

"Long enough," Alexander said, as he fumbled in his pouch for one of the vials of deathwalker-root powder that Lucky had given him. He carefully sprinkled the powder into Boaberous's mouth and onto his upper lip so that he would inhale it the moment the paralyzation spell failed.

"Will that be enough to keep him out for a while?" he asked Lucky.

"That should render him unconscious for several hours," Lucky said.

"Good. Empty your bag and help me get him inside," Alexander said. "It's the only way I can think of to take him through the shield guarding the top chamber of the tower."

Lucky nodded and started emptying his many belongings onto the table. Once the magical bag was empty, Anatoly helped move Boaberous inside it.

Alexander hoisted the bag onto his shoulder and turned to Jataan. "I'm sorry," he said.

"As am I," Jataan said. "Boaberous swore to serve the Reishi. He would willingly face death in battle. This is no different, except his death will achieve a greater victory than most."

"You're going to sacrifice one of your own?" Regent Samuel asked indignantly. "If you're going to kill someone, it should be your wife. She's the real threat. You all heard what Prince Phane said. She is the reason the shades are in the world in the first place. If we must sacrifice someone, it should be her."

"Don't be a fool, Samuel," Regent Cery said, as he sat with his back against the wall trying to recover from Boaberous's attack.

"Lord Reishi himself said that the shades are the most dangerous threat we face," Samuel said. "If Lady Reishi's sacrifice can save the world, then we must consider it."

"Maybe he's right," Isabel whispered.

Alexander whirled on her and took her by the shoulders.

"He's not! I'll find a way to send the shades back where they came from without hurting you. I promise."

"What if you can't?" she asked. "I will not be the doom of the world. If I can save all that I love with my death, then I have to consider it."

Alexander pulled her to him and hugged her fiercely. "No! It's not an option."

"Promise me, Alexander," Isabel said. "If you have to choose between me or the world, you'll let me go and choose the world."

"I can't," he said, his voice breaking.

"You have to. You're Lord Reishi," Isabel said. "It's your duty."

Alexander couldn't speak past the lump in his throat. He held her, shaking his head back and forth.

"We'll find another way," he said, once he'd composed himself. "For all we know Phane was lying. Right now, I have work to do. We'll reconvene in two hours," he said as he headed for the door with Anatoly, Jack, and Abigail trailing behind him.

He walked in a daze through the halls of the giant Keep. So many thoughts fought for his attention. He couldn't lose Isabel, and yet he feared that Phane was telling the truth.

"My Love, I can see a dark thread in the aether leading from Isabel to the south," Chloe said in his mind. "I'm so sorry."

He swallowed hard, fighting the tears that threatened to overcome him. His friends didn't try to console him or even talk about all that had transpired, they simply followed, offering their silent support.

His blindness wasn't getting any better. He'd hoped that the effects of the cold would be temporary. Without his magical vision, he would've been helpless. Even with his all around sight he was still a bit disoriented.

Through all of the terrible things that were swirling around in his mind, he felt a nagging guilt for his willingness to sacrifice Boaberous. The giant had been a steadfast ally since the moment Alexander had bonded with the Sovereign Stone.

He told himself that Shivini was too dangerous to be left alive. He told himself that only he had ever survived Shivini and then only through Isabel's magic. He told himself that Boaberous had stood with him in battle time and again, risking his life for Alexander's cause, that he had volunteered to face Alexander's enemies, yet none of it seemed to assuage his guilt.

He had sworn to protect the Old Law and he was choosing death for another to spare the world the horror of Shivini's presence. No matter how hard he tried, he couldn't reconcile the conflict. He had no right to take Boaberous's life and yet he knew that he would. He had to. Shivini was simply too dangerous.

He had to be destroyed, even if it cost Alexander his soul.

He touched the mark on his neck and lamented the turn of events that had brought him to this place. He'd long since embraced his duty, but he still longed for a simple life spent with those he loved in a world free of the ambitions of those who would rule over others.

As he ascended the seemingly endless stairs leading to the top of the tower, he imposed order on his emotions and focused his mind. He was fighting for a world where people could be free to live and love without fear of those with the ambition to rule. His cause was just. His sacrifices were necessary.

He reached the top room of the tower and laid Boaberous out on the floor of Mage Cedric's Wizard's Den.

"I'm sorry, Boaberous. I wish there was another way."

He looked at the sleeping giant for a long time before he stepped out of the Wizard's Den and drank the transference potion that Lucky had made for him. Only a moment passed before he felt the effects. He closed his eyes and found the place of stillness within himself. After a moment of final deliberation, he decided that his course was set.

With a word, the door to the Wizard's Den closed, sealing Shivini and Boaberous away for eternity.

Alexander sat down, put his face in his hands and cried.

Chapter 20

When the war council reconvened, Wizard Ely reported that he had found the device that allowed Phane's projection spell to reach so far. It was a metal disc six inches in diameter that had been affixed to the underside of the table. After Mage Gamaliel carefully examined it, he handed it to Abigail and asked her to cut it in half with the Thinblade. Alexander watched the aura of magic fade as the device was destroyed. They speculated that Shivini had brought it into the Keep when he originally entered in the body of a Ranger or a soldier.

The afternoon session of the war council was spent discussing Phane and his revelation that Isabel would turn against Alexander and his cause. He listened to the nobles and his friends and family explore every option from imprisoning Isabel to attempting some form of magical intervention.

He allowed them to go on because he wanted to give them the opportunity to surprise him with some way of saving her from the terrible fate that Phane had devised for her, but he knew in the end that they wouldn't. Phane had spent considerable time and effort engineering this outcome and it was unlikely that anyone at the table would have more insight into the situation than the Reishi Sovereigns.

Alexander already knew his course. He'd told Phane that he was coming for the wraith queen as a ruse. He knew full well that he didn't have the power necessary to penetrate the underground fortress where Phane was holding the linchpin of his plan. Alexander intended to pursue the only other option available to him: the potion that the sovereigns had described. That course would take him where he needed to go anyway.

During the discussion, Isabel sat straight-backed, listening to others debate her future. After a heated argument between Hanlon and Regent Samuel over killing her to eliminate the threat of the shades once and for all, Alexander stood up. The table fell silent.

"If you wish her dead, then come try to kill her," he said to Regent Samuel. The tension in the room was heavy and oppressive.

Regent Samuel blinked, then swallowed as the truth of what he was calling for became real to him. He remained seated.

"Here's what's going to happen," Alexander said. "We're going to follow through with our plan as it stood before Phane's visit. Nothing has changed … except the death of Boaberous and Shivini."

"And you've been blinded," Bella added. "You might want to reconsider your part in the plan. Surely there are others you could send to recover the keystones and the ingredients you need."

"No, Mom," Alexander said, shaking his head. "This is my part. Even blind, I can see better than most, and what I can't see, Chloe can."

Prior to the resumption of the war council, Lucky had given him a healing draught but it didn't restore his vision. He surmised that the complete coldness of the aether had literally frozen his eyes, rendering him permanently blind …

barring some extraordinary healing magic. Isabel cried quietly at her inability to call on the light to restore his vision, but he just smiled at her and told her that she had lost her light saving him from a fate far worse than blindness.

Alexander fixed Regent Samuel with his glittering eyes, even though he could only see him with his magical vision.

"I will hear no more talk of murdering my wife, not for any reason. Is that clear?"

Samuel started to say something but thought better of it and simply nodded stiffly.

"Our course is set," Alexander said. "In one week, Abigail will lead the bulk of our forces into Fellenden and I will depart for the Reishi Isle. We have much to do before then. Let's make the most of the time we have."

With that he took Isabel's hand and left the war council with his wife.

After breakfast the next morning, he and Isabel went to the Hall of Magic to see Kelvin and Hax. They'd sent word of progress with the books that Alexander had retrieved from Benesh Reishi's keep.

Lucky was also in Kelvin's workshop when they arrived. "Ah, there you are, my boy," Lucky said. "How are your eyes?"

"They hurt and I still can't see," Alexander said.

"I suspect the pain will subside over time," Lucky said, "but I doubt they will heal without powerful magic. I'll begin doing some research into more specific healing concoctions. Perhaps I'll be able to find something that will help."

"Don't make it a priority," Alexander said, turning to Hax. He hadn't told Isabel about Lucky's assignment and now that Phane had gotten his hooks into her, he didn't intend to. He loved her and wanted to trust her with everything but he knew better than to underestimate the Reishi Prince.

"What can you tell me about these books?"

Wizard Hax placed the first of the volumes on the table before him.

"This one contains information about the unique nature of an adept's magic," Wizard Hax said. "I've read it through and can summarize it for you, but you'll benefit more once I've had the time to make a complete translation."

"Tell me what you can," Alexander said.

"Of course. It's really quite fascinating," Wizard Hax said. "The vast majority of wizards experience the firmament in the same way, as a limitless reservoir of potential that's separate and distinct from their consciousness. Benesh Reishi reached the conclusion, after a great deal of well-documented and painstaking research, mind you, that an adept's consciousness and the firmament are somehow fused together.

"Where a normal wizard is at risk of falling into the firmament and becoming lost to the endless possibilities, you are able to merge your consciousness with the firmament, in essence becoming one with the source of reality. The implications are staggering.

"First, there's the issue of locality. A normal wizard can inject his will into the firmament and cause effects within his local area, but the farther away he tries to change the nature of reality, the more difficult it becomes, until he reaches a range where he's unable to manifest any change at all.

"Your descriptions of the way your clairvoyance works would seem to bear this out. You are able to see across vast distances without difficulty. That fact seems to substantiate Benesh Reishi's claim that an adept has no restrictions on the range of his magic. In effect, you can wield your power anywhere within the firmament without regard to your physical location.

"Second, there's the issue of sheer power. A typical wizard must guard against the pull of the firmament or become lost, but you are able to join with it without fear. The result is vastly more potent. Unfortunately, Benesh Reishi wasn't unable to discover how to inject his will into the firmament in the way that other wizards do. Like your magic, his was based on perception rather than substance. He was able to make others see and hear nearly anything he could imagine, yet he couldn't cause any type of actual physical effects within the world of time and substance.

"Your magic is similar, in that you can see a great deal, yet you are unable to actually cast spells in the conventional sense."

"This is all very interesting, and I'm looking forward to reading your translation," Alexander said, "but it doesn't offer me anything that I can use right now."

Wizard Hax nodded. "Yes, of course. Benesh Reishi discovered that his magic was similar to a muscle. The more he used it the stronger it became. Over time, with ongoing practice, he was able to increase the size, duration, and detail of his illusions. He set out a rigorous practice schedule for himself and followed it closely to expand his abilities. Similarly, I believe that your abilities will only reach their full potential with regular use and practice.

"From the information in this volume, I can't say if you will develop further abilities, but I can say with relative certainty that the abilities you have will become more readily available and controllable with routine use."

"All right," Alexander said, nodding. "That's confirmation of the advice the Reishi Sovereigns gave me. Not exactly what I was hoping for, but good enough for now. Did any of the other books deal with the nature of an adept?"

"I'm afraid not," Wizard Hax said. "The next most promising was the treatise on Mindbender. I still have more to translate, but I've been able to learn some things of interest. It describes how the sword was created, which Mage Gamaliel has expressed great interest in, but it also deals with how the sword can best be used."

Alexander sat forward.

"It seems that it was designed to function with the unique connection to the firmament possessed by an adept," Hax said. "In other words, it probably wouldn't work for anyone except you. Benesh Reishi was quite ambitious. He sought to essentially duplicate his mind and therefore his link with the firmament within the sword. His goal was to create a sword that could offer him the perception necessary to project his illusions anywhere he could see.

"Essentially, he was trying to create a sword that had your gift of clairvoyance. He reasoned that the combination of being able to see anywhere, coupled with his ability to manifest illusions anywhere, would allow him to act anywhere in the entire Seven Isles from the safety of his keep.

"Unfortunately, he didn't achieve the result he desired. While he was successful in creating a semisentient sword with an adept's link to the firmament, the powers the sword manifested didn't live up to his hopes. Instead of clairvoyance, Mindbender was able to see into the minds of the enemy he faced while also duplicating his talent with illusions.

"He was actually disappointed by the result, doubly so when he realized that creating the sword had imbalanced his own connection to the firmament, eventually leading to his death. In the end, he considered the sword to be a curse and ultimately his greatest failure."

"Is there any information about using it more effectively?" Alexander asked.

"It seems that the sword's magic is similar to an adept's link to the firmament," Hax said. "Practice is the key. After a while, Benesh Reishi learned how to condition his mind so that the sword would believe he was in a fight. Once he developed that mental discipline, he was able to practice with the sword much more often.

"He found that creating illusions with Mindbender was much the same as using his own magic. He simply visualized the result he wanted and released it into the sword, much the same way a wizard releases an image of his desired effect into the firmament. He found that many of the more traditional visualization exercises taught to wizard apprentices were very helpful in training his mind to create more detailed and therefore more believable illusions."

"I can help you with that," Isabel said. "I learned a few of those exercises while training to take the trials on the fortress island."

"I guess I'm going to be spending a lot of time practicing then," Alexander said. "What about the other two books?"

"This next one deals with the magic magnifying effects of crystals," Hax said. "It seems that crystals have the innate ability to shield a wizard's mind from the pull of the firmament, thereby allowing a more full and complete connection to be made with less possibility of being drawn in and lost. Conversely, crystals also possess the ability to draw out and contain a wizard's link to the firmament. I don't quite understand the significance of this property just yet. The dialect used in this section is unfamiliar, so I may be misunderstanding it somewhat, though it is clear that Benesh Reishi was quite excited about this particular aspect of crystals.

"He created a crystal chamber to test the limits of this theory and found that it had little effect on his magic. It did, however, allow other wizards to substantially increase the power of their spells."

"Could we use the crystal chamber in the Keep to help Kelvin enchant items with greater power?" Alexander asked with renewed interest.

"Perhaps," Hax said.

"I'd like you to try, Kelvin," Alexander said. "The Reishi Sovereigns believe that they could create a device that could draw a shade in and imprison it permanently, but they also believe it would take the power of an arch mage to construct such a device. If the crystal chamber can increase your connection to the firmament, then maybe you can create such a device."

"I'll give the matter some thought," Kelvin said, "but I believe it would be wise to attempt lesser enchantments first to test the limits of the chamber."

"I agree," Alexander said. "I'll dispel the barrier and command the sentinel to allow you and my father passage into the lower chambers while I'm away. Please continue, Wizard Hax."

"The last book contains a line of research that Benesh Reishi was pursuing in his final year that is staggering in its implications if it's possible at all.

He was trying to create an item that would function as an artificial link to the firmament similar to Mindbender, except that it would allow the wielder to cast spells in the same way as a wizard without requiring a connection to the firmament."

"Was he successful?" Alexander asked.

"No," Hax said, "it appears that he was in the final stages of researching the possibility when he died. His research is promising, though. I haven't studied it enough to make a determination and I believe that the Guild Mage should review it as well, but I suspect that it may be possible, although very difficult."

"Would such an item allow one who hasn't survived the mana fast to cast spells?" Alexander asked.

"That's unclear, but I believe it may be possible," Hax said.

"How complete a connection to the firmament could such an item create?" Alexander asked.

"He believed that a full and complete connection similar to that of a mage could be created and his research seems to support his belief."

"Keep this information secret for now," Alexander said. "The last thing we need is Phane creating these items and arming his soldiers with them."

Chapter 21

The week that followed was busy with the mundane details of preparing an army to march. Alexander spent the time consulting with the Reishi Sovereigns, practicing his magic, and training Abigail to use the Thinblade more effectively.

He learned a great deal about magic and the netherworld in his conversations with the sovereigns, although none of what he learned could help him immediately. He made a careful record of each exercise that Lucky would need to practice in order to ascend to the rank of mage alchemist. Lucky had reservations about staying behind while everyone else left to face the enemy, but he accepted the tasks that Alexander had assigned him nonetheless.

Isabel worked with Magda learning a force-push spell. It was less deadly than the light-lance spell, but it could be cast more quickly and was still a formidable weapon at relatively close range. The effect was to create a wave of magical energy that would strike an enemy and knock them backward, often disorienting them or even rendering them unconscious. The choice of the spell was Magda's suggestion, more for the time it would take to master than for any other reason.

Magda and Cassandra spent time exchanging knowledge about magic and history with the wizards. Wizard Hax was especially interested in their perceptions of magic and spent many hours engrossed in deep conversations with the witches about esoteric topics.

Kelvin worked tirelessly on the creation of a new collar of binding that could be used against a shade or a wraithkin. Alexander intended to find and face Jinzeri somewhere on the Reishi Isle and he needed every advantage he could get.

A flight of Sky Knights arrived during the week and moved into the aerie, bringing a significant military capability to Blackstone Keep. Within a day, they were flying aerial patrols over the northern half of Ruatha. Duncan sent a wing to support Duane in the north. He wanted to eliminate Elred Rake's legion of troublemakers in the northern wilds without risking too many of his men. The Sky Knights would be invaluable as scouts and support when the time came to attack. He wanted Duane and his Rangers to learn to work with the Sky Knights prior to the battle that was coming.

A second flight of Sky Knights, commanded by Mistress Corina, was preparing to fly to Fellenden to augment the assault force that would attack through the Gate.

Lieutenant Wyatt was promoted to captain and given his pick of any Rangers in the army to reconstitute his force. He chose a number of the most skilled and experienced men and women that he could find. Alexander asked him to accompany Abigail to Fellenden.

Captain Sava split his forces in two, leaving half on Ruatha under Duncan's command and taking the other half with the bulk of the army to Fellenden. Two platoons of dragon-armored cavalry mounted on rhone would be a significant addition to Abigail's forces.

Abigail's command staff was selected—Conner Ithilian, Mage Dax, Wizard Sark, Mistress Magda, General Markos, and General Kern would accompany her, along with Anatoly, Mistress Corina, and Knight Raja, who would be her wingman when she was riding Kallistos. Another six wizards were selected to join the assault force to offer their expertise and assistance against Zuhl and his minions.

Duncan was to remain behind on Ruatha with Hanlon, Kelvin, Lucky, and the majority of the wizards who were still busy exploring and cataloging the contents of Blackstone Keep. In addition to Duane's legion, three would remain behind as well to provide security in northern Ruatha in the event that Phane managed to land another force.

Jataan was healing slowly but was no less busy for it. He had called forth the Reishi Protectorate to Blackstone Keep and many of his agents were already arriving. After a personal interview with each, he made careful notes of their capabilities and skills so that he could decide how best to use them. He was building a royal guard force, an intelligence service, and a group of operatives who could be sent on missions of vital importance.

Alexander visited him occasionally during the week, ostensibly to receive reports on his progress, but actually to see how he was healing. He wished the battle mage would be accompanying him. Without Jataan or Boaberous or Anatoly, Alexander would have no protector. While he was confident in his own abilities and knew Isabel and Jack could hold their own in battle, he wanted a bit more muscle … and another person to stand guard wouldn't hurt.

Jataan solved the problem when a pair of his agents arrived: twin brothers from Karth named Hector and Horace Lal. They had served as infiltrators within the Reishi Army Regency for several years, sending reports to Jataan whenever the means presented itself. When they heard the summons, they abandoned their posts and deserted the Regency Army to make their way to Ruatha.

After Jataan had interviewed them thoroughly, he asked Alexander to speak with them. They were identical in appearance, save the scar on Hector's right cheek. Each stood just over five and a half feet tall and had a medium build, nondescript brown eyes and brown hair. All in all, they looked completely ordinary, except Alexander knew with a single glance at their colors that they were anything but. Both had the subtle magic of a sorcerer, their abilities manifesting in very different ways.

Hector was capable of transforming himself and all of his belongings into a gaseous cloud of vapor that vaguely resembled his solid form. He could make the transformation with breathtaking speed, one moment being solid and the next becoming insubstantial. While in his vaporous form, he could flow through the cracks in a door with ease and was virtually immune to normal weapons, however, he was also unable to attack.

Horace was able to manifest an invisible being of limited capability within a hundred feet or so. His magical servant wasn't very strong and couldn't attack very effectively, but could be highly useful for performing a variety of tasks at a distance.

Alexander asked both men to demonstrate their powers while he watched their colors closely. He was becoming accustomed to relying on his all around sight. He could still see colors through it so the only real limitation due to his blindness was a lack of distance vision. Within a hundred feet, he was able to see everything quite clearly.

His evaluation of their colors told him that they were both loyal to the Reishi and were both accustomed to handling themselves in dangerous situations. Each was competent in his own right, but together they were formidable, relying on the strengths of the other and communicating with an almost telepathic link.

Each was skilled in combat, their weapons of choice being a pair of short swords. They were also talented spies, capable of moving silently, picking locks, climbing walls, concealing themselves in plain sight, and blending into the background of nearly any gathering. Neither looked particularly intelligent but after an hour of questioning, Alexander discovered that both were highly trained, expertly skilled, and quite capable operatives who had survived undercover within a hostile force for years without being detected.

When he asked them if they would like to accompany him on a mission of great importance and great danger, they were both eager for the assignment. While Alexander didn't know them well, Jataan assured him that they were loyal to the Reishi. Their colors confirmed it and Alexander felt better having them along.

***

The morning of departure arrived. Kelvin had given Alexander the newly fashioned collar of binding the night before, and Lucky had given every member of his party a pouch of potions for their journey, including several healing draughts and a jar of healing salve each. Alexander had split his supply of fairy dust into two vials, keeping one with him and secreting the other in the tower. Isabel's life might depend on having the fairy dust when he needed it, and he certainly didn't want to risk losing all of it on his journey. He also took one of the vials of Wizard's Dust back from Kelvin and put it with the fairy dust, just to be sure he would have what he needed for the potion when the time came.

The army had gathered around the Ruathan Gate and preparations had been made for the assault into Fellenden. Prior to opening the Gate, Alexander sat down on the platform to meditate, sending his awareness to Fellenden to make sure that everything was as he expected it to be. Two legions were still encamped around the Gate. He was about to ruin their morning.

The last of Kelvin's larger explosive weapons was loaded onto a wooden ramp so it would roll through the moment Alexander opened the Gate.

He looked to his friends and family for confirmation that everything was in order, then placed his hand on the Gate. It shimmered momentarily before opening to the plains of central Fellenden. The weapon rolled through into the midst of a platoon-sized guard force arrayed before the Gate and an encampment of thousands more sprawling away in every direction. Before they could raise their weapons, Alexander closed the Gate and gave Kelvin a nod. The Guild Mage crushed a small enchanted pebble under his boot.

Alexander waited for a count of thirty before opening the Gate again. This time the scene was very different. All of the soldiers within several hundred feet had been blown to the ground, most of them dead. The enemy in the distance was in a state of sudden panic as they scrambled to make sense of the tremendous explosion that had just eaten a hole out of the middle of their encampment.

Alexander's heavy cavalry thundered through into the heart of Fellenden, followed by the infantry and archers. Once the lead force of three legions led by General Kern was through the Gate, Alexander and his friends followed. There was nothing but devastation for as far as he could see with his all around sight. He felt a pang of frustration at his blindness. As much as he tried to tell himself that he could overcome it, he had to admit that it limited him in some important ways.

He sent his mind to Chloe and surveyed the scene of battle through her eyes. She flew up a hundred feet over the encampment to get a better perspective. The forces guarding the Gate had been completely unprepared for such a violent and sudden attack. The initial explosion had killed thousands and wounded thousands more. Those who were unscathed were disoriented and unorganized.

Ruathan forces in the initial attack were prepared and fought with a plan. The cavalry split into two forces, turning left and right, cutting the enemy force in half. The infantry followed, creating a battle line facing the enemy soldiers that remained in front of the Gate, while the cavalry moved to engage the forces behind it.

Archers came through next, forming a line behind the infantry and immediately attacking the soldiers at the front of the Gate. It took only a few volleys from the legion of longbowmen to send the enemy in front into an all-out retreat.

The plan was to rout those in front of the Gate, then collapse back onto the group caught behind the Gate, run them down and kill or capture the lot of them. Zuhl's soldiers were fearsome and skilled, but they didn't fare well against the superior numbers and coordinated attack launched from within their midst. Within an hour, the two legions had broken and were fleeing from the rapidly growing Ruathan army.

It took the better part of the day for Abigail's army to move through the Gate. Command tents were erected nearby as the soldiers and supply trains poured through. Alexander and Abigail presided over a meeting to reiterate their battle plan and contingency plans for the coming struggle against Zuhl's forces.

A flight of Sky Knights commanded by Mistress Corina would be joining them by nightfall, and the Ithilian armada was moving into position to participate in the attack against the shipyards.

Near dusk, after the last of the soldiers had arrived and the army was busy setting up a hasty camp, Alexander prepared to return to Ruatha with his parents and many of his advisors.

"Be safe, Abigail," he said. "Remember, you don't have to fight the enemy, you just have to lead the army in battle, but lead from behind."

"I know, Alexander," Abigail said, giving her brother a hug. Take care of Jack for me," she whispered.

Alexander nodded and turned to Anatoly. "Watch out for her."

Anatoly gave him a grim grin and a big hug. "I'd feel better if Commander P'Tal was going with you."

"Me too, but the pair of men he picked to accompany us look promising," Alexander said. "I'm sure we'll be fine. I'll look in on you from time to time. Pay attention to your dreams."

The big man-at-arms nodded and clapped him on the shoulder.

Isabel and Abigail shared a hug.

Jack didn't say a word to Abigail, but instead took her in his arms and kissed her tenderly but passionately. They shared a look for a moment before he turned away from her and walked quickly back through the Gate.

"I've set the Gate so you can open it with the Thinblade," Alexander said to his sister. "With Kallistos, you should be able to reach it relatively quickly if you need to send word back to Ruatha. Dad will be posting a squad to run messages."

"Alexander, I know all of this," Abigail said. "We've gone over every detail several times."

"I know," Alexander said. "I just want to make sure. I love you, Abigail."

"I love you too, Alexander. I'll see you soon."

With that, he and those of his friends and allies who wouldn't be taking part in the campaign against Zuhl returned to Ruatha. The regiment he would lead to the Reishi Isle was camped nearby and had already set up his tents. He went to bed early after a quiet dinner with Isabel.

She was becoming increasingly on edge. He could see anxiety in her colors and it worried him but he didn't ask her about it. She would talk to him in her own time.

The next morning he rose before sunrise and prepared for his journey. At breakfast, a rider arrived with an urgent message from Baron Buckwold. The young man entered, out of breath and coated with road grime. "Lord Reishi, I have news of invasion in Warrenton," he said.

"Do you have any details?" Alexander asked.

"Only that it's a legion or more from Andalia," he said. "They attacked in the night, led by a small force of wizards. They took the ports. Once the first of the Lancers were ashore, the home guard of Warrenton was overpowered and forced to retreat. The Lancers are waging a scorched-earth war against the villages up the coast. They left Warrenton standing but are focusing their attacks on the food crops and livestock."

Alexander closed his eyes and shook his head.

"All this time I've been so concerned about the south, I didn't even think about the east coast," he said. "It makes sense, though. Buckwold and Warrenton would have had the best crop of any territory in Ruatha. Makes for the perfect target."

"Ithilian harvest estimates are good this year and we have quite a bit of grain stored away for hard times," Abel said. "I'd say this qualifies. Your people won't go hungry this winter."

Alexander nodded. "Thank you, Abel. Dad, you'd better take the remaining legions in the north and see what you can do about the Lancers."

"I read General Talia's report on his fight with the Lancers down south," Duncan said. "With the Sky Knights' help, I think we might be able to lure them into a bad spot again. I'll set the infantry and archers moving and take a legion of cavalry east today."

"It's a good bet Phane is sending more to the port in Warrenton," Alexander said. "We'd better see about reinforcing Buckwold's defenses, and I'd like the Sky Knights to begin patrolling the coastline."

"I've already talked with Mistress Constance," Duncan said. "For some reason her people are eager to fly patrol, so that shouldn't be a problem."

"I have a team trained and equipped to make firepots," Lucky said. "The Sky Knights are armed and ready. In fact, they've been practicing with stones to hone their aim."

"Good, I'll feel a lot better if we can drown those Lancers rather than fight them," Alexander said. "Dad, as much as I'd like to stay and help with this, I have to go."

"I know, Son," Duncan said. "We all have to fight the enemy we're best prepared to fight. Between the wizards, Sky Knights, and the legions I have under my command, we'll manage against the Lancers."

***

Within an hour, Alexander was standing on the Gate platform with Isabel, Jack, Chloe, Hector, and Horace. Wizard Jahoda and Commander Perry were there as well. The severe and highly disciplined commander had volunteered for the most dangerous mission of all. His regiment of a thousand battle-hardened soldiers would take and hold the Reishi Keep in the midst of the most wild and untamed scrap of dirt in all the Seven Isles while Wizard Jahoda would supervise the building of a wall around the Keep. Two wizards had been handpicked by Kelvin to accompany the task force, and Cassandra would be sending a wing of twenty-four Sky Knights to assist as well.

Alexander feared it wouldn't be enough. He'd traveled across the Reishi Isle and knew how perilous it was. More worrisome was the tentacle demon loose within the Keep. There was no telling what it might do or how many men it might kill before they brought it down … if they could even kill it.

With a deep breath he opened the Gate to the Reishi Isle. It opened to the plain outside the Keep, as Alexander knew it would.

"Commander Perry, secure the area," Alexander said.

"By your command, Lord Reishi," Commander Perry said, then motioned for his cavalry to move through. Two hundred men on heavy horse stepped onto the Reishi Isle and fanned out around the Gate, followed by six hundred infantry and two hundred archers. Alexander and his party were the last through. He closed the Gate behind him, cutting off any hope of escape for the task force he'd assigned to secure the Keep.

"Work quickly," Alexander said to Wizard Jahoda. "The nights will be the most dangerous. The sooner the wall is built, the safer you will all be. I'll be back in two or three weeks. We'll assess your progress at that point and determine if more resources are needed from Ruatha."

"Be safe, Lord Reishi," Jahoda said. "We'll begin construction immediately."

"Stay sharp, Commander," Alexander said to Perry.

"Always, Lord Reishi. Safe journey," Commander Perry said with a crisp salute.

With that they were off into the wilderness of the Reishi Isle.

Chapter 22

They traveled for two uneventful days through the thick forest. Occasionally, they heard a predator in the distance, but nothing that was interested in a group of five. A few times they thought they were being watched but nothing ever came of it.

The forest teemed with life, most of it small but all of it very busy with the business of survival. The Reishi Isle had been bereft of civilization since the fall of the Reishi Empire. Worse, the island was home to some of Malachi Reishi's more ambitious experiments and summonings.

Dark things stalked the wilds of the Reishi Isle.

Alexander was wary. Every step brought him closer to Jinzeri. He remembered all too vividly how hopeless and powerless he felt in the brief time that Shivini had been in possession of his body.

He also remembered the feelings of despair and self-doubt he was experiencing at the moment when Shivini had taken him. His emotional weakness had opened him up to the shade. He had no intention of allowing that to happen ever again.

As he walked, he reflected on how poisonous such feelings were. He already had enough going against him … he couldn't allow his own mind to entertain thoughts that plotted against him as well. He renewed his silent vow to remain ever vigilant lest his thoughts betray him again, and he resolved to entertain only those thoughts that accurately reflected reality or the vision of reality that he was attempting to create.

Self-doubt, worry, negative fantasies, and guilt were no longer welcome within his mind.

And yet, he did feel guilt, a nagging and terrible guilt deep within his psyche that he couldn't shake.

He had killed Boaberous.

His purpose had been just and necessary.

His need had been great.

His friends and family, allies and advisors all agreed that it had to be done.

And yet, he had killed an innocent man—violated the Old Law … the very law that he'd sworn to protect.

He couldn't reconcile the conflict within himself and so it played out on the battlefield of his mind, unbidden and unwanted, yet inescapable.

He snapped back to the present moment when Hector suddenly stopped in midstride, urgently signaling for stillness. Alexander froze, stretching his hearing and his all around sight to the edge of its range. Within seconds, a rustle in the brush brought his attention to the wolf that was stalking them. After a closer look, he breathed a sigh of relief. It was a grey wolf, just an animal.

"Wolves," he whispered.

Isabel tipped her head back and closed her eyes, sending her vision to

Slyder.

"I count seven," she said.

Alexander saw her colors flare with power as she called on her ability to control animals.

"They're mine now," she said. "They've accepted us as part of their pack … for the time being anyway."

Alexander smiled at his wife. She had truly come into her own. She was Lady Reishi by marriage, by right, and by virtue of her power. He was proud of her and he loved her completely, but he was also afraid for her. Her colors held the taint of Phane's darkness and he wasn't sure if he could save her.

As the thought entered his mind, he forced it aside and replaced it with of a vision of them happily growing old together, then told himself, yet again, that he wasn't going to feed dark thoughts with his attention.

Two more days passed without incident. They were making steady progress toward their objective, even if it was slower than Alexander would have liked. The forest was thick and overgrown, untended and wild. Finding a path was challenging at times, cutting a path was tedious and time-consuming, but occasionally necessary.

Alexander's all around sight was becoming clearer the more he used it, but it came at a price. He was beginning to have headaches, especially late in the day. It took some measure of concentration and effort to see with his magic and using it all the time was taking a toll.

On the fifth day, the gently rolling hills of the Reishi Isle's northwestern forests gave way to the foothills of the mountain range that formed the northwest corner of the island. Alexander felt a sense of expectancy as they neared his goal. If he could secure the keystone from Jinzeri, he would have plenty of time to figure out a more permanent solution to the problem of the Nether Gate.

They were struggling through some particularly dense underbrush when Isabel stopped, looking up and closing her eyes.

"We're being followed," she said. "I count over two dozen."

"Two dozen what?" Alexander asked.

"They look like primitives, similar to some tribes that live in the eastern wilds of the Great Forest. They're armed with stone-tipped spears."

"Stone-tipped spears can be pretty sharp," Jack said.

"How far back are they?" Alexander asked.

"Ten minutes, maybe less if they can move through this brush faster than we can," Isabel said.

"I don't want to fight them if we can help it," Alexander said. "Maybe I can scare them away with Mindbender."

"They might not be looking for a fight at all," Jack said. "They could just be curious."

"I'd rather avoid them altogether," Alexander said. "We don't have time for distractions."

Before he could make a decision, there was a terrifying roar from the south. It came from a good distance away, but not nearly far enough for his liking. Whatever made that noise had to be big.

Everyone froze, waiting expectantly.

"That was unsettling," Jack whispered.

Alexander nodded and gestured to the northwest. Hector set out again but more quietly and cautiously than before. The forest had gone silent. The birds and small animals that had only moments before filled the forest with activity and song had all gone to ground.

"The wolves are spooked," Isabel said.

"I know how they feel," Alexander said. "Can you get a look at that thing?"

Isabel nodded and closed her eyes for a moment. She inhaled sharply as her eyes snapped open.

"It's huge, and it's headed straight for us," she said. "There are some cliffs to the north where we might find cover."

"How big is huge?" Jack asked.

"Twelve feet at the shoulder and twenty feet long," Isabel said. "It runs on all fours and has massive shoulders and huge jaws with lots of teeth."

It roared again, only this time it was much closer. They could hear it crashing through the dense forest.

"Run!" Alexander yelled.

They headed for the cliffs and the hope of cover. As they fled through the brush, they heard the dying yelp of one of the wolves that Isabel had been using to scout for them. She released her hold on the rest so they could flee the beast and at least have a chance for survival.

The forest thinned as they neared a sheer cliff face that reached several hundred feet into the sky. Alexander scanned it with his all around sight, looking for any break or opening that they could hide in, but found nothing.

The beast broke through the thick underbrush into the shade of the cliff and stopped to roar at them. It was terrifying and awesome all at once. Alexander saw in a glance that it was a creature of magic and darkness rather than a natural-born species. At least there was probably only one.

"I've found a cave, My Love," Chloe said in his mind. "Come quickly."

The beast charged. Alexander drew Mindbender and called forth the illusion of a dragon, rearing back, wings spread wide as though preparing to strike.

The beast's charge faltered and it roared in challenge but held its ground against the illusion.

"Run along the cliff," Alexander said. "Chloe's found a cave."

They raced along the base of the cliff through the ferns that covered the forest floor. Alexander split his focus between running for his life, maintaining the illusion of the dragon, and watching the creature with his all around sight. It was a delicate balancing act. When the beast attacked the dragon and found nothing but empty air, it roared in rage and frustration before turning its attention on Alexander and his fleeing friends.

They reached a narrow crack in the cliff face and filed in one by one. Alexander was the last to enter and squeezed into the safety of the fissure just as the beast reached him, snarling and snapping. Alexander was just out of reach but still close enough to smell the beast's fetid breath as it roared in frustrated rage at his narrow escape.

The fissure ran for twenty feet into the cliff before opening up into a cave. Alexander was so focused on the beast that he had paid no heed to the cave. When he stepped into the large semi-round cavern, he realized that he and his friends were surrounded by more than thirty men armed with stone-tipped spears. From the looks of the cave, the primitives took refuge there regularly.

Hector and Horace stood in front of Isabel with swords drawn. Jack was nowhere to be seen. Isabel's colors flared with power as she cast her shield spell. The colors of the men surrounding them showed mostly fear and apprehension, but no malice.

"Hold," Alexander said as he deliberately sheathed Mindbender and stepped forward with his hands held palms up.

"We don't want to fight you," he said.

The man leading the group of primitives stepped forward and appraised Alexander for a moment before he gestured for him to follow. He turned on his heel and headed through the gloom to a passage leading out of the cave on the far side. The primitives encircled them, motioning for them to follow their leader.

"I guess they've invited us in," Alexander said. "Remain vigilant," he added for Jack's benefit. As long as the bard was unseen, they had an advantage. Chloe also remained invisible, and Isabel kept Slyder in the trees outside the fissure in the cliff.

The primitives led them through a series of natural passages cut through the stone by water and time. Yellow lichen grew on the walls, casting an eerie glow that illuminated the cave system. Alexander considered using his night-wisp dust but decided against it. These people might not react well to such magic.

The passages led steadily up as they wound through the gut rock of the cliff. Occasionally, they came to stairs cut into the stone that eased their passage up particularly steep sections of cave.

The primitives spoke guardedly amongst themselves in a language that was totally foreign and unintelligible to Alexander. He wondered if Jack could understand anything they were saying but didn't want to risk exposing the bard to find out.

After half an hour they emerged onto a natural shelf on the side of the cliff face. It was nearly two hundred feet wide from the back wall that rose several hundred feet above them to the edge of the cliff that fell nearly five hundred feet to the forest floor. The shelf ran a mile or more along the face of the cliff, forming a naturally safe place for their village. Spread out among the sparse trees were huts made of wood and grass.

More primitives began to approach as the hunting party brought Alexander and his friends into the village. Soon they were surrounded by hundreds of people who had stopped the mundane chores of their day to come see the newcomers.

They seemed both curious and afraid. Alexander imagined that these people didn't often have guests and he wasn't sure how they might decide to react, but he was hopeful that they would be peaceful and maybe even helpful. Their colors revealed a simple people without malice or guile.

They were dressed in skins or furs, wore leather sandals, and used stone or bone tools and weapons. In spite of their lack of advancement and the absence of metals, woven cloth, and agriculture, they seemed well fed and even happy with their isolated lives.

Alexander wondered how long they must have lived like this. It was entirely possible, even probable, that these people were the descendants of those who had survived on the Reishi Isle after the war ended and the rest of the island went wild. He wondered if this was the only village on the island or if there were other isolated enclaves of human habitation that had survived the millennia.

An older man approached with six others trailing behind him. He was dressed similarly to the rest of the people but wore a necklace adorned with the teeth of several predatory creatures. He carried a staff that was capped with a human skull, bleached white and carved with scores of intricate symbols.

When Alexander saw the faint colors of magic emanating from the staff, he sent his all around sight closer and examined the details of the skull as the elder approached. Many of the symbols were unknown to him but he did see each of the seven symbols of power used to draw a circle of protection—the very same symbols forged into Mindbender's blade.

The leader of the hunting party bowed his head deferentially to the elder as he approached. They spoke for a moment before the elder stepped up to Alexander. The crowd fell silent as the elder gazed intently into his golden eyes. After several moments, he took a deep breath and let it out slowly, nodding to himself before turning to the six men behind him and speaking briefly.

The six bowed respectfully and turned as one, heading for a large hut in the center of the village. The village elder bowed formally to Alexander, then motioned to his heart with one hand and Alexander's heart with the other before clasping his hands together firmly.

Alexander saw a mixture of hope, expectation, and fear in his colors. He had no idea what to make of it but at least he didn't see hostility or guile.

"Little One, do you have any idea what he's saying?" Alexander asked Chloe in his mind.

"No, My Love, but I advise caution. Primitives often make very significant agreements with strangers. He could be welcoming you to stay the night or he could be offering you his daughter in marriage."

"Let's hope it's just a place to stay for the night," Alexander replied silently. "I'd rather not go back down there with that thing roaming around."

"You sure you know what you're doing?" Isabel whispered.

"I hope so," Alexander said.

He nodded to the elder and repeated the series of gestures back to him.

The crowd seemed to relax and started talking again as if something had been decided.

The elder escorted Alexander and his friends to a large wooden hut in the center of the village.

Alexander took in the interior of the structure with his all around sight. Each long wall was lined with rows of rough-cut wooden benches worn smooth from use. A well-crafted, stone fire pit filled the center of the room with the embers of a fire still glowing softly. The floor was covered with woven-grass mats and there were seven low chairs surrounding the pit—little more than timber rounds topped with cushions made of woven grass and filled with wool or feathers.

Six other elders were already seated around the burned-out fire. The chief elder motioned for Alexander and his friends to sit on the nearest bench as he took his seat around the fire and the room filled up with members of the village.

Alexander picked out Jack from his colors and gave him a nod.

What followed was a lively debate between the elders with occasional input from several villagers, including a very old woman and the leader of the hunting party. The chief elder said nothing but listened intently.

Alexander watched with a mixture of curiosity and wariness. All he really wanted from these people was a safe place to stay for the night in the hopes that the beast in the forest would lose interest and move on to other prey. From the tone and emotion of the discussion, it was apparent that these people had other ideas.

"What do you think they're talking about?" Isabel asked.

"Us," Alexander said with a sidelong grin.

She poked him in the ribs.

The debate lasted for the better part of an hour before the chief elder stood and the room fell silent. He spoke briefly in a manner that suggested he was proposing a course of action. Once he finished speaking, he looked to each of the other six elders for their consent. Each nodded in turn.

"Looks like they've made a decision," Alexander said quietly.

The chief elder pointed at Alexander with his staff and motioned for him to follow. Alexander and his friends followed the elder to a smaller hut off to the side of the village and closer to the cliff. It was a tiny structure, barely big enough for two people. The elder held the leather flap aside and motioned for Alexander to enter.

When Isabel tried to follow after him, the elder barred her path with his staff and shook his head gravely.

"I'll be all right," Alexander said.

"I don't like this," Isabel said.

"It can't be much worse than that beast down below," Alexander said. "Stay sharp."

The elder followed him inside and allowed the tent flap to fall closed, plunging the tiny room into darkness. In the center of the room was a small table with a shallow stone bowl resting on it. Woven-grass mats covered the dirt floor on opposite sides of the table. The elder motioned to one as he lowered himself onto the other.

As Alexander sat down, the elder withdrew a small wooden box from under the table and gingerly selected three dried flower buds one by one which he placed within the shallow stone bowl. He took a hot coal from a small stone pot and placed it into the bowl. Within seconds the flowers started to smoke, quickly filling the small hut with a sweet, pungent aroma. The elder breathed the smoke-laden air deeply and encouraged Alexander to do the same. He was a bit unsure about it but as he breathed, he began to feel more relaxed and present in the moment.

A few minutes later the old woman who had spoken at the gathering of elders entered, carefully carrying a bowl half filled with a dark liquid. Without a word, she handed it to the elder and then left.

The elder took the bowl, spoke a few words over it and drank deeply. Then he handed it to Alexander, who was becoming more dubious about the whole thing but he reasoned that the contents were probably safe, so he took a drink of the sweet liquid and handed it back to the elder. The elder nodded approvingly, set the bowl aside and closed his eyes.

Within a few moments Alexander felt a deep calm settle over him. His eyes closed involuntarily and quite suddenly he found himself standing in a forest with the elder.

He looked around for any sign of a threat but all he saw were ancient trees and the undergrowth of a wild and healthy forest.

"My name is Rentu," the elder said.

"I'm Alexander. Where are we and how are we speaking the same language?"

"We are dreaming together," Rentu said.

"Why are we here?"

"I've brought you here to determine if you are a threat to my people," Rentu said. "We have dreamed many prophecies that speak of a time when outsiders will bring war and destruction to our home. We are here to see if you are the outsiders our dreams have warned us about."

"I don't understand," Alexander said. "How can you see into the future?" Even as he asked the question, a thrill ran up his spine because he had experienced future sight himself. The implications of being able to see even farther into the future were staggering.

"In the dream, time does not matter," Rentu said. "We cannot know with certainty what will happen, but we can see some of your possible futures. Ultimately, free will and chance will determine how your life unfolds, but this place allows us to follow some of the more likely paths that you might travel."

As dubious and wary as Alexander was about the claims Rentu was making, he couldn't help being curious. He'd witnessed magic do impossible things, used his own magic to see a few crucial moments into the future when it mattered most. If Rentu could help him see some of the challenges he might face in the coming months or years, he would be better prepared to meet them.

"I don't know what to do," Alexander said.

"I will guide you," Rentu said. "All that is required is your consent."

Alexander nodded. "I consent."

"We will travel through time to many possible futures," Rentu said. "We can only observe. Those living in the futures we will visit will not see us or know of our existence. I must warn you, Alexander, dreaming the future is sometimes traumatic and difficult, often showing us frightening possibilities. Accept what you see with the understanding that it is only one possible future."

"I'm ready," Alexander said.

Rentu nodded, and the forest abruptly vanished and just as quickly they were standing on a rocky outcropping overlooking a beach on the northern coast of the Reishi Isle. Alexander wasn't sure how he knew their location, just that he was certain of it.

A great armada of enormous ships was anchored offshore and the ocean was filled with longboats ferrying troops onshore. A great battle was being fought between Alexander's forces and the army of Zuhl.

Alexander scanned the battle and found his future self fighting toward a raised platform erected on the beach where several wizards were casting terrible black magic into his forces. Jataan was fighting at his side, but Anatoly, Abigail, and Isabel were nowhere to be seen.

When he looked at his own colors, he saw resignation and loss. Zuhl was winning.

"Perhaps these are the outsiders we have seen in our dreams," Rentu said.

"This is Zuhl's army," Alexander said. "He's trying to conquer the world. If he succeeds, everyone everywhere will suffer for it. He's one of my enemies."

"It appears that your forces are vastly outnumbered and yet you fight," Rentu said.

"If we're fighting on this beach, it probably means he's already taken all of the other islands," Alexander said. "This looks like my last stand and it doesn't look good. Can you show me the events that led up to this time and place?"

"The dream doesn't work like that," Rentu said. "It only reveals turning points and significant events that change the outcome of the dreamer's life."

"Does this answer your question? Are these the outsiders you saw in your dream?" Alexander asked.

"In some of the futures we dreamed that men such as these were the destroyers," Rentu said, "but not all. There are still many other possibilities to explore."

The beach faded away and they were standing in a stone room. Phane was there with Isabel at his side. Her colors were the dark and muddy colors of evil. She had been turned. Alexander felt a sickness well up within him, but he schooled his emotions and reminded himself that this was only one possible future.

He scanned the room and found his future self kneeling in shackles.

"You have carried the day, My Lord," Isabel said to Phane. "The pretender is at your mercy and only Zuhl remains between you and your rightful place as Sovereign. May I kill him quickly, as you promised?"

"No," Phane said. "It displeases me that you still have feelings for this upstart. He has caused me no end of trouble and I believe I would like to see him suffer before he dies."

"My Lord, please don't be angry," Isabel said. "My loyalty to you is absolute and unshakable, but you gave me your word that he would die quickly and without suffering if I brought him before you."

"Did I?" Phane said. "I don't recall ever saying that. No, he will suffer before I send his soul into the netherworld where he will suffer even more."

"Don't do this, Isabel," Alexander's future self said. "I know you still have goodness in you. You have to fight this."

Isabel looked at him quizzically and frowned. "But I don't want to," she said.

Phane made a dismissive gesture and two big guards roughly dragged Alexander off to the torture chambers.

Alexander swallowed hard and fought to still the trembling in his stomach. That he had lost to Phane was bad enough, but that Isabel had delivered him into his enemy's grasp was intolerable. He looked at Rentu beseechingly.

The elder nodded and the world changed again. This time they were standing in a cave. Alexander recognized the place. He had seen it with his clairvoyance. It was the cavern where the Nether Gate was hidden.

A battle was taking place. He and Isabel were fighting against several Reishi Army Regency soldiers led by a wizard and a wraithkin. Jack was there, as were Hector and Horace. Rexius Truss, possessed by Jinzeri, was standing behind the Nether Gate watching the battle unfold.

The Regency soldiers fell easily to Mindbender and Isabel's magic.

Hector and Horace fought well, without flash or wasted movement but deadly quick and accurate with their short swords. As Alexander and his friends fought the soldiers, the wraithkin stole the keystone from Jinzeri and fled the cavern with the shade in pursuit.

Alexander and his friends were victorious against the remaining soldiers and the wizard, but they lost the wraithkin and the keystone in the bargain.

"We have not seen this place before," Rentu said, "but I recognize those soldiers as the other group of outsiders that we have seen in our dreams."

"Those are Phane's soldiers. They're here to get the keystone to the Nether Gate," Alexander said, pointing.

"This Nether Gate looks to be a most dangerous device," Rentu said with a frown. "We have not seen it in our dreams."

"If Phane opens it, everything is doomed," Alexander said. "That's why I'm here. I have to get the keystone before my enemies do."

"So that you can open it?"

"No!" Alexander said. "I want to ensure that it never gets opened by anyone."

Rentu nodded thoughtfully. After a few moments, the world shifted again. They were in the same cave as before.

Rexius Truss, possessed by Jinzeri, was there. Phane, possessed by Rankosi, was there. And the Nether Gate was there.

He and Isabel were there along with Jack. All three of them were in shackles, lined up on their knees with soldiers behind them. Another woman was there with Phane. She was in her early twenties and beautiful, with strawberry-blond hair and deep blue eyes.

"It's time, my dear," Phane said.

"And you're sure we can defeat Zuhl with this?" the woman asked.

"Of course. Zuhl will be crushed and Fellenden will be free. You will have saved your people."

She thought it over for a moment longer, clearly struggling with the decision. Alexander saw his future self try to speak around the gag in his mouth as she opened the little magical box that contained the third keystone.

When the lid came open, revealing the final keystone, both Jinzeri and Rankosi started laughing maniacally. Rankosi used Phane's magic to unceremoniously hurl the young woman against the wall of the cave with such force that her body fell to the floor in a broken heap.

"This is the worst possible outcome," Alexander said.

"I'm coming to see that the threat is much greater than we feared," Rentu said.

The scene changed yet again. It was night and they were on the coast of Andalia. Alexander had gained access to the Sovereign Stone's Wizard's Den and the door was open. They had just pulled themselves from the surf after their boat had been sunk by a fleet of pirates. Wreckage was washing ashore as a company of Lancers bore down on them from inland and the pirates' longboats were coming from the sea.

Alexander and Jack were in the Wizard's Den with Chloe, but Isabel stopped at the threshold, snatching the pouch with the keystone from Alexander's belt and stepping out onto the beach.

"I'm sorry, Alexander," she said through tears, "but the darkness is stronger than I am. You're not safe around me anymore."

"Isabel, come inside," Alexander's future self pleaded. "We don't have time for this right now."

She shook her head. "Close the door before it's too late. I love you, Alexander," she said as she raised her hand and her aura flared with magic. Alexander willed the door to the Wizard's Den closed a moment before her light-lance spell stabbed out into the night.

Alexander closed his eyes and shook his head.

"She won't betray me," he whispered. "She's strong enough to resist Phane's darkness."

The scene shifted again and they were in a chamber deep underground. Alexander recognized it as the place where Phane had the wraith queen imprisoned. The dark, insubstantial-looking creature from the netherworld was trapped inside three metal rings suspended over a magic circle. Each of the three rings was positioned ninety degrees to the next so that one was horizontal and two were vertical at right angles to one another.

Isabel was there, at Phane's side. Alexander's future self was kneeling in shackles with Jack right beside him.

"All this time, I've been trying to hunt you down," Phane said. "I never imagined that you would walk right into my home and deliver not only the Sovereign Stone to me but the final keystone as well. I guess the right bait makes all the difference." He pulled Isabel close to him with a lewd smile.

"It really is a shame, Cousin. We could have done great things together. But alas, you're too stubborn to see the big picture and now you've lost everything, when you could have had it all. Your own island kingdom, your beautiful wife, your family and friends … all you had to do was kneel before me." Phane shook his head sadly as he raised his hand and called forth his magic. Alexander watched himself die. Isabel closed her eyes as he slumped over to the floor. At least she still had some feelings for him in spite of Phane's insidious magic.

"I've seen enough," Rentu said, and suddenly they were back in the forest where they started. "I do not believe that you have come to destroy us. I now believe that you are here to preserve us from those we have seen in our dreams, but your wife will betray you and put your efforts in jeopardy. She cannot be trusted, Alexander."

"Phane has infected her with his magic," Alexander said. "That's another reason I've come here. I know how to help her, but I need to get some very rare ingredients first. One of them can only be found near here."

"The dreams show us many possible futures, but in most that we have seen she has betrayed you." Rentu frowned deeply, shaking his head. "We must help you in order to preserve ourselves. I know of the place you seek, where the ancient tree grows. I can guide you there, but I require that Isabel remain here in our care until you have preserved the world from the outsiders that we have seen. We will care for her and protect her, but she will not be allowed to leave."

Alexander stiffened and absentmindedly reached for his sword. He'd gained invaluable insight into the future from Rentu and he was grateful for the experience, but he wasn't about to leave Isabel behind.

"You can't do that," Alexander said.

"I must," Rentu said. "Her betrayal is your doom. Without her, your chances of success will be much greater. I know this pains you, but it is the path that wisdom commands me to follow."

"This isn't wisdom," Alexander said. "It's the worst mistake you could make."

"It must be done," Rentu said. "We will wake now."

The forest faded away and Alexander found himself sitting in the little hut filled with aromatic smoke.

"Are you all right, My Love?" Chloe asked within his mind.

"Yes and no, Little One," Alexander replied silently. "I was shown several possible futures where Isabel betrays me. Rentu, the chief elder, has decided that she has to stay here for now."

"Oh, My Love, what will you do?"

"I'm not sure yet," Alexander said silently, "but I am sure that I'm not leaving Isabel behind. Tell Jack what's happened."

"At once, My Love," Chloe said.

Alexander stood facing Rentu with his blind eyes glittering. He wanted to rail at the elder, to argue his case with passion and reason, but he knew the elder wouldn't understand him. Instead he turned and strode from the tent.

Isabel was waiting for him with Hector and Horace. Surrounding the tent were a hundred men with spears and blowtubes loaded with poison darts. Alexander surveyed the scene and decided that bold action was a sure path to a quick death. Rentu had said he would help Alexander find the vitalwood tree and the cavern where the Nether Gate was hidden. Patience was called for.

As Rentu emerged from the little hut, the six other elders approached and listened intently to his account of the dreaming. At one point, they glanced furtively at Isabel.

"What happened in there?" Isabel asked.

"He showed me a number of possible futures," Alexander said. "In several, you're turned by Phane's magic and you betray me."

Isabel stepped back with a stricken look, shaking her head. "I love you, Alexander. I would never betray you."

He drew her into his arms. "I know, but Phane's magic is powerful. You may not have a choice."

"I won't," she pleaded. "I can't."

"Hush. I know your soul," Alexander said. "You'll never betray me of your own free will, but Phane's magic may overpower you. Right now, it's not important, but these people want to keep you here to protect me."

"What?" Isabel was suddenly alarmed. "I'm not staying here."

"I know, but we have to be smart about this," Alexander said, motioning with a nod to the armed men arrayed around them.

"So what do we do?" she asked.

"We play along," Alexander said. "When we make our move, we'll have to do it quickly and they'll probably be right behind us."

She nodded, then looked around. "The odds aren't exactly in our favor."

"They never are," Alexander said.

Rentu approached with the six elders and motioned for Alexander and his friends to follow. He led them to a large gathering area where a community meal was being prepared. They were treated like guests of honor and brought large portions of roasted wild boar, berries, and nuts. The fare was simple but good nonetheless. During the entire meal, the hundred armed men remained ever vigilant, standing in a loose cordon around the gathering place.

Once the meal was finished and darkness began to settle on the Reishi Isle, the elders led them to two huts, motioning for Alexander and Isabel to take one and Hector and Horace to take the other.

"Be ready," Alexander said to the brothers.

"Always, Lord Reishi," Hector said with a humorless smile.

As Alexander drifted off to sleep, he worried about Isabel. The thought of her betraying him left him sick to his stomach, but it was also a very real possibility that he had to face if he was going to have any chance of defeating Phane.

Chapter 23

Jack shook him awake in the dead of night.

"It's time," he whispered. "Hector and Horace are ready."

"Good," Alexander said and then he woke Isabel and they quietly packed their things. He handed Jack a blowtube filled with deathwalker-root sleeping powder and sent his all around sight out into the night. The armed men were still there, but only half as many and they looked tired. "We're ready," he said.

"I'll be right back," Jack said, tossing up his hood and vanishing from sight.

Alexander and Isabel slipped out of the tent and found Hector and Horace waiting for them in the shadows. Hector pointed toward the cave entrance that led back to the forest below and they started moving slowly and quietly toward their escape.

Jack returned after a minute or so.

"The guard's out cold. We have a gap of about thirty feet in their line of sentries."

Alexander nodded, motioning for Jack to lead the way. They crept through the dark, testing every step and taking what time they needed to move as quietly as possible. Once through the cordon, they moved toward the cave. When Alexander saw the colors of the two men guarding the cave entrance, he tapped Jack on the shoulder.

"Looks like we have a problem," Alexander whispered. "Two guards at the cave entrance."

"We can eliminate them quietly, Lord Reishi," Horace whispered.

"I don't want to kill any of these people if we can help it," Alexander said.

The brothers looked at each other and nodded. "We can take them quietly without killing them," Hector said.

"All right," Alexander said.

Hector and Horace faded into the shadows, moving silently and without a trace. Alexander found himself holding his breath as he watched their colors converge with the colors of the two guards. They moved into position behind the guards slowly, without a sound. As one, they attacked from behind, taking each guard in a choke hold that both prevented them from raising an alarm and rendered them unconscious within a minute.

Alexander used his remaining blowtube of sleeping powder to ensure that the two men wouldn't wake anytime soon, then he and his friends moved into the caves that led down to the forest below the village.

They moved through the darkness for the rest of the night, trying to gain as much distance as possible before the tribe of primitives realized that their guests were gone. Alexander didn't want to fight them. They weren't evil. They weren't even working against him, but they'd chosen to help him in a way that was totally unacceptable.

An hour after dawn Isabel reported that Slyder had seen a hunting party leave the cliff-side village. They were a half a day behind and moving quickly. Alexander picked up the pace. He was tired and his head hurt from the constant concentration of using his all around sight but he pressed on, hoping to reach the hidden fortress before the primitives caught up with them.

As the day wore on, the terrain became more mountainous and the path became steeper. By evening, they were nearing the limits of their endurance, but Alexander didn't let up. He pushed them until darkness and exhaustion overcame them.

He woke in the middle of the night to Isabel murmuring in her sleep, struggling with something dark in her dreams. He could see her colors darken as she fought with her nightmare. It made his stomach squirm to see her like this. Phane's hold on her was growing. When he shook her awake, she sat bolt upright with a start, then shuddered with relief as she lay back down in the comfort of Alexander's arms.

"It's getting worse," she whispered. "Maybe Rentu's right. Maybe you would be better off without me."

"Not a chance," Alexander said. "Go back to sleep."

Exhaustion overpowered his worry for Isabel and he drifted off again within a few minutes.

He woke before dawn, his head still hurting from the day before and the pain was becoming more severe. He started to wonder if Shivini's attack had actually done more harm than he first thought. His magical vision had saved him from the crippling consequences of being blinded but he was paying a price for constantly using his magic.

Before they set out, Alexander sat down and drew a magic circle in the dirt. He cleared his mind in spite of the pain and focused on finding the state of empty-mindedness that was his passage to the firmament.

It took longer than usual but he eventually found his way into the endless ocean of potential. He started with their current location, rising high into the sky, taking in the surrounding terrain and looking for a path to his destination. At first he couldn't see the fortress entrance, but when he focused on Jinzeri, he quickly found himself in the cavern where the Nether Gate was hidden. Before the shade could notice his presence, he drifted through the stone of the mountain until he was high above it. From there, he marked his location and worked backward, plotting a course through the increasingly steep and treacherous mountains.

Once he was satisfied that he knew the way, he sent his awareness to the hunting party. There were easily thirty men and they were already on the move. Alexander had no idea what they would do to Isabel if given the chance and he didn't want to find out. He returned to his body and they set out for the hidden fortress. They were less than a day away.

By midmorning, Isabel reported that the primitives were gaining ground. They moved through the forest quickly, being more familiar with the terrain. Alexander set a fast pace but he feared that they wouldn't make it to the fortress in time to avoid a fight.

By midafternoon, he could hear the primitives in the forest behind them. Alexander and his friends ran as fast as their fatigue would allow, but they were being outpaced by their hunters. He estimated that they were still an hour from the entrance to the hidden fortress and he knew they wouldn't be able to keep up their pace for that long.

He stopped in a narrow canyon with steep walls rising on both sides.

"We'll make our stand here," he said, breathing hard. "Hopefully, I can scare them off, but if not, then we fight. Make ready for battle. They'll be here within a few minutes."

Isabel cast her shield spell, enveloping herself in a bubble of protective magical force. Hector and Horace dropped their packs and drew the pair of short swords they each carried in crossed scabbards on their backs. Jack put up the hood of his cloak and flickered out of sight.

Alexander grasped the hilt of Mindbender and settled his nerves. He was in a fight and he had a sword in his hand. Everything else faded away. Before the primitives arrived, he cleared his mind and visualized an image of the beast that had chased them into the cave the day before. He released it into the sword and the enormous creature materialized in front of them, facing the direction of the approaching hunting party. As they came around a bend in the ravine, Alexander made his illusionary creation roar. The sound was deafening in the confined space, staccato echoes reverberating off the stone walls.

The primitives stopped in their tracks, then turned and fled. Alexander breathed a sigh of relief until he heard another roar from the real beast not too far off. His illusion had just alerted it to their location.

"Just keeps getting better and better," Jack said with a sardonic smile.

"It's never easy," Alexander said. "Let's get moving."

They moved as fast as their weariness would allow. The occasional roar of the beast from off in the distance and the threat of the hunting party somewhere behind them spurred them on. In just under an hour, they came to a mountain meadow. One side was bordered by a sheer cliff reaching several hundred feet into the sky. Several ravines led into the meadow through the mountains surrounding the other three sides. A waterfall cascaded down one smaller cliff between two of the ravines and collected in a small mountain lake before meandering off in a burbling little stream flowing out of the meadow and down one of the other ravines.

It was a beautiful setting—or at least it would have been had it not been for the beast standing on the opposite side of the meadow. Alexander quickly scanned the area for cover but found nothing except for the ancient stone archway carved into the base of the sheer cliff. Weather-worn glyphs and runes decorated the entrance to the hidden fortress, giving it an ancient and foreboding look.

The stone door that had once barred entrance was long ago broken and lay in scattered, moss-covered rubble underneath the archway. The entrance was a good hundred feet away and the beast was nearly two hundred feet behind them.

It roared and stamped its feet as if making ready to charge.

"Run!" Alexander shouted as he broke into a sprint with the last bit of his strength.

The beast charged as they raced toward the safety of the entrance passage. Alexander noticed the hunting party peering out from behind a field of boulders littering the mouth of one ravine. They watched as the beast closed the distance, perhaps hoping that the creature would do their work for them.

The beast gained terrifying speed, closing the gap too quickly. Just as

Alexander was about to stop and make a stand, Hector broke off from the group, charging toward the beast.

Alexander started to slow to help his bodyguard, but Horace pushed him toward the safety of the cave entrance.

"He'll be fine, Lord Reishi."

Alexander didn't quite understand, but he accepted Horace's assurances and continued to run for the entrance. Once they reached the threshold, Alexander stopped to catch his breath and turned to see the battle unfolding between Hector and the beast.

The beast was bleeding from the belly along two deep gashes. Hector stood his ground as the beast lunged forward, snapping with its huge jaws. At the last moment, when Alexander was certain that Hector would be killed, he transformed into a vaporous cloud in the shape of a man. The beast's jaws landed on insubstantial vapor. Hector flowed out between its giant teeth and beneath it, where he became solid once again before driving his twin short swords into the belly of the beast.

It roared in pain and Hector once again transformed into vapor before the beast could kill him. When he noticed that Alexander had made it to safety, he disengaged, drifting toward the cave entrance. The beast roared in frustrated rage, turning away from the prey that had bitten it back.

"Well done, Hector," Alexander said.

"Thank you, Lord Reishi. I suspect it'll be back once it's had a chance to lick its wounds."

"Hopefully we can get what we came for and be on our way before then," Alexander said, turning to the darkness of the fortress entrance and holding up his vial of night-wisp dust.

"Stay alert. The hunting party is right behind us and might follow us into the fortress."

The corridor ran straight for several hundred feet into the stone of the mountain before it came to a large octagonal room with several other corridors radiating away from it. The arched ceiling was thirty feet high with glowing crystals embedded in the stone that cast a pale light into the chamber. Alexander stopped at the threshold, scanning the room.

There were a number of relatively fresh footprints leading into the fortress. It looked like a squad of soldiers had spent some time searching for just the right passage before moving on.

"It seems we aren't the first ones here," Jack said.

"I was hoping the things Rentu showed me were just possibilities," Alexander said.

"What did you see?" Isabel asked.

Alexander saw the trepidation in her colors. She was worried about the prediction that she would betray him, but Alexander suspected he knew which prophecy they were walking into.

"I saw us in a battle with Regency soldiers led by a wraithkin and a wizard in the cavern where the Nether Gate is hidden. Truss was there too, possessed by one of the shades. In the prophecy, we defeated the soldiers and the wizard, but the wraithkin escaped with the keystone, and Truss chased after him.

"These footprints look recent and they're from boots, not sandals or bare feet. It looks like Phane's men have beaten us here."

"Perhaps there is some good news," Jack said. "The soldiers' tracks are liable to lead us right to the chamber we want. It's a good bet that Phane knows the layout of this place and gave his men directions."

"It's worth a try," Alexander said.

"I'll take point," Hector said.

The walls were made of large blocks of stone cut with exacting precision and fitted together with virtually no tolerance. Even after thousands of years, the walls were nearly seamless.

Hector moved carefully and quietly down the hallway. Very suddenly, the floor gave out beneath him and he fell into a pit concealed under a trap door. In a blink, he transformed into vapor and drifted back up to the hallway on the opposite side of the trap.

Alexander and Isabel peered down the shaft as the door slowly closed, resetting the trap. Forty feet below was a floor filled with three-foot spikes. A soldier from the Reishi Army Regency was impaled by several of them.

"Well, I guess that confirms it," Jack said.

"Hopefully, this place will thin them out a bit," Isabel said.

"Just so long as it doesn't thin us out, too," Alexander said.

It took them half an hour, but with the aid of a rope they were able to traverse the pit trap safely. Once on the far side, Alexander marked the floor as a warning for their return trip.

They continued on through the halls of the hidden fortress, following the footprints of the enemy soldiers as they led the way deeper into the bowels of the mountain. At one time, the fortress could have housed thousands, but now it was broken down and dilapidated. The air was still and heavy.

The place made Alexander uneasy. His headache didn't help.

They had just descended a flight of stairs when Alexander saw a section of the floor glowing with a slight aura.

"Stop," he said.

Hector stopped midstride and looked back quizzically.

"There's something wrong with the floor up ahead," Alexander said.

"If it's a trap, maybe I can spring it," Horace said.

Alexander nodded. Horace stepped forward and closed his eyes for a moment. Alexander watched the aura of Horace's magical servant appear just ahead of them. It was roughly three feet tall and vaguely shaped like a man, or at least its colors were; it was completely invisible to normal vision. It ambled forward until it reached the place in the floor.

Horace looked to Alexander for confirmation.

"That's the spot," he said.

The magical servant jumped up and landed with a slight thump. A five-foot-wide section of the floor stretching across the hall glowed intensely for just a moment. Horace staggered back as his magical servant was destroyed.

"It seems to respond to pressure," he said. "I won't be able to conjure my servant for another hour or so."

"Are you injured?" Isabel asked. "I mean, can you be hurt when your magic is dispelled like that?"

"It causes pain for a moment," Horace said, "but no damage. When my servant is destroyed by violence or magic, I simply can't call on it again for a while."

Jack carefully approached the edge of the magical trap. He looked closely at the floor and frowned.

"I suspect there's a mechanism that deactivates the trap for a time," he said. "It looks like the soldiers walked right over it without difficulty."

They spent several minutes searching before Jack found a small stone in one wall that moved with pressure. When he pushed on it, Alexander saw the light of the aura fade away. Once they were all across the spelled section of floor, Alexander marked the spot by scraping a line on the floor.

They continued down the passage until it came to a tee. Hector looked around the corner and pulled his head back quickly. They heard shouting from down the hall.

"Looks like we found them," he said, drawing his twin short swords.

"How many?" Alexander asked.

"I saw four, but I suspect they're just the first line."

Alexander sent his all around sight down the hall to survey the enemy. Four men lined up at the entrance to a large room. All of them were armed with crossbows.

"Once they've fired their crossbows, we charge," Alexander said. "Remember, as soon as we're past these four, there will be more soldiers, plus a wizard and a wraithkin."

Isabel started casting a shield spell, Jack tossed up the hood of his cloak, Horace drew his short swords. Alexander drew Mindbender and focused on the fight. He created the image his enemy most expected to see and sent it into the sword.

An illusion of him and his friends rounding the corner, weapons drawn and charging came into being, lifelike and real. The four soldiers loosed their crossbow bolts as one. What would have been a deadly attack fell on empty air.

"Go," Alexander said as he slipped around the corner, racing toward the enemy. The four men drew swords and held their ground. Before Alexander could reach them, a shaft of brilliant white light lanced past him and burned a hole three inches in diameter through the chest of the man on the right.

Alexander reached them first. He knew his first opponent's intention even as the man formed the thought. He slipped past the thrust to the right of the center man and drove the point of his sword through the soldier to his right as he shoved the center man into his companion on his left. Before they could recover, he had his blade free and stabbed one man in the throat as Hector reached the last man and dispatched him with two quick strokes.

Jack flickered back into view. "Not quite as dramatic as the Thinblade, but I think your new sword definitely has potential."

Chloe buzzed into view. "Darkness is near, My Love, in the chamber below."

"It's a good bet they know we're here," Isabel said.

"Can you scout for us, Little One?" Alexander asked.

"Of course, My Love. Send me your mind and I will show you the room."

"Be ready," Alexander said as he sat down and closed his eyes.

Chloe buzzed into a ball of light and vanished into the aether. Alexander watched the world through her eyes as she drifted into the chamber below. It was a large cavern, one that Alexander had seen before. Nearly a dozen soldiers with weapons drawn were arrayed before the Nether Gate, with three more guarding the staircase leading into the chamber above.

A wizard and a wraithkin stood side by side in front of the soldiers, facing the Gate and Truss, who was still possessed by Jinzeri. They seemed to be arguing.

"You are of no consequence, Wizard," Jinzeri said. "If you kill this body, I will simply take yours."

"You won't take mine," the wraithkin said. "Mother won't allow it."

"Yes, how very clever of Phane," Jinzeri said. "I am well acquainted with your mother. I'm quite sure she would much rather help me than Phane."

The wraithkin twitched.

"We will have the keystone, Shade," the wizard said.

"Come and take it," Jinzeri said, holding the small stone pyramid out in Truss's good hand. "I grow tired of this broken body and your magic would be useful, not to mention entertaining."

In a blink the wraithkin vanished, leaving only wisps of blackness where he had been standing, and reappeared in front of Jinzeri. With a tormented smile, the wraithkin hit Jinzeri hard. He staggered back, dropping the keystone. The wraithkin snatched it up and vanished, only to reappear twenty feet closer to the staircase leading up to the room where Alexander and his friends were preparing for battle.

"Tell your master, I'll take him for this," Jinzeri shouted in rage as he regained his feet.

The wizard finished his spell just as Jinzeri stood, and a wave of magical force blew him onto his back without killing Truss.

The wraithkin vanished and reappeared on the other side of the three soldiers guarding the staircase.

"Flee!" the wizard commanded. The soldiers at the base of the stairs started up toward Alexander as the remaining soldiers and the wizard followed.

Alexander snapped back into his own body.

Chapter 24

"Here they come, wraithkin first," he said. "Spread out."

The wraithkin appeared at the top of the stairs and smiled. Alexander advanced toward the man mixed with darkness, listening through Mindbender for his thoughts. The wraithkin vanished and Alexander spun. The wraithkin reappeared ten feet past him, running fast.

Alexander flipped Mindbender to his off hand and hurled his throwing knife at the fleeing wraithkin, hoping to hit his head, but the blade drove into the creature's back instead. The wraithkin shrieked and vanished, reappearing twenty feet down the hallway fully healed and running even faster.

Alexander was torn. There were more than a dozen soldiers, a wizard, and a shade coming up the stairs. It would be suicide to give chase to the wraithkin and leave themselves defenseless to the threat behind them and he dared not divide his force.

"Take the Regency soldiers first," he said as he turned back to the staircase, advancing toward the three men who had just reached the landing.

The soldiers drew swords as Alexander advanced with Hector and Horace on either side of him. He met the first soldier with a quick parry, deflecting his blade to one side and following with a thrust to the heart, followed by a kick to drive him off Mindbender and send him toppling down the stairs into his companions.

Hector and Horace each engaged a soldier, wielding their twin short swords with the kind of fluid grace that only comes from the combination of long practice and too much real-world experience. Each of them used his leading blade to trap his opponent's weapon while striking out with his following blade. Both men killed their opponents in a way that looked almost routine.

Alexander waited at the top of the stairs for the soldiers to come to him, not wanting to give up the high ground. Once they'd recovered from the corpse he'd cast into their midst, they began to advance again. The first one to reach him died quickly from a thrust to the eye.

The next was more wary, making a stab for Alexander's legs. Through Mindbender, he saw the attack coming and jumped to avoid the blade, coming down with an overhead stroke that split the soldier's helmet and skull.

A crossbow bolt broke against his armor shirt, then another whizzed past his head. Alexander held his ground, waiting for the next soldier to come close enough to kill, when he saw the wizard pull a man aside and stretch his hand out over another man's shoulder. Alexander tried to duck, but he was a moment too late. The wave of magical force caught him full in the chest, tossing him backward ten feet. He landed hard on his back.

Hector and Horace took his place at the top of the stairs, but the remaining soldiers didn't charge. Before Alexander could regain his feet, a shell of magical energy emerged from the top of the staircase and pushed out in a bubble, driving Hector and Horace back as the enemy soldiers filled the space within.

With his all around sight, he watched ten soldiers form a battle line at the top of the stairs while the wizard cast another force blast down the stairs at Jinzeri, followed by a spell that caused the stone of the staircase to rapidly grow like crystals until the entire passage was blocked behind him, trapping Jinzeri in the cave with the Nether Gate.

Alexander regained his feet just as the bubble of force protecting the soldiers dissipated. They fired a volley of crossbow bolts as one. Hector transformed into a vapor, saving himself from injury. Horace took a bolt in the leg and one in the shoulder. He went down to one knee.

The crossbow bolts meant for Isabel bounced harmlessly off her magical shield.

One bolt hit Alexander in the thigh, driving straight through but missing the bone. He remained standing, almost automatically retreating into the place within his mind where pain was less important. Two more bolts broke against his dragon-scale armor.

Jack was off to the side where the bubble of force met the wall, waiting for the chance to strike. The soldier at the end of the battle line died with a knife across his throat.

The remaining soldiers dropped their crossbows, drew swords and charged. The lead man fell back with a hole through his chest from Isabel's light-lance spell. Alexander held his ground, waiting for the enemy to come to him rather than risk using his injured leg any more than he had to. Hector rematerialized in position to strike at two men at once. They both fell with stab wounds to the gut.

Another went down from Jack's knife as the first three men reached Alexander—or where they thought he was. He had projected an illusion of himself several feet to one side while making his true position invisible to the advancing soldiers. As they committed their attacks to striking down his illusion, Alexander dispatched them one by one.

Mindbender's power was becoming more accessible and more natural, flowing freely from his imaginative mind in the heat of the battle. He was learning to trust the power of deception and the foreknowledge that the sword gave him. It was a far more subtle weapon than the Thinblade, but its reach was greater and its potential was staggering.

Another man fell from Isabel's light-lance spell. Alexander saw her colors swelling with rage as she fueled her anger to protect herself from the pull of the firmament.

The remaining two soldiers reached Alexander and Hector as the wizard stepped into the room. The two men fell quickly but the wizard had time to cast his spell. Six narrow wedges of blue magical force shot forth from his outstretched hand at Isabel, one after the next. Her shield absorbed most of them but failed when the fifth hit. The sixth magical blade drove hard into her stomach, penetrating her armor and driving into her gut. She went down with a shriek that made Alexander's blood run cold.

A moment later, Jack slipped up behind the wizard and cut his throat. The look of surprised horror on his face was only matched by the horror Alexander felt at seeing Isabel fall to the ground.

"Hector, guard the door," Alexander said as he limped toward Isabel.

"Jack, see to Horace."

He had to clench his teeth to keep from crying out in pain as he went to a knee next to Isabel. She was bleeding through her armor and breathing shallowly.

"This is going to hurt, but you have to let me get to the wound," Alexander said, as he rolled her onto her back and fished around in his pouch for his jar of healing salve.

Her leather armor was rent as if she'd been stabbed by a blade. Alexander unbuckled it quickly and lifted her shirt to reveal a deep wound. She gasped in pain as he packed the wound with healing salve and she gritted her teeth as he wrapped her belly with a strip of cloth. Next, he unstoppered one of Lucky's vials of healing draught and helped her drink the contents.

As she drifted off into a magically induced sleep, Alexander examined the crossbow bolt in his leg. With his brass-pommeled long knife he scored the bolt so he could snap it off several inches below the point. He nearly screamed as he pulled the shaft through his leg, feeling light-headed and nauseous the moment it came free.

He lay still, focusing on his breathing for a minute or so before he tore his pant leg open and applied healing salve to the wound on both sides of his leg. He knew the wound was too deep for the healing salve alone, so he reluctantly drank one of his healing draughts. Lucky had given them each three vials of the potent magical liquid, and Alexander knew they may need them all, given the dangers they faced. But he also knew that he wouldn't heal completely with just the salve and he would need his full strength in the coming days and weeks.

Jack tended to Horace's injuries and soon the wounded were sleeping soundly as the magic did its work. Alexander woke to Jack watching him.

"How are you feeling?" he asked.

"Much better," Alexander said. "How's Isabel?"

"Her wound is closed but she's still sleeping," Jack said. "The stone wall in the staircase is holding and everything's quiet. Horace is mending as well but he isn't awake yet either."

Alexander stared at the ceiling as he played the battle over in his mind. He'd seen a similar battle unfold in the dream with Rentu. All of the people were the same and the place was identical, but the events had unfolded slightly differently. In the dream, Jinzeri had followed the wraithkin, and the battle had taken place in the chamber below.

"It's strange," Alexander said. "The vision I had of this battle was very similar, yet the details were quite different. I guess prophecy can only get the broad strokes right."

"Still, the insight was invaluable," Jack said. "Knowing that we would encounter the enemy allowed us to face them on our terms rather that stumbling into them, and it helped us find this chamber in the first place."

"I just hope the rest of what he showed me turns out differently," Alexander said. "In this case, the wraithkin did escape with the keystone. That was the most important part of the prophecy and it came to pass."

"What now?" Jack asked.

"I doubt we can catch the wraithkin," Alexander said, shaking his head. "We probably can't even track him and it'll be hours before we're ready to travel. Once we heal, we'll look for the vitalwood tree. Hopefully, we can get some of its nectar without too much trouble. After that, we'll head back to the Reishi Keep and through the Gate to Tyr."

Jack nodded thoughtfully. "How do you suppose the wraithkin plans to get off the island?"

"They must have come by boat," Alexander said. "It's probably waiting for them in a cove somewhere. I think I have some work to do."

He sat up and started drawing a magic circle around himself.

"I wish I could get word to Cassandra at the fortress island," he said as he worked on the circle. "They're close enough to make sure that ship sinks in deep water, keystone and all. Maybe the Sky Knights at Blackstone can reach it in time."

With that he carefully crossed his legs and began his meditation routine. He had refined it down to a familiar process and it came easily. Within minutes his mind was quiet and he was floating on the firmament.

First he floated through the stone wall blocking the staircase down to the chamber below and scanned about in the dim light, looking for Jinzeri … but the shade was nowhere to be seen. A more careful search of the room revealed two concealed passages leading deeper into the mountain.

Alexander shot straight up through stone and earth, rising thousands of feet into the sky over the Reishi Isle. He picked a point on the southern coastline that had a distinctive stone jutting from the surf and began his search there. It didn't take long moving at the speed of thought to find a boat moored in a small lagoon on the southeast shore. It was a fast-looking ship with a crew ready and waiting.

He had no idea how long it would take the wraithkin to cover the distance. On foot he thought it would take a man the better part of a week, but the wraithkin could move with frightening speed using its ability to teleport short distances. A day, maybe two, and the creature would be making best speed toward Karth and Phane.

With a flick of his mind, Alexander was in Blackstone Keep, looking at his message board. He was almost relieved that the board was blank.

He went to the sleeping chamber and drifted into the dreams of a Ranger. He told him to relay orders to Mistress Constance to send Sky Knights to sink the ship if at all possible. As he slipped out of the Ranger's mind, the man came awake and started pulling his boots on.

His message sent, he moved to Buckwold in a blur. The world flashed by and then he was floating over the sprawling city. A single legion of Buckwold regulars was dug in south of the city; the soldiers were working feverishly to fortify their defenses.

Alexander floated higher into the sky and found the smudge of color on the horizon that was his father's legions. Then he turned and found the legion of Lancers to the south in Warrenton. He moved closer to the enemy to estimate their numbers and saw more than a legion. Next he went to the Warrenton docks and saw more troop ships arriving. Phane had his port and was landing an army that Ruatha wasn't prepared to defend against.

He floated out over the ocean and saw a steady string of transport ships moving up along the wild eastern coast of Ruatha from Andalia. They had chosen a route that put them out of reach of the navies operating out of Southport and

Kai'Gorn.

Phane had outflanked him.

Seeing the scope of the danger, he nearly faltered and lost his connection to the firmament. A moment later he was back at Blackstone Keep in the sleeping room, where he found two more Rangers still sleeping quietly. He drifted into one and relayed the news and his orders that all available Sky Knights move to attack the Andalian transport ships.

As he slipped out of the Ranger's dreams, Alexander focused on General Talia. The world blurred and he was suddenly floating in a quiet office with the well-groomed commander of Ruatha's southern forces. The man was reading a history of the border wars.

Alexander drifted out of the office and into the keep that overlooked Kai'Gorn's port. He searched for several minutes until he found a serving girl who was sleeping restlessly. He gently slipped into her dreams.

"Don't be alarmed," Alexander said.

"Who are you?"

"My name is Alexander. I need your help."

She frowned. "How can I help?"

"I need you to take a message to General Talia."

She shook her head. "But he's an important man. I'm just a serving girl. I can't bother him."

"Many lives depend on swift action," Alexander said. "Tell him that a fleet of Andalian transports is moving up the east coast bound for Warrenton. Tell him to do all that he can to stop them without jeopardizing Kai'Gorn."

"But he won't believe me," she said. "I'm nobody."

"Tell him that Alexander spoke to you in your dreams. Please, this is so important."

She nodded timidly.

"Thank you," Alexander said as he drifted out of her dreams and watched her wake. She seemed unsure at first, but after some internal struggle, she left her room and went to the part of the keep that Talia used for his command quarters. A guard stopped her but after a brief conversation he escorted her to General Talia.

Alexander was gratified that she repeated his instructions verbatim. General Talia went to work immediately, summoning his command staff and the Wing Commander of the Sky Knights that had been assigned to assist him.

Within twenty minutes, two scout riders were airborne and heading east to determine the accuracy of the message.

Next he visited Abigail. She was riding in the midst of her army, heading for the shipyard on the northwest coast of Fellenden. It looked like she was still a week or more away. Satisfied with her well-being and her progress, he slipped back into the firmament.

One last errand. He thought of the young woman he'd seen in his dream with Rentu, the one with the strawberry-blond hair and blue eyes. His awareness coalesced in sparse woods somewhere in southern Fellenden. The woman he'd seen in his dreams was hiding in a thicket as six big, brutish-looking soldiers searched for her. He could see the palpable fear in her colors. She was afraid and desperate, yet underneath it all, he could see resoluteness about her. She was on a mission and she was determined to succeed.

Right next to her was a man. It looked like they were hiding from the soldiers together, but the thing that caught Alexander's attention was the man's colors—he was without conscience, a killer, no, a murderer, a man who would kill with complete indifference. The woman was in greater danger than she knew.

If Rentu's dreams were right, and Alexander suspected that the important parts were, she was Lacy Fellenden and she was carrying the third keystone. He needed to find a way to help her. If she were asleep, he could deliver a message, tell her about Abigail. Then another thought occurred to him and he slipped back into the firmament and returned to his body.

He opened his eyes and grasped the hilt of Mindbender, then focused on the mindset of being in a battle. With a firm hold on that mental state, he tried to find the place of empty-mindedness that led to the firmament. But the two frames of mind were mutually exclusive. Try as he might, he couldn't be both calm enough to reach the firmament and believe he was in a fight at the same time. He opened his eyes again, frustrated by his failure.

Jack was leaning against his pack, watching him meditate.

"I can't help but wonder what it's like to leave your body and travel across the world in an instant," he said.

"Sometimes it's terrifying," Alexander said. "Andalia is sending an armada of transports up the east coast into Warrenton. I warned everyone I could, but I'm afraid we just don't have the strength to defend against them while the bulk of our army is in Fellenden."

"Phane is certainly persistent," Jack said. "Hopefully, the Sky Knights will be able to thin their numbers a bit before they reach Warrenton."

"Even if they do, my father is going to have his hands full," Alexander said. "I wish I had the time to go destroy the Andalian Crown. Without the power of their force lances, the Lancers are just oversized cavalry."

"Perhaps a detour is in order," Jack said.

Alexander thought about it and shook his head. "The Nether Gate has to come first. It breaks my heart to risk Ruatha, but the consequences of allowing Phane to gain control of the Nether Gate are too terrifying to contemplate."

"So we go to Tyr and the dragons, then?" Jack said with a slight tremor of uncharacteristic nervousness.

"I'm afraid so," Alexander said. "Bragador has the one of the keystones. One way or another, we have to get it before Phane does."

"I just hope she's open to reason," Jack said. "We already have enough enemies."

"I couldn't agree more," Alexander said. "Get some rest. I have some thinking to do. I'll keep an eye out."

Chapter 25

Alexander examined the stone wall across the staircase leading down to the chamber where the Nether Gate had been hidden for so many years. Even though the wall had been created by the wizard's spell, it seemed to be ordinary stone without any aura of magic.

"Can you sense the shade?" Alexander asked Chloe.

"No, My Love," she said. "He's no longer in the chamber below."

"I saw a couple of passages leading deeper into the mountain," Alexander muttered. "I wonder where they go."

"This keep seems to be pretty extensive," Jack said. "There's no telling how far its halls and chambers spread through the mountain."

"The shade could be anywhere by now," Alexander said. "If I had to guess, I'd say he's chasing after the wraithkin and the keystone." Alexander looked at the wall and sighed. "Sometimes I actually miss the Thinblade. Without it, this wall is going to take a while to break down."

"I could send it away, My Love," Chloe said.

"What do you mean, Little One?"

"I can send it into the aether, out of the world of time and substance," Chloe said.

Alexander smiled at his familiar. "Sometimes I forget how special you are, Little One." She buzzed into a ball of light at his praise, then went to the wall and it vanished into the aether with her.

They moved into the natural cavern cautiously. Chloe brought the wall back again once they were through, sealing the staircase behind them. The chamber was large, easily a hundred feet across in an irregular oval shape with a rough stone ceiling thirty or forty feet overhead.

Against the wall opposite the stairway was the Nether Gate. It was fashioned from a single piece of jet-black stone that stood twelve feet high and eight feet wide at the base. The side facing them had been cut cleanly and polished smooth. The stone was an odd shape, with the left side rising nearly straight from the floor to its apex and the right side describing a gradual arc to the ground.

Alexander saw the familiar aura of Reishi magic that he associated with the Gates, but there was more. This device had a darkness to its colors that made his head hurt. The light of their night-wisp dust fell into it, leaving the surrounding area shrouded in shadow. He knew with terrible certainty that they had no power at their disposal capable of destroying it.

As if to confirm his belief, Isabel sent a shaft of pure white light into the center of the polished face of it. The Nether Gate absorbed the light-lance spell without a blemish.

She took a deep breath, mastering her rage before she spoke. "That spell was powerful enough to burn a hole three feet through solid granite," she said.

Alexander put his arm around her and shook his head. "We don't have anything that can destroy it," he said. "And I doubt we could move it either."

"We can't just leave it here," Isabel said. "That thing is the end of everything if Phane gets his hands on it."

"We don't have a choice, but I do have an idea," he said without elaborating. He didn't want to risk Phane learning what he had planned, and as much as it pained him, he couldn't risk letting Isabel know what he had in mind.

"Well?" Isabel said.

Alexander smiled. "Later, I still have to work out the details."

"Over here, Lord Reishi," Horace said. "I've found a passage and fresh tracks."

A single set of footprints led into the dark of a small natural passage.

"According to the sovereigns, the grotto of the vitalwood tree is only accessible through natural passages leading from this keep," Alexander said. "We can't risk the shade finding that tree. Hector, lead the way. And be careful."

The passages were irregular and the floor was uneven. At one time, water had flowed through this subterranean network of caves. The caverns turned and twisted, forked and meandered through the gut rock of the mountain. Horace marked their passage on the walls as Hector tracked the footprints of the shade. For over an hour they traveled through the dank and silent darkness until they saw a flicker of light in the distance.

Jinzeri was standing at the end of long stretch of relatively wide tunnel. He saw them, but didn't make any move to flee. Instead, he held his ground and watched.

Alexander stopped, wary of the shade, and sent his all around sight down the passage. He saw hundreds of strands of silk hanging from the ceiling, dripping with venom. The ceiling was dotted with tiny glowing worms that were waiting mindlessly for their next meal to become entangled in their lines. The colors of the drops of sticky liquid slowly dripping down the silk threads reminded Alexander of the colors of the deathwalker root.

"Stop," Alexander said as Hector started moving toward the shade.

Jinzeri smiled before he slipped around a corner and vanished into the darkness.

"We have to find another way around," Alexander said as a drop of venom splashed against the back of his neck. He looked up and saw that they were standing underneath dozens of glow worms and they were all spinning their strands of silk, droplets of venom slowly drizzling down each one.

He felt cold numbness where the drop had hit him, and it was spreading.

"Retreat," he said, backing out from under the glow worms. Within two steps he stumbled, unable to command his legs to carry him. He tried to regain his balance but failed, toppling to the ground.

"Alexander," Isabel cried out, racing to his side.

Hector and Horace picked him up and carried him to a chamber several dozen feet away from the threat of the glow worms and laid him down.

Alexander was aware of his surroundings but he'd lost the ability to move of his own free will. He was completely paralyzed by the fast-acting toxin.

"Alexander," Isabel said frantically. "Can you hear me?"

He was powerless to respond with words but he could still communicate with Chloe. She spun nervously into a ball of light before regaining her normal form.

"He's paralyzed, but conscious and aware," she said. "A drop of glow-worm venom landed on the back of his neck."

Isabel nodded to Hector and Horace and they carefully rolled him over. An angry red splotch stood out on his neck. She carefully scraped the venom off his skin with her knife, then slathered healing salve over the mark.

"He says the cold has stopped spreading," Chloe reported.

"All we can do now is wait," Isabel said. "I don't want to risk choking him with a healing potion."

"That's a remarkably fast-acting toxin," Jack said. "I suspect Lucky would appreciate a sample, if we could collect some without further risk."

"I can," Horace said, "provided you have a suitable container."

Jack smiled. "Lucky asked me to collect any rare or unusual ingredients we came across and he gave me a number of vials and containers," he said.

After Jack handed him a small glass vial and a little spoon, Horace concentrated for a moment and then handed them to his invisible magical servant. Jack provided light as the vial and spoon floated down the hall to gather the sticky venom from the puddles on the floor under each strand of glow-worm silk. The stuff had the consistency of honey but it was as clear as water. Within a few minutes the vial was full. Horace handed it to Jack, who carefully wiped it off with a scrap of cloth. He discarded the cloth, then slipped the vial inside a metal tube that Lucky had provided to safeguard dangerous ingredients.

Then they waited, with Chloe providing frequent reports on Alexander's well-being. After about an hour, he started to regain some feeling in his fingers and toes. An hour after that, he was nearly fully recovered.

"That's some potent stuff," he said. "One drop put me down. I suspect a few more would have killed me."

"How did the shade get through there?" Isabel asked.

"I don't think he did," Hector said. "I've reexamined his tracks and it looks like he went that way initially, but backtracked in his own footprints and then very carefully stepped on stones to cover his real path out that passage over there."

"So he tried to walk us into a trap and was waiting for us so he could watch," Alexander said. "Let's see if we can catch up with him and at least leave him without a body."

They continued into the dark by the light of their night-wisp dust, moving slowly and cautiously. The encounter with the glow worms had made them all more wary.

Several hours later the Sovereign Stone pulsed with red light, went back to its normal soft glow, then pulsed again. Alexander stopped dead in his tracks. Everyone looked at him with curiosity.

"Why did it do that?" Isabel asked.

"The Wizard's Den," Alexander said. "The sovereigns told me the Stone would pulse with light about a day before the Wizard's Den opened. This changes things. As soon as we're done here, we have to get back to Ruatha as quickly as possible."

"I don't understand," Isabel said.

"There are spellbooks in the Wizard's Den," Alexander said, "including a banishing spell. Our wizards need to study those books and learn everything they can from them."

"You mean we could be rid of the shades, once and for all?" Isabel asked.

"And the wraith queen," Alexander said.

They traveled through the dark for the rest of the day. It was a confusing maze of twisting and turning caverns. Occasionally, they became disoriented or ran into dead ends and had to backtrack. Alexander stopped several times and used his clairvoyance to chart a course but it was difficult because it was so dark. Even with his magical sight, he couldn't get a clear picture of their environment.

They came upon glow worms a few more times and had to backtrack to avoid them. The time lost was worth it though. Alexander didn't want to find out what would happen if several drops of the potent poison got on one of them. When they were exhausted, they stopped in a larger chamber and made a small camp. It was cold and dank but they slept well from sheer fatigue, waking some time later, though none of them knew if it was day or night. In this place such a concept had no meaning.

Three hours later, they rounded a corner and saw a glimmer of light in the distance. Alexander wanted to hurry but he knew this was the most likely place for Jinzeri to spring another trap, so they moved with a measured and cautious pace. The cavern passage was broken on one side; a crack in the stone of the mountain wide enough to pass through led into a small valley filled with a lake.

They stepped out onto a stone shelf ten feet above the water of the deep lake and caught their first glimpse of the vitalwood tree.

The valley was actually a deep pit in the mountain with stone walls rising hundreds of feet on all sides. It was only about three hundred feet across at its widest point and there were no other entrances. In the middle of the deep blue waters of the lake was a small island, fifty or sixty feet across, with lush green grass blanketing its surface. The vitalwood tree stood directly in the center of the island.

Alexander had seen the colors of dragons, wizards, and fairies … but this surpassed them all. It radiated vital life energy in waves of undulating power. Physically, it looked like a giant oak tree with lush, broad leaves and thousands of pure white flowers all in bloom. It was beautiful and awe-inspiring—for a long time they just stood there, taking in the sheer majesty of the tree. It was a thing of such beauty that Alexander felt a deep sense of gratitude for the privilege of simply looking at it.

Chloe buzzed into a ball of light, floating higher into the air as she did.

"My kind came to the world of time and substance from the realm of light to frolic under the shade of the vitalwood. I never fully understood why until now. I can only imagine an entire forest of such magnificent trees covering the world."

"For the first time in my entire life, I think I'm actually at a loss for words," Jack said.

Alexander took Isabel's hand.

He could not only see the aura of the tree, he could actually feel it. It permeated him with calm tranquility, a feeling of belonging and acceptance that he had only found before in Isabel's love. In the presence of the vitalwood tree, everything felt right with the world.

Before them, at the edge of the stone shelf, a being of pure white light coalesced out of nothingness, taking form and substance between them and the tree.

"I am Selaphiel," he said. "You may not pass."

He stood ten feet tall in the form of a man, but that's where the similarity ended. His skin was pure white and he glowed so brightly that no one, save Alexander, could look directly at him. He had no hair and wore no clothes, nor carried any weapons, yet it was obvious that he was more than a match for any power they had at their disposal.

"I am Alexander Reishi," Alexander said, drawing the Sovereign Stone from under his tunic. "I have come for three drops of nectar from the vitalwood tree and nothing more. I have seen a great many things, but nothing of such surpassing beauty as this tree. I will do no harm, but I must have the nectar to save the one I love."

"I have been charged by one of your ancestors with protecting this tree," Selaphiel said. "For millennia, I have watched over her, waiting for the day when she would choose to spread her seed into the world again. Why should I grant you what you seek?"

"Because my need is driven by love," Alexander said.

"And yet there is darkness within the one you would save," Selaphiel said, turning to Isabel, "although, there is also light."

"We wish to banish the darkness from her," Alexander said. "The Reishi Sovereigns have told me of a potion that can save her, but it requires the nectar of the vitalwood tree."

Selaphiel turned to Chloe as if Alexander was of little consequence. "You are a long way from home, Chloe."

"As are you, Selaphiel," Chloe said, flitting up to within a few feet of his face.

"You have bound yourself to this mortal," he said.

She nodded.

"So you will be coming home soon."

"Yes."

"And he is worthy of your love?" he asked.

"He is," she said.

Selaphiel thought for a moment.

"I will permit you to gather the nectar he has requested, but the mortals must not pass," he said.

She looked to Alexander. He nodded, smiling.

"Bargain struck," Chloe said.

She spun into a ball of light at the same moment that Selaphiel's entire body pulsed pure white.

"Darkness nears," he said. "Jinzeri, I can smell you. Show yourself."

The shade stepped out of the crack in the stone wall and scanned the scene. When he saw the tree, his face contorted in a mixture of rage and lust—rage that such a thing of beauty existed and lust to destroy it.

Selaphiel looked from Jinzeri to Isabel.

"This demon is bound to the darkness within you," he said.

"She gave birth to me," Jinzeri said mockingly. "Of course, Alexander here helped. Without him, she would never have been a viable conduit between the netherworld and the world of time and substance. And my favorite part—

Alexander did it all for love." He tipped his head back and laughed. "He has doomed the world, and all for love," he said, still laughing.

"The world has not fallen yet," Selaphiel said, "and you will not be here to see the day when it does."

"Are you threatening me, Selaphiel?" Jinzeri said. "You know the price of what you suggest. You cannot banish me without relinquishing your post."

"I could just kill you," Alexander said.

"When will you learn?" Jinzeri said. "You can't kill me … because I'm already dead."

"Maybe I can't kill you, but I can leave you without a body," Alexander said.

Jinzeri shrugged, "I'll find another." He turned back to Selaphiel as if dismissing any threat Alexander posed.

"If you banish me, who will guard the tree and all it represents?" Jinzeri asked in a knowing sort of way.

"I can place the tree beyond your reach, beyond anyone's reach," Selaphiel said.

"For a time, perhaps," Jinzeri said. "But my brothers and I are patient. Now that I know where it is, we will finish the job we started so long ago."

Selaphiel pulsed with light and Alexander saw an undercurrent of rage undulate through his puissant colors. Alexander's mind raced. He was missing a vital piece of information and he knew better than most the value of complete information. He also knew that the time for words would soon end. Above all, he needed what he'd come for.

"Gather some nectar for me, Little One," Alexander said silently to Chloe. She spun into a ball of light and vanished into the aether.

"You remember that time, don't you, Selaphiel?" Jinzeri taunted. "Soot and ash blotted out the sun for an entire season. The wail of anguish that tore through the world at the death of the vitalwood forest brought despair to all. It was a delicious triumph, or it would have been had it not been for this one tree."

"You failed then and you will fail now," Selaphiel said. "The forest will be reborn and you will be cast down into the darkness where you belong."

"Go ahead, then," Jinzeri said. "Banish me. I'll find my way out again. I always do." Jinzeri waited a moment with feigned expectation. When Selaphiel took no action, he laughed derisively.

"You are as powerless as these mortals," Jinzeri said, "bound by your own empty values. Without the will to act, all the power in the world is meaningless."

"Sometimes the greatest thing you can do with power is withhold it," Selaphiel said.

Alexander began to feel a strange sensation building in his head. Pressure behind his forehead grew swiftly. He staggered with the sudden pain of it as the Sovereign Stone pulsed with crimson light and the door to the Wizard's Den opened.

The room beyond was a fifty-foot square with arched ceilings, twenty feet high and dotted with a dozen glowing stones that cast a warm illumination. A single door occupied the center of the far wall. The center of the right wall held a hearth with several comfortable-looking chairs arrayed before it. The middle of the room contained an elegantly carved table large enough to seat four to a side and one on each end surrounded by ten matching chairs. The left wall held a four-poster bed in the far corner with a large footlocker pushed up against it and a small night table and lamp beside it. An ornately carved and polished desk sat in the corner to the left of the door with a large set of bookshelves occupying the space between the desk and the bed.

Alexander registered all of these things at a glance, but the thing that demanded his immediate attention was the swirling ball of soot-black smoke floating over the central table. It was darker than night with colors to match.

A moment after the door opened, Selaphiel pulsed with light so bright it would have blinded Alexander had it not been for his magical vision. His companions all shielded their eyes against the brilliance.

Jinzeri tipped his head back and cackled. "Destroy the tree," he commanded.

The swirling ball of smoke seemed to expand as if awakening. It shot forth in a two-foot-diameter jet of blackness straight for the vitalwood tree. Despite its frightening speed, Selaphiel was faster. In a blink, he stood on the island between the tree and the demon. He raised his hand and a shield of magical force tinged with white formed a shell around the tree. The demon scattered as it crashed into the shield. Wisps of blackness slid through the air, reforming into a ball of thick black smoke.

"Flee!" Selaphiel commanded.

Everything was happening so quickly. Alexander couldn't quite make sense of it all. He had no idea why a demon was waiting within the Wizard's Den. Jinzeri had commanded it to destroy the tree and it tried to obey. From the brief conversation between the shade and Selaphiel, it was obvious that the vitalwood tree was far more important than Alexander understood.

"I have the nectar, My Love," Chloe said in his mind.

Selaphiel spoke a word of power and a shell of shimmering blue-white light encased the entire vitalwood tree and a large part of the island.

"You will not succeed!" he shouted as he cast a bolt of light at the smoke demon.

Alexander felt a tremor ripple through the air as light met darkness.

Somewhere in the background of the chaos, Jinzeri laughed.

"You will have your wish, Shade," Selaphiel said. From his outstretched hand, an arc of brilliant light reached out and took hold of a point in space before him. With a jerk, he tore the light away and the fabric of the world was rent, revealing a place beyond time and substance.

The tear in the world began to draw everything toward it.

"Quickly, My Love," Chloe said, "we must take refuge within the Wizard's Den or we'll be lost."

"Inside!" Alexander shouted above the fury of the vortex drawing everything into it.

His companions didn't hesitate. They filed into the Wizard's Den quickly, even as the vortex pulled on them.

Alexander watched the scene unfold from the threshold of his Wizard's Den. The hole in the world sucked everything toward it, siphoning water from the lake into the emptiness beyond, sucking small stones and sand, tugging at

Alexander.

The tree was protected by the shield that Selaphiel had erected, but everything else was fair game. The smoke demon was drawn into the vortex, swirling around the hole in tighter and tighter circles. Selaphiel had lost his form and was just a streak of bright light spiraling into the tear in the world as well.

The pressure increased and Alexander saw Chloe start to slide toward the door. In a panic, he willed the door closed and it vanished, leaving nothing but a wall where a moment ago was a passage leading to chaos. The sudden silence was deafening.

The turbulence stopped abruptly and Isabel staggered against him. He caught her, helping her to a chair.

"What's wrong?" he asked, worry creasing his brow.

"It's the darkness."

Chapter 26

Abigail stood in the ruins of Fellenden City. Anatoly, Magda, Conner, and Captain Wyatt and his platoon accompanied her. It was unusually cold for autumn and the sky was grey and bleak.

It had been weeks since Zuhl's forces had sacked the city, but the stench of death still lingered in the damp air. Fellenden was a lifeless shell of what it had once been. The streets were littered with corpses, decaying or picked clean by scavengers. Rats ran freely through the city, fat from the abundant carrion. Buildings were smashed or burned out and abandoned. The few people they'd seen were hiding, no doubt terrified that the army responsible for such barbarity had returned to pick the bones of the city.

Abigail fought the feeling of nausea welling up inside her. She had been warned by her scouts that the city was broken and dead. Her advisors had suggested that there was nothing to gain by entering the city, but she needed to see it for herself. She wanted to have a clear picture of what she faced, who the enemy was.

The people, if they could be called that, responsible for such enormity were the problem with the world. Such an act of wanton destruction for the sake of power, without any regard for the suffering of others, was the reason the world was embroiled in war. Whether it was Phane or Zuhl didn't make any difference. People who craved power and those who followed them were the enemies of civilization.

Abigail thought about the events of the past several months. She remembered how many times she had quietly wished that her family wasn't at the center of events, that she could have gone on living her blissfully boring little life.

As she looked around in dismay at the carnage scattered through the streets of Fellenden City, she was grateful. For the first time since this ordeal had begun, she felt a deep sense of gratitude that she *was* at the center of events. In that moment she understood her brother a bit better. He had reluctantly embraced his fate. She had resisted, supporting him out of love, but never fully committing to any cause other than the preservation of those she loved.

Seeing the horror that had befallen Fellenden, she finally understood the only just use for power. Power was good for one thing: crushing those who would kill for it. And that's exactly what she intended to do. She looked around at the faces of those with her.

Anatoly wore grim determination. She knew that look. It was the look he always had just before he spun his war axe off his shoulder and stepped into battle. She understood completely.

Conner wore a mask of desolation. The people of Fellenden were close friends and trading partners with Ithilian. The two islands shared much in the way of cultural values and work ethic. He looked like he was trying to reconcile the fact that other human beings were capable of such malice.

Magda's face was set and devoid of expression, yet her eyes flashed with anger. Having been secluded for so long in the fortress island, she was coming to see that Phane wasn't the only evil in the world worthy of her wrath.

Wyatt was detached and distant, focusing on his duties and maintaining a vigilant watch on the nearby buildings for any hint of a threat to his queen. Even though he was doing a good job of hiding his feelings, there was a tension about him that revealed the turmoil within.

"I never wanted power," Abigail said, almost to herself. "But I've never been more grateful for anything in my whole life than the fact that I'm leading an army against the people who did this."

"I know how you feel," Magda said. "We've always had our petty squabbles and political infighting within the coven, but we've never been at war. Now that I see this, I want blood."

"You're going to get your wish," Abigail said. "Alexander said the primary objective is to take or destroy the shipyards, and that still stands, but our secondary objective is to kill every single one of these brutes in the process. We will offer them no mercy, no quarter, and no remorse. If they offer to surrender, we'll accept it, disarm them and then execute them to a man. Their crimes are so horrendous, their violation of the Old Law so beyond redemption, that I sentence each and every soldier of Zuhl to death."

Anatoly nodded in agreement.

"This is so much worse than we feared," Conner said. "I need to send word to my father. The scope of the destruction we've seen here will give him greater reason to mobilize our people."

"Flight Commander Corina will provide you with message riders," Magda said.

"The scout riders will be back before dark," Abigail said. "Once we have their report, we'll plan our first attack." She mounted up without another word and turned her horse toward the broken city gate.

***

They had arrived on the island the day before. The initial battle had been very one-sided. Zuhl's forces guarding the Gate were taken completely by surprise and quickly overwhelmed. Once Abigail's army was through and the Gate was closed, she had issued orders to move northwest toward Zuhl's shipyard and the bulk of his forces. It would take weeks to reach their target but Abigail expected to encounter his raiding parties along the way. She intended to pick him apart a piece at a time, weakening his forces before engaging the bulk of his army.

Flight Commander Corina had arrived with nearly a hundred Sky Knights just after dark the night before. She was tall and lithe with a gaunt face, severe eyes, and dirty-blonde hair that she wore tied back in a long braid.

Abigail had ordered her to send out scouts to assess the damage to Fellenden and to locate the enemy. They'd lifted off at dawn and were scheduled to return before dark. Forty teams of two were each given an area of the island to survey. Given the range and speed of the wyverns, they would be able to cover the entire island in a cursory way, providing vital information that would help Abigail formulate her strategy and decide where to focus her scouting activities in the coming weeks.

It was just past dark when the last of the scouting parties returned. The Wing Commanders each accepted reports from their Sky Knights, then reported to the command tent with Mistress Corina. Abigail had assembled her command staff including Connor Ithilian, Mage Dax, Wizard Sark, Mistress Magda, General Markos, and General Kern, along with Anatoly, Knight Raja, Captain Sava, and Captain Wyatt.

Each Wing Commander spoke in turn, reporting the results of the scouting parties under their command. Half of the enemy forces were encamped and dug in around the shipyard on the northwest coast at the edge of the Iron Oak Forest. The scouts estimated four legions. The remaining four legions were spread out across Fellenden.

Each had targeted a city. Wakefield and Bredon were under siege. Bristol Bay had fallen. Reports spoke of fire and carnage on a scale that rivaled the devastation at Fellenden City. The fourth legion was just beyond the mountain pass south of Fellenden City and turning west toward Suva.

The cities that hadn't yet been targeted by Zuhl's raiding legions were busy fortifying their defenses and preparing for a battle they knew they would eventually lose. Of the twelve large cities on Fellenden, two had fallen and three more would fall before Abigail could do anything about it.

Raiding parties ranged through the less densely populated areas attacking smaller villages, pillaging what resources they could carry to supply their army and shipyard, raping the women, killing or enslaving the men.

There was virtually no organized resistance to the enemy invasion. Fellenden hadn't fielded any sort of army to speak of with the exception of small companies of militia who had taken it upon themselves to defend against some of the smaller raiding parties.

One report spoke of a large number of people hiding deep within the Iron Oak Forest. From the description, they appeared to be at least partially military with an ordered encampment beneath the giant trees, scouts posted all around, and warning fires that signaled when the Sky Knights passed overhead. She suspected they were the refugees Alexander had spoken of.

Abigail looked at the updated map and picked her target: Bredon, a city to the north of Fellenden City. The scouts had reported that it was surrounded by ten thousand enemy soldiers and that several buildings were burning within its walls. Its gates were holding—for now. More importantly, it was on the route to the shipyard.

Abigail wanted to strike out at Zuhl's soldiers, she wanted to crush them, more than that, she wanted to protect the innocent people of Fellenden, but she had a duty that was more important than any of that.

Zuhl had a horde of unimaginable size waiting for ships to carry them to the far corners of the Seven Isles. Her first responsibility was to stop that from ever happening. The future depended on it, but in order for her to fulfill that duty, many innocent people would suffer and die.

Abigail swallowed the bitter taste in her mouth and stabbed the point on the map where the first battle of Fellenden would be fought.

"There," she said. "We'll move to Bredon with haste, kill Zuhl's scouts from the air, and attack with the full force of our infantry and archers. The cavalry will flank to the west and run north to cut off any escape. We won't stop at Bredon any longer than we have to. The objective is to destroy this legion quickly and continue toward the shipyard."

"If I may," General Markos said.

"Of course, General," Abigail replied.

"Perhaps we should systematically destroy the raiding legions before we move against the shipyard," General Markos said. "That way, we won't end up fighting on two fronts when the raiding legions learn of our presence and regroup to counterattack."

"I considered that, General," Abigail said, "but our first priority must be the shipyard, and we have to take it before winter sets in. I'm afraid that several engagements will cost us the time and manpower we'll need to defeat Zuhl's defenses at his main encampment."

"Your strategy is risky," General Markos said.

"I know, but it's a necessary risk," Abigail said. "I'm hoping we can destroy the enemy at the shipyard and take their defensive position for our own. From there, we can work the shipyard through the winter and hopefully have a few vessels of our own to lend to the battle come spring."

"Perhaps we could divide our forces," Conner said. "The people are suffering terribly. We could use the cavalry to go after the raiding legions while the infantry and archers move against the shipyard."

"No," Abigail said. "We're going to keep our forces together as much as possible. Conner, I want to help the people of Fellenden, but not at the risk of failing to secure the shipyard. If Zuhl can hold it long enough to get his ships in the water, then no one will be safe. He'll do to Ithilian and Ruatha what he did to Fellenden City."

"I agree with Lady Abigail," General Kern said. "But perhaps we could send some smaller teams to infiltrate the raiding legions, collect information about their leadership and objectives, and possibly find a way to disrupt their activities."

"Volunteers only," Abigail said. "If we can learn about them or hurt them without a direct fight, then I'm all for it, but I won't send men on such a risky mission unless they ask to go."

"I'll put out the word," General Kern said.

"Good," Abigail said. "Anything else?"

"I suggest we attempt to make contact with those hiding in the Iron Oak Forest," Magda said. "Our scouts report a sizable number with some military organization. Perhaps, with some help, they could add to our force strength."

"I agree, but let's wait until after we engage the enemy at Bredon," Abigail said. "We'll have more to bargain with if we can demonstrate that we're on their side."

***

Several days later, Abigail sat atop her horse on a hillock overlooking a broad plain that stretched for miles in every direction. Her army was well behind her and moving slowly but inexorably toward Bredon.

On the horizon, she could see a pall of smoke hanging over the city from dozens of fires burning within its walls. Bredon had fallen to Zuhl's soldiers, who were no doubt busy looting and pillaging the homes and shops of the inhabitants.

Abigail felt a sense of urgency building within her. She knew she couldn't save all of the cities of Fellenden, but she could at least salvage what was left of Bredon—if she could get there in time. It would be at least another day before the main body of her army reached the outskirts of the city.

Her plan to use the Sky Knights to eliminate Zuhl's scouts had worked better than expected, presumably because the barbarians were too preoccupied with pillaging Bredon to notice the absence of scouting reports.

The cavalry had separated from the infantry and archers days ago and were skirting the city to the west, cutting off any hope of escape. Abigail wanted to utterly destroy these invaders, but more practically, she didn't want reports of her army's advance to reach the enemy forces at the shipyards.

This first battle would be a test, of sorts. The soldiers in her army had fought against the infantry of the Reishi Army Regency and the soldiers of Headwater, but they had never faced Zuhl's forces. She didn't know what to expect and was glad to have such a lopsided engagement be their first against this new enemy. From their treatment of Fellenden City, she was convinced that they were cruel and barbaric but their capability on the battlefield was unknown. This fight would help her formulate a strategy for attacking the legions guarding the shipyard.

"Doesn't look like they've noticed us yet," Anatoly said.

"No, but it's only a matter of time before they do. I just wish I knew how they would react."

"You and everyone who's ever commanded an army marching toward battle," Anatoly said with a grin.

Abigail smiled as she nodded. "I know, I know, all I can do is formulate a sound strategy and then execute my plan."

"At least you were listening during your lessons, even if they were meant for your brothers," Anatoly said.

Abigail was quiet for a long moment. "I miss him, Anatoly. Sometimes I wonder how events would have played out if Darius had been marked instead of Alexander."

"I loved Darius like my own son," Anatoly said, "but honestly, I'm not sure if he would have fared as well as Alexander has."

Abigail nodded. "I wonder how Alexander's doing. I keep hoping he'll visit my dreams and at least say hello."

"I'm sure he's all right," Anatoly said. "Jack, too," he added with a sidelong glance.

Abigail tried to suppress a smile as she turned her horse toward her army.

She ordered General Markos to pick up the pace and march until sundown. They made a dark camp and ate a cold dinner to prevent the enemy from seeing them in the night. Abigail found it hard to believe that Zuhl's soldiers hadn't noticed her army yet, but she was willing to take any stroke of luck that broke her way.

They marched on at dawn, moving as quickly as she could motivate such a large group of people to move. As they neared the outskirts of the city about midday, a warning bell tolled. The invaders began to pour out of the city and started forming a battle line, but seeing the size of the enemy they faced, they quickly changed their strategy, re-forming into company-sized units of a hundred men or so and moving away from the city in all directions.

Abigail cursed under her breath. At first she suspected cowardice, but the discipline of the soldiers was too great. They didn't just scatter and they didn't all head off toward the main encampment near the shipyards. Instead, they seemed to be forming into units large enough to be more than a match for most towns or villages, yet small enough to move quickly.

"So much for that plan," Abigail said.

"No plan ever survives contact with the enemy," Anatoly reminded her.

"So you've said," Abigail muttered. "Mistress Corina, send word to General Kern and the cavalry to separate into hunting parties of five hundred men each and range out around Bredon, killing as many of the enemy as they can find. Dispatch a wing of Sky Knights to assist them. General Markos, continue around the city. We march for the shipyard with haste. Captain Wyatt, assemble your men. You'll accompany me into the city."

By the time they reached the broken city gates, the enemy had all but abandoned the place, leaving the survivors in a state of stunned and almost disbelieving relief.

The gates were torn from the gatehouse and one tower had been smashed, leaving rubble strewn across the street. Several dozen men in armor, all wearing the crest of Bredon, were scattered across the roadway just beyond the gate, their broken bodies left to rot where they'd fallen. They were the lucky ones.

Abigail surveyed the scene and nearly vomited. An elderly man, scrawny with unruly hair, was nailed to the wall of a nearby shop. He may have been the owner or just an unlucky passerby but now he had a dozen six-inch nails driven through each outstretched arm and into the wall of the building. His feet were several inches off the ground. Streaks of blood dripped down the wall beneath each nail. His head hung forward, limp and lifeless.

Bodies were haphazardly scattered about. Some were women who'd been raped and left for dead. Others were children, casually murdered and discarded.

A frantic young man came running up to them. Wyatt's Rangers stopped him before he got close to Abigail.

"Have you seen her?" he asked urgently. "Have you seen my Emma? They took her from our house."

His face was coated with grime and his clothes were dirty and torn. A lurid bruise lit up his cheek and his right eye was swollen shut. He didn't seem to notice or care.

"Dear Maker, I have to find her," he said, before hurrying off on his search.

Abigail swallowed the bile rising in her throat.

Now that the invaders had fled, the people of Bredon were returning to the streets. Some were stunned by the sudden absence of their tormenters. Others were desperately looking for lost loved ones. A few just sat on the edge of the road and cried, perhaps for what they'd lost or perhaps because they'd been spared.

"I've seen enough," Abigail said, wheeling her horse and heading for the gate.

Chapter 27

She marched her army relentlessly, pushing them to the limits of their endurance. Time was the greatest enemy now. She needed to engage the legions guarding the shipyard before the raiding legions could regroup with them.

The cavalry reported some success against the legion that had disbanded from Bredon but they also reported that the enemy was fearless and fearsome. They were big men, most over six feet tall and few under two hundred pounds. Some stood nearly seven feet tall, and three hundred pounds was not uncommon within their ranks. They fought with a variety of weapons and wielded them all with a kind of skill and familiarity that only comes from experience. They were ruthless and brutal. Their commanders were cunning and treacherous, several times luring cavalry hunting parties into close quarters and turning the tables on them.

Zuhl's horde had few horses and the ones they did have were big and slow, but powerful. A few of his soldiers carried javelins but none carried bows; they seemed to view such weapons as beneath them, preferring to wield swords, battle-axes, spears, and heavy maces in face-to-face combat.

That was one weakness that the Rangers knew how to exploit. After a week of hunting the enemy, it became apparent that Abigail's heavy cavalry were less effective and more vulnerable. They relied on size and mass to attack effectively, but these soldiers happily stood their ground against a cavalry charge, more often than not unhorsing those on the leading edge of the attack.

The Rangers, on the other hand, discovered early on that they could use the speed and mobility of their light horses coupled with the deadly accuracy of their composite bows to pick the enemy soldiers off one at a time.

Abigail ordered her single legion of heavy cavalry to regroup with the rest of the army and left the two legions of Rangers to hunt Zuhl's raiders. The Rangers were adept at the tactic and started to take a real toll on the legion that had sacked Bredon.

Unfortunately, they were not the only ones exacting a toll. A company of barbarians sneaked into a Ranger encampment one night and attacked. The battle went poorly for the surprised Rangers. They fought fiercely and many managed to mount up and escape to a distance where they could make use of their bows, but nearly two hundred were lost before the battle ended.

As the days stretched into weeks, the tension within the ranks built as stories of the barbarians' brute strength, size, and ruthlessness began to circulate. The Sky Knights reported that the raiding legions were abandoning the cities and moving to regroup behind Abigail's army. She'd known that this was a possibility all along, even hoped for it. Drawing the enemy into an engagement with her army was the best chance she had for sparing the people of Fellenden the horrors that had befallen the people of Bredon and Fellenden City.

Once she was certain she would reach the shipyard several weeks before the raiding legions could regroup and attack her army's flank, she decided it was time to go in search of allies.

Anatoly held his tongue, but he obviously didn't relish the idea of a ride on Kallistos. Abigail just grinned as he grumbled while strapping himself into her saddle. Conner strapped in behind Knight Raja, and the two wyverns lifted off. Abigail had become used to flying and even found it exhilarating, but Anatoly had never been in the air before and his nervousness showed in his death grip on the saddle.

The air was crisp and the sky was clear as they flew toward the Iron Oak Forest and the camp of refugees hiding under its canopy. It took several hours to reach the forest and then another hour to locate the camp. Tens of thousands of people were busy building fortifications and homes under the sheltering branches of the giant trees. Abigail made a low pass and dropped her message. She'd written a letter, sealed it in wax with the butt of the Thinblade, and put it in a small pouch with a stone.

As they flew over, alarms began to sound within the camp and warning fires were lit, signaling other parts of the sprawling camp that danger was near. Abigail gained altitude, wheeling toward the bare hillock she'd chosen for their meeting place. The scouts had provided her with a detailed description of the area, including several spots that were open enough to land a wyvern.

Anatoly heaved a sigh of relief when his feet hit the ground.

"That just isn't natural," he muttered.

"Maybe not, but it's a lot faster than horses," Abigail said with a smile, patting Kallistos on the side of his giant jaw.

Knight Raja and a slightly shaken Conner approached.

"That was terrifying and strangely exciting at the same time," Conner said. "I have half a mind to apply for Sky Knight training, although I suspect my father would forbid it."

"You never know," Abigail said. "Abel is a reasonable man. He might see the value of it."

Anatoly shook his head and muttered, "If the Maker wanted us to fly, he'd have given us wings."

Abigail and Knight Raja chuckled.

"How long do you think they'll be?" Conner asked.

"Probably an hour or so," Abigail said. "We're a ways from their camp and they'll want to send a sizable force to meet us in case we're unfriendly."

"Are you sure we can trust these people?" Anatoly asked.

"I've known Torin and Lacy since we were children," Conner said. "Our fathers saw to it that our families spent time together to cement the bond of friendship between Ithilian and Fellenden."

Nearly an hour later, a hundred men armed with bows and spears stepped out of the forest all at once, completely surrounding the hillock. Anatoly twitched but refrained from spinning his axe up into his hands. Abigail held her ground and waited.

Three men warily approached while the rest maintained a cordon around the hillock.

"Surrender your weapons," the lead man commanded.

Abigail smiled tightly. "No," she said. "We're not your enemies. We only wish to speak to your leaders."

"You're surrounded and outnumbered," the lead man said, glancing nervously at Kallistos. "Surrender your weapons."

"No," Abigail said again, this time with a bit more edge in her voice. "We're here to offer an alliance against Zuhl. I have an army of ten legions marching against him as we speak. We are your allies."

"I don't believe you," he said. "It's far more likely that you're in league with Zuhl."

Conner stepped forward. "I'm Conner Ithilian. Is Torin or Lacy Fellenden among your leaders?"

"Prince Torin is the commander of our forces," the lead man said. "I'm acting under his orders."

"Very well then," Conner said. "Take us to him. You have enough men to overpower us so it won't be necessary to disarm us. Torin and I are friends. He'll understand once we have a chance to speak with him."

"No, you will not be permitted to leave this hilltop unless you relinquish your weapons."

"Then send word to Torin that I've come to speak with him," Conner said. "We'll wait."

The lead man conferred with his subordinates before they agreed.

"It will be some time before Prince Torin arrives," he said. "Do not attempt to leave."

"We're not going anywhere," Abigail said as she unhooked her pack from her saddle. They ate lunch while they waited under the wary eye of Torin's soldiers.

Two hours later Torin and a dozen bodyguards emerged from the forest. He was cautious at first, but broke into a broad smile when he saw Conner.

"It's good to see a friendly face," Torin said. "I take it Lacy made it through."

"No," Conner said. "We heard a report that she was coming to Ithilian, but she never arrived."

Torin's face went white and he closed his eyes in pain. His family was gone. He and Lacy were all that remained of their line.

"I'm sorry, Torin," Conner said. "It's possible that she just couldn't get through."

Torin swallowed hard and set aside his worry for his sister.

"There's nothing we can do about it right now," he said after he composed himself. "Who are your friends?"

"Prince Torin, this is Queen Abigail Ruatha; her champion, Master Grace; and her wing rider, Knight Raja," Conner said.

"I've heard rumors that the throne of Ruatha has been reclaimed by one called Alexander," Torin said. "Is he your husband?"

Abigail smiled. "No, he's my brother."

Torin frowned. "I don't understand. How are you queen if he is king?"

"He's abdicated the Ruathan throne so that he can fulfill his duty as the Reishi Sovereign," Abigail said.

Torin tensed, looking around quickly as if he'd walked into a trap.

"The Reishi are the ancient enemy," he said.

"They're our enemy as well," Abigail said. "Phane Reishi is waging war against us on Ruatha. My brother is leading the fight against him."

"I still don't understand," Torin said. "How can your brother be Lord Reishi if he's Ruathan? And why would he fight against his own house?"

"Apparently, the Reishi are a branch of the Ruathan line," Abigail said. "When Alexander recovered the Sovereign Stone, it bonded to him; hence, he has become Lord Reishi. As for fighting against his own house, he serves the Old Law—Phane does not."

"The Sovereign Stone has returned to the world?" Torin said. "You bring dire news. The Reishi are widely reviled on Fellenden for the destruction they caused during the war. How can I trust you, knowing that you're part of that family?"

"Because I say you can," Conner said. "Lord Reishi came to Ithilian while his home was under attack. When he learned that Phane had abducted Evelyn, he set out to return her to us. Without his help my sister would be dead or still in our enemy's hands. I've stood with Lord Reishi in battle. I trust him with my life and I count him as a friend."

"Your word carries weight with me," Torin said, "but I'll need more to convince the others."

"We've come with an army of ten legions," Abigail said. "Ruatha is under attack even now by Andalian Lancers acting on Phane's behalf and yet Alexander chose to send the bulk of his army to Fellenden. We're marching against Zuhl's shipyard because the Seven Isles will fall to him if he's permitted to build an Iron Oak navy, but more than that, Alexander looked upon the suffering of your people and chose to help you. We're natural allies, Torin. We have the same enemies and the same desire to live in a world free of tyranny and war."

"How is this possible?" Torin asked. "How did you move so many men so far so quickly?"

"We came through the Reishi Gate," Abigail said.

"It's true then," Torin said. "We believed that Zuhl's army came through the Gate. Scouting reports later confirmed it, but I'm still confused. What is there to stop Zuhl from sending more men when he becomes aware of your army?"

"He can't open the Gate," Abigail said. "Alexander controls the Gates now and he's locked everyone else out. Zuhl can't send more men unless he manages to build his navy."

"Even if everything you say is true, it will be very difficult to persuade many of our people to help you," Torin said. "We've suffered greatly. The atrocities Zuhl's horde inflicted upon us are unspeakable. Most of those who've escaped into the forest want no part of violence … though there are those who crave vengeance."

"This war started for me the day Phane murdered my older brother and burned my home to the ground," Abigail said, holding Torin's eyes with a steady gaze. "Since that day we've fought with everything we have, first just to stay alive, then bit by bit to gain the power necessary to strike back at those who would rule by force for the sake of their own ambition. Now I stand at the head of an army poised to drive a killing thrust into the heart of Zuhl's forces on Fellenden. I've seen the ruins of your city. I rode through the streets of Bredon only hours after the enemy fled our approach. I know all too well the suffering you speak of and that's why I'm here.

"I want their blood, and I mean to have it.

"If you wish to stand with me, then gather those who will fight and come forth. If you wish to cower in the forest while we avenge the barbarity inflicted upon your people, so be it."

Torin clenched his jaw but held his tongue until he'd regained his composure.

"You speak unfairly, Lady Abigail," he said.

"I speak truth," Abigail said.

"Don't you want to take this war to the enemy?" Conner asked. "You owe them vengeance, this is your chance. Ride with us against them and help us drive them into the sea."

"Of course I want to destroy them," Torin said, unable to fully contain his turbulent emotions. "I've lost my home, my father, probably my sister as well. I'm all that remains of House Fellenden. I want vengeance as much as anyone, but I have a responsibility to protect my people. They've suffered so much and I can't leave them defenseless."

"Do you really believe you're safe here?" Abigail asked. "Zuhl has all the time in the world. He hasn't come for you yet because you aren't important to him. He has an army of nearly a million soldiers just like the ones who violated your home and nearly extinguished your line. All he needs are ships and he'll bring more men to your shores, enough to completely subjugate and enslave every single man, woman, and child on the entire Isle of Fellenden. If you want to protect your people, then help me destroy Zuhl's shipyards and his army."

"How can you know this?" Torin said, alarmed by the news.

"My brother is a wizard," Abigail said. "He's seen Zuhl's army. The only hope the Seven Isles has is to keep his horde confined to the Isle of Zuhl."

Torin shook his head in dismay. "If that's true, then we're truly lost. I've been monitoring his work at the shipyards in hopes that I could free some of my people. He's enslaved thousands, working them long hours, killing those who become exhausted, flogging those who work too slowly, torturing any who speak out against him. We watched the first of his ships slip from its berth into the water just days ago. The other nine are nearly complete."

Abigail shared a look with Anatoly, his face set and grim.

"Then we don't have any more time," Abigail said. "I intend to attack within the week. Stand with me, gather what men you can and ride against Zuhl with me."

Torin thought for a long moment, torn between the safe course and the necessary course.

"I will gather those who choose to fight," he said. "We'll move through the forest and attack from the east on your order."

Abigail smiled fiercely and extended her hand. Torin took it, though somewhat less sure about the coming battle.

"Now, tell me about your sister," Abigail said.

"Father sent her south with Wizard Saul," Torin said. "She was to go to the family crypt and recover an item from Carlyle Fellenden's sarcophagus. My father called it the legacy of the Fellenden line."

"Did he say what the item was?" Abigail asked.

Torin shook his head. "I'm not sure he even knew, only that it was entrusted to our house at the end of the Reishi War and that it must not fall into Zuhl's hands."

Abigail and Anatoly shared another look.

"Do you think it could be?" she asked.

"It's possible," the big man-at-arms said.

"What do you know of this?" Torin asked.

"I'm not sure yet," Abigail said, "and I'm not willing to speak more of it lest Phane is watching."

"How could he be watching?" Torin asked incredulously, looking around nevertheless.

"Magic," Abigail said. "I'll send a company of riders to find your sister and bring her back to you."

"Thank you," Torin said. "Of all the troubles I face, my sister's well-being weighs on my mind the most."

"I understand completely," Abigail said.

***

They returned to the army just as the sun was setting. Abigail strode into the command tent and found her general staff crowded around the map table.

"Welcome back, Lady Abigail," General Markos said.

"Thank you, General. Report."

"We're five days from the enemy encampment," General Markos said. "The Rangers have reported that the remaining soldiers of those occupying Bredon have all turned and are making best speed for the nearest of the three remaining raiding legions. Our commanders estimate that we killed nearly half of their number. The raiding legions will regroup within the week and number just under four legions, including the survivors of the attack on their two legions at the Gate. Admiral Tybalt of the Ithilian Navy reports that he has sixty-eight ships holding station off the coast of Ellesmere awaiting orders."

"Very good," Abigail said. "Recall the Rangers and send word to Admiral Tybalt to commence his attack in five days. Advise him that Zuhl has at least one ship that's seaworthy and perhaps more. He's to focus his attack on those ships first, then on the ships still in their berths. Prince Torin will gather what men he can and be in position to attack from the northeast by the time we arrive."

"Did he say how many men he will bring to the battle?" General Markos asked.

"No. Unfortunately, many of his people would prefer to remain hidden in the forest. Plan as if he will not bring significant numbers."

"Understood," General Markos said.

"Captain Wyatt, I have a mission of great importance for you," Abigail said. "Lacy Fellenden was sent south by her father to retrieve an item from their family crypt and take it to Ithilian. She hasn't been heard from since. Find her and the item she's gone to retrieve and bring them both safely back to us."

"Of course, Lady Abigail," Wyatt said. "If I may, who will protect you?"

"Captain Sava and his men will serve as my guard," Abigail said.

Wyatt nodded approvingly.

"Mistress Corina, assign two Sky Knights to assist Captain Wyatt,"

Abigail said. "They'll be leaving in the morning."

Abigail surveyed her command staff. Everyone in the tent fell silent.

"We must take those shipyards at all costs," she said. "Many will die, but far fewer than if Zuhl is permitted to build his fleet. As soon as we've driven them into the ocean, we'll secure the encampment and fortify our position. There are many innocent people working as slaves in Zuhl's shipyard—protect them as best you can."

Chapter 28

Abigail looked down over Kallistos' wing. The encampment was butted up against the shore, docks linking ten enormous berths to dry ground. A berm wall, wooden spikes jutting from it at all angles, surrounded the entire camp with a deep trench running in front of it. Towers stood just inside the perimeter at odd intervals, some armed with ballistae, others armed with catapults, still others manned by lookouts.

The camp was busy. Slaves milled about fortifying the defenses, cutting timber into lumber suitable for building ships, and keeping the smith fires stoked to work iron into steel hard enough to cut the dense branches of the Iron Oak trees.

A steady stream of horses, carts, and wagons, all overseen by Zuhl's brutish soldiers, moved to and from the edge of the forest where slaves were cutting trees, removing the limbs, and loading the wood for transport to the mills within the camp.

Most troubling were the three empty berths and the three giant ships anchored just offshore. Each boat was as big as a small town, easily capable of carrying a thousand men with horses, supplies, wagons, and weapons for them all. Worse, each of the three boats bristled with armaments. Longboats lined the sides of each hull, a hundred oars jutted from each side, and dozens of sails stretched between the seven masts rising out of the deck of each massive warship.

Abigail banked, circling high overhead, evaluating the strengths and weaknesses of their defenses. Zuhl's men were barbarians but they were industrious, strong, and well-ordered. In just weeks, they had built a small city.

She knew from the reports of her Ranger hunting legions that this enemy eschewed bows, crossbows, and even javelins in favor of close combat. They were big men, powerful and hardy, accustomed to rule by strength. She intended to use their misguided belief in brute force against them. They would want to meet on the battlefield, facing their opponents in close-quarters combat. Abigail would deny them a direct confrontation as much as possible. She cared nothing for how the enemy died, only that they did, and sooner was better than later.

She signaled to Knight Raja. They wheeled their wyverns and headed back to her army, a day out and traveling as quickly as a force of nearly a hundred thousand could move. By nightfall they would be within half-a-day's march.

With the exception of those on the road leading to the forest, the enemy had withdrawn inside their encampment. They'd made what preparations they could to defend against Abigail's approaching army and now they seemed to be working feverishly to complete the seven ships still occupying their berths.

She landed behind her troops and dismounted, giving Kallistos the haunch of a cow from the feed cart before mounting up on her horse and riding to the head of the army. She pushed the army on until sunset, then called a halt. She spent an hour or so walking among her soldiers, offering encouragement and listening to their stories. Most of these men had seen battle on Ruatha, many were seasoned warriors, but all were nervous about the coming fight. Zuhl's soldiers were fearsome and they were defending from a secure position. Tomorrow would be the beginning of a battle that would probably last for days. Many would die.

She went to her tent, tired from her day of scouting the battlefield. She had received reports and reviewed maps of the area, but she also wanted to see the terrain, the enemy positions, and the fortifications for herself. She remembered one of her father's lessons: Accurate information about the enemy and battlefield is the first step to victory.

That she would destroy the enemy was a certainty; she outnumbered them two to one. She was less certain if she would defeat them before the ships were completed and she was concerned about the losses she would take. From a human perspective, each life lost was an unspeakable tragedy, but she didn't have the luxury of such considerations.

She was worried that the battle for the shipyards would diminish her force strength enough so that the next engagement with the regrouping raiding legions would cripple her army. She knew there would be many more battles before this war was won or lost, and she would need to preserve as many of her soldiers as possible so they could stand and fight in the battles to come.

She hated it that these were her concerns. So many would die. So many families would suffer the terrible loss she had grappled with since Darius was murdered. She consoled herself with the knowledge that many more would be lost if she failed, and so she vowed to herself that she would not fail—no matter the cost.

***

Anatoly woke her just before dawn. He wore his armor, his broad-bladed battle-axe strapped across his back and his short sword at his side.

"The army's started moving," he said quietly. "General Markos estimates we'll reach the enemy by noon."

After strapping on her leather armor, her quiver, and the Thinblade, she picked up her bow and left the tent. Captain Sava was standing just outside with several of his dragon-plate-clad Strikers in a loose cordon around her tent.

They followed her to the mess tent, constantly vigilant. After a quick breakfast, she went to the stables and mounted her horse. Anatoly shadowed her without question or conversation. He was mentally preparing for the battle to come. He often said that he fought best when he was in a foul mood. From the frown he wore, Abigail suspected he was nursing his anger. She left him to it as she reviewed her plan of attack yet again.

Dawn broke over a clear sky. There was a chill in the air and the wind was still, as if the world was waiting expectantly for the events of the day to unfold.

She'd gone over every angle of attack, every capability at her disposal, every weakness, every terrain feature and come up with the best strategy she could. She'd listened to the counsel of her generals, the Sky Knights, wizards, and witches. Now her plan would be put to the test and she was certain of only one thing: It would not survive contact with the enemy.

Once the fighting began, she would have to be flexible, seizing opportunities as they presented themselves and defending against threats as they became apparent.

By midmorning, she could see the enemy encampment in the distance. It was a large camp, sprawling away from the sea in a haphazard arrangement of tents, hastily constructed buildings and towers, all surrounded by a berm wall and trench. She heard the alarm bell toll in the distance, alerting the enemy of her approach.

By noon, they were nearing the outer berm. It looked quite a bit taller from this angle than it had from the air. She stopped on a little hill and surveyed the scene. Her army spread out around her in all directions.

"General Markos, move the infantry and archers into position," she commanded. "Commander Corina, send out the scout riders and prepare the attack wings for launch on my order. Make contact with Admiral Tybalt and Prince Torin. Tell them to attack at will. General Kern, deploy the cavalry on the southern flank and await orders."

Her commanders saluted and left to carry out her instructions, leaving Abigail with Anatoly, Conner, Magda, Wizard Sark, Mage Dax, and Knight Raja. Captain Sava's Strikers surrounded them as the soldiers began moving into position.

Abigail expected the enemy to react ... but they didn't. Instead, they held their position inside the berm wall and waited as their slaves worked furiously to load the lumber necessary to complete the construction of the remaining ships.

She waited with the outward appearance of patience, though she was anything but patient within. The battle would begin on her command, but she had to wait for her men to move into position first. It was a painstaking hour before the infantry had advanced to within a hundred feet of the berm wall and formed a shield line. Behind them were several rows of pikemen backed up by another ten ranks of infantry. Next came row after row of archers armed with longbows. Abigail had been careful to ensure that they had plenty of arrows—her plan depended on it. A heavy rope soaked in oil was laid out before each rank.

Once all was in place, she double-checked everyone's position and nodded to herself. It was time. She withdrew the arrow from her quiver, yellow feathers standing out in stark contrast to the grey-and-white fletching of her other arrows. She nocked the arrow and drew, aiming into the sky. When she released it into the air, a piercing shriek rose into the clear sky, alerting all for miles around that the battle had begun.

Things moved slowly at first. The ropes before each rank of archers were ignited, providing a source of flame for their arrows. Each archer nocked an arrow, touched it to the rope and raised the flaming point toward the sky. The first volley lifted into the air, trailing smoke and embers in its wake. Before it reached the apex of its trajectory, a second volley was away.

Abigail meant to kill the enemy with flame and arrows. If she could destroy them without ever crossing blades, then so much the better. It didn't matter how they died, only that they did. Another volley of arrows rose into the air as the first volley ripped into the enemy encampment. Horns blew in warning. Shouting rose above the screams.

The enemy's few ballistae and catapults began to fire into Abigail's army. The weapons were powerful but they were too few to cause significant damage—unless you happened to be the unfortunate man who got hit with a small boulder or large spear-sized ballista bolt.

After ten volleys of arrows, the attack wings flew overhead in formation, heading for the ships still berthed in the shipyard. Fifty Sky Knights joined the battle, armed with firepots and tasked with burning the shipyards and Zuhl's ships before they could launch.

The enemy didn't appear to be putting up much of a fight, which was fine with Abigail. As she watched the arrows rain down on them and the fires begin to build, she started to get the feeling that it was all too easy.

That's when she saw the dragon.

Chapter 29

Alexander took Isabel by the shoulders and peered into her piercing green eyes with his magical vision. Her colors had changed. There was still a slight taint but the growing, festering darkness in her colors that had been keeping him up at night was gone.

"What about the darkness?" he asked.

"It's gone," Isabel whispered. "Dear Maker, Alexander, I didn't realize how much it had worked its way into me until just now. Azugorath's magic must not be able to reach into the Wizard's Den."

"Makes sense," Alexander said. "Shivini wouldn't have remained trapped if there was a connection between the outside world and a Wizard's Den."

"What happens when you open the door?" Isabel asked.

"I don't know," Alexander said, "but I suspect the wraith queen will be attracted to the taint infecting your magic."

"I didn't even realize how loud the voices were," Isabel said. "I've been trying so hard to ignore them. Now that they're gone ..."

Alexander waited as she stared off into the distance, lost in thought.

"I don't think I can resist for much longer," Isabel said. "I'm terrified that I'm going to betray you."

"I don't believe that you will ever betray me," Alexander said. "I know your soul. If Azugorath influences you to act against me, it won't be you making that choice."

"But what if I hurt you? Or worse?" Isabel said.

"You won't," Alexander said. "I'll see the danger before you succumb to the wraith queen's will. If worse comes to worse, we can always use the Wizard's Den to shield you."

"I'm not sure that would be wise," Jack said, "at least not until you have a chance to empty this place out and refurnish it."

Alexander looked at the bard and then at the bookshelf he was staring at intently. It was a finely crafted cherrywood case with glass doors. The books within were all magical tomes, but the thing that made Alexander's blood run cold were the dark colors emanating from most of the volumes.

They were books of necromancy.

Alexander carefully looked around the rest of the room. A number of other items radiated colors that indicated magic.

"You might be right," he said. "There are quite a few magical things in here and there's no telling what any of them do. If Malachi left that smoke demon in here, he might have left other deadly things, as well. Let's not touch anything over there." He motioned toward the desk and bookshelves. "The table and chairs look safe enough."

Hector opened the door on the wall opposite the entrance and wandered out onto a balcony. "Curious," he said.

Alexander joined him. The balcony was about ten feet wide, jutting six feet from the doorway with a four-foot-high wall. It opened into a luminous fog that was neither warm nor cold. With a frown, Alexander went to the hearth and found a piece of charred wood. Stepping up to the railing, he tossed the wood into the fog. It fell out of sight without a sound. Everyone waited for several moments for any hint of noise but there was nothing.

"I think I need to talk with the sovereigns about this place," Alexander said, returning to the main room, "especially Malachi."

"Any idea how long we need to stay in here?" Jack asked.

"At least several hours," Chloe said. "Selaphiel tore the world open. He and the demons will be drawn into the aether and then to the netherworld and the realm of light. The rift will heal naturally within a few hours but it isn't safe until then."

"Do you think he managed to banish Jinzeri?" Isabel asked.

"Probably," Chloe said. "A rift to the aether draws creatures from the light or dark into it. Without the Wizard's Den to take refuge in, I would have been drawn in as well."

"If that's true, then Rankosi is all that's left," Alexander said, turning to Isabel. "I've been thinking about that. Phane said the shades would be banished if you were killed."

Isabel nodded. Alexander could see the flare of guilt in her colors. She still blamed herself for freeing them into the world.

"I wonder if it works the other way around, too," he said. "If we get rid of all three shades, maybe the passage to the netherworld within your mind will close."

She blinked a few times as the possibility sank in. "Do you really think?"

Alexander shrugged. "We can hope. I'm not sure if Phane was telling the truth about that, though. He may have just been trying to dupe me into killing you," Alexander said, drawing her into his arms. "He's obviously never been in love."

"That will be his undoing," Isabel said with a gentle smile as she looked into his eyes.

"That would be fitting," Alexander said, letting her go with a wink. "While we wait, I think I should try to get some answers."

He went to the hearth and found a cold piece of charred wood. After surveying the room for a moment, he pushed the table out of the center and started drawing a magic circle on the stone floor.

"Do you think your clairvoyance will work in here?" Jack asked.

"Yes, but I doubt I can see anything outside the Wizard's Den," Alexander said. Once he finished with the circle, he took a cushion off one of the chairs and placed it in the center.

"I'm going to have a chat with Malachi," he said. "The rest of you should try to get some rest. We have a lot of ground to cover."

Chloe floated over and landed on his knee as he sat down and closed his eyes.

"I will watch over you while you're away, My Love."

"Thank you, Little One."

He touched the Stone and abruptly found himself in the Reishi Council Chamber. He took his seat and fixed Malachi with a hard look.

"Why was there a demon in the Wizard's Den?" he asked.

Malachi scowled. "How could you have bested such a beast? You should be dead."

"I didn't best it. Selaphiel did," Alexander said. "The Wizard's Den opened while we were talking to him."

Malachi spat in disgust, shaking his head. "Pure dumb luck," he said.

"Why was it in there?" Alexander asked again.

"I was afraid Phane might kill me," Malachi said with a shrug.

"How lonely your last years must have been, my son," Demetrius said. "You are such a disappointment. Had you obeyed the Old law and taught your son right from wrong, you would've had nothing to fear."

"Bah," Malachi said to his father.

"What else did you leave in there for Phane?" Alexander asked.

"Everything," Malachi said.

"Is there anything else in the Wizard's Den that's deadly?" Alexander asked.

"Yes," Malachi said with a contemptuous smile.

Alexander glared at him as he formulated his next question. "Are there any magical items within the Wizard's Den that are designed to harm those who use them?"

"Yes," Malachi said, his smile turning to a sneer.

"Which items?"

"The book on the top shelf, third from the right," Malachi said. "Also the onyx sphere on the desk."

"What does the book do?"

"If you read a single word of it, your soul will be instantly drawn through the book into the netherworld," Malachi said.

"And the onyx sphere?"

"If you gaze into it, your mind will become lost in the firmament," Malachi said.

Alexander nodded, appraising the Sixth Sovereign. "Did you really hate your son so much?"

"Not at all, but his ambitions were obvious," Malachi said. "He murdered all of my other children to ensure that he would inherit the Stone. Such ambition is rarely patient."

"Which book contains a banishing spell?" Alexander asked.

"Second shelf from the top, fourth book from the left," Malachi said.

"Is that the only one?"

"Of course not," Malachi said.

And so it went for nearly an hour. Alexander asked Malachi a string of questions, narrowing his focus with each until he had a clear picture of the items of danger and importance within the Wizard's Den. He was still not confident that he'd uncovered all of the danger hidden within the magical room by its previous occupant, but he had a better idea of the contents.

Many of the spellbooks detailed the process for summoning specific demons—their appetites and desires, powers and proclivities, weaknesses and temperaments. Each demon was carefully catalogued so that Malachi could summon just the right creature for the task at hand with full knowledge of what it would take to bring the demon forth from the netherworld, what it would take to bind it to service, and what unique abilities it possessed.

Several books contained different versions of banishing spells: some that relied on the realm of light to drive a demon into the aether and then into the netherworld, others that opened a rift in the fabric of the world of time and substance much the same as Selaphiel had, and still others that opened a portal directly to the netherworld that would allow passage in only one direction.

Other tomes contained painstaking records of careful research conducted by Malachi Reishi over the many years of his life. Whatever else he was, he was not stupid. He took the pursuit of knowledge very seriously, and his tomes represented the definitive body of research into the netherworld. No one before or since had explored the darkness as thoroughly as Malachi had. While Alexander was wary of the corrupting influence of such knowledge, he had high hopes that Kelvin and his wizards could use the information to develop new ways of fighting creatures from the netherworld.

A few books contained spells that relied on dark magic but did not involve summoning. One spell caused the one touched to age twenty or more years in the space of seconds, another could bring a recently deceased person back to life for an hour or so, during which time they were bound to serve the caster of the spell. Malachi suggested that this spell was the most effective tool of interrogation he had ever devised.

Several spells were designed strictly for killing. One projected a shaft of darkness that would enshroud the target in a black haze that consumed his life force over a period of several seconds. Another sent a wave of dark force at the enemy that desiccated his body as it passed through him, leaving nothing but a dried husk that crumbled into dust moments later.

One tome in particular gave Alexander chills. It described the process for transforming a living person into an undead creature, still possessed of all knowledge and memory, yet dead and lifeless … an animated corpse that was impossible to kill because it was already dead. Malachi had been researching a perverse form of immortality and he'd been nearly ready to attempt the spell. Had he succeeded, the world surely would have fallen under his dominion and would probably still be under his boot.

There were a number of other items of interest as well.

A sacrificial knife lay on the desk. It was enchanted to ensure that the soul of one killed by the blade would be bound to the will of the person wielding the blade, guaranteeing that the wielder could use the soul as a bargaining chip when summoning a demon. Apparently, in his early years of studying the dark arts, Malachi had encountered a few creatures from the netherworld that were dishonest, stealing the soul of his sacrifice before he could extract his price.

There was a box of six gold rings, each of which allowed the wearer access to the magical protections and capabilities of the Reishi Keep, much the same as the rings Alexander had found in Blackstone Keep.

One of the more useful items was a flagon that poured an endless stream of clean water.

But of all the treasures contained within the Wizard's Den, none compared to the small stone box filled to the brim with Wizard's Dust, enough to create dozens of wizards, enough for several mage fasts, enough to tip the balance of power in Alexander's favor.

Once he had thoroughly grilled Malachi, he turned to the other sovereigns for advice.

"Balthazar, what can you tell me about the Wizard's Den?" Alexander asked.

"It can be opened by you and you alone, and then only when you hold or wear the Stone," Balthazar said. "I added that feature to ensure that you couldn't close the door while the Stone was inside unless you were inside as well. Within the Wizard's Den with the door closed, you are in a world all your own. Nothing outside can reach you; conversely, nothing within can reach outside. Your clairvoyance will not work beyond the walls of the Den as long as the door remains closed. Time does not pass within the Wizard's Den unless there is a living being inside. If you put someone in the Wizard's Den and close the door, they will experience the flow of time as the rest of the world does, but if there are no living beings inside the Den, then time does not pass. Hence, you can leave a plate of steaming hot food on your table, close the door and return days later to find the plate of food still hot and fresh.

"I added the balcony and endless fog for a very specific reason. Some items of magic cannot be destroyed without prohibitively dangerous consequences. The fog exists to give you a place to dispose of such items that is quite beyond anyone's reach. Simply toss the item over the balcony railing and it will fall through the fog for all time; but be certain, because once you cast an item into the fog, it's lost forever.

"The room will remain at a comfortable temperature regardless of conditions outside, provided the door is closed. I added the hearth because fire soothes me and I occasionally like it warmer. As for light, you have no doubt noticed the glowing stones in the ceiling. They are controlled by your will, providing a range of illumination from sunlight bright to total darkness. The fog provides ambient light as well but the door to the balcony will close out any light from beyond if you want total darkness.

"Of all the powers conferred by the Sovereign Stone, the Wizard's Den is one of the most helpful. There are countless uses for such a place and it has served us all well during our service to the Seven Isles."

"Thank you, Balthazar," Alexander said.

Then he proceeded to detail everything that had happened since he last spoke with the council. He told them how he had defeated Shivini and the price he'd paid. He told them about the campaign he was waging against Zuhl's forces on Fellenden and about the invasion of Ruatha by yet more Andalian Lancers. He told them about his journey to the Reishi Isle and his dreams with Rentu. Finally, he told him about the Nether Gate and the vitalwood tree. They listened with interest, absorbing the details and integrating them into their understanding of the state of the world.

"Your move against Zuhl is wise and correct," Balthazar said. "If he's permitted to build a fleet, he will dominate the world through sheer numbers. Your effort to secure one of the keystones of the Nether Gate is also vitally important, though I fear Phane is ahead of you on that score. Securing the nectar of the vitalwood tree is an excellent first step toward defeating Phane's hold on Isabel. What is your next move?"

"I intend to return to Blackstone Keep and clear out the Wizard's Den, have the wizards examine and study everything we find, and refurnish the Den with items that I know won't try to kill me."

"A wise precaution," Balthazar said. "You might suggest to the Guild Mage that he adapt one or more of the banishing spells into enchantment spells so that he can empower weapons to destroy creatures from the netherworld. In that way you can arm yourself directly without having to rely on another wizard to cast a banishing spell for you."

"I hadn't considered that," Alexander said. "I'll definitely suggest it. Also, I plan to ask Kelvin to take the mage's fast with some of the Wizard's Dust we found. I'll need any suggestions you can offer for improving his chances of success."

"Of course," Balthazar said. "Although, I must caution you, properly preparing for the mage's fast is a lengthy process. It will take some time and I suspect the heartstone of the Keep will fail before he's ready to enchant another."

"I know, but there's nothing else I can do about it," Alexander said.

"I suggest you bring the bridge into the world of time and substance before the Keep's magic fails completely or else your people will be trapped," Balthazar said.

"You're probably right," Alexander said.

"Have you given any thought to securing the keystone on Tyr?" Constantine asked. "The Nether Gate is still the greatest threat you face."

Alexander nodded. "Once I'm done at Blackstone, I'm headed for Tyr. I'm hoping that I can reason with the dragon Bragador. If not, things might get more complicated."

"Indeed," Balthazar said. "I would not advise a direct confrontation, especially with her brood nearby. Dragons are exceedingly powerful, especially those that have lived for several centuries. Fortunately, they're also quite intelligent and not beyond reason. If you can convince her of the danger the Nether Gate poses, she might agree to allow you to cast the keystone into the endless fog of the Wizard's Den to permanently eliminate the threat. Although, I expect she will demand a price and probably a costly one."

"I'll pay it," Alexander said. "I have to. One last thing, I might know where the last keystone is. Apparently, Carlyle Fellenden was given an item at the end of the war by Barnabas Cedric. A small box. Could a container be enchanted to prevent divination spells from locating its contents?"

Balthazar nodded. "Yes, of course. If Mage Cedric was unable to destroy the keystone, he would probably have sought to hide it from the world. Such a device could also be keyed to a specific bloodline, much the way the Thinblades are."

"So only someone from the Fellenden line could open it?"

"I'm speculating, but that's what I would have done," Balthazar said.

"Thank you, gentlemen," Alexander said.

With that, he walked away from the table and opened his eyes to find his friends resting quietly while they waited for the chaos outside the Wizard's Den to subside. Chloe smiled at him and flew up to eye level.

"Were they helpful?" Chloe asked.

"Yes, very much so," Alexander said. "There are a number of things over there," he gestured toward the desk and bookshelves, "that are deadly in the extreme. I think we'll wait until the wizards can help us before we start going through Malachi's stuff. There are also a number of things that will help us greatly, maybe even tip the balance of this war in our favor."

Chapter 30

Before Alexander opened the door to the Wizard's Den, he and his friends lined up against the inside wall to either side of the door to protect themselves against the effects of Selaphiel's power. They'd spent several hours resting and waiting until Chloe believed it would be safe.

Alexander braced himself and willed the door to open. With a popping noise, the stylized archway opened to reveal a calm and quiet grotto.

Isabel's scream shattered the still air and sent a thrill of fear racing through Alexander. He whirled to see her slump to her knees with her hands on either side of her head as if she was trying to keep it from flying apart. He knelt before her, helpless and terrified.

Jaws clenched, eyes shut against the world, breathing deliberately through her nose, Isabel struggled to overcome Azugorath's tendrils as they once again bored into her soul. After several moments of struggle, she relaxed and staggered to her feet with Alexander's help.

"The darkness is back," she said weakly as she put her head against his chest and wept.

He held her tenderly as quiet tears streamed down his cheeks. He wanted to tell her that everything was going to be all right, he wanted to banish the darkness within her, he wanted to strike out at Phane for doing this to his love … but he was powerless. So he just held her. She cried for several minutes before mastering her emotions and scrubbing the tears from her face.

"Is there anything I can do?" Alexander whispered.

"You're doing it," she said. "I'm all right now. I just wasn't expecting the darkness to come rushing in so quickly or so forcefully. It's like it was waiting for me and I wasn't ready for it."

"Are you sure you want to go with us?" Alexander asked. "You could stay in the Wizard's Den while we travel."

She shook her head. "Every time you open the door, it's going to be like this. I'm better off keeping my mental defenses up against it than hiding from it. It's a constant struggle, but I can manage to keep it at bay, for now anyway."

Alexander closed his blind eyes in an effort to shut out a reality that he didn't want to face. He was losing Isabel to Phane's vengeance.

Panic and despair threatened to overpower reason.

With an effort of will, he shifted his focus from the problem to the solution. He had succeeded in obtaining the vitalwood nectar he needed for the potion that would heal her. The last ingredient was blood of the earth. Once he had that, she would be saved. As he focused on that thought, a renewed sense of urgency began to build within him. He wished he could tell her about it, but the sovereigns' warning had been emphatic—no one could know about the blood of the earth.

"Are you ready?" he asked.

She nodded with a weak smile.

He cautiously stepped out into the world from his Wizard's Den and surveyed the scene. The vitalwood tree was completely enclosed in a shimmering sphere of magical force. The leaves didn't flutter and the boughs didn't sway in the gentle breeze whirling around the deep mountain valley.

Within the sphere of force that Selaphiel had wrought, time ceased to pass, shielding the tree from any who would do it harm and depriving the world of time and substance of its vital essence.

The lake was almost gone, the water having been sucked up into the vortex. The stone shelf they stood on was scoured clean of sand. Even the small stones that had littered the surface were gone, leaving the shelf bare as if it had been meticulously cleaned.

There was no sign of the smoke demon that Malachi Reishi had left within the Wizard's Den for his wayward son, no sign of Selaphiel who had stood guard over the vitalwood tree for millennia, and no sign of Jinzeri or his host.

"Do you think Selaphiel's rift banished Jinzeri?" Alexander asked Chloe as she orbited his head.

"Almost certainly, My Love. Creatures of the light or the dark can't long resist the pull of a rift in the world. When it opened, Jinzeri was too close to escape."

"What about Truss?" Isabel asked.

"That is harder to know," Chloe said. "Jinzeri may have been pulled from him before he was drawn bodily into the rift. Otherwise, he is lost forever as well."

"If Truss is still out there, I suspect he'll be looking for a way to cause us problems," Alexander said. "Let's stay alert on our way out."

Jack pointed to the muddy slope of the island that had just hours before been submerged and said, "What's that?"

Alexander sent his all around sight to the place where Jack was pointing. There, stuck in the mud, was a branch from the vitalwood tree.

"That's something worth taking with us," Alexander said. With help from Hector and Horace, he climbed down to the water and waded across the lake. The branch was about seven feet long and six inches thick. Alexander could see the powerful colors of the wood as he wiped the mud from it. He put it in the Wizard's Den before wading back across the lake and climbing up to the stone shelf. After he changed into dry clothes, they set out.

By an unspoken agreement, Hector took the lead and Horace brought up the rear. The group slipped back through the crack in the wall, moving slowly through the dark of the caverns by the light of their night-wisp dust, always wary of the glow worms and always alert for the passage or presence of Rexius Truss.

When they reached the chamber that held the Nether Gate, Hector knelt to examine the ground.

"This is odd," he said. "A set of tracks leads into this chamber but then the same set leads right back out."

Alexander chuckled, motioning toward the stone wall conjured by the dead wizard. "Looks like Truss is alive … and trapped," he said. "Let's make sure he never gets out of this place."

"That is a terrible way to die, My Love," Chloe said.

"I know," Alexander said with a sigh, "but the important part is that he dies. Truss is a surprisingly resilient little weasel and there's no telling what his experience with Jinzeri has taught him. He may know things that we can't allow Phane to learn. Besides, I still owe him for abducting Isabel."

Chloe came to a stop in her orbit around his head, floating several feet in front of his face.

"This man stole Isabel from you?" she asked.

Alexander nodded. "I got her back from him, though, and put an arrow through his shoulder in the bargain."

"He sounds like a very bad man, My Love."

"He is, Little One. If we had the time, I'd hunt him down and finish him myself, but we have more pressing concerns right now."

She nodded and flew to the stone wall, buzzing into a ball of light and vanishing into the aether, taking the wall with her. Once they filed past, she returned to the world of time and substance, returning the wall with her and sealing the chamber below, trapping Rexius Truss alone in the dark with nothing but the Nether Gate and glow worms to keep him company.

"Jack, can you draw a map of the route we took to get here?" Alexander asked.

"Of course," Jack said, taking his tablet from a pocket. "How much detail would you like?"

"Enough to guide some soldiers back here safely," Alexander said. "Make sure to note the traps we found."

"Not a problem," Jack said as he started drawing.

They retraced their path to the entrance of the hidden fortress, stopping occasionally to allow Jack to add the most recent passages to his map, and carefully peered out into the meadow beyond. Isabel tipped her head back and linked her mind with Slyder, who had been waiting for them in the treetops.

"I don't see the beast anywhere," Isabel said, "but Rentu and about twenty of his men are camped on a high stone shelf on the other side of the meadow and they have three pairs of scouts watching the fortress entrance. If they haven't seen us already, they will the moment we step out into the light."

"Then let's give them what they expect," Alexander said. "Little One, I need you to follow the illusion I'm going to project and let me see through your eyes so I can maintain it long enough to lure Rentu away from here. I guess we'll find out the range of Mindbender's magic."

"Of course, My Love," Chloe said before buzzing into a ball of light and vanishing into the aether.

Alexander grasped the hilt of his sword and focused his mind. The world narrowed down to the moment—he was in a fight and he had a sword in his hand. Everything else faded away.

He visualized images of himself and his friends running from the entrance of the ancient fortress across the meadow. It was a bit disorienting at first, seeing himself through Chloe's eyes while she followed his illusion, but within a few moments that too faded into the background.

Rentu's scouts called out an alarm, and the hunting party started clambering down from their perch atop the stone shelf. Alexander's illusion reached the edge of the meadow and entered a ravine that led in the opposite direction of where he really needed to go. He found that the range of his illusion magic didn't seem to matter, as long as he could see what he was doing. The possibilities were nearly distracting enough to make him lose his focus on the task at hand.

Within a few minutes, the clearing was empty and Alexander was leading his pursuers away into the forest. He maintained the illusion for almost ten minutes to ensure that Rentu and his men would be far enough away that Alexander and his friends could escape and gain a significant lead.

Through Chloe's eyes, he saw a small cave entrance in the side of a rocky outcropping and sent his illusion into the cave, waiting just long enough for the lead men in Rentu's hunting party to see them enter.

"That ought to do it," he said, drawing his awareness back from Chloe and asking her to return to him. "We should have a good twenty minutes head start."

They left the cave quickly, looking this way and that for any sign of a scout left behind just in case, but saw nothing save the wild mountains. Within an hour, they were making headway through the dense forest, traveling in the general direction of the Reishi Keep.

Slyder flew from treetop to treetop keeping watch for the hunting party, but Isabel reported that they were well behind and still confused by the ruse. Alexander had gained them the time they needed to avoid a confrontation.

They traveled as quickly as they could through the forest of the untamed Reishi Isle, occasionally coming upon a predator, but most were natural creatures, easily commanded by Isabel's magic. The darker creatures that inhabited the island were mostly absent from this area, probably due to the presence of the beast.

Alexander played over the problems he faced as they marched. He had so many threats to deal with that he couldn't seem to focus on one long enough to arrive at a satisfactory solution. Always in the back of his mind was the threat building within Isabel. He reminded himself to focus on the solution lest the problem plunge him into despair.

As a means of distraction, he deliberately returned to his many other problems. Even with the immediate dangers of the Reishi Isle and the more distant, yet all too insistent, dangers of Phane and Zuhl, the shade and the Nether Gate remained the gravest threats to the Seven Isles. Phane had one of the keystones and he knew the location of the Nether Gate itself.

There were still two keystones out there and Alexander knew right where he had to go to find one of them. He'd been trying to avoid thinking about that conversation. He remembered how impossibly powerful Tanis had seemed, aloof and detached from the petty concerns of humanity.

Bragador, no doubt, held similar opinions. If Alexander couldn't persuade her to help him, he wasn't exactly sure how he was going to get the keystone from her. A direct confrontation against one dragon was suicide, never mind a whole mountain full of them. That left stealth and thievery. He wasn't sure if that was acceptable either. He was sworn to the Old Law—its champion and protector. How could he justify stealing the keystone from Bragador?

He puzzled over the dilemma for several days as they made their way toward the relative safety of Commander Perry's regimental encampment around the Reishi Keep. He finally decided that he would have to find another way to stop Phane if Bragador wouldn't help him. He simply couldn't justify stealing the keystone. Bragador hadn't violated the Old Law. She was living in her home, minding her own business and making a deliberate effort to avoid the conflict consuming the Seven Isles. Although Alexander knew she wouldn't be able to avoid it forever, he decided that he had to respect her decision.

He was acutely aware of Isabel's condition as well. She had been mostly silent since they emerged from the Wizard's Den, no doubt struggling with the darkness working to overpower her free will. He wanted to console her, to sweep away the danger, to protect her, yet he felt helpless, helpless in a way that led to despair. When the dull haze of hopelessness descended on him, he struggled to remind himself that he was doing everything within his power to protect her. When that didn't work, he distracted himself with one of his many other problems.

The brief and contentious conversation between Jinzeri and Selaphiel also puzzled him. He played it over in his mind several times in an effort to extract all of the salient facts. He gathered that both Selaphiel and Jinzeri had been present when the vitalwood forest died. From the sounds of it, Jinzeri had played a role in its destruction.

"What can you tell me about the death of the vitalwood forest, Little One?" Alexander asked Chloe silently as they walked.

"It was a very sad time, My Love," she said in his mind. "The death of the vitalwood led to the extinction of many beings that used to inhabit the Seven Isles. For thousands of years the world was home to a wide variety of different creatures, many drawing their vital essence from the realm of light. The vitalwood forest was the conduit through which the Maker shared his life-giving light with the world. When the forest died, many of those creatures could no longer survive. Many died."

"When did it happen?" Alexander asked.

"Several thousand years before I came to the Seven Isles," she said. "It's hard to be more specific because time means less in the realm of light."

"What would happen if the last vitalwood tree were destroyed?"

"It's hard to say for sure, but I believe many of the creatures that rely on the light for sustenance would whither and die."

"Would you die?" he asked.

"No, but my longevity would be diminished," she said. "Fairies have a natural connection to the realm of light that is the source of our long life, but the presence of the vitalwood adds to the light we bring to this world and makes us effectively immortal."

"So that's why so many of the creatures you spoke of died."

"Yes, their life spans were no longer extended by the presence of the life-giving energy of the vitalwood forest. Over the centuries that followed the death of the forest, most perished." She hesitated, as if trying to decide to continue. Alexander waited patiently. "In some ways, the death of the forest brought about the rise of mankind. Humans are short-lived because they are creatures of the world of time and substance with only a very limited connection to both the light and the dark. When the forest was destroyed, there was a sudden die-off of other creatures, which freed up vast space and resources. Humanity flourished."

Alexander thought about everything she had said for as they walked through the forest.

"What would happen to humanity if the vitalwood forest was reborn?"

"That's hard to say," she said, "but I suspect people would live longer, healthier lives with more interest in love and life than power and death. That's why the shades waged a war to destroy the forest. As long as it was present in the world, the darkness couldn't find purchase here."

"So the vitalwood forest eliminates evil?"

"No, evil is a choice, born of free will," Chloe said. "The vitalwood simply encourages us to keep our better nature in mind."

He knew that the potential for evil was a necessary result of free will, but then he remembered how warm and safe he'd felt in the presence of the tree. It was as if he'd found his way back to a home that he never knew he'd lost. He couldn't imagine conceiving an evil thought while in the presence of such life-affirming energy. And it wasn't as though the tree had altered his mind or his thinking so much as it had reminded him of the truth of his nature, reminded him that life is a thing to cherish, that beauty abounds, and that love is worthy of reverence.

He had spent countless hours puzzling over the dilemma of evil and he still wasn't sure he understood it, yet he was all too certain of its existence in the world. It always felt like those who chose evil were missing some piece of essential information. Perhaps the vitalwood could provide it for them.

At dawn of their sixth day of travel, Isabel reported that they were only a few hours from the Keep. They were all tired and anxious for a safe place to sleep without all of the unsettling noises that haunted the night on the Reishi Isle. Alexander had kept the Wizard's Den closed. Even though it would have been a safe place to sleep, he didn't want to subject Isabel to the trauma of the darkness insinuating itself into her over and over again. She was struggling enough as it was. As they broke camp, they heard the roar of the beast from the general direction they were traveling.

Alexander looked to Isabel as she tipped her head back and linked her mind with Slyder. She opened her eyes and pointed off into the forest.

"The beast has Rentu and his men cornered about half a league that way. Looks like they're in trouble."

Alexander sighed, shaking his head. "All right, let's go help them."

He ignored the look Hector and Horace gave each other as he hoisted his pack and set out through the forest.

As they neared a clearing, they could hear grunting and growling intermingled with frightened shouts in an unknown language.

Alexander sent his mind to Chloe as she floated through the aether. When she cleared the treetops, Alexander saw the beast gnawing and clawing at the base of a large tree that Rentu and his men had climbed for refuge. Parts of three men were scattered about at the base of the tree, remnants of the beast's breakfast.

Alexander grasped the hilt of Mindbender and visualized dozens of wild boar racing through the clearing, squealing and snorting as they ran. The beast stopped and spun to face the commotion. It looked torn between Rentu's men and the boar, but then it abandoned the tree and charged into the forest in pursuit of easier prey. After a moment, Rentu and his men clambered to the ground and vanished into the forest. Alexander called Chloe back to him and they set out toward the Keep with haste.

Several minutes later, they heard a roar of frustration somewhere behind them as the beast realized that both of its intended prey had escaped. Alexander picked up the pace. The beast was stupid enough to be deceived but still dangerous in the extreme. He didn't want to risk a confrontation.

They stopped for a moment on a little hill to get their bearings and catch their breath when they heard shouting behind them. Rentu and his men had spotted them and were closing fast. Alexander looked out across the forest at the Reishi Keep looming in the distance and calculated that Rentu would probably catch them before they could reach it. He sent up a whistler arrow to alert Commander Perry, and then they started running. Alexander set a grueling pace. His whistler arrow had alerted everyone and everything, including the beast, to his position. He only hoped Commander Perry would understand and send help in time.

They could hear the primitives racing through the forest behind them, moving through terrain and territory that they were familiar with and accustomed to. They were gaining ground as Alexander and his companions were becoming exhausted and slowing down. It was only a matter of time before they would reach the end of their strength. He slowed the pace, knowing full well that doing so would ensure that Rentu would catch them, yet also knowing that they would need some of their strength for the fight that might result.

They reached the tree line and stepped out into the gently sloping grassland that surrounded the Reishi Keep just as Rentu and twenty of his men emerged not fifty feet away. At the same time, a hundred men on horseback were thundering toward them from the Keep.

Rentu's men spread out, arrows at the ready, but hesitated as the company of soldiers approached. The soldiers fanned out, surrounding both Alexander and Rentu's men. Commander Perry rode through his cordon of men accompanied by Wizard Dinh.

"Lord Reishi, what are your orders?"

"Release these men unharmed and escort us back to your encampment," Alexander said with a sigh of relief.

Commander Perry snapped several orders to his subordinates and they shifted their cordon to surround Alexander and his companions, leaving Rentu and his men looking unsure of what to do next. Rentu started complaining loudly, pleading to be heard and pointing at Isabel. Alexander couldn't understand what he was saying, but he knew what he wanted. He stepped in front of Isabel, shaking his head.

Wizard Dinh dismounted. "Lord Reishi, I can allow you to speak with him if you wish," he said.

Alexander looked at the wizard for a moment, once again struck by wonder at all the possibilities magic had to offer, before nodding his consent.

Wizard Dinh motioned for the soldiers to clear a section of ground and then began muttering a spell. Several moments later the grass flared brightly and burned away to reveal a perfect magic circle drawn in charred lines.

"Both you and he must stand in the circle," Wizard Dinh said.

Alexander nodded, stepping into the circle, then pointing at Rentu and motioning for him to approach. Once Rentu cautiously stepped into the circle, Wizard Dinh began casting another spell.

Alexander felt the familiar tingle of magic race over his skin as the spell took effect.

"You may speak and be understood," Wizard Dinh said.

"Hello, Rentu," Alexander said.

Rentu frowned and cocked his head to the side for a moment before he spoke.

"How is it that I can understand you?" he asked.

"Magic," Alexander said with a smile. "Like the dream, but different."

Rentu thoughtfully nodded his acceptance of the explanation. "Please let us take your wife," he said. "She is a threat to everything. We will keep her safe and care for her well. You can have her back when the threat of darkness passes."

"No," Alexander said firmly. "She's my wife."

"She will betray you," Rentu said. "The dreams don't lie."

"She won't betray me," Alexander said. "The darkness within her may overpower her free will and use her against me, but she will never betray me. More to the point, I won't betray her. She stays with me."

"You risk everything," Rentu said with dismay.

"Perhaps, but the future isn't set," Alexander said. "You said as much yourself—the dreams are only future possibilities."

"But she betrays you in most of the futures we saw," Rentu said.

"I remember," Alexander said, but before he could continue, the beast charged out of the forest several hundred yards from where they stood and roared in fury and triumph.

Alexander's focus narrowed in an instant. He scanned the surroundings for an advantage as the beginnings of a plan formed in his mind. The wall surrounding the Reishi Keep was more than half finished on the side opposite from where they stood.

"I need a horse," Alexander said to Commander Perry.

Perry snapped at the nearest soldier, who dismounted immediately and handed Alexander his reins.

"Stay here and don't let Rentu take Isabel," Alexander said as he mounted.

"Lord Reishi, let us help you," Hector said.

"There's no time," Alexander said as he drew Mindbender and wheeled his horse toward the beast.

First he formed the image of a cliff face running through the open field, creating an illusion of a hundred-foot rock wall behind him but in front of the others. He wanted the beast to see only him. With his illusion in place, he called out to the beast in challenge and turned his horse toward the Reishi Gate. The beast gave chase, bellowing in rage.

Alexander spurred his horse into a wild gallop, charging across the field with all the speed he could muster, but the beast was faster, gaining with each stride. Alexander focused his mind once again on the image of his desired outcome and released his illusion into Mindbender. An area surrounding the beast suddenly went dark. Not the darkness of the netherworld, but the simple darkness of an absence of light. A cloud of magical blackness surrounded the beast and blinded it, causing enough confusion to slow it down, giving Alexander precious distance from his pursuer.

He raced on toward the Gate. The beast broke through the illusionary darkness and renewed its charge, but Alexander had gained the time and distance he needed. He dismounted at a run, stumbling and nearly falling from the momentum, but regaining his balance and racing for the little map of the Seven Isles on the side of the Gate.

He touched the outline of the Isle of Karth. The Gate shimmered for an instant before it opened to a walled courtyard surrounded by a heavily fortified military encampment. Soldiers started shouting and bells started tolling. Alexander ignored them and focused his mind on creating another illusion.

He sent an image of himself through the Gate into Karth, yelling a challenge for the beast, while obscuring his true position. The beast dutifully charged toward the illusion and into the midst of a thousand enemy soldiers hastily making ready to repel an assault. Alexander touched the Gate again and it closed behind the beast.

He was sitting on the edge of the Gate platform, deliberately willing the anxiety and tension of the previous moments away, when his friends rode up.

"Well done, Lord Reishi," Commander Perry said as he dismounted.

"I'll say," Jack said. "Did you send it to Phane or Zuhl?"

"Phane," Alexander said with a chuckle. "I just hope he can't make a pet out of it."

"There is that," Isabel said. "At least it won't be a problem around here anymore."

Chapter 31

After retiring to the command tent for a hasty lunch, Alexander asked Commander Perry for a report on their status.

"The wall is just about halfway complete," Commander Perry said. "I've lost one hundred and twelve men to the Reishi Isle and have sixty-eight men injured. The beasts come in the night, most from the wilds but some from the Keep itself. Since we've fortified our encampment, the number of casualties has diminished greatly, though some of the creatures still manage to penetrate our defenses."

Alexander swallowed hard. He knew the mission to secure the Reishi Keep was going to be hazardous, but he hadn't expected to lose so many men.

"I'm sorry for your losses, Commander. Unfortunately, I'm going to have to ask you to remain and complete your mission. The contents of that Keep may prove to be decisive in the battles to come. I'll send reinforcements and ask Kelvin if he can spare another wizard."

"We'll get the job done," Commander Perry said.

"Maybe we should go in right now and take a look around," Isabel said. "We might find something we could use."

"We might," Alexander said, "but we might just waste time." He shook his head. "We have more pressing matters to attend to right now. As much as I'd like to take a look at the sovereigns' library, we can't spare the time."

"If I may, Lord Reishi," Commander Perry said. "How would you like us to deal with the natives that were pursuing you?"

"With respect and courtesy," Alexander said. "They may prove to be important allies in the near future. They're not bad people … we just have a difference of opinion. After lunch, my companions and I will be returning to Ruatha. Expect reinforcements tomorrow. And Commander, the Nether Gate is on this island and Phane knows it, so be ready for anything."

"Understood, Lord Reishi," Commander Perry said.

Over lunch, they discussed all of the beasts that had attacked them during their time on the Reishi Isle. Alexander listened carefully and offered suggestions for combating the creatures that he'd fought in the past. He had expected to hear about the tentacle demon, but much to his relief, it hadn't ventured forth from the Keep.

Commander Perry had fought gorledons, nether wolves, and ganglings, as well as a number of other things that they had no names for. His men had done well in the face of all they'd encountered, but they'd also paid a heavy price.

When he was ready to leave for Ruatha, Alexander asked Wizard Dinh to cast his translation spell again so he could speak with Rentu before he left. After a contentious discussion, Rentu agreed to help Commander Perry and his men. Rentu was adamant that Isabel should remain with them, but Alexander flatly refused. Aside from that point of disagreement, they were able to come to an understanding. Both wanted the same outcome, they just disagreed on the best way to get there, and Rentu had to admit, he was grateful that the beast was gone.

***

Alexander stepped through the Gate to a cold and rainy day on Ruatha. The Rangers guarding the Gate stood down immediately when they saw him, and the Lieutenant in command of the hundred-man guard force saluted crisply.

"Welcome home, Lord Reishi," he said.

"Thank you, Lieutenant," Alexander said. "We need horses."

"Right away," the lieutenant said.

Some time later they were approaching the bridge leading across the chasm to Blackstone Keep's paddock. The fact that the bridge was present in the world of time and substance was a reminder that the Keep's magic was failing. One more problem that Alexander didn't have the time or power to address at the moment. He added it to his mental list of the things he needed to do before they departed for Tyr in the morning.

When they reached the paddock, a horn sounded from one of the platforms above, signaling their arrival. As they were approaching the entrance to the Keep, Bella and Emma came out to great them.

"It's so good to see you both," Bella said, hugging Alexander and Isabel in turn.

"With everyone gone, we have nothing to do but fret over you all," Emma said. "Come inside out of the cold and have something to eat."

Alexander and Isabel shared a smile as they followed their mothers. Adele was waiting for them in their quarters. Their friends had all gone to their own quarters to get cleaned up.

"Welcome home, Lord Reishi," Adele said with a bright smile. "I've stoked your fire and have water boiling for tea."

"Thank you, Adele," Alexander said. "We'll be leaving again tomorrow, so I'd like to have dinner with family tonight. Also, I have an important task for you. I'm going to need furnishings for a large room, about fifty feet square. I'll need a double bed, five single beds, a desk, table and chairs for six, another six comfortable chairs, a sitting-room table, bookshelves, two barrels of water, enough travel food to feed six for a month, a footlocker, an armoire, and enough firewood for a month."

She frowned, a bit confused, but said, "I'll see to it personally."

Alexander nodded with a smile and willed the door to the Wizard's Den to open. With a pop, the chamber outside of the world of time and substance stood open before them. Adele stared in disbelief and shook her head.

"That is truly astonishing, Lord Reishi," she said. "If I may ask, many of the furnishings in your magical room look quite nice. Why don't you use them?"

"Everything in that room belonged to Malachi Reishi and I don't trust anything he ever touched," Alexander said. "As soon as I get cleaned up, I'm going to have the wizards help me clear everything out of this room and then I'm going to clean it from top to bottom."

"Very good, Lord Reishi," Adele said. "I'll have everything you asked for by this evening."

"Thank you, Adele," Alexander said as he headed for his washroom to draw a bath.

***

"I'll be with the wizards for a few hours," Alexander said. "Why don't you see if you can find Wren and invite her to dinner?"

"Are you sure you don't need some help?" Isabel asked.

Alexander smiled, shaking his head. "We'll just be moving furniture. Get some rest. I'm sure Wren would love to hear all about the Reishi Isle."

"You're right about that," Isabel said. "She loves stories, and I would like to see her."

"It's settled then," Alexander said. "I'll see you at dinner." He kissed her goodbye and headed for the Hall of Magic. Alexander loved Isabel with all his heart but he didn't trust the darkness that Phane was using against her. He had a contingency plan in mind for dealing with the Nether Gate but it hinged on secrecy. He knew Isabel would never betray him of her own free will, but he also knew that she might not have a choice in the matter. It hurt him to keep things from her, but the stakes were just too high.

Jataan P'Tal was waiting for him at the archway leading to the Hall of Magic. He sat in a hard-backed chair, looking uncomfortable. When Alexander rounded the corner he stood with some effort and the assistance of a cane.

"Lord Reishi, Hector and Horace reported your return," he said. "Can I be of assistance?"

"Shouldn't you be in bed?" Alexander asked.

Jataan's brow twitched. "Perhaps, but I grow weary of resting while others struggle against your enemies."

"You won't do anyone any good if you reopen your wounds," Alexander said.

"So Mistress Lita tells me … frequently," Jataan said. "I'm taking appropriate precautions to ensure that I heal as quickly as possible, but I would very much like to accompany you this afternoon, if you will permit it."

"Of course, Jataan, just take it easy, all right?"

"As you wish."

On their way to Kelvin's workshop, Alexander stopped at Lucky's laboratory and stuck his head in the door. The place was in a state of orderly disarray, every surface covered with something, from books, to glassware, to a sheet pan of steaming biscuits. Lucky was busy setting up a complex network of glass beakers, tubes, and basins.

"Hi, Lucky," Alexander said with a broad smile.

"Ah, my boy," Lucky said. "Are you hungry? I have some fresh biscuits. I'll pour you a cup of tea and you can tell me all about your adventures."

"I'm afraid I don't have time at the moment," Alexander said with an apologetic smile. "I was just headed to see Kelvin. If your work can wait, I have something to show you."

"Always in a hurry," Lucky said with a sigh. "Well, let's go then. Does your mother know you're home? She tries not to let it show but she worries about you and your sister … and your father. In some ways, I think it's harder being here where it's safe while you're out there in danger."

"I know what you mean," Alexander said. "I looked in on Abigail a week ago. She was moving toward the shipyards as planned."

"Glad to hear it," Lucky said.

Kelvin was busy at work, directing a crew of nearly twenty craftsmen and a few wizards. His expansive workshop was bustling with activity as he choreographed half a dozen projects. Alexander smiled at the sight. The big mage was in his element and he looked like he loved it. Kelvin stopped abruptly when he noticed Alexander standing just inside the doorway and issued a few quick orders to his chief assistants before winding his way through the forges and worktables to greet him.

"You're back sooner than I expected," he said.

"We'll be leaving again tomorrow," Alexander said, "but I needed to talk to you first."

Kelvin nodded and motioned to the door of his office. Once inside with the door closed, Alexander willed the door to the Wizard's Den open. All three men stared in shock for a moment before Lucky and Kelvin began to chuckle.

"Please step inside," Alexander said.

Once they were all inside, he closed the door and took a seat at the table.

"Malachi Reishi left us some very useful, and dangerous, gifts," Alexander said. "There are a number of items in particular that I wanted to talk to you about. Then I want to remove everything and refurnish the place so we can use it without fear of activating some trap or other."

"Why would Malachi Reishi have left traps within his own Wizard's Den?" Jataan asked.

"Apparently, he was afraid that Phane was planning to kill him," Alexander said. "A lot's happened since we left." He proceeded to report everything that had transpired on the Reishi Isle: the encounter with Rentu, the fight with Phane's agents, the loss of the keystone, the encounter with Selaphiel and the smoke demon, their narrow escape from the beast, and the effect that the Wizard's Den had on Isabel.

"Sounds like you had a busy trip," Lucky said. "Is Isabel all right?"

"I don't know," Alexander said. "She's strong, but the darkness is gaining a foothold within her. That's one reason we're having this conversation in private. What we discuss in this chamber must remain secret. I have a contingency plan for the Nether Gate but I need your help, Kelvin."

"Anything within my power," Kelvin said.

"I need one of your smaller explosive weapons," Alexander said. "I'm going to send reinforcements to Commander Perry tomorrow before we leave for Tyr and I want to send one of your wizards along as well. Only the wizard you select can know his true mission."

"Very well," Kelvin said. "What's your plan?"

"I want the wizard to bury the weapon in the chamber with the Nether Gate," Alexander said. "If all else fails, we can destroy the chamber and bury the Gate under tons of stone. Who knows? We might even be able to lure Phane into a trap."

"I have just the man for the job," Kelvin said. "And I'll ensure that the wagon carrying the weapon looks like nothing more than supplies for the soldiers."

"Good," Alexander said. "Prepare the weapon and give me the activation stone in a protected container. Hopefully, we can get the keystone from Bragador, but if we can't, I want to have a backup plan."

"A wise precaution," Kelvin said. He looked over at the desk and bookshelves. "Have you consulted the sovereigns about these items?"

"I have," Alexander said, "and that's another reason I came straight back here." He got up and retrieved the little stone box full of Wizard's Dust and set it on the table. Holding his breath, he carefully lifted the lid.

All three men stared speechlessly at the treasure until Lucky began to chuckle.

"That may be the most beautiful thing I've ever seen," he said.

"There's enough there for dozens of wizards," Kelvin said. "More than enough for every apprentice we have who's ready for the trials."

"Probably enough for all of Ithilian's apprentices as well," Lucky said.

"It's also enough for the mage's fast," Alexander said.

Kelvin nodded slowly. Alexander saw the flare of anxiety within his colors. The mage's fast hadn't been attempted in centuries, and for good reason.

"I don't want to rush you, Kelvin, but the Keep's magic is failing," Alexander said.

"You're right, of course," Kelvin said. "I will begin making preparations for the fast immediately, although it will be some time before I'm ready."

"I understand completely," Alexander said. "I'll consult the sovereigns tonight and ask them for their guidance in the matter. With their help, I believe you have a very good chance of surviving. How would you recommend we use the rest?"

"I could use a small portion for enchantments," Kelvin said, "and I suspect that Lucky could use some for his potions, but the rest should be used for the mana fast. Ultimately, adding to the ranks of our wizards and witches will prove most valuable."

"Set aside enough for the mage's fast and as much as you each need for your work," Alexander said. "Portion out the rest into vials sufficient for a single mana fast each. We'll divide them up between your guild, the wizards on Ithilian, and the Reishi Coven."

"Lord Reishi," Jataan said. "There are also a number of promising candidates in the Reishi Protectorate on Tyr. We have always maintained a training academy for wizards and are ever on the lookout for caches of Wizard's Dust."

"All right," Alexander said. "I'll take a few vials with me and give them to the Reishi Protectorate once I'm satisfied they intend to stand against Phane."

"I assure you that they will bow to your authority," Jataan said. "Once they see the Sovereign Stone, their loyalty will be absolute. I'll also write a letter in case they need more convincing."

"I hope you're right," Alexander said. "There are a few other matters we need to discuss."

One by one, Alexander selected items from the shelves and the desk, placing each on the table in front of him. He selected the book that had been spelled to draw the mind of any reader into the netherworld, the onyx sphere that would scatter a wizard's mind into the firmament, the sacrificial knife, and the flagon of endless water.

"I need a secure container for these three items," Alexander said, motioning to the book, the onyx orb, and the knife. He spent a few moments explaining the workings of each.

"We might wrap a ribbon around that book and send it to Phane as a gift," Lucky said.

"I would if I thought he was stupid enough to actually read it," Alexander said. "The only way that might work is if he really has to work to get it from us. He'd have to believe it's something other that what it actually is, and I have an idea about that, but it'll take some doing."

Alexander selected another book from the shelf.

"This book is truly terrifying, and it just might be enticing enough to draw Phane out. It details the process for transferring your soul into a specially prepared object while you still live, effectively killing your body, yet making you immortal at the same time. As I understand it, a wizard that undergoes this process can't be killed except by destroying the item imbued with his soul. Malachi was very close to attempting the spell when he was killed. Had he succeeded, he'd probably still be ruling the Seven Isles."

"That is such a disturbing concept it makes my skin crawl," Kelvin said. "But I think you might be right. If knowledge of this book made its way to Phane through just the right channels, he might take action to secure it for himself. Once he had it, he would trust no one with it. It might be just the ruse we need to ensure that he reads from this book instead." Kelvin tapped the cover of the cursed book to punctuate his remarks.

"My thoughts exactly," Alexander said. "For the time being, I don't want to take these items out of the Wizard's Den, but the rest of these books might be extremely valuable. A number of them are filled with research into the netherworld, several contain summoning spells, a few detail very dangerous destructive spells that call on the darkness, and most importantly, a handful include banishing spells. The sovereigns suggested that you might be able to adapt the magic of the banishing spells into enchantments so we could arm our forces against Phane's summoned minions."

Kelvin's eyes lit up. "I believe the sovereigns might be right. It will take some time and study, but I'm certain I can adapt the spells, provided they work in the first place. Speaking of books, we've been studying the four volumes you retrieved from Benesh Reishi's tomb.

"Wizard Hax has discovered that the crystal chamber was not created just for the purpose of magnifying a wizard's connection to the firmament. Apparently, it was a necessary element in the creation of Mindbender. In essence, the crystal chamber is the central part of a very powerful spell capable of stripping a wizard of his connection to the firmament and transferring it to an item. Benesh Reishi used this spell to transfer his link to Mindbender and came to believe that it could also be used to strip a typical wizard of his magic, though with very similar consequences.

"As for the magnifying effects of the chamber, I can confirm that they are indeed powerful but not sufficient to increase my magic to the level of an arch mage. I've made three attempts to create a device capable of trapping a shade and failed on all three attempts, although in each case I've learned a great deal. I'm confident that I will succeed once I've survived the mage's fast."

"Good," Alexander said. "One last thing." He retrieved the branch from the vitalwood tree and placed it reverently on the table. "This limb came from the vitalwood tree. The sovereigns tell me that it has the potential to be made into a very potent magical staff."

Kelvin lifted it carefully and examined it as a smile grew on his face. "I believe they're right," he said.

"Use your best judgment," Alexander said. "The vitalwood is a thing of beauty and power; it's only fitting that a staff made from its branches be worthy of it."

"I already have an idea in mind," Kelvin said. "It will take some study and testing, but I think you will be pleased with the result."

"All right," Alexander said, "let's find a chamber where we can empty this place out. And I'd like a strong lockbox for these more dangerous items."

They relocated to a room reserved for summoning and went to work with the help of several of Kelvin's aides. It took more than an hour to empty the entire Wizard's Den of everything save the strongbox with the items too dangerous to remove. After they were finished, they scoured the room clean.

Chapter 32

Kelvin and his wizards immediately went to work studying the books that Malachi Reishi had stored away from the world, while Alexander headed back to his chambers with Jataan following dutifully yet slowly behind. When they arrived, they found Mistress Lita standing at the door as if she had been waiting for them.

"I thought I might find you here," she said. "How many times have I told you to stay off your feet?"

Jataan sighed, "Several times too many, Mistress Lita."

"You aren't going to heal if you push yourself too much," she said. "You need bed rest."

"I need something useful to do," he said.

"Healing is useful!"

Alexander got the impression that they'd had this argument before.

"We were just going to have dinner," Alexander said. "Why don't you join us, Mistress Lita? That way you can keep an eye on your patient."

"Thank you, Lord Reishi," Lita said. "Someone has to keep him from tearing his wounds open again. The Maker knows he'll never heal if he keeps this up."

Alexander opened the door to a room full of people. Isabel was talking with Bella, Erik, and her mother, filling them in on the details of their recent journey. Jack sat by the fire sipping a cup of tea, adding details here and there. Wren sat quietly in an overstuffed chair, listening intently and looking like she was trying to not be noticed, lest someone send her on an errand.

Alexander found a chair as his mother poured him a cup of tea, adding cream and honey, just the way he liked it. He smiled his thanks as he took the steaming cup.

Lita ushered Jataan to a comfortable chair and tried to help him sit, but he managed on his own with a grimace which was met by a reproving scowl from Lita. He ignored her.

"Isabel was just telling us how you sent Phane a rather unpleasant gift," Bella said.

"I hope he likes it," Alexander said with a mischievous grin. "I've just come from a meeting with Kelvin. He's pretty excited about the contents of the Wizard's Den. His wizards went right to work studying the spellbooks we found, and Lucky is busy measuring out the Wizard's Dust as we speak. He should be here in a few minutes."

"Isabel tells us that you're planning to leave again tomorrow," Emma said.

"Yes. We're headed to Tyr to ask Bragador for the keystone. Once we destroy it, we'll be in a good position to start working on an attack strategy."

"Are you sure this potion you're collecting ingredients for will help my daughter?" Emma asked, worry etched in every line of her face.

Alexander took a deep breath and sighed. "As sure as I can be," he said. "The sovereigns have more knowledge of magic than anyone alive. Besides, the only alternative is simply beyond me at the moment. Even if Kelvin can fashion a weapon capable of banishing a demon, the wraith queen is too well defended to reach."

"It'll work, Mom," Isabel said.

"It has to," Wren whispered.

"Any news from Buckwold?" Alexander asked.

"I received a letter from your father yesterday," Bella said. "Apparently, the Lancers are content to hold Warrenton while they build their strength. For now, anyway. Although, the way your father tells it, Mistress Constance is making that very difficult. She has three wings of Sky Knights flying constant patrols and making attack runs against any ship that even tries to sail up the east coast.

"Phane has resorted to using only a handful of his biggest transport ships protected by wizards to move his troops into port. Lancers are still getting through, but far less than before.

"Your father is busy building a berm wall and a ditch across the entire southern border of Buckwold. His soldiers are working night and day, even though the Lancers don't seem to be in a hurry to begin their attack."

"Hopefully, they'll stay put through winter," Alexander said. "At least that would buy us some time."

"Any word from Kevin or Duane?" Isabel asked.

"The last letter I got from Kevin reminded me of your father in his early years as Forest Warden," Emma said. "He sounds exasperated by the nobles and totally immersed in his job. He and General Talia are working closely together to ensure that the south and west coasts are well patrolled and defended. His shipyards are working ceaselessly to build those attack boats he designed, while the rest of Southport is busy sending timber and food to help the people of Kai'Gorn. Talia kept one squad of Sky Knights under his command to run messages so they can coordinate the defense of the south more quickly.

"As for Duane, he sounds bored. Rake and his legion are dug in deep and don't appear to be going anywhere soon. He did mention that they seem to be looking for something in the mountains. He's managed to get a few spies into Rake's camp and they report a systematic effort to find something that's supposed to be buried there from the time of the Reishi War, though no one can say what it is."

"That's unsettling," Jack said.

"If he's looking for something in the northern wilds, it's a good bet Phane told him to," Alexander said. "Maybe I'd better take a closer look."

"Couldn't hurt," Isabel said. "The last thing we need right now is for Rake to come riding down out of those mountains with some ancient weapon."

"It's always something," Alexander said. "But at the moment, he's the least of our worries. Jataan, how are your teams coming along?"

"I have three assembled and ready for assignments," Jataan said. "Each team is comprised of uniquely skilled individuals, each complementing the skills of the other members."

"Good work," Alexander said. "I want to send one team to my father, one to Abigail, and one to Duane. Instruct the one you send to Duane to infiltrate

Rake's camp, determine what he's looking for, and then kill Rake and his inner circle."

"That's such nasty business, Alexander," Bella said.

"I agree, but it has to be done. Whatever Rake is looking for could be a serious threat, and he's already forfeited his life under the Old Law." Alexander turned back to Jataan. "Is one of your teams capable of such a mission?"

"Yes," Jataan said. "Do you have instructions for the other two teams?"

"No, I just want to give my dad and Abigail more options," Alexander said. "Have them all ready to leave in the morning."

"Yes, Lord Reishi," Jataan said and started to get up, using his cane for support.

Lita sprang to her feet and scowled at him so intently that he sat back down. It was all Alexander could do to keep from laughing.

"You stay right there," she said. "I'll send for a messenger to relay your orders."

Jataan clenched his jaw but said nothing until she turned and went to the door to speak with a Ranger standing guard in the hallway.

"There must be some way that I can come with you tomorrow, Lord Reishi," Jataan said.

"Not until your wound is healed," Alexander said. "I know this is difficult, Jataan, but I need you to get better and that won't happen if you push yourself too hard."

"As you wish, Lord Reishi."

"How are you feeling?" Alexander asked. "It looks like you're making progress."

"I'm much better than I was, yet not nearly well enough," Jataan said. "I grow weary of resting, but Mistress Lita is most vigilant. I'm finding it more and more difficult to elude her."

"Let her help you," Alexander said. "You'll heal faster."

"How are things going here, Erik?" Isabel asked her brother.

"Well enough," Erik said. "Since most of the refugees have returned to New Ruatha, it's almost mundane around here. The wizards keep to themselves and stay busy with whatever it is they do. I spend most of my time coordinating the flow of information and supplies. We haven't had any threats since you got rid of the shade."

"Good," Alexander said, then turned to Wren with a smile. "And how are you doing? Do you like it here?"

She nodded earnestly, her big eyes sparkling with excitement. "Master Owen is teaching me to sing. I never imagined there was so much to learn, but he says I have natural talent, and I love it so much. I just have to get over my fear of singing in front of other people. I'm also learning how to fight with a knife," she admitted timidly.

"I'm glad to hear it," Alexander said. "People should be able to defend themselves."

"Your mother suggested it," Wren said. "After the shade beat me up, she helped me understand that I didn't have to be afraid—I could take my safety into my own hands."

"Good advice," Alexander said with a gentle smile for his mother.

"Who's your teacher?"

"Commander P'Tal," Wren said. "He leads a class in knife fighting for anyone who wants instruction. Mistress Lita makes him lecture from a chair while his assistants demonstrate the techniques. I'm not very good, but I'm getting better."

"Your capability with a blade is quite good for one with so little experience in the art," Jataan said.

Wren blushed at the praise and the sudden realization that she was the center of attention. Adele saved her by announcing that dinner was served.

Lucky bustled through the door not a moment later. "Ah, looks like I'm right on time," he said with an unabashed smile.

They spent dinner talking of little things, avoiding the more important topics in favor of enjoying the time they had with their friends and families. All too soon the meal was over and Alexander still had things to do. With a sigh he pushed away from the table.

"Adele, that was wonderful. Thank you, and give my compliments to the chef," Alexander said. "I wish I had more time to sit and enjoy the evening, but I still have some preparations to make before tomorrow."

"Of course, Lord Reishi," Adele said. "I have the items you requested in a room down the hall. I took the liberty of selecting a number of each so that you could choose those that best suit your needs."

"Outstanding. Let's start there," Alexander said.

They spent the rest of the evening moving furniture into the Wizard's Den. Six beds lined the left wall with a footlocker at the end of each. A sturdy and functional table sat in the center of the room with six high-backed chairs. Another six comfortable chairs faced the hearth in a semicircle with a low table in front of them. A desk and a bookshelf occupied the far right corner along with a secure lockbox. Two barrels of clean water, a month's worth of food for six and an ample supply of firewood filled the right corner just beside the entrance. In the left corner of the room, next to the entrance, was a low round table with a magic circle inlaid in gold.

At one point, Lucky pulled Alexander aside to report that he had measured out Wizard's Dust for thirty-seven mana fasts in addition to the quantity set aside for Kelvin to take the mage's fast. Alexander instructed him to distribute fourteen to the Ruathan Wizards Guild, ten to the Ithilian Guild, ten to the Reishi Coven and three to the Reishi Protectorate. With that task complete, he and Isabel returned to their quarters. Before bed, Alexander went to his meditation chamber.

First he went into the Sovereign Stone and gave the sovereigns a full report of all that had transpired since last he spoke with them. He asked them to help him guide Kelvin in preparation for the mage's fast and they were only too happy to provide him with several exercises that would expand Kelvin's ability to emotionally detach and maintain a firm grip on reality even in the face of the limitless possibility the firmament represented.

Next he slipped into the firmament. He focused on Jinzeri but was unable to find the shade. He'd suspected that Selaphiel had banished Jinzeri along with the smoke demon but he'd wanted confirmation. That left only Rankosi to contend with. While still dangerous in the extreme, one shade was far better than three.

Then he thought of his sister and found her encamped half a day from

Zuhl's shipyard, making preparations for battle. She seemed determined and focused. He watched her for a while, not to second-guess her decisions, but simply because he missed her.

Satisfied that she was well and that her mission was progressing, he slipped back into the firmament and coalesced his awareness over the northern wilds in Ruatha. After a minute or two of searching, he found Elred Rake's encampment. His men were dug into a box canyon with impassible mountains on three sides and a narrow ravine for the only entrance. They appeared to be reasonably well supplied and were building fortifications and makeshift barracks. Apparently, Rake intended to stay where he was for the winter. Further searching led him to the network of caves where Rake's men were making a systematic effort to find something within the mountain.

Unfortunately for them they didn't have Alexander's magical sight.

He started moving his awareness through the stone of the mountain in a grid pattern, looking for whatever it was that they were searching for. After almost an hour, he found it, nearly losing his connection to the firmament when he did.

It was the third Bloodvault.

And it was deep underground.

From the looks of Rake's progress, it would take him all winter to find the chamber and then he would discover that he couldn't get inside anyway. Alexander decided to leave him to it. Might as well have his enemies do the hard work for him. Once Rake reached the chamber, Alexander could move against him. Before he left the mountain, he had a thought and tried to slip inside the Bloodvault but was unable to. It didn't scatter his awareness the way the fortress island did, but he couldn't pass through the wall.

Next, he went to Tyr and found that isle's Gate. It was abandoned in the rocky highlands of the southernmost island of Tyr. As far as Alexander could tell, there was no one within a league of it.

Finally, he went to Karth to see what the beast had done to Phane's forces. The wall surrounding the Gate was breached and there were bodies of Regency soldiers scattered around the courtyard. It looked like the beast had gone on a rampage through Phane's army, killing hundreds before escaping into the jungles and swamps of Karth. Good enough. At least the enemy had something to fear. It was a small victory … but a victory nonetheless.

***

Alexander was up before dawn to oversee the preparations for the day's events. He had a busy morning ahead of him. After several hours of coordination and work, he arrived at the Gate with two hundred men to reinforce Commander Perry. He would be traveling to Tyr with Isabel, Jack, Chloe, Hector, and Horace. Lucky would remain behind to continue working toward becoming a mage.

Alexander opened the Gate to the Reishi Isle first. Commander Perry was waiting with Wizard Dinh. Jahoda was busy working on the wall. The troops went through with Wizard Crocious, Kelvin's handpicked man who would lead the mission to bury the explosive weapon in the chamber of the Nether Gate.

Next, he opened the Gate to Ithilian and sent a messenger to find a representative of the Wizards Guild. King Abel and Mage Lenox came riding up several minutes later. After a brief conversation, Alexander gave Mage Lenox ten vials of Wizard's Dust. The mage was nearly giddy with excitement as he thanked Alexander on behalf of the ten apprentices who would now be able to take the trials. Before he closed the Gate, Alexander spent a few minutes briefing Abel on everything that had transpired since the war council.

Finally, he opened the Gate to a cold and windy day on Tyr and he and his companions rode through. Hector and Horace were familiar with the island, having grown up there, and they led the way toward the headquarters of the Reishi Protectorate.

Chapter 33

What they found when they arrived was the burned-out husk of a town with the broken shell of a keep at the heart of it. There wasn't a soul around and the place had an eerie quality about it, as if something dark was stalking the ghosts of those who'd died there.

Alexander reined in his horse and dismounted when he saw the track. It was bigger than any wolf's print with deep gouges where the long, sharp claws had scored the earth.

"Nether wolves," he said. "Phane must have done this when he learned that the Stone had bonded with me."

"It's been months," Isabel said. "There's no telling what damage a pack of nether wolves might have done in that amount of time."

"One thing's for sure, there's no one left here," Jack said.

"Where would the Reishi Protectorate go?" Alexander asked.

"There are a number of fortresses in the mountains and several along the coastlines," Hector said.

"Can we reach the nearest one before dark?" Alexander asked.

"If we ride hard, we'll make it just after sunset," Horace said.

"Then we don't have any time to waste," Alexander said, mounting up. "We don't want to be caught out in the open when darkness falls."

They pushed their horses to the limits of their endurance, racing the sun to the nearest fortress, which was located in the mountains occupying the center of Alta, the southernmost island of Tyr. Alta was rocky and mountainous, rich in minerals and stone. Where there was soil, it was dark and rich, ideal for farming. Trees were sparse and stunted by the wind that seemed to constantly blow over the island, which had served as the base of operations for the Reishi Protectorate since the fall of the Reishi Empire. The coastline was heavily fortified and there was a network of well-made roads linking the numerous fortresses together.

As they traveled, they came upon several small villages, all abandoned. Alexander didn't take the time to investigate further but he suspected they would find the remains of some of the townsfolk scattered about if they did.

They caught a glimpse of the fortress as they crested a ridge. It was an impressive fortification, built into the side of a mountain with stout stone walls extending to the edge of a natural stone shelf. The only route to the gatehouse was a series of switchbacks cut into the mountain. From the tops of the walls, the occupants of the fortress could easily cast stones or shoot arrows down onto the road. More encouragingly, there were numerous lamps lit and a large signal fire burning on the top of the tallest tower.

Only minutes after the sun slipped behind the horizon, they heard the telltale howl of the nether wolves, a mixture of metal scraping metal and a dying pig's squeal. They had no trouble urging their horses to make better speed up the road toward the gatehouse.

They reached the drawbridge just as the sky was fading from deep blue to sparkling black. The chill mountain air was colder still from the periodic howls that echoed in the mountains.

They were getting closer.

"That sounds like quite a few," Jack said.

Alexander nodded, taking his night-wisp dust from his pouch and holding it high to get the attention of the men in the guard tower. Within minutes a dozen men with bows lined the tower wall.

"What's your business here?" one called down.

"We seek refuge from the nether wolves," Alexander called back.

"What hold to you hail from?"

"We're travelers from Ruatha," Alexander yelled. "Let us in and we'll explain everything."

"I need a name that I recognize before I can let you in."

"Hector and Horace Lal," Hector yelled.

"Darkness comes, My Love," Chloe said in his mind.

Alexander stretched out with his all around sight but the nether wolves were still too far away for him to see, yet close enough to hear them racing up the road below.

The drawbridge lowered slowly. Alexander waited tensely. He expected he was going to have to face the nether wolves eventually, but he wanted to do so on his own terms, on a battlefield of his choosing.

They rode across the stout drawbridge on their skittish horses. As they passed under the portcullis and the drawbridge began to rise again, Alexander glanced back with his all around sight and saw nine nether wolves charging toward them. The creatures stopped at the edge of the precipice, howling in fury that their quarry had escaped.

Alexander and his friends entered a courtyard ringed with archers along the walls. A dozen armed and armored men approached, most with weapons drawn.

"I'm Captain Mithras of the Reishi Protectorate, commander of this stronghold. Last I heard, the brothers Lal were assigned as spies on the Isle of Karth."

"We have since been reassigned," Hector said.

"On whose authority?" Captain Mithras asked. He was a big man, taller than average and barrel-chested with powerful-looking arms, a cleanly shaven head and a long beard braided into three strands secured with a bone bead at the end of each.

"Commander P'Tal," Hector said.

"We've not heard from him since Prince Phane sent him to kill the pretender," Mithras said. "How is it that you've been in contact with the Commander?"

Hector looked at Alexander for an indication as to how he should proceed. Alexander nodded.

"Captain Mithras, I am honored to introduce Lord Alexander Reishi, Seventh Sovereign of the Seven Isles," Hector said, extending his hand toward Alexander. At the same time, Alexander withdrew the Sovereign Stone from under his tunic and let it fall against his chest.

Everyone froze for a moment before Mithras drew his sword. His men all stepped forward, raising their weapons as the men on the walls nocked arrows.

Alexander's focus sharpened and narrowed down to the present moment. His left hand found the hilt of Mindbender but he didn't act.

"Stand down, Captain," Hector said. "Lord Reishi is your rightful master. Prince Phane is the pretender and the enemy of the Reishi Sovereign."

"Last word we had was news of the destruction of Protectorate Headquarters," Mithras said. "Prince Phane disappeared the same day, and since that day, the night has been haunted. No one is safe outside the walls of our strongholds. Thousands have been slaughtered. Those that remain are overcrowded and our food supplies will not last the winter. We hunt these foul beasts by day but they elude us. By night we dare not venture forth.

"Now you come before us at the side of the man responsible for our plight and claim that he is our rightful master."

Hector leaned forward in his saddle. "He is your rightful master. He bears the Sovereign Stone."

Mithras looked more closely at the softly glowing red teardrop ruby hanging around Alexander's neck and his colors flared with indecision and doubt.

"I did not summon the beasts that stalk you in the night," Alexander said. "Phane did. He also destroyed your headquarters. He did these things because I claimed the Sovereign Stone and he knew that the Protectorate would turn against him. Phane is your enemy, Captain Mithras."

He lowered his blade slightly.

"What's more," Alexander said, "I've faced the nether wolves that are menacing your people and I know how to defeat them. I can also offer you food for the winter, but I need your help in return."

"For two thousand years we've waited for Prince Phane to awaken," Mithras said, "and now I'm supposed to believe that he is our enemy? The Sovereign Stone is rightfully his. You should surrender it to him so that he may claim his proper station."

"That's not going to happen, Captain," Alexander said. "Phane is a necromancer. He calls on the netherworld for his power and he is thoroughly evil. He's waging a war against the Old Law as we speak. The time has come for you to choose. Will you serve the Old Law or will you serve the tyrant who loosed darkness upon your home?"

"I serve the Reishi," Captain Mithras said. "Prince Phane is the only Reishi left."

"You're wrong, Captain," Alexander said, tapping the Sovereign Stone. "I couldn't have bonded with the Stone if I wasn't Reishi."

"The tradition of the Reishi Empire is clear," Hector said. "The Sovereign is the one who bears the Stone."

"This is difficult to accept," Mithras said, his sword lowering further still.

"Would a letter from Commander P'Tal help you decide?" Alexander asked, withdrawing a sealed parchment from his pouch and extending it to the nearest soldier.

The commander took the letter from the man and examined the seal carefully before breaking the wax and reading the letter.

"This is in the Commander's hand," Mithras said, sheathing his sword. "I don't fully understand all of this, but I'm not foolish enough to defy an order given by Commander P'Tal. You're welcome in our stronghold, Lord Reishi."

"Thank you, Captain," Alexander said.

Chapter 34

"There's no way we can run that blockade, Lord Reishi," Captain Rastus said. He was a weather-worn sailor with a greying beard and long hair tied back in a ponytail. Alexander had boarded his ship two days prior over the captain's strenuous objections.

Alexander had been on Tyr for nearly two weeks and he was beginning to feel the all-too-familiar feeling of urgency building in his gut. He hadn't expected to spend so much time working with the remnants of the Reishi Protectorate but the damage done by the nether wolves was extensive. Thousands had been killed in the night, but more than that, the spirit of those left alive had been broken. For two thousand years they had waited for the return of the Reishi Prince, and upon his arrival, they had been ravaged by creatures from the darkness.

The trauma of it had been enough to cause many of the people living on Alta to question their purpose, to question their loyal service for so many years, to question the Reishi.

Overcoming their dismay and earning their trust had taken some effort. Alexander spent the better part of a week, aided by the few men brave enough to volunteer for such a task, hunting nether wolves. The first night only three men from Captain Mithras's stronghold were willing to venture forth from the walls after dark.

They lured three nether wolves into their trap that night and killed all three without taking any casualties. Alexander's experience with the beasts, aided by the light of his night-wisp dust, almost assured their victory. After the other men of the stronghold heard the stories of the battle, many more were willing to venture forth the next night.

They were not so fortunate. Several of the men lost their courage when the nether wolves howled in the darkness. Three of the seventeen that accompanied Alexander broke formation and fled into the night. They died quickly. But another two nether wolves fell, and Alexander's hunting party managed to track the remaining four into a box canyon and hold them at bay with the night-wisp dust until dawn.

The next night went much better. Alexander located the place where the nether wolves had gone to ground and was waiting for them when the sun set. Using the light of the night-wisp dust to keep them from rematerializing, he was able to allow one at a time to rise from the ground, only to be hacked apart by men of the Reishi Protectorate.

With the destruction of the nether wolves, the spirit of the men stationed at Captain Mithras's stronghold soared. They sent forth riders with word of the victory and stories of their new leader to all of the other holds on Alta. Although Alexander was anxious to be on his way, he decided that consolidating his command of the Reishi Protectorate was worth the delay, so he waited for the captains of all the other holds to assemble. They were skeptical at first, but after reading the letter written by Jataan and listening to the stories of the men who had stood with Alexander against the nether wolves, they began to come around.

When he opened the Gate to Ithilian and asked Abel to send food, they decided that he was indeed the Reishi Sovereign and threw their support behind his cause with enthusiasm.

Two days' ride had brought him to the northernmost port town and Captain Rastus's ship.

The sailor accepted Alexander's title and pledged his loyalty to the Reishi, but was reluctant to sail north as Alexander requested. He reported that ships from Tuva, Lorraine, and Kalmar, the three small islands of Tyr to the north, had been blockading the straits they would need to sail through to get to the Spires, as they called the dragon isle. He flatly refused to take his boat past the Spires until Captain Mithras told him he would lose his command if he didn't.

"Captain's right," the first mate said. "They'll sink us for sure."

"No they won't," Alexander said. "They won't even see us."

"What's your plan?" Isabel asked.

"I need you to spot for us from the air and guide the captain's course," Alexander said. "It's about to get very foggy."

He stood on the bow of the ship, holding the hilt of Mindbender and focusing his mind's eye on visualizing an enormous fog bank rolling in around them. Stretching out with his all around sight, he envisioned a heavy blanket of dense white fog for as far as he could see. When he released his illusion into the sword, the air rapidly condensed into a thick fog bank that reached for several hundred feet in every direction.

They sailed blind for the next hour, threading their way past the blockade that stretched from the east coast of Tuva to the west coast of Lorraine. Alexander could hear shouting in the distance from the enemy sailors as they passed through their line but he ignored them and focused on maintaining his illusion.

Not long after the cloud of artificial fog had passed the blockade, one of the ships began to give chase. As it neared the edge of Alexander's illusion, a wave of magical energy emanating from the other ship swept through them, dispelling Alexander's illusion. In the span of two breaths' time, the fog bank vanished.

"It would seem that they have a wizard," Jack said.

"I really wasn't expecting that," Alexander said.

The rest of the ships in the blockade began to turn and give chase as well.

"Best speed," Alexander shouted to Captain Rastus.

The captain started barking orders at his men, who leapt into action, raising more sail and putting oars into the water. Within minutes they were racing north as fast as the wind and the strength of the rowers could propel them, but it wasn't fast enough. A few of the enemy ships were gaining on them.

"That nearest ship is within weapons range," the first mate said.

"Fire at will," Captain Rastus said.

The men manning the aft ballista went to work loading a firepot and cranking the winch to arm the weapon. The first shot missed.

"Why aren't they firing at us?" Horace asked.

Alexander tapped his chest where the Sovereign Stone bulged under his tunic. "They don't want to sink us, they want to board us."

The second shot hit squarely on their foredeck, sending men scrambling to douse the flames before they could ignite the mainsail. Two more ships raced past as a third came up alongside the burning vessel to render aid and take on crew.

The ballista fired again. The firepot sailed in a gentle arc, coming down on the nearest enemy vessel, but before it could reach its target, Alexander saw a wave of magical energy rise from the deck of the ship and shatter the firepot, sending the flaming contents harmlessly into the ocean.

"More than one wizard," Jack said.

"I told you this was a bad idea," Captain Rastus said.

"I never said it was a good idea," Alexander shot back, "only that it was necessary."

"It looks like we're faster than all but three of the remaining ships," Isabel said. "The gap is widening between them. Unfortunately, it also looks like two of those faster ships have a wizard standing on the deck waiting for us to take another shot at them."

"Hold your fire, Captain," Alexander said. "Don't waste the firepots, we may have a chance to make better use of them later."

"What do you want me to do?" Captain Rastus asked.

"Make best speed north," Alexander said. "It's all we can do for now."

"And when they get closer?" Rastus said.

"We fight," Alexander said, straining to extend the range of his all around sight. He could see farther now than he could the day after he'd been blinded but still not as far as he could with his natural vision. He was frustrated by the limitation but told himself that he could still see better than most. Without his magic, he would be completely blind.

The pain behind his eyes came and went, depending on how far he tried to extend his all around sight. On the days he was content to see within a hundred feet or so, he felt no pain at all, but when he pushed to see farther, it hurt, yet with each effort to stretch his ability he could see farther than the last, so he ignored the pain. He could see out to about five hundred feet, farther than ever, yet still not far enough.

They raced north all afternoon, rotating rowers to keep them fresh. The three pursuing ships gained on them steadily but slowly. The other vessels fell farther behind but showed no sign of giving up. Isabel reported that they'd formed a flotilla and were pursuing doggedly even though the gap was widening.

"Start looking for a cove to hide in, Captain," Alexander said.

"They'll see us," Rastus said.

Alexander shook his head, pointing to a place on the coast of Tuva that might work. "Do you know if that cove is deep enough?" Alexander asked.

"It is. But they'll see us and then we'll be trapped."

"Head for it," Alexander ordered. He went to the aft deck and grasped the hilt of Mindbender, sending his vision into the sword. He visualized them sailing north along the coastline into the gloaming while obscuring their true course.

The captain was reluctant but obeyed nonetheless. They slipped into the secluded cove and the enemy sailed right past them into the night.

"Might make tomorrow interesting," Jack said.

"Tomorrow's going to be interesting no matter what we do," Alexander said. "At least this way, the men can get some rest."

***

They sailed out of the cove before first light. Again, Alexander lamented his loss of sight. Prior to his encounter with Shivini, he would have been able to see the colors of the men aboard the ships in the night but they were well out of range of his all around sight. He stretched out as far as he could, straining through the pain to see farther still but the enemy just wasn't close enough to detect.

Luckily, dawn broke over an ocean shrouded in mist. The enemy would have a harder time finding them with the limited visibility. Captain Rastus ordered his men to make best speed north as quietly as possible. Normally, the ship was a noisy place with men yelling and the row master calling out the stroke of the oars, but everyone understood the situation and made an effort to keep the noise at a minimum.

By midmorning the fog started to burn off and Isabel reported that the enemy ships were holding position in a blockade line across the narrowest point between Tuva and Lorraine. Seventeen ships formed a line across the strait, most of them large, sail-driven ships, capable of good speed out on the open ocean but lacking the banks of oars that gave the smaller ships an advantage when the wind was calm.

Alexander picked a point in the blockade where there were several of the larger, slower ships.

"We'll run the line there," Alexander said. "Captain, have your fore ballista loaded and ready to fire. Hit that ship as soon as we're in range, then hit it again. Once its sails are on fire, attack the next nearest ship."

The remnants of the morning fog helped them reach firing range before any of the enemy sailors saw their approach. As the first firepot lifted off the deck, the enemy sent up a whistler arrow.

The firepot shattered against the side of the nearest ship, sending the sailors scrambling to pour water on the growing flame before it reached the sails as the captain turned the ship to make for a smaller target. The second firepot was away quickly, arcing through the salt air and crashing into the mainmast, splashing fire across the sails.

The next nearest ship was closing fast, bringing its ram into position to hit Alexander's ship broadside. Captain Rastus ordered his rowers to step up the pace as the fore and aft ballistae swiveled to target the approaching ship. They fired in unison, each scoring a direct hit on the deck, causing the enemy's ram attack to falter.

They raced through the hole in the blockade as the rest of the ships adjusted course to give chase.

"One of those faster boats is going to catch us," Isabel said. "It turned early and got out ahead of us as soon as the alarm went up."

"Adjust course," Alexander said to the captain. "Head straight for it. Target the nearest ship behind us with the aft ballista and sink it."

"It's almost out of range," Captain Rastus said.

"Then you don't have much time, Captain," Alexander said. "Do what damage you can without slowing down, then prepare to engage the ship out in front of us."

Rastus seemed to give up his ingrained reluctance and threw himself into the task at hand with a mixture of anger and resignation. The aft ballista fired moments later, scoring a hit against the prow of the nearest trailing ship, but failing to ignite the sails.

As soon as they were in range of the ship out ahead of them, the fore ballista fired but the wizard on the deck of the enemy ship deflected the firepot with a spell that sent it harmlessly into the ocean.

"I figured that ship had a wizard on it," Alexander said. "Isabel, I need you to put a hole in the bow right at the waterline. Captain, prepare both ballistae but hold until you can fire both at once. Hopefully, the wizard can only defend against one shot at a time."

Alexander took up his bow and went to the bow of the ship with Isabel. He could feel the tension build as the two ships approached. When they entered the range of his all around sight, he nocked an arrow.

"Captain, prepare to turn hard to starboard," Alexander shouted.

They closed to within three hundred feet and Alexander loosed his arrow at the wizard standing on the foredeck just as Isabel unleashed her light-lance spell. The wizard conjured a shield to deflect the arrow, allowing Isabel's spell to strike her target unhindered, burning a hole the size of a grapefruit through the bulkhead of the ship just below the waterline. Steam rose in a puff, then dissipated quickly.

The enemy ship fired two grappling hooks into the sails of Alexander's ship, both trailing rope and both scoring direct hits in the mainsail.

"Turn!" Alexander commanded.

Captain Rastus spun the wheel, turning the ship to starboard and bringing both ballistae to bear on the enemy ship, both firing in unison. The enemy wizard deflected one firepot into the ocean but the other scored a hit against the deck cabin just behind the mainmast. Sailors raced to douse the flames but the sails ignited before they could put out the fire.

At the same time, the enemy started pulling on the two grappling hooks entangled in the mainsail, tearing gaping holes in it before the tethers could be cut. Captain Rastus barked orders to the row master below deck to row harder and to the deckhands to prepare the spare sail. Alexander knew it would take more time than they had. The enemy was going to board them and more ships were coming from behind.

The enemy fired their ballistae again, this time aiming for the broadside of the ship with barbed harpoons trailing rope. Both struck home, lodging deeply into the hull. A dozen men pulled on each rope in rhythmic cadence, drawing both vessels closer together with each heave.

One of Rastus's sailors scrambled down a net draped over the railing in an effort to cut one of the tethers, but before he could reach it, a narrow wedge of blue magical force leapt from the enemy wizard's hand, driving straight into the man's heart. The sailor fell into the ocean and slipped under the waves.

Alexander sent another arrow at the wizard but he deflected it easily. Isabel fired a light-lance at one of the tethers, severing it cleanly. The ballistae fired again, this time both firepots shattered into the already burning sails, engulfing them in flames.

The enemy started to deploy their longboats, even as the men on deck heaved on the one remaining tether, pulling the ships closer together. Another of Rastus's sailors attempted to reach the remaining tether by climbing down the side of the ship. This time Alexander was prepared. He cast an illusion of a curtain of darkness between both ships so the enemy wizard couldn't see his target. The sailor reached the harpoon and cut the tether, but a moment later three men appeared on the deck of Alexander's ship, wisps of black smoke fading quickly in the wake of their arrival.

"Wraithkin!" Alexander shouted. The meaning of his warning was lost on the crew, but Alexander's friends understood the threat at once. Hector and Horace stood back to back, as did Alexander and Isabel. Jack flickered out of sight.

Alexander dropped his bow as he drew Mindbender and stretched out with his magic to see into the minds of his enemies.

He was in a fight and he had a sword in his hand … everything else faded away.

The first wraithkin killed a sailor with almost casual ease, then vanished and reappeared next to the first mate. The second in command of the ship stabbed the wraithkin in the gut with his dagger, but the wraithkin just winced in pain as he slashed the man's throat and then vanished, only to reappear right in front of Isabel.

With the tethers cut, the gap between their ship and the now fully blazing enemy ship was widening even as the remaining fourteen ships in the flotilla were gaining on them. The rowers below deck were pulling against the water with all their might but the mainsail was offering little thrust and the sailors on deck were now engaged in a pitched battle with an enemy beyond their understanding.

The second wraithkin vanished before a sailor could bring his blade around in a slashing attack that would have decapitated him, only to reappear behind the commander of the fore ballista crew. He stabbed the man in the back and vanished again.

The third wraithkin easily sidestepped the thrusting attack of a deckhand, cutting him deeply on the outside of the arm before vanishing. A moment later, Alexander heard a shout of terror come from below decks in the rowers' cabin.

Isabel sent the wraithkin before her flying over the railing toward the water with a hastily cast force-push spell, but he disappeared in midair and reappeared to the side of Hector and Horace, stabbing at Hector the moment he appeared.

Hector turned to vapor almost instantly, using his innate ability as a sorcerer to once again save his life. The wraithkin looked almost puzzled as his blade thrust through the insubstantial form of his target. Horace seized the opportunity the wraithkin's hesitation gave him and stabbed him under the chin, driving his blade up through his head and out the top of his skull.

Alexander waited, listening to the intent of his enemies. The wraithkin that had killed the commander of the fore ballista appeared beside him, as Alexander knew he would. When Phane's dark creation materialized amid wisps of blackness, Alexander was poised to strike and his thrust was true, stabbing into the wraithkin's right eye socket and driving through his skull. The man mixed with darkness slumped off Mindbender to the deck of the ship.

Another scream from below decks sent Alexander scrambling for the ladder. The rowers were their only means of propulsion and the lone remaining wraithkin was slaughtering them. Alexander reached the base of the ladder and found six of the sixteen rowers dead. The wraithkin saw him and smiled before vanishing.

Alexander heard a shout from the deck above and scrambled back up the ladder. Captain Rastus lay bleeding. The wraithkin reappeared behind another sailor and killed him with a quick thrust. Alexander reached out to see into his mind as he vanished.

"Beside you, Horace!" he shouted.

The wraithkin appeared beside Hector and Horace, poised to strike when Jack flickered into view, stabbing down through the back of the wraithkin's skull with his dagger, dropping him to the deck with the force and violence of his blow.

Sudden calm descended on the ship. Alexander took a moment to assess his situation. It was bad. The captain and first mate were dead, as were the commander of the fore ballista, six rowers, and as many sailors. The mainsail was torn, and fourteen enemy ships were closing on them.

Just as he made up his mind, a deafening crack reverberated through the ship. The wizard, standing on the longboat rowing toward them, unleashed a spell that sent a whirling disc of blue-white magical energy scything through the mainmast, cutting it off just above the cabin and sending it toppling into the water.

"How close is land?" Alexander asked Isabel.

"A league, maybe less," she said.

Alexander grabbed the nearest sailor.

"Take the wheel, head for the coast," Alexander said, pointing to the coast of Lorraine off in the distance.

"You men go below decks and row," he commanded the crew of the fore ballista before racing to the aft ballista.

"Sink that longboat," he ordered.

The ballista crew had a firepot loaded and fired quickly, but it shattered against a shell of magical energy and dripped off into the ocean.

"Be ready to fire on my order," Alexander said. He visualized a cloud of dense white fog surrounding the longboat and sent it into Mindbender. An instant later, fog materialized around them, enshrouding the enemy longboat. Alexander held the illusion and waited. He didn't have to wait long before the wizard dispelled the fog; it dissipated nearly as quickly as it had come into being.

"Fire!" Alexander commanded.

From a distance of fifty feet, the ballista launched a firepot into the longboat, scoring a direct hit. The wizard leapt into the water in a panic as his robes went up in flames.

"Cut the mainmast free and rig the secondary sails to give us best speed," Alexander shouted to the stunned sailors.

After only a moment's hesitation, they sprang into action.

"Take a shot at that ship," Alexander said to the commander of the aft ballista, pointing at the boat that was nearest and gaining. The firepot narrowly missed.

"We only have three firepots left," the commander said.

"Very well, hold your fire," Alexander said, "but keep one at the ready."

The pursuing ships stayed just out of range of Alexander's ballistae, but that was fine by him. His plan of sailing through the enemy blockade had failed, and badly. He stood on the bow of his damaged ship, stretching out with his all around sight in spite of the pain it caused him, and considered his limited options. He would soon be on dry land in enemy territory with fewer than two dozen sailors to stand against fourteen ships' worth of sailors and soldiers, not to mention whatever enemy he might find on the island of Lorraine.

"Hector, Horace, what can you tell me about Lorraine?"

"It's the second largest of the subislands of Tyr," Hector said. "Rich in minerals and stone with some timber, used mostly to build ships. It's ruled by five warlords that seem to be in a constant state of conflict. They almost routinely make and break alliances with one another to gain some advantage or other. They trade primarily with Andalia and Karth, but only sail in well-protected flotillas to defend against piracy, which is rampant in the waters of Tyr."

"Any idea who the ships chasing us belong to?"

"Most are flying the flag of Tuva, the subisland across the strait," Horace said, "but a few are sailing under the flag of the warlord who controls the southwest coast of Lorraine. We're headed right for his territory."

Alexander sighed.

"At least we'll have solid ground under our feet," Jack said.

"And it'll probably take some time for them to get organized," Isabel said. "We can probably make it out of this territory before they can send enough men to be a threat."

"Let's hope so," Alexander said. "I'd like to move north and find another boat as soon as we can. Going to ground might throw off the ships chasing us enough for us to get to the dragon isle."

They ran aground in shallow water and took longboats to shore. Alexander had twenty-three frightened sailors left. As they set foot on dry ground, the enemy ships began putting longboats into the water.

The coast rose rapidly into a small range of lightly forested, rocky hills. Alexander led the way directly inland over the rugged and wild terrain. This part of the island didn't appear to be inhabited but he was wary nonetheless. They reached a vantage point with a good view of the coast and Alexander turned to see how close his pursuers were, but they were well beyond the range of his all around sight.

"Lend me your eyes, Little One?"

"Of course, My Love."

Through Chloe's eyes, Alexander saw a dozen or more longboats lined up along the shore, each capable of carrying ten to twenty men. The flotilla of enemy vessels was holding station off the coast in a long line stretching north and south.

"We'll head north along this ridgeline," Alexander said.

"And then what?" one of the sailors asked.

His colors were bright with fear and dismay. Alexander understood how he felt but he didn't have time to argue the necessity of his objective, so he ignored the man and started out. At first, the sailor was reluctant to follow, but Hector spoke quietly in his ear. The sailor stiffened for a moment before he nodded quickly and fell in line with the rest of the crew.

They traveled through the sparse forest for the rest of the day. Isabel reported that nearly two hundred enemy soldiers were following their trail about an hour behind. Worse, she saw at least one wizard with the small army, and

Alexander suspected that there were probably a few more wraithkin among the soldiers.

"There's a village on the coast about a league ahead," Isabel said.

"Are there any ships big enough for all of us?" Alexander asked.

"Three. And they're all flying the same flag as the ships we fought this morning."

Alexander led them as close to the village as he dared before they stopped to wait for dark. He used the time to do some reconnaissance. When he opened the door to his Wizard's Den, the sailors that had been reluctantly following him fell silent to a man, staring in awe at the magical portal. Alexander sat down in his magic circle and quieted his mind. Horace stood guard at the doorway while Alexander slipped free of his body and sent his mind to explore the village he intended to raid.

It was primarily a fishing village with a number of docks extending like fingers into a deep lagoon protected from ocean turbulence by a jetty made of large stones. The villagers didn't seem to know or care about the battle that had taken place just south of their little community but they did openly fly the flag of the warlord who ruled over the area, the same warlord who had sent ships to kill Alexander.

He scouted the three larger ships in port and found his target, the only warship of the bunch, the only vessel armed with heavy weapons, the only vessel loaded for combat, the one vessel that was most likely preparing to join the enemy flotilla that was hunting him. The other two ships were cargo transports. While either was large enough to carry Alexander and his crew, neither was armed and both were heavily laden with freight, either waiting to be unloaded or just recently loaded for transport to another port.

Alexander surveyed the security of the small village and found it lacking. They were not prepared for an attack. The few men aboard the warship were playing dice and drinking rum. He floated through the village and found the rest of the crew in three taverns that lined the main street running through town.

Once he was satisfied with his plan, he sent his mind up the coastline in search of other enemy vessels that might be waiting for him farther north, but found none. Next he moved in a blur to the dragon isle. He understood in a glance why the people of Tyr called it the Spires. There was a ring of black stone spires surrounding the central volcanic island, each spire reaching up out of the ocean a thousand feet or more. The orange-red glow emanating from the top of the volcano beyond painted an ominous picture.

He moved closer, searching for a place to hide his ship. He was counting on Bragador being reasonable, but he wasn't foolish enough to approach a dragon's lair unprepared. He had no intention of revealing the presence of his ship until he had his prize ... maybe not even then.

The entire island was the product of an all-too-active volcano, the cauldron sputtering and smoking, rivulets of bright red lava flowing down the sides of the mountain from a number of cracks and fissures. As he delved deeper into the mountain, he discovered a labyrinth of caves, caverns, and passageways. While many of the areas in the center of the mountain were occupied by molten rock, steam, and smoke, the periphery was far less dangerous.

All throughout the mountain were dragons of many different colors and sizes, which was surprising to him. He assumed that dragons were all the same as Tanis, but these were far different, smaller, though still larger than a wyvern, scaled in a variety of colors from bright reds to dark greens to black and displaying a wide variety of horns, spikes, and bone ridges along their backs, necks, and heads.

After some searching, he found a cave that met his needs. It was large enough to sail a warship into, far enough away from the main entrances to the network of caves inhabited by the majority of the dragons, yet linked to the labyrinth of passageways permeating the mountain.

Having learned what he needed to know about his destination, he brought his awareness back to his location and then set out in search of the enemy soldiers and sailors pursuing him. He found them easily, not two leagues away and moving slowing through the forest in his general direction.

They would reach his position before sunset.

He slipped back into the firmament and listened to the song of creation for a few minutes, simply allowing his mind to take in the totality of the present moment. He could feel the strife unfolding in the world, hear the angst of countless people struggling with the hardships of war, and feel the desperation of people everywhere trying to preserve a future worth having.

He returned to himself quietly and sat for a moment longer, collecting his thoughts and mentally preparing for the night to come. Stepping out of his Wizard's Den, he closed the door and faced his band of wayward sailors.

"They'll be here within an hour so we have to move now. We'll get as far as we can with stealth, then I'll provide a distraction for the townspeople so we can reach the ship. Once we're aboard, we need to remove the crew and cast off as quickly as possible. Who's the ranking officer?"

There was a palpable hesitation among the crew before one of the men raised his hand.

"I'm the weapons officer," he said.

"Good, what's your name?"

"Dreven Kalderson," he said.

"All right, Dreven, you are now the captain," Alexander said. "Assign duties to your crew so everyone knows their place once we board.

"We move in ten minutes."

***

They moved quietly toward the road that ran down the coast from the north and then turned east in the middle of town, heading up into the rugged hillside. The people seemed to be preoccupied with their day-to-day business and didn't take much interest in Alexander and his group, until they entered town.

He led his sailors straight down the road toward the docks, watching the townsfolk closely for any sign of a threat. Most of them eyed him curiously, a few vanished between buildings as they approached, either out of fear or, more likely, to warn what passed for authority in the little town of the arrival of a group of strangers.

They had nearly reached the docks before a small group of townsmen armed with spears approached. The lead man gestured for his men to fan out.

Alexander counted sixteen.

"What's your business here?" the lead man asked.

Alexander ignored him, gesturing for his sailors to continue toward the ship as he grasped the hilt of Mindbender and conjured the vision of a dragon. He brought his illusion into existence high in the sky so it would pass across the sun, casting a shadow over the town as it flew overhead.

The men froze at the sight of the magical beast.

When it roared, the people of the village panicked, running in every direction.

"Move!" Alexander shouted.

They reached the dock amid the confusion and chaos, racing up the gangplank in single file and taking the few sailors aboard by surprise. The crewmen started to put up a fight but stopped abruptly when they saw how badly they were outnumbered. Within a few minutes, Alexander's men had the entire eight-man crew at sword point and the ship was pulling away from the dock.

"I have no cause to harm you men, but I need this ship," Alexander said. "I suggest you jump overboard before we get too far away from the docks."

One by one they stepped off the plank, splashing into the shallow water of the bay.

"Can you disable those other two ships?" Alexander asked Isabel.

She nodded with a little grin as she stepped up to the railing and started muttering the words of her light-lance spell. After she'd burned an eight-inch hole into the hull of each ship, Alexander released his illusion and turned his attention to formulating a plan for approaching Bragador.

As the sun slid past the horizon, the ship slipped past the jetty and into the deep waters of the strait running between Lorraine and Tuva. The sailors seemed to be somehow more at ease than they had been since Alexander had ordered their ship to run aground. They took to the task of manning the warship with enthusiasm.

Most of them manned the banks of oars until they reached deeper water, then they unfurled the sails and set a course north toward the Spires. They sailed through the night using the few lights from settlements onshore as a guide for their course.

Captain Kalderson was tentative about his new command at first, but stepped into the role without reservation once they were under way, issuing orders to his crewmen with confidence and surety. Alexander left him to it.

Dawn broke over a crystal clear sky. The air was cold and the wind blew steadily, propelling them with good speed toward the dragon isle. Alexander saw no sign of his pursuers, though he knew they were probably taking advantage of the wind to catch up.

They sailed for the rest of the day and into the next before they saw the spires rising up out of the ocean to their north. Beyond was the volcanic island at the heart of Tyr and the home of Bragador and her brood. The sailors became nervous as they drew closer.

"Two ships, one on either side of that spire," Isabel said.

Alexander had been relying on Chloe's eyes to see things at a distance but her eyes weren't as sharp as Slyder's.

"Captain Kalderson, come twenty degrees starboard," Alexander said.

"Prepare the ballistae."

Captain Kalderson barked orders to his crew as if he'd been captaining a ship for years. They responded without hesitation, bringing the ship about and preparing for battle.

The two ships holding station at the Spires unfurled their sails and put oars into the water.

"Those ships will have Phane's agents aboard," Alexander said. "Hopefully, they won't follow us into the dragon isle, but we have to be prepared for them if they do."

"I suspect the dragons might be unhappy to see us," Jack said.

"That's why they won't see us," Alexander said, patting the hilt of Mindbender. "I'm hoping Bragador will take care of those ships for us if they're dumb enough to follow us in."

The wind was with them and they reached the gap between the two spires that Alexander was aiming for well ahead of the two enemy ships. As he stood on the prow, holding the hilt of Mindbender, he envisioned a calm sea and obscured the wake of their passage to ensure that the dragons wouldn't detect their position.

The two enemy ships turned north, following Alexander into the waters surrounding the dragon isle, the wind adding to their speed. Not long after they passed between the spires, a dragon roared from the rim of the volcano's cauldron as it took to wing.

"Here it comes," Isabel said.

"Steady," Alexander said, focusing intently on his illusion.

The crew watched nervously as the dragon coasted on the wind high overhead. It didn't seem to notice them, but it did see the enemy ships. The dragon gained speed as it lost altitude in a graceful dive toward the encroaching ships. It flew over them at an altitude of three hundred feet, roaring with terrible fury.

Both ships pulled hard to starboard and came about, rowing against the wind to retreat from the waters encircling the dragon isle and avoid the wrath of the magical beasts.

Alexander smiled to himself as he focused on maintaining his illusion. Isabel pointed out the spot that Alexander had selected, and Captain Kalderson set a course that brought them in a gentle arc toward the mouth of the deep-water cave. As they slipped into the darkness, out of view of the watchful dragons, Alexander released his illusion and stretched out with his all around sight.

The cave was large enough to accommodate their ship without risking a brush against its rocky walls, and even large enough for the ship to turn around, though only by carefully rowing forward on one side and backward on the other. After a tense few minutes of expert navigation by Captain Kalderson and his crew, the ship was securely anchored two hundred feet inside, facing the entrance.

"Well done, Captain," Alexander said. "Hold your position here, very quietly, until we return."

Alexander and his companions climbed into a dinghy. Hector and Horace rowed to a sandy little beach within the cave and pulled the dingy ashore. Then the group cautiously made their way through the gloom to one of several entrances to the labyrinth of caverns and passages that riddled the island.

Hours of picking their way through treacherous passageways brought them to the rocky shelf that Alexander had selected for his meeting with Bragador.

It was a level spot high over the ocean, and the passageway leading to it was big enough for them to pass through but far too small to accommodate a dragon.

After carefully inspecting the place, he nodded his approval. It was large enough for a dragon to land but small enough for only one.

"Is everyone ready?" he asked.

"I'm not sure I'd go so far as to say I'm ready," Jack said. "But I have to admit, this will make for an interesting chapter, provided I have the opportunity to write it."

"You will, Jack," Alexander said. "Kelvin says Bragador is reasonable."

"Let's hope he's right," Jack said.

Alexander sent a whistler arrow into the early evening sky, then held his vial of night-wisp dust high to mark their position.

Chapter 35

They didn't have long to wait. Within a minute a dragon passed overhead, banking sharply and corkscrewing down to the shelf. It landed hard, sending reverberations through the stone. Crouching low, coiled like a spring, it brought its giant head down to their level, scrutinizing them intently with catlike eyes.

He was beautiful and terrible all at once, dark green scales with just a hint of iridescence, three rows of sharp black spikes running down his spine, forked barbs on the end of his long, sinewy tail.

Alexander held his ground, hands open and out at his sides.

"You are not welcome here, Human," the dragon said.

"All of the Seven Isles faces a great danger," Alexander said. "I've come to ask for Lady Bragador's help."

"She is not interested in your war," the dragon said. "Leave us in peace."

"The war isn't the danger I'm speaking of," Alexander said. "There's a shade loose in the world and he's searching for the keystones that are capable of opening the Nether Gate, a portal to the netherworld. If the shade succeeds, nothing will survive—not even you."

The dragon's eyes narrowed, as if he was weighing a decision. "Wait here," he said before launching himself into the air. The downdraft from the beating of his giant wings sent dust flying.

"A dragon of few words," Jack said.

"Do you think he's going to get Bragador?" Isabel asked.

"I'm hoping," Alexander said.

Not five minutes later, the sky was full of dragons. Nearly a dozen of the majestic magical creatures floated overhead as the largest among them descended toward Alexander. He waited somewhat nervously … so much rested on Bragador. If she agreed to help him, he could end the threat of the Nether Gate permanently. If she refused, he wasn't sure what his next move would be.

She flared her giant wings, landing gracefully on the stone shelf. Her scales were jet black with a tinge of red iridescence, a dozen or more horns swept back from her brow forming a crown that transitioned into a single row of spikes running the length of her spine, her talons dug into the volcanic stone, and her golden catlike eyes shone with intelligence and ancient wisdom.

She wasn't as big as Tanis but she was every bit as magnificent, with colors of rich vibrancy and clear hue. She was a queen among dragons.

"Why are you intruding in our home, Human?" Bragador asked.

"I've come to seek your aid," Alexander said. "I believe you are in possession of an item that I wish to bargain for."

She sniffed the air and eyed him more closely.

"How is it that you have come to wear my scales?"

Alexander lifted his tunic, revealing the armored shirt he wore underneath.

"Mage Gamaliel gave me this shirt of armor as a gift," he said. "It has saved my life more times than I can count."

"Then it seems you are already in my debt, and yet here you stand, trespassing in my home and beseeching me for yet more aid."

"I wouldn't have come if the need wasn't great," Alexander said. "Will you hear me out?"

"Very well. Your presence here is a curiosity," Bragador said. "Not many humans have the nerve to come before me."

"A mage told me you are in possession of a keystone to the Nether Gate," Alexander said. "It's a small pyramid of black stone. I've come to ask that you allow me to destroy it. I've also come to request a single dragon tear."

She actually laughed, a deep rumble emanating from her chest.

"I know the bauble of which you speak," Bragador said. "Surely Mage Gamaliel told you how greatly we dragons value our treasure. Why would I part with such an ancient item?"

"It's one of three keystones needed to open the Nether Gate," Alexander said. "If you allow me to destroy it, the Gate will remain closed and the world will be safe from the gravest threat it has ever faced."

"I have no intention of using it to open this Nether Gate you speak of," Bragador said. "As long as it remains in my hoard, the world is safe from the darkness you fear."

"There is a shade loose in the world searching for it," Alexander said. "Phane is also searching for it. Both of them are powerful and resourceful."

"Are you suggesting that either of your adversaries could best me in my own lair?" she asked, somewhat bemused by the idea.

"No, but they may be able to steal it from you," Alexander said. "As long as it exists, the world is in jeopardy."

"Stealing from a dragon's hoard is unhealthy," Bragador said. "I've heard tales of the shades, and while formidable, their hosts are just flesh and bone. If it should be foolish enough to trespass in my lair, it will never leave. As for the arch mage, he has already visited us and fled, barely escaping with his life. I doubt he will be back."

"Probably not in person," Alexander said, "but he will send his minions, one after the next, until he has his prize. I know from personal experience just how relentless he is. At the very least, you will face a stream of constant intrusions as long as you possess the keystone."

She frowned, considering his argument.

"Do you know the history of this item you seek?" Bragador asked.

"I know it was created by Malachi Reishi," Alexander said. "Beyond that I only know that it needs to be destroyed."

"My grandsire was entrusted with it by the Rebel Mage at the end of humanity's last great war," Bragador said. "It has been a part of my family treasure hoard for nearly two thousand years. My sire spoke of it to me before he passed from this world. His only instruction was to never let it fall into the hands of a human … any human."

"Lady Bragador, please, I implore you to reconsider," Alexander said. "Your sire knew the danger it poses or he wouldn't have been so insistent about protecting it. I only wish to destroy it, nothing more."

She seemed to be weighing his words when Chloe buzzed into existence in a ball of scintillating white light. She floated up to Bragador. The dragon seemed slightly startled by her sudden presence.

"Hello, Lady Bragador. My name is Chloe and I've bonded with Alexander. I give you my word of honor that he speaks truth. His need is great and the burden he carries is terrible. Please help him."

"You're a long way from home, Little One," Bragador said. "I didn't think your Fairy Queen permitted you to leave her valley."

"She made an exception for Alexander," Chloe said. "And he is worthy of her trust, as he is of yours."

"Even if he could be trusted, the item he seeks cannot be destroyed," Bragador said. "My sire tried. He couldn't shatter it. And his fire, hot enough to melt stone, had no effect either."

Alexander pulled the Sovereign Stone from under his tunic and let it fall against his chest. With a thought, he opened the door to the Wizard's Den.

"I am Alexander Reishi, Sovereign of the Seven Isles. Within the Stone's Wizard's Den is a balcony and beyond that is an endless mist. If I cast the keystone into the mist, it will be gone from this world forever."

Bragador peered into the Wizard's Den and snorted.

"I have seen many things, Human, but this is a curiosity beyond my experience," she said. "For showing me such a thing, we are even for the use of my scales to protect you. But while impressive, I'm still not convinced that I should give you the keystone and even if I were, you have not offered me anything in return for such a rare item."

"Name your price for the keystone and a dragon tear," Alexander said, hoping she would name something he had the power to give.

She scrutinized him closely, her golden eyes narrowing.

"You possess two items that are both unique and ancient," Bragador said. "That bauble hanging from your neck and the sword at your waist. Either would do."

Alexander swallowed hard but he didn't hesitate. With a deep breath, he lifted the baldric over his head and extended Mindbender to Bragador.

"Alexander, are you sure about this?" Isabel asked.

"What choice do I have? The keystone and your life are both more important than a sword."

"I did not expect you to meet my price," Bragador said. "But you still haven't convinced me that you can destroy the keystone. Until then there can be no bargain."

"How can I convince you?" Alexander asked.

Before she could answer, a dragon roared from overhead, followed by another and then another. The large dark-green dragon that had first greeted them landed on a rocky prominence nearby, fury flashing in his eyes.

"Anja has been taken!" he roared.

Bragador reared back, her nostrils flaring, her wings spread wide.

"Deceiver!" she said.

Alexander grasped the hilt of Mindbender and threw up an illusionary wall of stone between himself and the now furious dragon.

"Run!" he shouted.

He and his friends raced back into the cave. They rounded one corner and then another as heat washed over them, singeing their hair and scorching their clothes. Bright orange fire illuminated the cave from behind as they ran, desperately trying to escape the dragon's fire.

"You will not survive this day!" Bragador bellowed.

They ran deeper into the mountain, twisting and turning through the labyrinth. For half an hour they fled, not caring where they went, so long as it was farther away from the dragons. Angry roars reverberated through the mountain, lending urgency to their flight.

They stopped in a small chamber to catch their breath.

"What just happened?" Jack asked.

"I'm not sure," Alexander said. "That green dragon said someone had been taken."

"Anja, I think," Isabel said.

"So who's Anja and who took her?" Jack said.

"I don't know, but I think we need to find out," Alexander said. "This smells like Phane's doing."

"What if they find the ship?" Isabel asked.

Alexander shook his head. "It won't be good. I just hope Captain Kalderson has the good sense to stay put. If he tries to run, they're sunk for sure."

He willed the door to his Wizard's Den open.

"If you hear anything coming, shake me until I come out of my meditation," Alexander said. "I'm going to have a look around."

He didn't waste any time. The moment he slipped free of his body and into the firmament, he focused on Bragador. His awareness coalesced in an enormous cavern. Dozens of dragons were arrayed around Bragador, who was sitting atop a mound of gold coins as big as a house. She was eyeing a single man standing casually before her as if he held the upper hand. He didn't seem nervous in the least to be standing in a dragon's lair.

Alexander looked more closely at the man. His colors were muddy, tainted with darkness and power. He was wraithkin.

"Our terms are simple, Dragon," he said. "You give us the keystone and secure the Sovereign Stone for us and we will return your egg, intact and unharmed."

"You are playing a very dangerous game, Human," Bragador said. "It is unwise to make an enemy of a dragon."

"Be that as it may, the deal is what it is," the wraithkin said. "We have no wish to involve you in our war but we require these items. Deliver them to us and we will return your egg."

"From your demands, I assume you are not in league with the bearer of the Sovereign Stone, the one who calls himself Alexander Reishi."

"No, he is a pretender," the wraithkin said. "He has stolen the Sovereign Stone from its rightful owner, Prince Phane Reishi."

"Yet the Stone is bound to this Alexander Reishi," Bragador said. "I know something about this item from stories told to me by my grandsire. By the tradition of the Reishi Empire, the rightful sovereign is the one bound to the Stone. So it would seem that Prince Phane is the pretender."

"Irrelevant," the wraithkin said. "We have your egg. Deliver the items we require or we will kill your unborn child."

Bragador leaned forward menacingly as if she was considering eating the wraithkin whole. Alexander saw the turmoil within her colors, the battle within her raged as she struggled to decide.

"Bargain struck," she said. "Be warned—if you harm Anja, my brood and I will come forth and wage war against Prince Phane with fury and wrath."

The wraithkin smiled and then vanished, reappearing twenty feet closer to the cave entrance, taking a step or two and then vanishing again. Alexander slipped into the firmament and focused on the dragon egg named Anja. Nothing happened.

He brought his consciousness back into the room with Bragador and started sweeping through the entire island in a grid pattern. The world passed by in a blur with each pass but he moved just slowly enough so that he could discern enough of his surroundings to find what he was looking for … and find it he did.

After nearly an hour of systematic searching, he located the cave where Phane's agents were holding the dragon egg. They'd found a cave similar to the one where he was hiding his ship, only theirs was bigger and had a number of large passageways entering from the mountain.

The egg was on a broad stone shelf resting in a pit of hot coals. Alexander examined the men surrounding the egg and found a formidable bunch: three wraithkin, two master wizards, and twenty armed men. As he assessed the enemy's strength, he stopped abruptly when he reached the captain of the vessel moored in the cave. He looked closer even though he knew his first glance hadn't been mistaken, couldn't have been mistaken.

At his waist, the man carried the Thinblade of Tyr. He was a pirate and a rogue. His colors were as disreputable as any Alexander had seen in a man, yet this man had the blood of the House of Tyr coursing through his veins, and he possessed the last of the three remaining Thinblades.

Alexander added yet another task to his list.

He marked their position and scouted a route to them, then turned his attention to the blood of the earth. After some searching within the bowels of the mountain, he found the ancient chamber where the potent magical liquid was collecting and traced a route back to his current position. It was long, treacherous, and circuitous but he was confident that it was passable. Satisfied with his reconnaissance, he returned to his body.

"Report," he said.

"All's quiet," Hector said from his position guarding the entrance to the Wizard's Den.

"What did you learn?" Isabel asked.

"Phane's people are here," Alexander said. "They stole Bragador's egg, then offered to exchange it for the keystone and the Sovereign Stone."

"She didn't agree, did she?" Isabel asked.

"I'm afraid so," Alexander said. "She didn't seem too happy about it, though."

"I don't imagine," Jack said, "but that does present quite a dilemma."

"We have an advantage," Alexander said. "I know where they're keeping the egg."

"You want to steal it back?" Jack asked.

"The thought crossed my mind," Alexander said.

"Once we get the egg back, what then?" Isabel asked.

Alexander noticed a subtle shift in her colors, as if some outside force was exerting influence on her. His focus sharpened.

"We give it back to Bragador," he said.

"We could use it to bargain for the keystone and her tears," Isabel said, muddy darkness swirling through her clear bright colors.

Alexander swallowed hard. Azugorath's influence was growing. He knew his wife well enough to know that she would never try to use another's child as leverage.

"Focus, Isabel," he said. "The darkness is influencing you."

She stepped back as if he'd slapped her, clenching her eyes shut and shaking her head vigorously. Her colors cleared and brightened, though the taint remained.

"I'm sorry," she said. "You have to believe that I would never suggest such a thing."

"I do," Alexander said, taking her into his arms. "Phane's influence is growing. We have to be vigilant."

"I hate this," Isabel said. "I'm so terrified that I'm going to hurt you, that I'll betray you when you need me most. I can't live like this, Alexander."

"We'll fix it, Isabel. We'll get the egg from Phane's people. Once we return Bragador's egg, I have to believe she'll honor her bargain and give me the keystone and her tears in exchange for Mindbender. As soon as we toss the keystone into the endless mist, we'll set sail for Ruatha. You just have to hold on until then."

"I don't know if I can," she whispered. "I can't even explain it. It felt like bargaining with Bragador's egg was my idea and I thought it was a really good one when it occurred to me. This is so insidious."

"I know," Alexander said, his stomach squirming. He was torn between his need to help Isabel, his rage at Phane for what he'd done to her, and the horrible realization that he couldn't trust the one person he loved most in the world. He'd known that this was coming, tried unsuccessfully to prepare for it and reasoned that he could handle it as long as he knew there was a way to save her. Now that she was starting to slip away from him, he wasn't so sure. It felt like something deep inside, something vital, was breaking.

"Quiet," Hector said, slowly drawing one of his short swords.

Alexander dimmed the light in the Wizard's Den and grasped the hilt of Mindbender. Closing the door to the Den would have protected them completely, but he didn't dare risk what it might do to Isabel, so he envisioned a stone wall and released it into the sword. Because he'd opened the door to the Den against the wall of the cave, it was a simple matter to project an illusion that blended with the natural stone.

Everyone held their breath as the sound of careful footsteps approached. They saw the light of fire first, flickering and dancing against the volcanic stone of the walls.

A man cautiously rounded the corner, as if he expected to encounter a threat. On his outstretched palm danced a flame, though there didn't appear to be any source other than his hand. He had a medium build with black hair and dark green eyes that almost seemed to glow and sparkle in the dim firelight. He entered the small cave and stopped, listening intently, then sniffing the air like an animal.

"I can smell you, Human," he muttered to himself. "You can't be far."

He left through another passage. Alexander quietly exhaled but didn't move. He stood, waiting and listening to the sounds of footsteps echoing softly in the distance. After several minutes, when he was sure that they wouldn't be heard, he increased the light in the Wizard's Den just enough for his friends to see his gestures and motioned for them to follow him.

They crept out into the cave and left through a different passage, moving slowly through the dark, feeling their way along the uneven stone walls. Alexander was following a map burned into his mind from his clairvoyant reconnaissance. They moved painstakingly, trading silence for speed. After an hour, they stopped again in a small cavern.

"Who was that?" Isabel whispered.

"I don't know for sure, but he had the colors of a dragon," Alexander said.

"How can that be?" Jack asked.

"I don't know that either," Alexander said.

"I know dragons are creatures of magic, but I never expected them to be able to take human form," Isabel said.

"This complicates things," Alexander said. "I figured we'd be safe from them in such narrow passages, but I'm starting to think otherwise. It might be safer to take a much longer route that takes us deeper under the mountain."

As they moved deeper, the temperature started to rise. They were able to move faster once they decided it was safe to use the light of their night-wisp dust. Alexander led the way, taking each turn only after carefully thinking through the path he'd scouted. He used his all around sight to peer down each twist to ensure they wouldn't blunder into anyone or anything, reminding himself that dragons and men weren't the only threats he might encounter.

The passages they traveled looked like they had once been channels for free-flowing lava, an unsettling thought, but under the circumstances, the least of their worries. At a few points they had to use ropes to continue down the path. Alexander stopped abruptly as they rounded a corner and the heat of a river of molten rock washed over them.

The path they needed to take ran for twenty feet along a shelf that paralleled the lava flow a few dozen feet below. The heat was stifling, scalding their faces red and singeing their hair. They backed around the corner and the heat diminished.

"This is going to hurt," Alexander said as he opened the door to his Wizard's Den. "Jack, Hector, Horace, you'll stay in the Den. Will your shield protect you from the heat, Isabel?"

She shook her head. "The heat is in the air, my shield only stops magic and solid objects."

"Alright, douse yourself in water and wrap yourself with a wet blanket."

Alexander dunked a blanket into one of the barrels of water and tossed it over himself, wrapping it across his face.

"We'll have to move quickly," he said. "Stay close."

She nodded as she prepared her blanket. They stepped out of the Wizard's Den and Alexander closed the door.

"Ready?"

Isabel nodded.

Alexander led the way, staying close to the wall. The air was scorching hot, burning his lungs with every shallow breath. The heat was suddenly almost unbearable but he pressed on as quickly as he dared until he reached the passage leading out of the chamber. He kept an eye on Isabel the whole time through his all around sight. She was faring worse than he was because she needed to expose part of her face to the unbearably hot air in order to see.

As he reached the turn, his blanket caught fire. Isabel's blanket ignited moments later. He pressed ahead a few more steps, then tossed the blanket off himself before it could burn through and ignite his clothing.

Isabel stumbled and went to her knees, choking on the hot air. Alexander tore her flaming blanket away, scorching his hand, and grabbed her by the back of her leather armor, hauling her away from the deadly heat. Around another corner and the temperature dropped significantly, though still sweltering, around the next corner it dropped further still. He willed the door to the Wizard's Den open and hauled her through it. Jack was there waiting for them. He took Isabel and helped her to one of the beds while Hector and Horace got water to cool them both.

Alexander felt as though his lungs were on fire, and his hand was blistered. Isabel was burned across her face and on her hand and knees. Worse, she was unconscious. Alexander set his own pain aside and went to his wife. She was breathing shallowly but steadily. Her lungs were no doubt as scorched as his. He propped a pillow behind her head and fumbled with his pouch for a jar of healing salve.

Gently, carefully, he dabbed ointment around her eyes. Her skin was red and blistered. Hector handed him a pail of water and a towel. Alexander put the cool towel on Isabel's forehead and sprinkled water on her neck and cheeks to cool her down. She woke with a gasp and whimpered at the pain in her lungs.

"Hush," he said. "You're burned pretty badly. Can you swallow a healing draught?"

She nodded without opening her swollen eyes. He carefully held the potion to her lips and tipped the vial slowly. She swallowed the draught in one gulp, then winced. Alexander lowered her back onto the pillow.

"Try to sleep," he said.

She nodded.

"Maybe you should take your own advice," Jack said.

Alexander nodded, taking another potion from his pouch and quaffing it. It felt like he was swallowing fire. He lay down on the bed next to Isabel's and closed his eyes, hoping that the magic of the healing draught would claim him quickly.

***

He woke with a start. It felt like bugs were crawling over him but he quickly realized it was just beads of sweat running down his body under his clothes. The heat was oppressive. Jack and Hector slept restlessly while Horace stood guard at the door, sipping a cup of water to replenish the water he'd lost to sweat. Isabel was asleep, breathing slowly and deeply. The healing draught had done its work, the burns across her face were nearly gone, leaving only redness where hours before there had been blisters and angry welts.

Alexander's lungs felt better as well. He could breathe deeply without pain but his head hurt, his tongue was thick, and his mouth felt like it was full of cotton. He got up and drank several cups of water one right after the other.

"How long have we been out?"

"A few hours," Horace said. "Jack suggested we all try to get some rest. I just relieved Hector about an hour ago."

"Any movement out there?" Alexander asked.

"Nothing, just the heat," Horace said.

"Go get some more rest," Alexander said. "I'll stand watch."

Horace started to protest but Alexander silenced him with a look as he pulled a chair up next to the barrel of water and sat down. He sipped at his water, periodically scratching where a bead of sweat ran down his body, and considered his next move. He was close to the blood of the earth. The stuff still frightened him, partly from the sovereigns' warning, but mostly from the brilliantly radiant colors it gave off.

It was powerful.

Powerful in a way that transcended anything else he'd ever encountered. He worried that the sovereigns were wrong about the potion, worried that it might kill Isabel instead of helping her, worried that he might have alerted Phane to the existence of the blood of the earth by coming here in the first place. But in the end, he decided he was following the best course he could, given the challenges he faced. He reminded himself to be driven by emotion but ruled by reason.

Isabel woke as he was working a plan to separate himself from his friends for long enough to find the blood of the earth without them knowing.

He handed her a cup of water. She took it eagerly and drank deeply. He handed her another.

Once her thirst was sated, she sat down. "It's so hot," she said. "I'm soaked with sweat."

"Me too," Alexander said. "How are you feeling otherwise?"

"The burns are mostly gone, even the ones in my throat."

"Good," he said. "I was worried about you."

She smiled at him. "You saved me again."

He pulled her chair closer to his so he could put his arm around her. They sat quietly together until Jack woke and scrambled over to the barrel of water. After drinking deeply, he poured a cup over his head.

"Dear Maker, it's hot," he said. "I remember almost freezing to death in that mountain lake on Grafton. When I was out of the water and couldn't seem to get warm, I imagined how good heat would feel. Now, I think I'd like to take a dip in that lake."

"I know what you mean," Alexander said. "We should get moving pretty soon. Hopefully it'll cool down once we get farther from the lava flow."

"I hope you're right," Jack said. "This is unbearable. I can't imagine how you two managed to get by that river of molten rock without cooking."

"We didn't," Isabel said, gingerly touching the redness around her eyes.

"Point taken," Jack said.

Hector woke next, followed a few moments later by Horace. After they drank their fill, everyone filed out of the Wizard's Den and Alexander closed the door. They moved cautiously through the winding natural caverns and were greatly relieved when the temperature began falling noticeably.

They spent the day navigating a confusing maze of passages. They moved slowly and deliberately. The footing was treacherous and the rock was sharp and jagged in spots. Occasionally, Alexander stopped to scout the path ahead with his clairvoyance, which was fortunate, because it allowed him to pick a course that avoided another chamber filled with a pool of molten rock.

When they reached a chamber that Alexander recognized from his clairvoyant reconnaissance, he called a halt. Everyone was tired and hungry. They'd been moving through the bowels of the mountain for at least twelve hours and the path had been treacherous and difficult. He opened the door to his Wizard's Den so they could eat and rest before moving on.

He picked this particular chamber because it was a fork in the road. One branch led to the blood of the earth, another led to a series of passages that wound through the mountain, eventually leading to the cave where the pirates were hiding Bragador's egg.

Alexander took the first watch so he could lay the groundwork for slipping away from his friends in the night. He adjusted the blankets and pillows in his bunk to look like a person was sleeping under the covers, darkened the room almost completely, and then stood guard through his shift.

"I need you to stay here, Little One," he said silently.

"Where are you going, My Love?"

"After the final ingredient for the potion that will save Isabel," he said. "No one can know what it is, or even that it exists, so I have to do this alone. Watch over everyone and let me know if they discover I'm missing."

"I will, My Love. Be careful."

After he woke Horace for his turn at guard duty, he went to his bunk, but instead of lying down, he grasped the hilt of Mindbender and released a vision into the sword.

Alexander vanished from view as an illusionary version of himself lay down and adjusted the covers. He held the illusion, watching Horace's colors carefully and waiting. After several minutes, he crept past Horace into the cave beyond, all the while maintaining an illusion that obscured his presence, rendering him invisible. Once he was down the passage leading to the blood of the earth, he stopped and sent his all around sight back to see if Horace had noticed him, but he was unaware of Alexander's ruse.

He wound deeper through the gut rock of the mountain. The volcanic passage gave way to cut stone. Alexander hadn't examined the room very closely when he'd searched for the blood of the earth through his clairvoyance. Now that he was here, he realized the place had been made by someone long ago. It was carefully cut and ancient. He proceeded with a mixture of awe and caution.

The passage led down at a shallow angle, passing through hundreds of feet of solid stone and opening into one end of a large rectangular room, thirty feet wide, a hundred feet long, and precisely carved from the heart of the mountain.

A raised platform with a large crystal bowl occupied the far end. The colors flowing from the bowl were almost blinding. They radiated away in undulating waves of power. Alexander stood motionless for a long time, trying to work up the courage to approach a thing of such surpassing power.

Finally, need drove him forward. As he neared the center of the room, the walls transitioned from black basalt to crystal shot with gold, creating a dazzlingly beautiful web of light, the colors radiating from the blood of the earth mingling with the pure white light of his night-wisp dust.

Within a few steps of the bowl he could see the blood of the earth itself. It seemed to exist with deliberate certitude, as if the rest of the world was ephemeral and incorporeal by comparison, and it knew it. Alexander was struck by the complexity of its colors and awed by the sheer power of it.

"Please don't do this, Alexander," a voice said from behind him.

Alexander whirled, drawing Mindbender in one fluid motion, leveling the blade at a lone man dressed in a simple robe, standing not ten steps away. He looked young, like a man in his midtwenties … except he wasn't young at all. Alexander could see a timeless wisdom in his eyes, but more than that, his colors were expansive and very subtly refined, as if he existed at a higher state than everyone else. Alexander wasn't sure what to make of him.

"Who are you? How did you get here? And how do you know my name?" he asked.

"My name is Siduri," he said. "I will not harm you."

Alexander lowered the tip of Mindbender slightly. Siduri's colors said he was telling the truth, but Alexander almost suspected that this man could make his colors lie.

"Are you working for the dragons?"

"No," Siduri said. He spoke deliberately, intentionally, as if he was remembering how to speak after being silent for a very long time.

"Did Phane send you?"

"No, I represent no one … and everyone," Siduri said.

"What's that supposed to mean?"

Siduri shrugged. "I am not in league with any of your enemies, Alexander."

Alexander frowned. "Have you been following me?"

"In a manner of speaking."

Exasperation started to build in the pit of Alexander's stomach. "I don't have time for this," he said. "Answer my question."

"I have been watching you for your entire life," Siduri said. "We are alike, you and I—one with source."

"You're not making any sense," Alexander said, turning back toward the blood of the earth.

"Please, don't do that, Alexander."

"Why not?"

"The blood of the earth is too powerful," Siduri said. "Leave it be. Find another way."

"What do you know about it?"

"A great deal and very little, I'm afraid," Siduri said.

Alexander clenched his jaw. His blind eyes started glittering.

"It is powerful beyond measure," Siduri said. "Surely you can see this as clearly as I, yet I have never touched it, so I do not know its true nature any more than I know the true nature of death, having never experienced it."

"I only need one drop," Alexander said.

"One drop contains the power of all that it is," Siduri said. "Find another way."

"There is no other way," Alexander said. "At least not one that I can hope to accomplish."

"This path leads to destruction," Siduri said. "Such power should be left alone."

"Ordinarily, I would agree with you," Alexander said, "but this is the only way I can save my wife."

"It is one way," Siduri said. "There are others."

"What others? And how do you know anything about this? And … how did you get down here?"

"Kill the wraith queen," Siduri said, holding up one finger. "I have been watching," he said, holding up a second finger. "I am one with source, hence I am everywhere," he said, holding up a third finger.

"There's virtually no chance that I can reach the wraith queen," Alexander said. "And even if I could, I don't have the power to banish her. I need the blood of the earth to save Isabel. Do you intend to stop me?" he asked, raising the point of Mindbender.

Siduri smiled, as if noticing something for the first time. "Do you know the true nature and history of your sword?"

"What?" Alexander said. "You aren't making any sense. What's my sword got to do with this?"

"It is a unique blade, forged by one like us," Siduri said.

Curiosity ignited within Alexander's mind. He lowered Mindbender again and stared at Siduri, trying to formulate a question that he thought might get a straight answer.

"One like us? You mean you and I are alike? We're the same as Benesh Reishi?"

"Yes, we are one with source," Siduri said.

"Source? What's that?"

"You call it the firmament," Siduri said.

"You're an adept?"

"Benesh Reishi used that term to describe himself," Siduri said.

"I thought I was the only living adept," Alexander said. "The sovereigns told me there have only been two others like me."

"They are mistaken," Siduri said. "I am aware of seven, though there may have been others that came before me."

"Wait … so you're saying you're the first of seven," Alexander said. "How can that be? How old are you?"

"I am many thousands of years old," Siduri said.

"How's that possible?" Alexander asked, reeling slightly from the implications.

Siduri shrugged.

Alexander shook his head and absentmindedly sheathed Mindbender, questions and possibilities tumbling through his mind.

"If what you're saying is true, there's so much you could teach me," Alexander said. "You've asked me not to use the blood of the earth, but I need it to save my wife. Help me understand. Help me find another way."

"It is not my place to interfere," Siduri said. "Your free will is your own, use it as you will. I am simply here to warn you of the danger, to ask you to find another way."

"All right, you're still not helping me understand," Alexander said. "Let's back up and take things one at a time. Tell me about Mindbender."

"Benesh Reishi created your sword using a process that he invented," Siduri said. "He was hoping to replicate his link with source and impart it on the sword, but he failed. Instead, he stripped himself of his link with source and transferred it to the sword. As a result, the normal aging process resumed and claimed his life. It was tragic really, the solution was so simple and yet he never saw it."

"What do you mean?"

"A link with source needs a place to reside," Siduri said.

Alexander sighed in exasperation. "I don't have time for riddles. If you aren't going to answer my questions, then let me do what I came here to do."

"I won't stop you," Siduri said, "but I beg you to reconsider. You're tampering with a power beyond your understanding. The result could be disastrous, and not just for you and your wife but for all of the Seven Isles."

"What will happen if I use it to help her?" Alexander asked.

"I cannot be sure, but I would have you consider the possibilities," Siduri said. "Using power always has consequences, often unforeseen. It may cure her. It may kill her. It may confer upon her a power so great that she would transcend her human existence. But then, she is in the grip of one of the Taker's minions, and so that power would pass to him."

"Wait … who's the Taker?"

"He is the enemy of the light, the Taker of life, the bringer of darkness," Siduri said. "He is the timeless and formless master of the netherworld."

Alexander felt a chill race up his spine. He stood stock-still, processing what he'd just learned. Before he could respond, Siduri continued.

"The Taker is always looking for a way into the world of time and substance. In the netherworld he cannot have substance, yet he craves it. Only in this world can he manifest in physical form, yet he is denied access by the very nature of the world of time and substance itself. The blood of the earth has the power to alter that essential nature, to unmake the rules of reality. This remedy you seek could deliver into the Taker's hands the power to come forth and consume the world."

Alexander swallowed hard as the magnitude of Siduri's words sank in.

"I have to try," he said. "I can't just let Phane take her from me." His voice broke as the weight of his emotional distress threatened to overwhelm him. "She's my wife. I love her more than anything. I have to save her."

"Find another way," Siduri said.

"The other way is beyond me!" Alexander said. "I'll do whatever it takes to save her."

"That will be your folly, Alexander. I speak from experience. Heed my words."

"No," Alexander said, his resolve hardening. He'd come this far. The last ingredient he needed was within reach. "I have to do this. I'll look for another way, but right now, I need this option if all else fails."

Siduri took a deep breath and let it out slowly.

"Let me tell you a story," he said. "Perhaps you will learn a valuable lesson from my mistake."

Alexander nodded, deflated and emotionally exhausted.

"I was born in a small village on what you call the Reishi Isle. My grandfather was the shaman. He took me as his apprentice because I demonstrated a keen insight at a very young age. Much like you, Alexander, I could see colors. Others have no concept of the power such vision confers. The insight is priceless.

"I studied diligently and learned quickly. When I was ready, I undertook my vision quest. From full moon to full moon I fasted, drinking only the water of a sacred and secluded mountain lake revered by our people as a place of magic. I faced pain and despair and fear like nothing I could have imagined, yet I survived. When I returned, my grandfather was disappointed that I couldn't learn the simple spells he wished to teach me, yet my insight increased. I could see farther and deeper than any other. Eventually, when my grandfather passed from this world, I became the shaman.

"I served my village for nearly three hundred years. Over those years my abilities developed. I gained the ability to see at a great distance, to become one with source, to see all around me even with my eyes closed, even the ability to walk with the spirits.

"Eventually, the people became fearful of me because I did not age as others do. It's expected that a shaman will live much longer than others, but I was different. I remained young, even though centuries passed.

"Seeing the fear in their colors was painful for me. I had served my people faithfully for my whole life but I realized that I could remain with them no longer, so I left my village and walked the world, exploring the Seven Isles for over a century. Still I did not age.

"Then I met a woman. She was beautiful and kind. I fell in love with her and discovered a joy like nothing I'd known before. For several short years we enjoyed happiness together, living a simple life in a little house. We had three sons and they were the center of our world. They were bright and full of life, exuberant and curious about everything."

Siduri stopped and took a deep breath, centering himself before he continued.

"One bright summer day, my sons went fishing in a little boat on the river. I found them washed up on the bank. All three had drowned. I can't express with words the depth of the pain I felt. The loss was total and all-consuming. The pain of the vision quest was a trivial thing compared to the limitless agony of such loss.

"As devastating as it was for me, it was doubly difficult for my wife. She was hysterical, simply unable to face a world without her children. Fearing she would harm herself, I gave her an herbal mixture to make her sleep."

He paused and fixed Alexander with a penetrating stare before continuing.

"Then I set out to bring my children back from the dead."

Alexander swallowed hard.

"I had not used my power for anything of consequence since meeting my wife. But now I slipped free of my mortal bonds and walked in the silvery world of the spirits. I sought out my sons and found them before they passed into the light. I beseeched their ghosts to wait, to remain in the spirit world. I told them that I could bring them back, that I would find a way.

"From there I found my way into the realm of light and begged the Lords of Light to help me, to grant a reprieve to my sons. I implored them to give my children life again. With great compassion and boundless sympathy, they refused to alter the natural order of the world to spare my wife and me the heartache we were suffering. I wept."

Siduri stopped again, staring off into the distance, a haunted look in his eyes.

"What I did next was driven by madness, desperation, and above all, hubris. Having failed to gain the aid I sought from the realm of light, I turned to the darkness. I would undo my children's deaths, no matter the cost." He fixed Alexander with a hard look.

He felt a tingle of dread wash over his entire body. He stood still, hanging on Siduri's every word.

"I traveled into the cold and lifeless void of the netherworld and was met by the broken souls that reside there. They assailed me, tearing at my living light with almost desperate viciousness, but I held my place and called out for the Taker. And he answered my summons.

"In abject desperation, I offered to pay any price if he would bring my children back to life.

"He named his price. It was what I had expected and I agreed willingly: When I die, he will claim my soul. In that moment, I believed it to be a triumph. I thought I had cheated death, overcome the natural order of the world to save my family. The price would be paid much later, and I was willing to bear it if it would bring my children back."

Siduri fell silent, wrestling with an ancient emotional burden that still haunted him.

"The Taker fulfilled his part of the bargain, in a manner of speaking. My children returned from the dead, but they were changed, tainted by the Taker's darkness. Would you like to know their names, Alexander?" Siduri looked up, his gaze boring into Alexander.

He couldn't move, couldn't breathe. He tried to swallow but his mouth was too dry. Cold dread rippled over his skin.

"My eldest son is named Shivini … my middle son is named Rankosi … and my youngest son is named Jinzeri."

Chapter 36

Lacy shivered with fear as the dragon's shadow passed over her hiding place beneath a large pine tree. Drogan was beside her, looking through the boughs toward the sky. They'd been on the run for days and Lacy was cold, tired, and hungry.

"There's the second one," he whispered as another shadow flickered overhead.

The dragons were new. She'd been hunted by soldiers since her home was overrun. She'd been hunted by something out of a nightmare since she'd recovered the obscure little black box from her family crypt. The dragons had only been hunting her since the previous day.

"I still don't understand why dragons are hunting me," she said, having difficulty reconciling her understanding of reality with the words coming out of her mouth.

"Zuhl has collared a number of dragons to serve him," Drogan said. "We'll have to move at night from now on."

Lacy nodded. Drogan had been her protector for only two weeks but he had already saved her life at least three times. She knew with chilling certainty that she wouldn't have made it through the night they met if he hadn't been there to help her.

She didn't quite trust him, though. There was something odd about him, something she couldn't put her finger on. She reminded herself yet again to be vigilant.

She had a duty to fulfill. Her father had trusted her in his moment of greatest need and she meant to live up to that trust no matter what. Drogan was necessary. She couldn't survive alone. Even without the soldiers, demons, and dragons hunting her, she wasn't prepared to live on the road. But she was learning quickly.

They had encountered a group of three thugs in the first days after Drogan had come to her aid. Lacy had heard stories about such men, but she wasn't prepared for the reality of meeting them on a deserted road. She knew without a doubt how her life would end if they'd had their way. Drogan had killed them with a kind of detached efficiency that both fascinated and frightened her.

The three ruffians were armed with rudimentary weapons: a woodsman's axe, a stout club of Iron Oak, and a knife. They spread out to surround them. Drogan simply waited, watching them casually, as if they posed no real threat. The man with the axe brought it over his head in an attempt to split Drogan's skull. He simply stepped aside at just the right moment. As the thug lunged forward, pulled by the momentum of his swing, Drogan grabbed him by the chin with one large hand and the back of the head with the other, a quick snapping twist and the man crumpled to the ground.

The other two were shocked by how quickly their companion had died. They hesitated. But Drogan didn't. He closed quickly on the man with the knife, grabbed his hand, crushing his fingers around the hilt, driving the blade up into his throat. The third thug turned and ran. Drogan casually picked up the fallen man's axe, eyed the fleeing man for a moment, then brought the axe over his head and hurled it, end over end, into the man's back. He died slowly, blood sputtering and frothing from his mouth. As he twitched in pain, Drogan searched him for anything of use and then left him lying in the road without the mercy of a quick death.

Lacy could still see the panic in his dying eyes. She hated that she was grateful for their deaths, but she knew what they would have done to her if they'd caught her alone. For now she needed Drogan and they both knew it.

***

She woke with a start. Drogan had a hand over her mouth but released it when she nodded. It was nearly dark, the sun having only just set. They'd spent the day under the pine tree waiting for the safety of night. Drogan said the dragons could see well in daylight but were just as limited as people at night. She hoped he was right.

He motioned in the gloom. She caught her breath when she heard a twig snap. The enemy was close. Carefully, quietly, she looked through the tree branches and counted six big brutish men spread out and moving slowly. They were searching for her.

"Their trail came this way, I'm sure of it," one of them said.

Another of the men looked up at the rapidly darkening sky and shook his head. "It's too dark to track them now. We'll make camp in this clearing and pick up their scent at first light."

Lacy schooled her breathing as she watched the men begin to make camp not thirty feet from her hiding place. Darkness fell as they built a fire. She held perfectly still, breathing slowly and evenly. The men cooked a meal of horse meat and washed it down with a jug of wine. After a painstaking couple of hours spent holding still while listening to the men joke and laugh about their very graphic plans for her when they caught her, she watched them finally lie down to sleep.

One man stayed awake, sitting by the fire, poking at the embers with a stick. When the rest were snoring, Drogan started to move. In the flickering firelight filtering through the branches, he took off his hat and long coat, then slipped a knife free of its sheath.

With deliberate slowness, he crept out from under the pine boughs and worked his way through the darkness. Lacy watched and waited. She knew what was about to happen—she knew it would be terrible and bloody, and she hated herself for wishing these men dead, but she also knew what would happen to her if they caught her.

Drogan was invisible in the dark, silent as a tomb. Lacy almost started to think he had simply crept out of the camp and left her to fend for herself when she caught a glimpse of his shadowy form behind the soldier sitting by the fire. Lacy's heart beat so hard she could feel it in her temples. When she caught herself holding her breath, she let it out slowly and silently.

Drogan inched closer to the soldier. Finally reaching striking distance, he lunged forward, driving the knife into the man's lower back just to the right of the spine, at the same time clapping his left hand over the man's mouth. The surprised soldier stiffened but didn't utter a sound as Drogan brought the blade up and cut his throat, spilling bright red blood down his tunic.

He carefully laid the man over, then froze still as a stone. No one stirred. He selected his next target, the nearest man. He didn't rush. Picking each step and testing his footing before committing weight to it, he glided in slow motion through the flickering light.

Lacy watched with a mixture of relief and dread as he slipped his blade under the man's ribs and up into his chest, slicing from side to side. The dying man's eyes opened in shock but he didn't offer any resistance, didn't utter so much as a whimper.

The third and fourth men died just as quietly. It had taken Drogan nearly half an hour to kill them as he traded speed for stealth. He reached the fifth man and positioned himself for the kill strike when the man rolled over and woke up. Drogan stabbed at him, but the soldier whipped his blanket up toward Drogan's hand, entangling the knife in the fabric as he shouted a warning. Drogan lunged forward, blindly stabbing through the blanket and hitting the soldier in the thigh. The man screamed in pain.

His lone remaining companion scrambled free of his bedding and looped a length of rope around Drogan's neck, hauling him back and away from the injured man. Drogan fought and flailed but he could neither reach the soldier with his blade nor free himself from the rope looped around his neck.

Before Lacy could think it through, before she could second-guess herself, she was moving out from under the pine boughs, in spite of the burning pain in her legs from holding still for so long, into the light of the fire, knife in hand. She darted across the camp, driving her blade into the middle of the soldier's back just to the left of the spine. Somewhere in the recesses of her mind, she vaguely remembered learning where to strike a man in the back to kill him quickly.

Drogan tore the loop of rope free, gasping for breath, and then choking, he fell forward onto all fours. The wounded man drew a sword and swung it wildly at him but Drogan was just out of reach. As the wounded man started to crawl forward to get close enough for a clean strike, Lacy grabbed Drogan and pulled him out of range.

He saw the danger and rolled backward from all fours to a sitting position where he could see the single remaining enemy soldier. He took a moment to collect himself, deliberately drawing each breath, wheezing past the injuries in his throat.

Lacy watched and waited. The soldier made another feeble effort to lash out at Drogan but he was still out of range. Doggedly, Lacy's protector got to his feet and scanned the campsite until he found what he wanted. Without haste, he retrieved a flask of oil, smelled it to confirm the contents, then poured it into the empty cook pot.

The soldier looked on with growing fear as he held his sword point between himself and his quarry-turned-predator. Drogan unceremoniously splashed the wounded man with a quart of lamp oil, picked up a flaming log and tossed it at him, igniting the oil with a whoosh.

The man screamed, then screamed again. Drogan ignored him as he began going through the other soldiers' belongings for anything of use.

Lacy watched the dying soldier burn. She was oddly fascinated by the spectacle. She had vowed to herself that she would learn about war and killing so that she could protect her people.

This was killing. And it was ugly. It was horrible.

And yet, it was necessary.

Even with all that she had heard from these very men about how they intended to rape her, viciously and brutally, she wouldn't have wished such a death on them, and yet, now that they were dead or dying, she was greatly relieved. She wondered if that made her a bad person.

Drogan snapped her out of her introspection with a hand on her shoulder. He didn't speak but instead motioned for them to go. She nodded tightly, and realizing that she still held her blood-soaked knife, wiped it off on the nearest dead soldier before they set out.

They moved slowly through the night. Lacy came to see the darkness as a friend, as an ally that shielded her from her hunters. Just weeks ago, she'd been afraid of the dark, but now daylight was her enemy. In the light of day, the dragons could see her from the sky. Whatever fear she had of the creatures that roamed the night paled in comparison to the visceral fear evoked by a dragon passing overhead.

By day, she and Drogan hid. By night, they walked south toward the coast and a ship that would take her to Ithilian and safety. For nearly a week they traveled this way, avoiding villages and roads as much as possible. Only when they ran out of supplies did Drogan agree to stop at a village.

They came across a road heading southwest, probably the road to Suva. Drogan insisted that they stay well off the road and travel parallel to it until they came to a village. Near dawn, they arrived at a little hamlet, more of a roadside rest stop than a village; it consisted of an inn, a general store, a stable, a blacksmith's shop, and a constable's office surrounded by a small number of houses. The forest was gradually giving way to farmland as they moved south, farther from the mountains and closer to the ocean. Plots of workable land were separated by copses of trees scattered haphazardly around the little town.

"Can we stay here for the day?" Lacy asked. "A warm meal and a decent sleep would do us both good … not to mention a bath." She wrinkled her nose.

Drogan looked at the town for a moment before nodding. "We'll stay until dusk and then be on our way," he said. "Suva is less than a week's walk. We can get passage on a ship there."

As they approached the town, a bell tolled. A dozen men armed with spears or bows came forth to meet them before they reached the edge of the village. Drogan stopped slightly ahead of Lacy and waited, hands at his sides.

The townsfolk spread out, surrounding Lacy and Drogan while a man wearing a badge of office from the territory of Suva approached.

"I'm the constable here," he said. "State your business."

"We're traveling south, hoping to get passage to Ithilian," Drogan said. "Low on supplies so we thought we'd stop here and buy a few things."

The constable nodded. "We've been getting a fair number of refugees fleeing the war up north. Have you seen any of Zuhl's soldiers nearby?"

"There's probably a hundred or so just north of here," Drogan said, "but they're pretty spread out, like they're looking for something. Don't know much more than that, since we've been trying to avoid them as best we can."

"Understandable," the constable said. "Well, you're welcome to go on into town so long as you obey the law. There's a caravan of refugees headed to Suva about midday, might consider joining up with them, strength in numbers and all. The roads aren't safe anymore."

"Thanks," Drogan said, "we might just do that."

They made their way into a town nervous with stories of horror to the north. People were suspicious of outsiders and it showed in their furtive glances and challenging glares. Drogan ignored them, Lacy tried to stay close to him.

They reached the inn only to find the door locked. Drogan knocked and waited patiently. Several moments later the peephole in the door opened.

"What do you want?" the man within said.

"A meal and a room," Drogan replied.

The innkeeper's eyes narrowed suspiciously until Drogan held up a gold sovereign. He nodded quickly, shut the peephole, and opened the door. As soon as they were inside he shut the door, threw the bolt, and dropped the bar.

"Can't be too careful these days, what with the war to the north and all," he said. "How long will you be staying?"

"Just for the day," Drogan said. "Do you have a room with two beds?"

The innkeeper nodded expectantly.

Drogan held up the coin.

"The room for the day and two hot meals each plus some travel rations," Drogan said.

"Agreed," the innkeeper said, taking the coin. "Have you come from the north? I hear the Reishi army is fighting the barbarian horde. Hardly seems possible."

"We've been working pretty hard to avoid being noticed," Drogan said. "I'm afraid we don't have much news to offer."

"One of the refugees said they saw the Reishi army," the innkeeper said. "He said it was a million men strong, soldiers from Ruatha and Ithilian all marching under the Reishi banner and taking the fight to Zuhl's horde. What do you think it means? What are they fighting over? And why here?"

Drogan shrugged. "If I had to guess, I'd say Prince Phane is trying to defend the people of Fellenden against Zuhl's aggression."

"Oh, I hope you're right," the innkeeper said. "Someone has to help us or we're all lost. I've heard such horrible stories about Zuhl's barbarians. I just can't believe they're as vicious as people say."

Lacy stayed stock-still and listened to every word of the exchange. In the back of her mind, she thought she should tell the man that Zuhl's brutes were worse than any of the stories he'd heard, but she was too focused on listening to the conversation to say anything.

All her life she'd learned that the Reishi had waged war on the Seven Isles, a war that had destroyed her House. The line of Fellenden had never regained its former station, not that it had mattered much to her. And now the Reishi army was on Fellenden once again, this time fighting against Zuhl's barbarian horde. She didn't understand and yet she hoped beyond hope that the rumor was true. Someone had to stand against Zuhl. If the Reishi Prince, risen from the ashes of history, was the only one powerful enough, then so be it. Her people didn't deserve what Zuhl was doing to them.

The innkeeper leaned in conspiratorially. "I also hear tell of dragons," he whispered.

Drogan nodded somberly. "The way I understand it, Zuhl's put a collar on a few dragons, turned them into pets, of a sort." Drogan paused for effect. "We saw them a few days ago, been traveling at night ever since."

The innkeeper blanched. "If that's true, then the Reishi Prince really is our only hope. It's said that he has powerful magic. Still, I don't know how anyone could stand against a dragon, magic or not."

"Having seen them with my own eyes, I'm inclined to agree with you," Drogan said. "Even Prince Phane will need some help if Zuhl has dragons serving him."

"This is all so much bigger than me," the innkeeper said, shaking his head. "I wish we could go back to the way things were. Oh well, let me get your room key and some breakfast."

The food was simple fare but it was hot and there was plenty. After the meal, Lacy felt better than she had in weeks, even though her mind was still reeling from the news that a friendly army was standing against Zuhl. She considered changing her plan and going back north to meet the army and offer what help she could, but then thought better of it. Her father had entrusted her with a mission that he believed was vitally important. She decided again that she would not fail him, no matter the cost.

The brief exchange with the innkeeper ignited a storm of new questions within her mind, questions that Drogan might be able to answer. Since they'd met, she had deliberately, or perhaps unconsciously, avoided asking him many questions. She told herself that it wasn't important, that questioning him might lead him to abandon her when she needed him most, but the truth was, she was afraid of the answers.

As she lay down on one of the two little beds in their room, bone-weary from traveling, she realized her curiosity wasn't going to let her sleep, so she steeled herself and plunged in.

"Drogan, are you awake?"

"I'm trying not to be," he replied.

"Why are you helping me?"

He was quiet for a moment before he answered, "I was sent to help you."

"By whom?"

"Prince Phane," Drogan said, "though indirectly. I work for the Reishi Army Regency out of Karth. They sent me here to gather information about Zuhl's invasion. Once I was here, I got an urgent order to look for you and help you reach safety."

"Why?" Lacy asked. "Why would Prince Phane care about me?"

Drogan shrugged as if the reason didn't really matter. "I suppose because you're a princess of the House of Fellenden. Truth is, I didn't ask."

"All of the stories say Prince Phane is a monster," Lacy said. "I don't understand why he would want to help me." She felt the inkling of suspicion start to build in the back of her mind. She hadn't told Drogan about the little black box she was carrying. But Prince Phane was supposed to be a powerful wizard … he might have ways of knowing about it, he might even know what was inside it. After all, he was alive when the box was hidden away from the world in Carlyle Fellenden's tomb.

"You've heard of the Rebel Wizard?" Drogan asked.

"Of course," Lacy said. "He led the Seven Isles against the tyranny of Malachi Reishi."

"Prince Phane was his inside man," Drogan said. "Prince Phane gave him the secret of Wizard's Dust. Prince Phane provided him with information about troop movements and battle plans. Without Prince Phane's help, the Rebel Wizard wouldn't have had a chance."

"Why don't the history books say that?"

"After the war was over, the Reishi Protectorate went underground," Drogan said. "They kept fighting against the Rebel Mage and his allies for almost a century. They were the ones who hunted Phane until he decided it would be better to give up and flee into the future. With him gone, the Protectorate systematically destroyed all of the history books that told the truth and replaced them with the stories you've heard.

"They were waiting for him when he woke," Drogan continued. "Nearly killed him, but he was too powerful for them. He managed to escape to the Reishi Army Regency, the last standing Reishi army in the world and the one place he knew he would find others loyal to the Old Law."

"This is all so hard to believe," Lacy said. "How can everything I've been taught my whole life be a lie?"

"For centuries, the Protectorate dedicated themselves to rewriting history," Drogan said. "Think about it, all we know about those years is what was written down. If the history books are full of lies, then it only makes sense that we'd believe them, especially since we didn't have anyone to tell us what really happened … until now, anyway. Prince Phane is going to change all that. He'll tell people the truth once this blasted war is over. I only hope he has the strength to defeat Zuhl and his dragons."

As Drogan drifted off to sleep and started snoring, Lacy thought about what he'd said. She decided she wasn't convinced of anything but she was willing to consider the possibility that Phane was an ally. The thought gave her more hope than she'd had in weeks. Someone powerful was standing up to Zuhl. Her people might have a chance.

***

She woke with a start. Drogan rolled out of bed and went to the door, his hand on the hilt of his dagger. She heard a scream, muffled by the walls between her and the source.

"Get your boots on," Drogan said.

Lacy didn't waste a moment. She was up and ready as quickly as Drogan. They grabbed their packs and went to the main hall of the inn. Several people were crowded around the innkeeper who was standing at the peephole, peering through.

"Dear Maker," he said. "We're under attack by a wizard."

"All I want is the princess from the north," Lacy heard from beyond the door. She recognized the voice—it was Wizard Saul. "Give her to me and I will spare you my wrath."

"Time to go," Drogan said, turning toward the kitchen.

Lacy followed silently, fear hammering in her chest. She didn't know what was inside Wizard Saul but whatever it was, she was viscerally afraid of it. They slipped out the back door of the inn as they heard pounding on the barred front door.

Drogan led her to the stables, furtively looking this way and that. The stable master was nowhere to be seen and the horses were skittish, but Drogan started saddling one anyway. Lacy stopped, frowning at him.

"What are you waiting for?" he said, cinching the straps. "Saddle that horse, we don't have much time."

"But these horses belong to someone," Lacy said. "We can't just take them."

Drogan looked at her like she was crazy, but didn't stop readying his horse.

"You can leave some gold for them if you like," he said. "Right now, we need the speed or we're both dead."

He finished preparing his horse and started saddling the one he'd selected for her.

Lacy wrestled with her conscience. Then she heard another scream, this time coming from inside the inn. Her fear got the better of her. She left four gold coins on the stall railing and helped Drogan finish preparing her horse.

She looked over her shoulder as they rode out of town and saw Wizard Saul step out the back door of the inn. He raised his hand toward her, but they rounded the corner of the building before he could cast his spell. They coaxed their horses into a gallop, racing the failing daylight to gain as much distance as possible before darkness slowed their pace.

They rode all night, sticking to the road for greater speed. Horses would cut the time needed to reach Suva by several days, but they would also make it much more difficult to hide during the day.

As dawn neared, sending streamers of crimson and orange across the sky, Drogan led them off the road and into a copse of trees. The terrain had transitioned from forested foothills into gently rolling fields interrupted by an occasional grove of trees hugging a small lake or lining the bank of a meandering stream. They were getting closer to the ocean and the promise of safety.

Lacy slept fitfully under the lone pine tree amidst the thinning hardwoods and woke midday to the sound of barking dogs. Drogan was up and pulling on his boots a moment later.

"We have to go," he said as he scrambled out from under the pine boughs and threw on his oilskin coat and broad-brimmed hat. Lacy was up and ready a moment later. The dogs were getting closer. She heard shouting off in the distance as she mounted her horse.

Through the thinning trees, she caught glimpses of soldiers on horseback, spread out in a long line, following three men with tracking dogs. Zuhl's soldiers had caught up with her. She swallowed her fear and spurred her horse into a trot through the trees, cautiously picking her path to avoid becoming entangled in the brush. As much as she wanted to bolt, to run for her life, she had to be smart. The forest floor was uneven and treacherous, moving too fast would only injure her horse.

Her fear spiked when she heard a whistler arrow shriek into the sky behind her. The enemy had her scent and was on the hunt. After what seemed like hours, she and Drogan finally broke free of the trees and into a rolling field, urging their horses into a gallop toward the road that ran along the tree line.

That's when they saw the soldiers. At least two dozen of the big brutish barbarians from Zuhl were waiting for the men with dogs to flush out their quarry.

Lacy's fear swelled into panic as she and Drogan veered away from the road and the onrushing soldiers. Everything seemed to happen at once. Coming up the road from the south was another force of nearly thirty men, all wearing the same brown leather armor trimmed in forest green and riding light, fast horses.

The dozen men behind them cleared the trees, spreading out and urging their horses into a gallop to prevent Lacy and Drogan from returning to the cover of the forest.

Wizard Saul came marching up the road from the north, undaunted by the soldiers. He began casting a spell as he quickened his pace.

Then Lacy heard the roar of a dragon. She looked up and saw two of the terrifying beasts in the sky above, flying in formation and wheeling to line up for an attack run.

She was trapped: barbarians to the east and west, unknown soldiers to the south, a wizard possessed by darkness to the north, and dragons overhead. Oddly enough, the panic that was just moments before threatening to overwhelm her reason faded away, leaving only calm clarity and a razor's-edge focus.

The soldiers to the south spread out into a battle line, the front rank wielding spears and shields, the back rank nocking arrows. They advanced on the two dozen barbarians to the east, sending a barrage of arrows into them as they closed the distance.

The barbarians to the west sent their hunting dogs racing out in front of them, easily gaining on Lacy and Drogan as they spurred their horses toward the narrow gap between the soldiers to the south and the grove of trees west of the road.

"She's mine!" Wizard Saul shouted as he released his spell. A black blob materialized just in front of his outstretched hand, streaking into the air and separating into three streams of a dark and viscous liquid. They spiraled around each other, traveling in an arc several hundred feet across the field and striking the three hunting dogs with unerring precision. Lacy looked back when she heard the dogs yelp. The black liquid tore into them, burning and melting their flesh away with terrifying violence, leaving only parts of each dog amidst a smoldering stain on the ground where they fell.

The dragons altered their attack run to target the wizard. Lacy expected to hear the roar of dragon fire but instead she saw a pair of javelins, one after the next, hurtle down from the dragon riders. Wizard Saul easily deflected the attack with his magic.

She raced on as the leather-armor-clad soldiers thinned the ranks of the barbarians with one volley of arrows after another, preferring to maintain a safe distance from Zuhl's brutes and pick them apart with their arrows rather than engage them in close combat.

The barbarians that had flushed them out of the trees were driving their horses hard to gain ground on Lacy and Drogan as they passed the unknown soldiers from the south, slipping out of the midst of the battle.

The leader of the leather-clad soldiers broke off from the battle with a squad of his men to give chase. He was yelling something, but Lacy couldn't hear over the rushing wind and the pounding of her heart. She leaned into her horse's neck, urging him to greater speed.

Just before she rounded the bend in the road, she looked back at the battle one last time. The leather-armored soldiers had broken into two groups, a squad-sized unit was racing after her while sending arrows into the barbarians that had flushed her from the trees, while the remaining soldiers were fighting a retreating action that seemed designed to prevent the barbarians from advancing past them to the south, putting this new enemy between Lacy and Zuhl's barbarians.

Wizard Saul unleashed a scything pinwheel of magical force that severed the wing of the lead dragon and sent it crashing to the ground in a horrendous cacophony of broken bone and wailing terror. Lacy couldn't imagine how much power it must take to kill a dragon, but now she knew that the monster chasing her was much more dangerous than she ever imagined.

When the dragon fell, the squad giving chase opted to focus on fighting the enemy soldiers rather than continue their pursuit, giving Lacy and Drogan precious minutes to make their escape.

They raced on through the late afternoon and into the evening, pushing their horses to the point of exhaustion and beyond, until just before dusk, Lacy's steed came up lame. They dismounted, took what supplies they could carry and headed off the road into the night.

"Who were those other soldiers?" Lacy asked.

"Reishi Protectorate," Drogan said as he carefully picked his path through the darkness.

"Why are they after us?"

"I couldn't say for sure," Drogan said. "I do know they can't be trusted. For now, we're on our own."

"I don't understand why they were fighting Zuhl's men," Lacy said.

"Zuhl hates everything Reishi," Drogan said. "He wants to destroy the Reishi Protectorate just as much as he wants to destroy the Reishi Army Regency."

For the next several days they traveled south, pushing themselves to the limits of their endurance each day before finding a hiding place to sleep for a few hours, only to wake and drive themselves to the point of exhaustion again. Speed was their best hope, their only hope. With so many enemies arrayed against her, Lacy thought it was a miracle that she was still alive. A month ago she wouldn't have thought herself capable of all that she'd done in the past weeks. Despite all of her troubles, she found that she was more sure of herself than she'd ever been. She wasn't a match for what she faced, she had no illusions about that, but she was learning and growing, becoming more capable with each passing day. She just had to make it to Ithilian. Lord Abel would help her.

Several days after the terrible battle, she and Drogan reached the city of Suva at dusk. She had no doubt that her pursuers hadn't given up but she saw no sign of them as they entered the city. The city watch was wary but they readily accepted the truth that she and Drogan were refugees fleeing the war to the north.

They went straight to the port and booked passage on a freighter converted into a passenger ship that was bound for Ithilian the following morning. The captain was only too happy to accept them aboard when he saw the five gold coins they offered in payment. Most of his passengers could only offer a few silver coins or livestock in trade. They were assigned to a cramped little stateroom with a bunk bed, but it was far better than a cot in the hold of the ship that most of the passengers were only too happy to get. She and Drogan locked the door of their stateroom and slept like the dead.

She woke the next morning from the noise of the crew casting off and went up on deck, trailing a silent Drogan behind her. As she stepped up to the railing, she saw three of the soldiers in leather armor on the dock. One noticed her and waved frantically.

She thought she heard the leader call out, "Princess Lacy!" But his voice was drowned out by the sounds of the crew and the seagulls. Lacy took a deep breath and let it out slowly. She was safe at last.

Then she saw Wizard Saul on the docks. He was looking straight at her as he cut his own throat and toppled into the water.

Chapter 37

The dragon was blue, the color of a glacier, twice the size of a wyvern, with a single row of spikes running down its spine and a pair of horns that coiled back from its brow. The first thrust of its wings lifted it a hundred feet into the air. It was magnificent and terrifying all at once. Not at all like Tanis, and yet just as potent.

"Didn't expect that," Abigail said. "Captain Sava, send a runner, have Knight Raja ready with Kallistos at a moment's notice."

He nodded curtly and gestured to one of his men.

"What are you thinking?" Anatoly asked, an uncharacteristic hint of nervousness in his voice.

"Not many weapons can pierce a dragon's scales," Abigail said.

The dragon lifted another hundred feet into the air with a second thrust of its wings. It roared, fury and puissance mingled to place the world on notice: A dragon had joined the battle.

Hundreds of long boards flopped over the front of the berm wall, covering the rows of spikes, stretching across the ditch and creating a multitude of paths from which Zuhl's barbarians poured forth. Like ants, they streamed out of their hill toward the shield line protecting the archers who had been raining death down into their camp.

"It has a rider," Wizard Sark said. "I didn't think dragons allowed people to ride them."

"They don't," Magda said.

The man riding the dragon started glowing, softly at first, growing brighter and brighter with each passing moment. By the time he was a thousand feet in the air, he was glowing so brightly that he challenged the sun's dominance of the sky. The dragon roared again as it turned to pursue the attack wings of Sky Knights that were moving to engage the ships.

"Signal the heavy cavalry," Abigail said.

General Kern had his order. If the barbarians came forth, he was to mount a charge along the berm wall into the enemy's flank.

The barbarians met the shield wall with a tumultuous crash that rippled through the still morning air. Many fell against the pikes set atop the shields, but many more made it inside the pike line and engaged the soldiers manning the shields.

The heavy shields, each locked to the next and set into the ground with two heavy spikes jutting from the bottom edge, held against the initial crush of the enemy. The soldiers jabbed their swords through gaps cut into the side of each shield, killing or wounding those directly in front of them. But still the enemy came.

The next wave of brutes climbed up the carnage and vaulted into the soldiers behind the shields.

A few at first, thrashing about against the soldiers all around them, then a few more, killing several men each before they fell to the infantry. A small cluster of barbarians turned back toward the shield line, killed two soldiers, unhooked their shields, hoisted them out of the ground and tossed them into the battle raging around them.

With the line broken, the enemy started to press forward, killing or maiming with each powerful stroke of their gruesome, battle-honed weapons. The fighting raged behind the shield line as the infantry struggled to stand against the bigger and more powerful barbarians. Zuhl's soldiers fought with reckless abandon, as if they had already forsaken their lives and simply wished to take as many as they could into the netherworld with them before they fell.

An enterprising captain commanding a company of archers ordered several of his men onto the back of a wagon, giving them a vantage point to fire from. They began sending a steady stream of arrows into the barbarians at the breach.

Another point in the line failed, buckling under the pressure, shields lying down on top of the men strapped into them, crushing them under the weight of the invaders clambering over the top of them.

Flaming arrows continued in a steady stream, arcing over the battle line and raining down into the enemy camp. Fires were growing behind their lines, but it wouldn't be enough. Abigail knew her army would have to advance before her archers could reach far enough into the camp to cripple the enemy.

"We have to press forward," she said. Everything was happening at once. She realized that the battle unfolding right in front of her was the least of her concerns as she looked out across the rest of the very big battlefield.

To the north, Zuhl's slavers were fighting in pitched battles against the soldiers Torin had mustered from the refugee camp. At a glance she estimated he led a force of five thousand, and they were gaining ground against the barbarians as they freed those slaves they could and sent them into the forest to the north.

To the south, the heavy cavalry was just reaching the flank of the barbarians spilling out of their encampment. General Kern had formed his men into a column twenty wide and five hundred deep. They crashed into the disorganized flank of the enemy, driving deep into the mass of men before Zuhl's brutes recognized the danger and turned to face them. As the cavalry slowed, the barbarians began to take a toll on them, dragging men off their horses or striking out at the mounts along the sides of the column.

Three catapults fired into the column, bringing down several horses and disrupting the momentum of the charge. Mage Dax started muttering a spell. A ball of crackling, blue-white energy formed between his hands, floating and sputtering with power. With a word, he sent it streaking at the nearest catapult tower. It struck with explosive force, splintering the tower and catapult, but it didn't stop there. It floated in place for a moment before it streamed in an arc of lightning-like energy to the next tower, shattering it in a shower of kindling, then arced to the third tower. In the space of three breaths, the nearest catapults were demolished.

"Thought it was time I got into the fight," Dax said.

"I agree," Sark said, before beginning a spell of his own.

Magda started casting a spell as well.

Out to sea, the Ithilian fleet, led by Admiral Tybalt, had begun firing on the three completed ships anchored in the bay. Abigail thought she saw the firepots burst against a half shell of magical energy hovering over each ship. Then they returned fire. Each of Zuhl's ships was armed with dozens of ballistae. Each targeted a single vessel with all of their weapons and fired at once.

Three of the vessels in the Ithilian fleet burst into flame as they were pelted by dozens of firepots.

Sky Knights hurled firepots down onto the docks and berths. The docks caught fire easily enough, but floating over each incomplete ship was a half shell of magical energy. The firepots shattered against the shields, coating the bluish shell of magic in angry but impotent burning oil.

The dragon, ridden by the man glowing as bright as the sun, swooped down on an Ithilian attack boat and breathed, not fire, but frost … air so cold it froze the ship and its crew solid in moments, coating everything in ice and solidifying the ocean for dozens of feet in every direction.

Several Sky Knights saw the dragon attack and broke off their futile attempts to destroy the ships. Two came in over the dragon, hurling firepots down at the rider, only to watch them shatter harmlessly against a magical shield. A streak of frosty-white magical energy stabbed out from the brilliantly glowing dragon rider and struck the lead wyvern directly in the chest. Almost instantly, the wyvern and rider froze solid. The wyvern's wings shattered against the wind and it plummeted into the water hundreds of feet below.

Magda finished her spell. An orb of bluish energy streaked from her hand and stopped abruptly over the barbarians several dozen feet in front of the slowing cavalry charge. It held there for a moment before it shattered into hundreds of shards of force, each beginning to swirl around the center point in an increasingly rapid whirl of deadly arcane power. With a gesture she lowered her creation into the barbarians, tearing into them with horrific violence, rending flesh from bone. She directed it to move along the ground, a twenty-foot-wide, five-foot-tall whirling vortex of magical blades, cutting down everything in its path for a hundred feet before the spell ran its course and dissipated, streamers of light trailing off in a whirl as each shard ceased to exist.

The carnage was so stunning that many of the barbarians momentarily stopped and tried to grasp the enemy they faced, only to be run down by the renewed momentum of General Kern's cavalry charge. The soldiers cut a swath through the horde, relieving the pressure on the front line and clearing the field for the shield wall to advance.

Abigail waited for the cavalry to clear the space between her infantry and the berm wall of the encampment.

"Push forward," she ordered.

General Markos nodded to a nearby soldier who was standing ready with a signal horn. He blew a long, steady note that drifted out over the field, penetrating the din of battle.

The shield bearers lifted and unhooked their shields, the pikemen dropped the points of their pikes between each shield man, and the whole line lumbered forward, slowly at first, scrambling over the fallen wreckage of the enemy piled up before them but gaining momentum as soon as they passed the jumble of bodies. A few remaining barbarians got through the lines, and while formidable in single combat, they fell easily to attacks from all directions by the infantry behind the shield bearers and pikemen.

Once they had gained a hundred feet, the shield line planted their spikes firmly into the ground and locked shields together, the pikemen dropped the hafts of their weapons into the guides atop each shield, and the whole line braced for the next wave of barbarians.

All the while, a steady stream of arrows rained down into the enemy. At least that part of the plan was working, Abigail thought to herself as she looked back out to sea.

The dragon ignored a direct hit from a light-lance spell hot enough to burn a hole through a man as it dove toward the Ithilian fleet. A gout of frigid dragon breath froze a swath of the ocean three hundred feet long into an instant iceberg, disrupting the path of two light warships intent on ramming the nearest of Zuhl's giant ships.

A wyvern dove at the dragon, pulling up at the last moment and whip-striking with its bone-bladed tail. The dragon folded its wings and twisted around upside down, grabbing the wyvern's tail with its powerful rear talons and clamping into the wyvern's soft underbelly with its powerful jaws. As it fell toward the ocean, the dragon thrust out one wing and spun around on top of the wyvern, driving both hind feet into the belly of the dying beast as it thrust its wings downward, gaining dozens of feet with a single stroke.

Over two dozen Sky Knights had refocused their attack on the docks and the soldiers within the encampment, this time with some success. They rained firepots and javelins into the surging barbarian horde, but the ships, the real target of the battle, remained unharmed.

Another Sky Knight made an attack run at the dragon, coming in high and from behind. The witch guided her wyvern into a talon-strike dive targeting the dragon's wings. Abigail watched as the brilliantly glowing rider turned and released his spell. A wave of translucent energy that looked like heat wavering over desert sands struck the wyvern and blew it backward, sending it spiraling into the ocean below. Then the dragon breathed on another ship, fusing it with the ocean around it and solidifying its crew in an instant.

Wizard Sark turned to vapor in a whirlwind and lifted off the ground, floating through the air, gaining strength until he touched down on the northern corner of the berm wall as a full-force tornado, sucking up dirt and sharpened spikes, cutting a swath big enough for a column of infantry to ride through. He continued to tear a path of destruction through the camp on his way toward the docks, sending Zuhl's soldiers and debris flying away from him as he went.

Abigail seized the opening before the enemy could respond.

"Send in the cavalry—all of them," she commanded.

General Markos issued his orders to the signalmen. Two horns blew, the first commanding the heavy cavalry to charge, the second calling for the two legions of Rangers held in reserve to attack.

"Conner, you have command, crush them to a man," Abigail said. "Magda, you're with me." She turned toward the rear of the camp, but Anatoly stopped her with a hand on her upper arm before she could take three steps.

"What are you going to do?" he asked, worry creasing his brow.

"I'm going after that dragon before it kills the entire fleet," she said, meeting his eyes without flinching.

"That's madness, Abigail. I can't protect you up there."

"I'll be right beside her, Master Grace," Magda said.

"I have to do this," Abigail said. "I'm the only one with a weapon that can get through its scales."

"And what about the wizard riding it?" Anatoly asked. "You're no match for him."

"I am if I can get close enough," Abigail said.

"I'll handle Zuhl," Magda said.

Both Abigail and Anatoly looked at the triumvir.

She shrugged. "I'm nearly certain Zuhl himself is riding that dragon. The spells I've seen him cast would require a mage or a high witch."

"I agree," Mage Dax said, pointing out to sea. "We'll win the ground war, but his ships are getting away."

Another of the giant ships slipped free of its berth, followed by another. Now five were in the water.

"Anatoly," Abigail said, drawing herself up and facing him like a queen, "take whatever men you need to board one of those ships and capture it before it casts off. We all have a part to play … mine is dealing with that dragon."

Anatoly clenched his jaw, struggling with his inner turmoil, then nodded once and hugged Abigail fiercely before turning away. "Captain Sava, you and your men are with me," he barked as he spun his war axe off his back.

Anatoly was angry, not at Abigail, but at the fact that he couldn't stand with her in this battle. He loved her like a daughter and it ate at him that he might never see her again. The enemy she'd chosen to fight was beyond her, beyond most mortal opponents, yet she was the best suited to defeat it because of the sword her brother had given her. He also worried about Alexander. If Abigail died in a battle because he had given her the Thinblade, he would never forgive himself. They were best friends, inseparable as children, closer than ever as adults, even with an ocean between them.

Captain Sava followed with two squads of dragon-plate-armored men right behind him. Anatoly set aside his concern for Abigail and turned his attention to the task at hand. He had a ship to capture and an army between him and his objective. A quick survey of the battlefield revealed his best chances for success. The shield wall had pushed forward to the top of the enemy berm and the fighting was fierce. Men were piling up in front of the interlocking shields but still more of the big, brutish barbarians hurled themselves forward.

Another of the ships slipped out of its berth into the ocean, lowering oars and pulling away into the bay. The cavalry charge along the inside of the north berm wall was making headway, allowing access into the enemy encampment that didn't involve climbing over the front line. Anatoly headed toward the breach, walking briskly behind the back rank of archers as they steadily emptied their barrels of arrows.

They reached the northern edge of the shield wall as the last of the Rangers poured past on their light horses. Anatoly stopped to let them by, motioning for the Strikers to gather around.

"We're going to follow the cavalry," Anatoly said. "We'll make our way along the inside of the berm wall toward the water. Don't stop to fight if you don't have to. Let the rest of the army kill the enemy." He pointed to the warship in the northernmost berth. "Our objective is that ship. Once we're aboard, we'll capture it if we can or set it on fire if we can't. Any questions?"

No one spoke. Anatoly nodded curtly and started out into the wake of the cavalry. There was little resistance near the gap in the berm wall. Most of the enemy soldiers were focused on repelling the main attack along the eastern front, and those nearest the gap had been trampled by the cavalry charge.

Anatoly ignored the battle taking place to his south as he moved purposely through the trail of carnage. Nearly two-thirds of the way into the enemy encampment, the cavalry had turned south and into the heart of the camp, disrupting the barbarians' efforts to mount an effective defense against the advancing shield wall and throwing the entire camp into chaos.

Wizard Sark had softened a path for them on his way through the camp toward the southern berm wall where he had blown another hole, allowing the cavalry a way out.

When they reached the place where the cavalry had turned, they started to encounter some resistance. Anatoly almost relished the opportunity to unleash his festering anger born of worry for Abigail, and more distantly for Alexander.

The first barbarian they came upon was a sentry posted along the northern berm wall. The Rangers had passed only a minute or so before and the barbarian was just coming out from behind an upturned wagon he'd used for cover against their arrows. He smiled when he saw Anatoly and the Strikers, then shouted for help from his companions.

Several dozen men emerged from similar hiding places, cautiously at first, then boldly when they saw that the threat of the Rangers' arrows was past.

"Finally, an opponent who will fight me face to face like a man," the barbarian said, drawing his enormous two-handed sword from the sheath on his back.

Anatoly brought his axe up into a ready guard position and advanced toward the barbarian, who brought his sword down over his head in a powerful stroke. Anatoly spun to his right and using momentum to fuel his stroke brought his battle-axe around in a whistling arc, cutting into the big barbarian from hip to navel. The man fell away screaming as Anatoly stepped into the next onrushing barbarian, thrusting the top spike of his battle-axe out straight into the man's belly. He didn't bother to finish the wailing man before he met the next attacker.

The Strikers formed a wedge behind him, fighting as a team, blocking with their dragon-scale shields for the man to their left and thrusting at the enemies that got close enough, but never breaking formation. Only one Striker was even forced to a knee by the barbarians. Kelvin's dragon-plate armor protected them flawlessly from any but the most blunt-force attacks. The one man who did go down blocked a downward stroke from a war hammer wielded by a barbarian who easily weighed three hundred pounds. The strike didn't even dent the dragon-scale shield but the force of it was enough to break the arm of the Striker who took the blow. A moment later, one of his companions killed the barbarian with a precision thrust of his sword to the throat.

They moved the rest of the way to the waterline, meeting pockets of resistance here and there but besting them without difficulty. Anatoly didn't shy away from the enemy that came his way, but he never took his eye off his objective.

At the water, they turned south and worked their way to the long dock linking the land with the giant construction berth cradling the warship. Most of the barbarians were east of them now, either fighting against the shield wall or moving toward it.

The cavalry had passed through the entire camp, leaving a trail of destruction behind them.

When Anatoly and the Strikers began advancing up the dock, the handful of men between them and the ship turned and ran toward the ship, shouting a warning.

The vessel was being prepared to launch. Ropes were being cut and the front scaffolding was being hastily pulled away, but it would still be several minutes before they would be free of the berth.

Anatoly reached the rear part of the berth and took the first of the staircases leading to the top wall where the gangplanks allowed access to the ship. As he rounded a corner in the switchback staircases, a barbarian thrust a sword at him, landing a glancing blow against his breastplate. He didn't bother with his axe in such tight quarters … instead, he grabbed the man by the wrist and threw him into the water.

They reached the top of the scaffolding and found that the gangplanks had been pulled onto the ship, except Zuhl's men had forgotten to retrieve a number of other planks that formed the topmost walkway of the berth wall. Anatoly set one of the stout boards across the ten feet separating the berth wall and the ship.

As he boarded the ship, two men rushed him. He met their charge, defending the gangplank as the Strikers filed aboard. Both men fell quickly, the first with a gash across his belly, the second toppling overboard.

Anatoly and his men moved along the deck toward the bow. The men onboard were mostly sailors or shipbuilders. Very few of the battle-hardened barbarians were guarding the ship, so they had a relatively easy time clearing the top deck, throwing most of the men they encountered overboard rather than killing them outright.

They reached the bow and turned down the other side of the deck to ensure they hadn't missed anyone. By the time they reached the aft deck and the anchor winch, Anatoly was convinced that the ship had nothing more than a skeleton crew aboard, just enough to sail it to the Isle of Zuhl where it could be loaded with troops.

He released the anchor, dropping it into the shallow water and ensuring that the ship couldn't leave the berth without becoming hopelessly entangled.

"That should hold them for now," he said. "Let's take the lower decks, one by one."

"We're right behind you, Master Grace," Captain Sava said.

Chapter 38

Abigail and Magda quickly changed into their riding armor before mounting their wyverns. Knight Raja and Flight Commander Corina were already mounted and waiting. Abigail took care with her locking pins to ensure that she was secure in her saddle. One final check and she goaded Kallistos into the air.

He thrust down with his powerful wings, propelling them dozens of feet off the ground. The next thrust brought them higher still and started them moving forward over the rear of the army toward the fierce aerial battle that was taking place over the ocean.

Knight Raja took his place to Abigail's right, just behind Kallistos' wing tip. Magda and Corina gained altitude more quickly, riding older and more experienced wyverns, and took a high overwatch position above and behind them.

They gained altitude, floating over the supply trains, then the soldiers held in reserve, then over the archers, and finally, over the melee taking place along the berm wall. Abigail surveyed the damage done by her army as she coasted on the crisp air.

It was a scene out of a nightmare. Dead and dying littered the ground, peppered with arrows. Fire burned everywhere there was fuel left for it to consume. Her archers continued to shower the enemy camp with their deadly rain. The shield wall had taken the top of the berm and the archers were reaching farther into the encampment, killing many of those that had attempted to avoid the fighting.

Abigail nodded to herself. These barbarians had sacked Fellenden City and Bredon. She'd seen the devastation they'd visited on the people of those cities. She'd seen the cruelty and depravity of the brutes from the Isle of Zuhl. Now she was watching them die, the logical consequence for such a vicious and wanton violation of the Old Law.

The heavy cavalry charge led by General Kern had cut a path of destruction along the inside of the northern berm wall and then turned south toward the heart of the camp, trampling barbarians underfoot with every yard gained. Rangers followed in their wake, sending arrows into the camp and cutting many barbarians down by surprise.

She turned her attention to the battle raging in the sky over the bay. Six of Zuhl's giant warships were in the water now, oars pulling them away from the shore, sails being unfurled and just beginning to catch the gentle breeze. The bulk of his fleet was getting away.

A swath of the ocean between Zuhl's ships and the Ithilian fleet was frozen into dozens of jagged chunks of ice floating mostly beneath the surface. Three Ithilian warships had attempted to pass the icy barricade only to collide with icebergs and suffer hull breaches.

A squad of Sky Knights broke off their attack runs against the soldiers within the camp and signaled as they passed that they were out of javelins and firepots, heading back to the rear to rearm.

Dozens of the Ithilian ships were damaged or destroyed, some frozen in place, bobbing on the ocean without direction, others were aflame, burning out of control, their crews abandoning ship.

The dragon made another pass against a fast-attack boat, freezing it solid with a gout of impossibly cold breath. Another ship scored a direct hit against the dragon's belly with a ballista bolt, only to have it shatter on impact, drawing the dragon's attention.

Abigail squinted against the brightness of the wizard riding the dragon as he pointed his staff toward the ship. A bolt of magical energy shot forth from the tip of it, streaking toward the offending ship and solidifying into a shard of ice ten feet long and two feet wide before it crashed into the deck, blasting a hole in the side of the ship as big as an ox.

Nearly a dozen Sky Knights, witches all, were commencing an attack run against one of Zuhl's ships that was sailing out to sea. One by one they targeted the ship, not with javelins or firepots, but with magic. Abigail watched with fascination as each witch in turn released an orb the color of the sky at the shield protecting the giant warship. Each orb hit home, one after the next, and with each impact, the shield pulsed and then dimmed, pulsed and then dimmed some more.

The Sky Knights still over the enemy encampment re-formed and started gaining altitude for an attack run against the same ship. As the second to the last witch passed over the target vessel, the shield failed and her spell fell harmlessly against the deck of the ship. Nearly two dozen Sky Knights turned as one and started a gradual dive toward the unprotected ship.

The dragon rider took notice and pulled away from the Ithilian fleet to engage the Sky Knights again. The witches were clear, gaining altitude and turning to make a run against another ship when the Sky Knights armed with firepots began their attack run. Two by two they flew over the ship, casting their firepots down through the masts and rigging onto the deck. The fires started small but grew quickly.

Then the dragon engaged. Coming broadside to the Sky Knights lined up for their attack run, the dragon breathed on one wyvern, freezing it in midair, sending it tumbling into the ocean, while the wizard riding the dragon unleashed a bolt of magical energy from his staff, hitting the second wyvern on the side and freezing it and its rider solid. Two dead in one pass.

Abigail and Knight Raja reached an altitude above the aerial battle and started their attack run. She signaled to Raja for a tail strike. They gained speed, wind roaring past them as they came down on the dragon from behind. He was wheeling away from them, lining up for another run against the wyverns attacking the vulnerable ship below, exposing his blind side as they soared in.

In unison their wyverns snapped their tails at the dragon, each hitting the bony ridge along its back. The dragon roared in pain, folding its wings and falling into a steep dive to escape the sudden insult it had sustained. Abigail and Raja pulled into a turn and angled up to maintain altitude over the dragon. A bolt of magical energy shot forth from the wizard's staff, just missing Raja's wyvern as he turned hard.

Magda and Corina were next, pulling sharply to maintain a viable attack angle on the dragon, each unleashing spells similar to the blue orbs that had depleted the ship's shield. Both scored direct hits against the wizard's shield, dimming it but not defeating it.

As the dragon roared in fury, it banked, thrusting hard against the open sky and gaining altitude faster that any wyvern could. It came for Abigail and Raja. She saw the danger of the rapidly rising dragon and attempted to pull her turn tighter as she tipped into a dive to avoid his attack … but she was too late. The dragon came around behind her; she had nowhere to run. She'd seen how quickly this dragon's breath could freeze a person solid. She had only moments now.

Then she felt it. Air so cold her skin burned, her hair felt suddenly hard and brittle, her riding armor grew stiff, resisting her effort to turn in her saddle. She reversed her direction, pulling Kallistos into another hard turn and looking back.

Knight Raja was falling away toward the ocean, frozen solid, already dead before he shattered against the surface of the water. He'd put himself between her and the dragon, saved her with his sacrifice, preserved her for one more try at the dragon.

Abigail swallowed her grief. Raja had been a good teacher and a loyal wing rider. She'd liked him. His gruff, no-nonsense demeanor only thinly veiled his sincere love for the Sky Knights.

The dragon matched her turn, coming around behind her again, but this time Magda and Corina were behind him. The rider saw the danger and banked away toward the Ithilian fleet, dodging a light-lance spell cast by Corina. Abigail turned back toward the dragon to rejoin the fight.

Magda cast her spell, an orb of darkness, not netherworld darkness, but simply a place where light could not be. It engulfed the wizard riding the dragon, shrouding his brilliance and dimming the morning. Abigail tipped Kallistos forward into a reckless dive, quickly gaining on the dragon, desperate to reach him before the wizard could unmake Magda's spell.

His staff came streaking out of the orb of darkness surrounding him, shooting toward the ocean below. It hit the water in the midst of the Ithilian fleet and stopped at the surface as if time itself had stopped, freezing it in place. One heartbeat passed, then two, and then the ocean began to freeze solid around the staff. It started slowly at first, a few feet in a second or so, then spread with terrible quickness, freezing the ocean to a depth of five feet for a league in every direction, encasing the entire Ithilian fleet in ice, locking them in place and rendering them impotent to pursue the now seven ships slipping out of the bay. The bulk of Zuhl's fleet was escaping.

Abigail took all of this in as she closed the gap to the dragon, the wind tearing at her, ripping the breath from her lungs. Her plan was madness. If she failed she would die—if she succeeded she would still most likely die, but she was the only one who could do what needed to be done.

The dragon banked again, bringing it closer to her and easing the angle she would need for her plan to work. The dragon rider was still blinded by Magda's spell, but it looked like the brilliant light emanating from his armor was starting to burn through the darkness surrounding him.

Abigail came in behind and above him. She tried not to think about the risk she was taking, tried to focus on the task at hand, but she couldn't help feeling a little relief when the dragon passed away from the frozen armada below and out over open ocean.

She slipped her hand through the leather thong she'd tied to the hilt of the Thinblade, pulled the loop tight around her wrist and drew her sword. With her left hand, she guided Kallistos directly above and just slightly behind the dragon.

The darkness was fading, allowing the brilliance of the wizard's armor to shine through again. A thousand thoughts raced through her mind, "what ifs" vied for her attention but she ignored them all as she yanked on the release cord, pulling dozens of locking pins free in a staccato cascade of pops muffled by the roaring wind.

She was free of her saddle.

Then she was falling.

Somewhere very far away she heard Magda shout her name.

It was only eight feet, ten at the most, but the instant she was in the air, unattached to her wyvern, utterly at gravity's mercy, she felt her heart rise up in her throat. Wild panic threatened to overcome her.

Then she crashed into the spiny back of the dragon and the desperate needs of the moment shoved everything else aside. As she scrambled for a grip, the Thinblade whipped around wildly, cleanly slicing off one of the dragon's back spines, almost without resistance. Abigail caught a saddle strap, stopping herself from sliding off the side of the dragon.

Magda's spell failed. The wizard's armor started glowing brighter and brighter until he was painful to look at, like staring into the sun. Abigail shut her eyes tight and held on with all her strength as the dragon banked to come around on Corina. Abigail dangled freely from the side of the dragon as it cut through the air. She heard the wizard begin to mutter arcane words but before he could release his spell, a series of half a dozen bluish magical spikes slammed into his shield from the other side. The repeated impact distracted him, breaking the concentration he needed to finish his spell.

Corina corkscrewed down, spiraling toward the ocean in a desperate attempt to avoid an icy death. The dragon banked sharply in the other direction and Abigail slammed into its side, gasping to catch her breath from the sudden impact.

She thrust her knees under herself, still holding on to the saddle strap, eyes still tightly shut against the brilliance of Zuhl's enchanted armor, and she lunged forward, bringing her sword around in a wild arc toward the brightness. She felt a slight tremor of resistance reverberate through the hilt of the Thinblade as it broke the magical barrier and cleaved Zuhl in half. The brightness evaporated, plunging the world into seeming darkness, even though the sun shone brightly overhead. She watched his upper body fall away toward the ocean, trailing a streamer of blood.

Abigail swung her leg over the ridge on the dragon's back, sliding in between two spikes and spinning the Thinblade around in her hand so she could thrust down into the back of the beast. Then she heard him speak.

"Stop!" the dragon said. "Free me and I will leave you in peace."

"Land," Abigail shouted over the roaring wind, the Thinblade still poised for a kill strike.

The dragon turned and settled into a gentle dive toward a section of the frozen surface of the ocean, flaring his wings gracefully and lighting on the ice.

Abigail didn't let go or lower the Thinblade but she felt a tremendous relief to be closer to the ground. Magda and Corina flitted past overhead, banking hard to come around again.

"Why should I spare you, Dragon?" Abigail said.

"I did not attack your people of my own free will," the dragon said. "The collar I'm forced to wear gives Zuhl the power to command me. Free me before he reasserts his control or you may find that you are not fast enough to survive."

"Reasserts his control? Zuhl's dead. I just cut him in half." The lower portion of his torso was still strapped into the saddle, blood spatter staining the side of the dragon.

"I've seen him killed before," the dragon said. "My sire killed him once, ate him whole, but before he could remove the collar, Zuhl rose from the dead and took control over us again."

"Us?" Abigail said.

"My sire and dam and my siblings," the dragon said. "Seven of us, my whole family lives in bondage, slaves to Zuhl. Free me and I will leave you in peace."

"What's to stop you from killing me the moment I free you?" Abigail asked.

"Only my word," the dragon said.

Abigail thought about it for a moment. She remembered how majestic Tanis looked gliding gracefully toward the dragon temple. Her nobility was humbling. The thought of her in bondage made Abigail flinch, recoiling against something that felt instinctively wrong.

She threw her leg over the side of the dragon and slid down to the ice, nearly losing her footing in the process. Carefully, she half walked, half slid around in front of the dragon that had killed so many Sky Knights and sailors.

"What's your name, Dragon?" she asked.

"I am Ixabrax," he said.

"Lower your head so I can reach the collar," Abigail said.

Ixabrax slowly and warily lowered his head, keeping his eye on the Thinblade.

"Hold still," Abigail said. "My sword's really sharp."

She carefully slipped the blade under the collar and pulled up through the enchanted metal. As it gave, a wave of force blew her backward to the ground. She shook off the daze and looked up into the sapphire-blue, catlike eyes of Ixabrax.

"I have never known a human to be honorable," he said. "My sire told me stories of human kindness but I have only known cruelty and dominance from your kind."

Abigail got back to her feet, wiping the frost off her backside.

"Turn your side toward me and I'll cut that saddle off you," she said.

Ixabrax frowned in confusion for a moment but complied without a word.

Abigail sliced the straps holding the saddle in place and let it fall, Zuhl's corpse splattering blood across the ice.

"I'm Abigail Ruatha," she said, sheathing the Thinblade. "I've freed you and now I stand defenseless before you." She held her hands out to her sides, palms facing him. "Will you honor your word?"

"I will, Abigail Ruatha," Ixabrax said. "You have made a friend this day."

With that, he thrust into the air, chilling Abigail further with the downdraft. He flew low over the ocean toward the nearest of Zuhl's ships, coming in under the shield, breathing frost into the side of the ship, freezing the hull solid before pulling up sharply and shattering the side of the ship with a tail strike. The ship shuddered with the impact and listed violently, throwing most of the crew on deck overboard as it began to take on water.

Ixabrax roared as he gained altitude, flying through the underside of the shield as if it wasn't even there, then turning north toward the Isle of Zuhl.

***

Abigail watched anxiously as the scouts returned, landing just south of the encampment. She hurried to her command tent with Anatoly right beside her. Her command staff was already there. The two scout riders arrived a few minutes later, still wearing their jangling riding armor.

The battle had lasted for the entire day and into the night, but the bulk of the four legions guarding the shipyard had been destroyed with a few thousand fleeing into the darkness. Abigail had sent the Rangers to track them down and finish them off. She'd also sent Sky Knights to determine where the rest of Zuhl's army was and where they were headed.

"Report," Abigail said.

"The enemy has regrouped and are moving northeast toward the forest," the Sky Knight said. "They appear to be headed for either Irondale or Dunston."

Abigail leaned over the map spread out on the table and frowned.

"I'd bet they're headed for Irondale, but we'd better send warning to both cities," she said.

"We certainly can't move the entire army to defend either city in time," General Markos said. "But we could do some damage with the Rangers and the Sky Knights, harass them a bit before they reach their objective, maybe slow them down."

"I like it," Abigail said. "General Kern, you'll take the two legions of Rangers. Don't engage the enemy, just pick at them. Bleed them a little bit at a time. Flight Commander Corina, you'll take two wings with General Kern. Leave the remaining two squads with us for message riders and scouts. As soon as we receive reinforcements from Cassandra, I'll send another wing north."

"Neither Irondale nor Dunston can hold against four legions of those brutes," Torin said. "Unfortunately, I don't think we can reach them before the snows start in the north. Once they do, it'll be almost impossible to move so many men that far without losing a great number of them to the cold."

"As much as I hate it," Abigail said, "I'm afraid we're going to have to wait for spring to attack what's left of Zuhl's forces. Let's focus on getting ourselves ready for winter first."

"I recommend we move the refugees back to Fellenden City," Torin said. "Now that we know the barbarians aren't looking for another fight at the moment, we have time to get people back indoors before winter sets in."

"Would there be enough room to barrack our entire army?" Abigail said.

"I don't see why not," Torin said. "Honestly, we could use their help rebuilding the city and disposing of the dead." Torin spoke like a man detached from his emotions.

"That would give the soldiers something to do for the winter," General Markos said. "I always feel better when the men have something to keep them busy."

"Admiral Tybalt, what's the state of the navy?" Abigail asked.

"Forty-seven seaworthy ships, including the one master Grace and the Strikers captured," Admiral Tybalt said. "We have a number of others we're scavenging materials and equipment from. I have crews for them all, and then some."

"Good, any progress figuring out those things?" Abigail asked, pointing to the five devices they'd found on board the captured ship. Each was a cube three feet on a side. The four sides were made of a clear substance revealing a crystal spinning in the center, balanced between opposing pyramids jutting up and down from inside the bottom and top of the cube. Another pyramid rose from the top of the cube, culminating in a crystal that seamlessly formed the top three inches of the pyramid.

"I believe they're the devices that projected the shields over Zuhl's ships," Mage Dax said, "although I have yet to discover how to operate them."

Abigail nodded. "Admiral Tybalt, deploy four of them on your four biggest ships. We'll take one back to Ruatha for Mage Gamaliel to examine."

"We might find a few more in the wreckage of the two vessels that sank," Wizard Sark said.

"How would we get to them?" Abigail asked.

He shrugged. "Magic, of course, Lady Abigail. My specialty is the manipulation of air. I know a spell that will allow me to breathe underwater. With the assistance of a ship and a few strong men to hoist the devices out of the water, I believe I can locate and retrieve the devices that went down with those vessels."

"Outstanding," Abigail said. "Admiral Tybalt, please offer Wizard Sark whatever assistance he requires."

"Of course, Lady Abigail," Admiral Tybalt said.

"The number of devices may provide some insight as to Zuhl's plans," Magda said. "If we assume that each of the ten vessels had five of the shield devices aboard, it stands to reason that he intended to build fifty of those vessels, enough to move five legions at a time."

"With that kind of navy, he'd be able to conquer the entire Seven Isles," Conner said. "No one would stand a chance."

"Especially if the dragon was telling the truth," Abigail said.

"About Zuhl rising from the dead or about him having seven dragons?" Anatoly asked.

"Both," Abigail said. "Any progress determining if he could still be alive?"

"Yes," Mage Dax said. "Mistress Magda and I have examined the remains and we agree—the wizard you killed was a simulacrum."

Abigail frowned. "I'm not familiar with that term."

"That's understandable," Dax said. "Such magic was only theoretical until now. Essentially, Zuhl created a duplicate of his body by some means as yet unknown to us and then endowed it with his consciousness and magic. It's highly likely that he is still alive."

"That's unsettling," Abigail said, suddenly thinking of Jack as the phrase passed her lips, hoping he was safe, but mostly just wishing she could see him. "So Zuhl is alive," she said. "He has seven ships capable of carrying a thousand men each and he probably has six dragons under his control. Prince Torin, is the sea passable between Zuhl and Fellenden in the winter?"

"Generally no," Torin said. "Some years the ice floes are worse than others but nearly every year Crescent Bay in Zuhl freezes solid. By the time he gets his ships home to load his troops, he'll be frozen in."

"So we can expect at least another seven thousand men come spring," Abigail said. "Assuming he takes Irondale, can he operate another shipyard there during the winter?"

"Maybe," Torin said, "but cutting Iron Oak timber in the winter is a difficult and dangerous job."

"General Kern, see to it that his men have a harder time than they expect," Abigail said. "General Markos, prepare the army to move to Fellenden City and coordinate with Prince Torin to provide whatever assistance we can to the refugees that will be moving with us. Admiral Tybalt, take your navy back to Ithilian, we may have need of you during the winter and I don't want you to get iced in up here."

"What should we do with the shipyard?" Conner asked.

"Burn it," Abigail said. "With the enemy headed for Irondale, we can't spare the men to work it and we can't leave it for Zuhl."

Chapter 39

Alexander staggered back a step. Siduri stood before him like a man awaiting judgment.

"Don't you see, Alexander," Siduri said. "I have called on powers beyond my understanding and doomed the world. I created the shades because I would not accept reality as it is."

Alexander's mind raced, trying to comprehend the nature of the man standing before him, trying to fathom the power he had unleashed on the world, yet understanding all too well the desperation that had driven him to such a tragic and fateful decision.

"I am trying to spare you and the world from the horror of making a similar mistake," Siduri continued. "After I made my bargain with the Taker, I went to the river bank to find my children, but they were gone. I followed their footprints back to our home and opened the door with triumphant joy. My family was whole again.

"My sons were there … but they were not really alive. Their bodies were still cold and dead, yet they walked and spoke. All three turned from the table where they had placed my wife and smiled at me, blood smeared across their faces like war paint."

Siduri swallowed a sob.

"They killed her, their own mother, my wife. My sons murdered her in a most gruesome way. Her entrails were pulled out of her belly and arranged around her dead body in a horrific display.

"Realizing my mistake, I sought to undo the damage." He paused, staring off into the distance. "I tried to kill them … my own sons … but they did not die. I watched as they rose from their corpses and floated off into the forest. I buried my wife in despair. My wonderful little life was shattered, contorted into something unbearable. I was contemplating suicide when I saw the fire.

"My sons had taken possession of three hunters. Through their hosts, they lit one of the vitalwood trees on fire. Such a thing was beyond imagining. The vitalwood were revered by all. Many of the beings that walked the world during that time worshiped the trees.

"What followed was a war that lasted nearly twenty years. The shades, as my children came to be called, destroyed the vitalwood forest despite our best efforts to stop them. I led the fight against them, and failed. Only at the end, when nearly all of the vitalwood trees were gone, did the Lords of Light heed my plea for help. Selaphiel came forth and confronted the shades, tearing a rift in the fabric of the world of time and substance and banishing them to the netherworld.

"I allowed myself to be drawn into that rift as well, thinking that the time had finally come for me to face the consequences of my hubris, but I did not die. I was a spiritwalker and so the aether did not destroy me as it would have any other.

"After a time, I returned to the world of time and substance, thinking that I would take my own life, but I couldn't bring myself to do it, more out of fear of paying the Taker's price than anything else. Then an idea occurred to me. My power had grown. My understanding of the nature of the firmament had grown as well. I didn't know if what I imagined was possible but I was willing to attempt it if it meant I could escape the Taker.

"I had ridden the wave of creation many times within my mind. This time I sought to transfer myself physically into source, to unmake myself and become one with source, to cease to exist without actually dying.

"I was successful, yet I did not cease to be. Instead, for the first time, I found that I was truly one with the source of all things. I had no form, no location, yet I was everywhere at once. I have been there ever since, watching the world, listening to the song of creation, content to simply observe.

"I watched the Reishi Empire rise and fall. I nearly intervened when Malachi Reishi discovered my children and summoned them into the world, but he always bound them to his will and sent them back when they were finished with the tasks he had assigned them.

"I took notice when you were born and I've watched you very closely since you freed the shades, but still I chose to simply observe. Only now, when you stand at the precipice of disaster, have I chosen to take physical form again. I wasn't even sure it was possible, but the course you have chosen compelled me to act."

Alexander was reeling from the magnitude of everything he'd just learned, but even in the face of it all, he couldn't let go of his desperate need to help Isabel. It felt a little like madness scratching at the edges of his sanity, urging him on. Even though he knew he was taking a terrible risk, even though his reason begged him to reconsider, he couldn't let go of the thread of hope that the blood of the earth represented. With it, he had a chance to save Isabel, without it, she was doomed.

"I'm sorry, Siduri," Alexander said. "I have to do this."

He could see the disappointment mingled with fear ripple through Siduri's colors.

"I know," Siduri said. "I only hope you will not come to regret your actions as I have come to regret mine."

Before Alexander could say another word, Siduri vanished, as if he'd never really been there at all. In a daze, Alexander turned back to the blood of the earth. Slowly, methodically, he took out a vial and a small spoon from his pouch. Very carefully, he scooped up a tiny amount of the black, iridescent liquid the consistency of quicksilver, and poured it into the vial. He placed the sealed glass vial inside a metal tube and screwed the cap on tightly before returning everything to his pouch.

All the while he struggled with the doubt building in the back of his mind. What if Siduri was right? How could he place even Isabel's life before the fate of the world? She would never accept such a thing, yet he had to try. The alternative was too much to bear. He couldn't imagine leaving the chamber without the blood of the earth, walking back to his wife with the knowledge that he had accepted her fate.

Hector was standing guard when Alexander returned to the Wizard's Den. He took care to cover his return, checking with Chloe in his mind to ensure that no one was aware of his absence. Satisfied, he projected an illusion of himself getting up and took the place of the illusion as he dispelled it.

He went to the water barrel, then to Hector.

"Any sign of the dragons?"

"No," Hector said, shaking his head. "It's been quiet."

Alexander nodded and went back to his bunk.

***

It took the better part of two days to navigate through the meandering maze of passages that led through the mountain to the cave where the pirates were hiding Bragador's egg.

Alexander sent his all around sight into the cavern, assessing the strength of the enemy he was about to attack. There were nearly a dozen men sitting around a fire, bickering over a jug of brandy. The egg rested on a nearby bed of hot coals with a single wraithkin standing watch over it and one wizard sitting nearby, intently studying a book.

The other wizard and the other two wraithkin that Alexander had seen before were gone. He also didn't see the pirate leader who carried the Tyr Thinblade. He liked the odds better than he had before, but he couldn't help wondering where the others had gone.

"Isabel, you take the wraithkin, I'll take the wizard," Alexander said. "If we get both of them, the men shouldn't be a problem. Watch the ship, they may have more men aboard. Little One, I need you to go to Bragador and lead her here."

"Are you sure about that?" Jack asked.

"She has every right to protect her young," Alexander said. "And I'd rather we tell her where to find her egg … might buy us some goodwill."

Chloe flitted up and kissed him on the cheek. "Be careful, My Love," she said, before she buzzed into a ball of light and vanished into the aether.

Alexander nocked an arrow and looked at each of his friends in turn.

"Hit them hard and fast," he said.

Jack tossed the hood of his cloak up, vanishing from sight.

From the shadows Alexander and Isabel picked their respective targets. The enemy was oblivious to their presence in the dim light of the passage.

"I'll release when your spell fires," Alexander whispered.

Isabel nodded as she started muttering under her breath. He saw her colors flare with anger and power as she prepared her light-lance spell.

A flash of brilliance lit up the cave, and light streaking from Isabel's outstretched hand burned a hole through the wraithkin's head, dropping him like a sack of beans. Alexander loosed his arrow an instant later, driving it hard into the chest of the surprised wizard. He didn't even have time to look up before his heart was pierced.

Alexander dropped his bow and drew Mindbender, stepping out into the firelight flanked by Horace and Hector, each drawing their twin short swords. The dozen men around the fire scrambled to their feet, shouting an alarm as they drew weapons.

As Alexander was closing the distance to the first man, two wraithkin appeared in their midst while the second wizard and the man with the Tyr

Thinblade stepped out of a passage on the far side of the cavern. Alexander cursed under his breath as he met the first man, slipping inside past his clumsy thrust and driving the point of Mindbender into his ribs.

A wraithkin appeared next to him but before he could bring his sword around, Isabel unleashed a force-push spell, blowing the wraithkin across the cavern. The second wraithkin appeared behind her, raising his dagger to stab her in the back, but then checked his strike and vanished again.

Hector and Horace engaged half a moment after Alexander. Horace parried the sword stroke of one of the pirates, trapped the blade with his second sword, and brought the point of his right-handed blade up into the surprised pirate's throat. Another of the pirates tried to charge him from the flank but tripped over Horace's invisible magical servant, sprawling on the ground in front of him. Horace stabbed him in the back and stepped up to meet the next attack.

Hector faced two men at once, slipping to the side and fighting a furious sword exchange, hacking, thrusting, and parrying until he gained the advantage and stabbed the first man in the thigh, dropping him to a knee screaming. His next thrust drove into the man's eye and out the back of his skull. The second man leveled a kill stroke at him, but Hector turned to vapor a moment before it struck, allowing the momentum of the man's swing to pull him off balance, then Hector solidified again and drove his sword into the man's gut.

A surprised pirate fell with a sliced throat as Jack flickered into view and then vanished just as quickly.

"Destroy the egg," shouted the man with the Thinblade. "Prepare to cast off."

A few men from the ship started racing to the battle while others scrambled to prepare the ship as the cavern lit up from another light-lance cast by Isabel, this time at the wizard. It hit a shield surrounding him and didn't even distract him enough to disrupt his spell. He unleashed a bubble of liquid fire at Isabel. Alexander watched it streak across the room even as he dispatched another pirate in his path to the egg.

Angry orange flame splashed over her shield spell, illuminating the bubble of magical force protecting her from harm.

Alexander reached the egg just as one of the wraithkin appeared before it, poised to strike the defenseless unborn dragon. He stabbed him in the back of the skull, killing him in a stroke, just as the last of the three wraithkin appeared behind him and stabbed him through the upper leg.

He felt white-hot, breathtaking pain shoot through him, radiating from the wound. The wraithkin jerked his tainted dagger free, sending another jolt of violent agony coursing through him, but Alexander detached from his feelings, almost instinctually, and listened to his enemy's thoughts. His blade whistled through the air, arcing toward the spot where the wraithkin would appear, catching him an instant before he could stab into the egg, cleaving his head in half at ear level. Alexander toppled to the ground as the momentum of the swing put weight on his freshly wounded leg.

Hector and Horace fought their way toward him but another pirate reached him first. Alexander just barely avoided his downward thrust and hacked at his ankle, toppling the man in a screaming mass.

Alexander staggered to his feet as the egg behind him cracked open and the head of an infant dragon peered out into the world for the first time. He met the beast's eyes, and she croaked at him. He was so captivated by the baby dragon that he nearly failed to block an attack that would have killed him. He swung his sword wildly, deflecting the downward stroke from himself and the hatching dragon just as Jack appeared behind the attacking pirate and cut his throat.

Another pirate swung a mace at Jack, catching him on the shoulder and sending him to the ground, vanishing as he fell.

Hector and Horace fought furiously, back to back, against five pirates surrounding them, all of them trying to find an opening past their deadly twin short swords. Alexander stood his ground in front of the baby dragon that had now broken almost completely through her shell.

The man with the Thinblade strode toward Alexander. Alexander held his ground, putting nearly all his weight on his good leg while warm blood coated his injured leg.

Isabel cast a force-push against the wizard but his shield deflected it. He cast a lightning bolt back at her, arcing brilliantly across the cavern and striking her shield. She staggered back as her magical protective barrier failed.

Another dozen men from the ship were nearly upon them when the man with the Thinblade reached Alexander. As he reached out with Mindbender, listening for the heir of Tyr's thoughts, a crossbow bolt struck him on the outside of the left arm, slicing deeply and painfully, distracting him for just a moment. Alexander gritted his teeth against the sudden pain as he met the enemy. Had he been listening to the man's thoughts, he would have shielded Mindbender, but he was too focused on the new and sudden pain in that one crucial moment.

The Thinblade came quick, cutting Mindbender off just above the hilt. Scintillating white light expanded from the broken sword, filling the cave with sparkling, dancing brilliance before it contracted back toward Alexander, surrounding him entirely and then fading away as if the light was soaking into him.

The wielder of the Tyr Thinblade frowned for a moment, then shrugged and casually flicked the blade at Alexander's head. He caught the Thinblade with his bare hand and punched the man in the jaw with the hilt of Mindbender, nearly falling again as he struggled to gain his balance but yanking the Thinblade out of the pirate's hand in the process.

"I've been looking for this," Alexander said, dropping the ruined hilt of Mindbender and flipping the Thinblade to his right hand. It felt good, like it was made for his hand. The man stared in surprise.

"How's this possible?" he said, more dumbfounded than afraid.

"It's my sword," Alexander said.

Another crossbow bolt hit him in the chest.

Chloe buzzed into existence. "Bragador comes," she said.

"Thank you, Little One," Alexander said silently.

"I'll take that scabbard now," he said.

"Not a chance," the man said. "That sword belongs to my line. You shouldn't be able to wield it."

Chloe flitted over to the man and grabbed his belt, vanishing with it into the aether. His scabbard, belt knife, and pouch fell clattering to the floor.

Isabel fired a light-lance spell at the wizard. He leaned into his shield as it failed under the heat of her spell. Hector and Horace fought the five men surrounding them to a stalemate. Jack was down and unconscious.

Everyone froze in place at the sound of a deafening roar. A moment later, two dragons flanking a woman with the colors of a dragon, her eyes glowing with fury and power, entered from another passage.

"Kill him!" the former wielder of the Thinblade bellowed, pointing at Alexander. The dozen pirates charged.

Alexander met the first man with the Thinblade. It felt familiar in his hand as he cut the man in half. The rest of the charging men faltered and began to surround him and the baby dragon cowering behind him.

He lopped the blade off a sword before it could come down on the dragon, exposing his back to a mace attack. It hit his armor, the force of it driving him to one knee.

One dragon roared, the second breathed fire on the pirate ship, engulfing it in flames in an instant and filling the room with bright orange light and heat. The woman who'd entered with the two dragons pointed her hands at the two men nearest Alexander and unleashed a stream of fire at each, igniting both and burning them alive in moments. Alexander could feel the heat wash off them as he struggled to gain his feet.

The wizard fled into a passage followed by the pirate heir of Tyr and half a dozen of his men. The few that remained fell quickly as the two dragons entered the battle with claws and fangs.

Hector and Horace positioned themselves between Alexander and the approaching dragons. Isabel came to his side, helping him to his feet.

"Stand down," he commanded. Hector and Horace lowered their weapons but didn't sheathe them.

"Hello, Lady Bragador," Alexander said as Anja poked her head out from behind him. "Your baby is safe."

"You stood against those who would harm my child," she said.

"I did," Alexander said.

"Why?" Bragador asked, wariness in her voice.

Alexander shrugged, wincing from the movement of his wounded shoulder. "She's innocent," he said.

Bragador's eyes narrowed. "You were injured fighting those who would have killed my Anja."

"Yes," Alexander said.

"I still don't understand why," Bragador said.

Alexander sighed, leaning heavily on Isabel.

"I've sworn to protect the Old Law," he said. "Anja is innocent. She doesn't deserve any of this. Also, I knew that you would stop helping my enemies if your child was safe."

He adjusted his weight and started to fall. Isabel caught him and helped him to the ground.

"He's lost too much blood," she said, drawing her belt knife and cutting his trouser leg open to get at the wound. "Oh Alexander, this isn't good," she said, tearing his pant leg into strips for a bandage.

"Hector," Alexander said, pointing toward Jack, who was still unconscious and invisible. "Jack is right there, feel for him and take his hood down."

Bragador and the other two dragons looked on with suspicion while Anja nuzzled in close to Alexander. Hector found Jack, removed his hood and started inspecting his wound.

"He's out cold," Hector said, "but his breathing is steady and he hasn't lost much blood."

"Lady Bragador," Alexander said, slightly slurring his words. "I spoke true when I said we come in peace. Those men we fought were Phane's. He sent them to steal your egg and use it as leverage against you."

Isabel tightened his bandage; he gasped in pain and took several deep breaths to steady himself.

"It seems that Anja has taken a liking to you," Bragador said.

Alexander smiled, gently stroking the baby dragon's brow. She leaned into his affections.

"You may stay here until your wounds are healed," Bragador said.

"Thank you, Lady Bragador," Alexander said, opening the door to his Wizard's Den. "I'm afraid I can't meet the price of our bargain. My sword was destroyed."

Bragador frowned, her slightly glowing eyes seeming to swirl with fire. "It would seem that the item you came to bargain for has been stolen by the same people who stole my egg."

Alexander closed his eyes, shaking his head.

"We'll get it back," Isabel said, as she slathered healing salve on his shoulder wound.

"I don't see how," Alexander said. "My leg wound won't heal for months."

"Don't worry about that right now," Isabel said. "You need to rest." She motioned to Hector and Horace. They carefully lifted Alexander and carried him into the Wizard's Den, placing him gently on the nearest bed, then carrying Jack to the next bed over. Anja followed after Alexander, resting her head on the side of his bed and whimpering softly.

Bragador pursed her lips and shook her head as Alexander drifted off to sleep.

***

Isabel couldn't quite focus. There was a thrumming in her head and she felt like she had to do something, but wasn't sure what it was or why it needed to be done. She was standing over a man. He seemed familiar but she couldn't quite understand why. The more she tried to concentrate, the louder the thrumming in her mind grew until it drowned out reason, replacing it with something else.

She looked down through the dim light and saw a knife in her hand. That was it, she was supposed to kill this man, but why? He was asleep, injured, harmless. The thrumming grew louder still.

She raised the knife, poised to strike, if only to silence the maddening noise coursing through every corner of her mind. Her thoughts were thick and gauzy, she struggled to understand what was happening, but the thrumming drowned out everything else except her purpose.

A brilliant flare of light erupted before her.

"Isabel, no!" Chloe said.

She stopped, blinking at the little woman floating on dragonfly wings, trying to understand why she looked familiar, too. Then she looked down again and the thrumming in her mind vanished as she remembered.

She looked at the knife in her hand, then back down at Alexander. As the realization of what she was about to do sank in, she dropped the knife, one hand going to her mouth, the other to her stomach, her head shaking back and forth in denial, tears streaming down her face. She backed away from him, staring at her love with a mixture of terror and gratitude, slumping to the floor against the wall. Alexander stirred but didn't wake.

She was trapped in her own skin. Phane's darkness was doing its work, undermining her free will, pitting her against those she loved most. Alexander was hurt, vulnerable. She had nearly killed him. If Chloe hadn't stopped her, she wasn't sure she would have realized what she was doing until it was too late.

"I have to leave, Chloe," she whispered through her tears.

"No, Isabel. He needs you," Chloe said.

"I need him too, but he's not safe with me around," Isabel said. "I didn't know what I was doing, couldn't understand what I was about to do. Oh Dear Maker, if I'd killed him …"

"But you didn't," Chloe said.

"Only because you stopped me," Isabel said, getting to her feet and looking around at her sleeping companions. She swallowed hard, then sniffed back her tears.

"I have to leave … now," Isabel said. "Tell him that I love him with everything that I have and everything that I am. Tell him that I will always love him, no matter what happens."

"I will tell him," Chloe said, "but he won't understand."

"I know," she whispered as she bent over Alexander and kissed him gently on the forehead. "But he'll live."

Isabel got her pack from the foot of her bed, strapped on her sword and headed for the door to the Wizard's Den without looking back, lest she lose her nerve.

"And Chloe," she said without turning, "watch over him."

"Always," Chloe said.

Isabel left, crying, not daring to look back. She made her way to the cave entrance and out onto the beach. It took the better part of the night but she found the entrance to the cave where Captain Kalderson was hidden.

She found her way to the little boat they'd used to reach land and pushed it into the water, rowing steadily toward the ship.

"Lord Reishi?" a man said from the railing. "Is that you?"

"No," Isabel said. "It's Lady Reishi. Help me aboard."

Captain Kalderson was there by the time she'd climbed the rope net and clambered over the railing onto the deck.

"Where's Lord Reishi?" Captain Kalderson asked.

Isabel swallowed hard and shook her head, tears streaming down her cheeks.

"Dead," she said. "Cast off … quietly or the dragons will find us."

Even in the dim light, Isabel could see the captain's eyes go wide. He nodded and started making the rounds, rousing his men and issuing orders in hushed tones. It wasn't long before they were sailing away from the dragon isle through the darkest part of the night.

Isabel stood at the aft railing watching the dragon isle recede into the night, the orange glow of the volcanic cauldron shading the clouds overhead in orange, tears flowing freely down her cheeks and rage boiling in the pit of her belly.

"We're nearly past the Spires," Captain Kalderson said to her quietly as if he didn't want to disturb her grief.

"Where are we going?" he asked.

"Take me to Karth," Isabel said, wiping the tears from her cheeks as she turned away from the only man she'd ever loved.

Here Ends Blood of the Earth
Sovereign of the Seven Isles: Book Four

www.SovereignOfTheSevenIsles.com

The Story Continues in…

Cursed Bones
Sovereign of the Seven Isles: Book Five

Made in the USA
Middletown, DE
13 August 2020